THE CYBERPUNK NEXUS
EXPLORING THE BLADE RUNNER UNIVERSE

THE CYBERPUNK NEXUS

EXPLORING THE BLADE RUNNER UNIVERSE

EDITED BY

LOU TAMBONE
JOE BONGIORNO

SEQUART ORGANIZATION   EDWARDSVILLE, ILLINOIS

THE MUSIC AND MANY VERSIONS OF *BLADE RUNNER*

I Dreamt Music: Replicating *Blade Runner* 89
    by Bentley Ousley

Why the Theatrical Cut is the Truest Version of *Blade Runner* 100
    by Paul J. Salamoff

Deckard: B26354 – Coming to Terms with Deckard Being a Replicant 111
    by Lou Tambone

All Those Moments Lost in Time: Deleted and Alternate Scenes..................... 122
    by Joeseph Dilworth, Jr.

The Creation of *Blade Runner*'s Unique 70mm Prints....................................... 131
    by Steven Slaughter Head

THE THEMES OF *BLADE RUNNER*

Mirrors for the Human Condition.. 143
    by Timothy Shanahan

On Death and Dying in *Blade Runner* 161
    by Ian Dawe

The Humanity of *Blade Runner*.. 171
    by Nelson W. Pyles

The Science and Technology of *Blade Runner*... 182
    by Sabrina Fried

THE LEGACY OF *BLADE RUNNER*:
ADAPTATIONS, COMICS, HOMAGES, AND SPIN-OFFS

Awe, Wonder, and Disappointment: The Summer of 1982 and the Box Office of *Blade Runner* 195
    by Robert Meyer Burnett

The *Blade Runner* Sequels You Never Read 206
    by Mike Beidler

Philip K. Dick on the Screen 232
    by Zaki Hasan

Cyberhomages: *Blade Runner*-Inspired Media 241
    by Jean-François Boivin

On the Marvel Comic-Book Adaptation of *Blade Runner* 250
    by Julian Darius

Creating the Graphic Novelization of *Do Androids Dream of Electric Sheep?* .. 265
    by Bryce Carlson

Earth to Earth: The BOOM! Comics 275
    by Mario Escamilla

Longevity and Incept Dates: The World-Building of *Blade Runner* Lives on in Multimedia 286
    by R. Lee Brown

I Want More Life, Smegger: How *Blade Runner* Influenced *Red Dwarf*'s Revival 298
    by Rich Handley

THE SEQUEL: *BLADE RUNNER 2049*

Calling Back Cyberpunk 311
    by Lou Tambone

"Dreadfully Distinct": The Symbolic Power of K's Baseline in *Blade Runner 2049* 321
    by Kelli Fitzpatrick

Building the World of *Blade Runner* without Breaking It: Why Unasked Questions are Answered but Our Most Enduring Question is Not 336
    by Nathan P. Butler

Skin Jobs and Snow Jobs: *Blade Runner 2049* as Cli-Fi Noir and Race Erasure . 354
    by Leah D. Schade

Looking for Love in Cyberpunk Places: Examining Love in *Blade Runner 2049* 375
    by Lou Tambone

Beyond 2049: An Afterword 395
    by Lou Tambone

About the Contributors 398

The original movie poster for *Blade Runner*.

Introduction

by Lou Tambone

The Dawn of Cyberpunk

Cyberpunk is generally defined as a genre of fiction that deals with "high tech, low life." It's that contrast of technical advancement and decaying society that makes it such a rich playground for writers and artists. Since its inception sometime in the late 20th century, it's become more than just a literary genre. It's spread out across several media and has even taken root in the worlds of fashion and design, much like its younger cousin Steampunk. Since the word Cyberpunk is part of this book's title, I felt that I should offer a proper, if brief, introduction for the uninitiated.

First, though, the word *nexus* (used in the film, the original novel, and also in this book's title) is defined as a relationship between people or things. It can also mean a causal link, a connected group or series, or the central focal point of something. You might say it's a hub of sorts. It's that first definition, though, that grabs me: a relationship between *people* or *things*. A little conjunction swapping and you find yourself very close to a central theme in *Blade Runner*: the relationship between people *and* things.

So where did the word *Cyberpunk* come from?

It's a common misconception that writer William Gibson coined the term Cyberpunk when he released his seminal science-fiction novel *Neuromancer* in 1984. While he was certainly a major player in defining the genre, he did not coin the phrase. That honor goes to writer Bruce Bethke.

Cyberpunk! by Bruce Bethke.

Bethke first used the word as the title of his short story *Cyberpunk*, written in 1980 but published in 1983. It wasn't some sort of literary happy accident either, according to Bethke. "The invention of the c-word was a conscious and deliberate act of creation on my part," he says. "I wrote the story in the early spring of 1980, and from the very first draft, it was titled *Cyberpunk*. In calling it that, I was actively trying to invent a new term that grokked the juxtaposition of punk attitudes and high technology. My reasons for doing so were purely selfish and market-driven: I wanted to give my story a snappy, one-word title that editors would remember."[1] While Bethke may have been the first to give the phenomenon a name, its conceptual origins go back slightly further.

Sometimes movements in art and literature creep into being slowly and somewhat organically. It's easy to look back in hindsight and identify the principal moments that make up such a phenomenon, but it's a bit harder to discern them while they are occurring.

A good example of this phenomenon can be seen in another artistic format: music. In the mid-1980s, certain bands (mainly from the west coast of the United States) started to become popular. They had funny names like Pearl Jam, Soundgarden, Alice in Chains, and Nirvana. Sometime in the 1990s, these bands found themselves labeled underneath an umbrella called *Grunge*, stylized by plaid shirts, loud guitars, and plenty of angst. The term hearkened back to the 1980s but was popularized in the 1990s, much to the chagrin of some of the bands allegedly responsible.[2]

By the time Bethke's *Cyberpunk* story was published, works by (but not limited to) William Gibson, Alice Sheldon (aka James Tiptree Jr.), John Brunner, John Shirley, Bruce Sterling, Rudy Rucker, *Métal Hurlant* magazine, and of course Philip K. Dick (whose *Do Androids Dream of Electric Sheep?* served as the inspiration for *Blade Runner*) had all seen the light of day. Again, looking back, it's easy to single out these works as significant moments in the history of Cyberpunk, but at the time they were simply regarded as good, forward-thinking science fiction. *Blade Runner* itself was released in 1982, *before* both Bethke's *Cyberpunk* and Gibson's *Neuromancer* were published.

However, it wasn't until Gibson coined the term "cyberspace" in *Neuromancer* that both publishers and the public took serious notice of the burgeoning underground sub-genre rising to the surface. In fact, most historians point to that book's publishing as the indisputable "birth" of the Cyberpunk genre.

So as you can see, the dawn of Cyberpunk was something that happened fluidly and over a number of years and publications. No one writer or filmmaker can be awarded full credit for creating something that was obviously a sum of its parts, no more than any one author, poet, or band can be credited with starting the counterculture movement of the 1960s. Many contributed to the

---

[1] The Cyberpunk Project:
http://project.cyberpunk.ru/idb/etymology_of_cyberpunk.html
[2] https://en.wikipedia.org/wiki/Grunge

genre's creation and at some point it was blessed with a name.

The rest, as they say, is history.

Longevity

The fact that we're still talking about *Blade Runner* today is nothing short of amazing.

I was a mere 12 years old when the film was released in 1982. My memories are hazy, but I'm sure that I convinced some reluctant relative with a car to chauffeur me to a local theater to see this film I had been reading and hearing so much about. I can't remember who it was or what theater I saw it in, but I can safely say I saw it before the US Television Broadcast version on CBS in 1986, and you best believe that when that broadcast happened, I was right there with a VHS tape at the ready. In fact, I still have it in a box in my attic. I've thrown away countless VHS tapes over the years, but for some reason I can't bring myself to part with that old Maxell tape with *Blade Runner* written on the label in my handwriting.

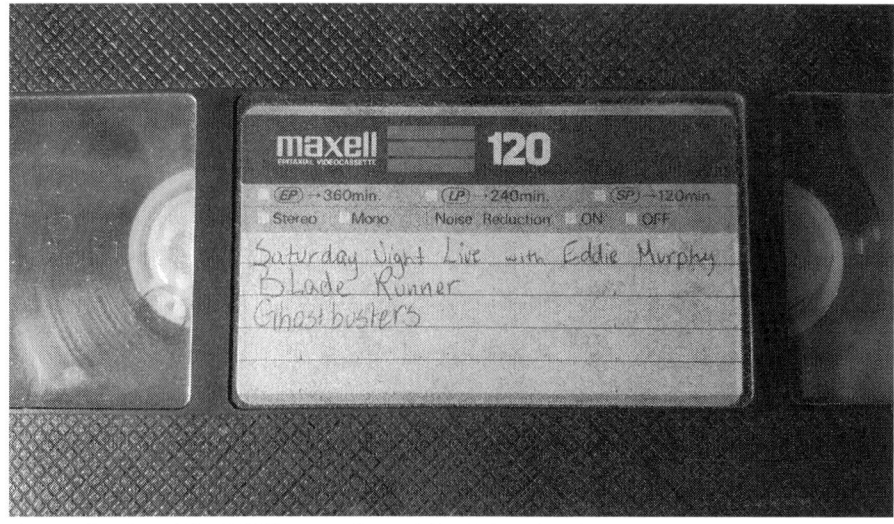

Your editor's original VHS recording of the U.S. television broadcast.

Harrison Ford had been my favorite actor since I saw him five years earlier in *Star Wars*. *The Empire Strikes Back* and *Raiders of the Lost Ark* were still fresh in my mind. I loved his acting so much that I kept up with him and his roles for a long time, never missing a chance to see him onscreen whenever possible. I followed *Blade Runner*'s production via magazines like *Starlog* for months before its release and kept reading about it for a long time after. In the pre-internet days, magazines were the best way to keep on top of such things.

At the risk of sounding retroactively revisionist, I'll admit that the movie somehow affected me *before I had even seen it*. Adults at the time might have found that hard to comprehend, but for a 12-year-old kid, it was an amazing feeling. All those images transported me into another world that was so familiar, yet so foreign at the same time. It was my first real experience with dystopia and cyberpunk (though I didn't know either of those words at the time) and I found it enthralling. Was this what the world was coming to? Was the film some kind of warning or harbinger?

It didn't seem all that far-fetched to me back then. We were smack dab in the middle of the Cold War and all I remember seeing on television were stories about nuclear devastation and it scared the hell out of me. When I finally got to see the film in the theater (complete with voiceover), I was shocked in all the right ways. I immediately started going through my magazines looking for images that weren't in the film because I wanted to see more.[3] I even obtained a copy of Philip K. Dick's novel *Do Androids Dream of Electric Sheep?* and read it several times. While I was initially confused at its complex theories and symbolism (I was a kid, after all), the fact that it was so different from the film didn't deter me. I wanted to understand the whole concept from start to finish. I wanted to know where this movie came from and how it became something else. I wanted all the pieces of the puzzle so I could make them fit together and make sense in my head. I created my own little nexus of information and digested it as best as a young kid could.

Fast-forward to the early 1990s.

My VHS tape, now weary from multiple plays, was finally swapped out with an official VHS copy of the Director's Cut in 1993. A version was originally released on Betamax and VHS back in 1983, but outside of video rental stores, I don't remember seeing it available for purchase. The DVD would find itself on my rack in 1997 and it was this Director's Cut that made the biggest splash, being one of the first DVDs ever released. While I thought I was alone in my love for the film, all of the sudden people were talking about *Blade Runner* again.

I started to realize the film had a cult status, much to my delight. The rise of the Internet only intensified the buzz. Then came computer games, spin-off novels, and (at last!) an official soundtrack, flawed as it was. This odd mix of science fiction and film noir that underperformed at the box office and seemed

---

[3] I was unaware of the many versions of the film, some still to come.

to disappear into oblivion soon after was now being viewed and discussed again with vigor.

Blade Runner isn't just a film I can watch over and over again, it's a film I can put on and *listen* to over and over again. The music, incidental and otherwise, along with the expansive sonic palette of noises and other sound effects provides a great inspirational backdrop for just about anything from writing to cleaning the house.

Today, it's hailed as one of the greatest science-fiction films of all time. You'll find the words "masterpiece" and "influential" used with regularity after a few simple Internet searches. That's a pretty big turnaround from the days it petered out at the box office and moved on to a mundane video rental life, as was the natural course of many films back then. How and why this happened will be discussed elsewhere in this book, as will many other things.

Blade Runner 2049 was released in October of 2017 and for a time it looked like things in the *Blade Runner* universe wouldn't be slowing down any time soon. However, much like its predecessor, it under-performed at the box office (depending on what your version of "under-performed" is, of course.) There are always rumblings of another film, but no one knows for sure. I had high hopes that the *Blade Runner* universe would expand to a size we have yet to encounter, which would be a good thing since these films are much too important to simply fade away into obscurity.

20 years from now, I want to once again be able to say that the fact that we're *still* talking about *Blade Runner* is nothing short of amazing.

I am very proud to be able to bring you this book, along with my co-editor Joe Bongiorno and the good folks at Sequart. The writers are a wonderful cross-section of hand-picked film aficionados, film industry folks, critics, writers, editors, and subject-matter experts, but most of all, they are all tried and true *Blade Runner* fans.

Some of the essays contain information that may overlap, so be patient because there's a lot of good information coming at you from a lot of different perspectives. The *Blade Runner* universe is a relatively small one when compared to other pop culture staples.

It's been an absolute pleasure working on this book and I hope you enjoy it as much as I've enjoyed putting it together with this wonderful team.

Have a better one.

The Death of Everything: *Blade Runner*, Entropy, and the Drums of Doom – a Foreword

by Paul M. Sammon

> The culture out of which punk (rock) arose reminds me of the Bertolt Brecht opera *The Rise and Fall of the City of Mahagonny*, where you can do anything you want if you got money, but if you don't have money, you're a criminal, you're scum, and you're a puke. And the milieu out of which punk arose also reminds me of the *Blade Runner* movie set—the kind of lifestyle where it's gritty, ominous, the drums of doom, only you don't know if they're the drums of doom or somebody's song. But there's always the drums underneath it all, drumming.
>
> — Ed Sanders. *Please Kill Me: The Uncensored Oral History of Punk: 20th Anniversary Edition*[1]

Listen.

Can you hear them? They're faint, but there. Whispered. Worrying. Despaired. The faint, persistent thrum of *Blade Runner*'s *true* soundtrack.

The drums of doom.

---

[1] Legs McNeil and Gillian McCain; Grove Press/Atlantic, Inc., Aug 2016.

Many only do eyes. They see detail, and design. Neon. Retrofitted sets. Weapons, costumes, smoke. Rain, perpetual rain. Noodles. Flying cars.

Some bypass their senses altogether, sieve *Blade Runner* through their brains. They analyze. Deconstruct. Talk character, plot, or the lack of it. Rhapsodize about subtext. Argue the essence of man.

We who listen also see, of course; who can escape *Blade Runner's* visual tsunami, its pictorial wipeout? We ponder, too. Evaluate. Think, yes, what *does* it mean to be human? But the lizard ears of our limbic-level souls cannot help but flinch at *Blade Runner's* primal, insistent scraping. We *feel* that constant, distant dirge.

Beneath *Blade Runner's* mesmerizing imagery, its seminal, still-astonishing showcasing of the melancholy beauty of decay trills a keening, unsettling wail. A futuristic siren song which inexorably leads us to wreck upon the black, annihilating reefs of entropy, and malice, and despair. And we cannot steer away. For *Blade Runner's* true destination is not spiritual redemption, or empathy, or love.

It is death. The death of everything.

The numerous essays in this volume which follow ably excavate the many other worthy aspects of Ridley Scott's classic science fiction/film noir hybrid. That is only to be expected. Since its release in 1982, *Blade Runner* has become one of the late 20th century's most cited examples of pop-culture post-modernism, a dusky gem whose darkly glittering facets long ago escaped the multiplex. Architecture, fashion, typography, production design, signage, graphics, textual and cinematic narratives; many of these real-world arts and crafts have today, in one form or another, absorbed or replicated the densely layered mash-up of the classical and the new for which *Blade Runner* remains justly celebrated. The various pieces herein do a man's job of explaining same.

Yet, for this author, one who was there from 1980 through 1982, who obsessively recorded first-hand *Blade Runner's* entire pre-production, principal photography, post-production, special effects work, publicity phase, and original theatrical release (a process recounted in my revised, updated 2017 edition of the HarperCollins book *Future Noir: The Making of Blade Runner*, now available as a trade paperback and e-book), the *Blade Runner* moment I most clearly recall does *not* involve any of the aforementioned filmmaking processes.

Of course, I was absolutely enthralled by *Blade Runner's* amazing, neon, smoke and rain-drenched sets, just as I was struck by the talents of its well above-average cast and crew and awed by the herculean, sometimes dreadful labors all endured to jointly create this cinematic monument. I likewise felt thrilled and humbled to be granted total, ongoing access to every soundstage, department, and crewmember involved in *Blade Runner's* making. As I was, and still am, touched by the eventual friendship I formed with author Philip K. Dick, whose 1968 novel *Do Androids Dream of Electric Sheep?* was the source novel behind *Blade Runner* itself.

Still, and for all that, the white-light *Blade Runner* moment that most strongly resonates for me today involves a brief exchange between Ridley Scott and myself, part of the first (and lengthy) interview I conducted with the director months before the *Blade Runner* shoot began. It went something like this:

Why, I asked Scott, had Ridley chosen to do *Blade Runner?* His answer was simple yet, retrospectively, profound. The director explained that he'd previously, immediately after the successful release of *Alien,* been struggling through a prolonged and difficult pre-production adaptation of Frank Herbert's epic science-fiction novel *Dune,* for Italian mogul-producer Dino De Laurentiis. At roughly the same time, the filmmaker's older, still relatively young brother Frank Scott unexpectedly died of events related to skin cancer.

"That shook me," I remember Scott saying. "*Dune* wasn't going anywhere, so I bailed. Then I looked at *Blade Runner.* I thought, 'I need to work and this is what I need to work on.'"

That admission, I think, is the secret key unlocking *Blade Runner's* most fundamental subterranean door. Yes, Scott was clear from the beginning that he intended *Blade Runner* to be a combination of a fully created futuristic world overlaid with the essential tropes of 1940s-era *noirs*; the morally ambiguous anti-hero, the eye candy of dutch angles and shadowy expressionistic lighting, the femme fatale, the downbeat feeling of encroaching, inevitable doom. But Scott noticeably grabbed those noir clichés and raised them to another order of magnitude.

Consider: in *Blade Runner*, nearly everything and everyone is touched with entropy or corruption. Most of earth's animals have gone extinct. Its central location, Los Angeles circa 2019, is a teeming, impossibly over-crowded mega-hive whose infrastructure seems barely functional. Its mean, filthy streets are riddled with violence, sex clubs, open-air bars, thievery and death. The planet's weather has also eroded, bathing L.A. 2019 in a near-perpetual downpour of acid rain. Meanwhile, older buildings have not been torn down or rebuilt; they have been retrofitted, slapped together with aging spare parts that nonetheless suggest that despite such "repairs," these structures could collapse at any moment.

There's more. The metropolitan police have become an ubiquitous paramilitary presence, whose sanctioned "blade runners" are, in reality, banally-bureaucratized, socially acceptable death squads. The finer angels of our nature have also fallen. Most of the human characters portrayed in Scott's film are deeply flawed: repressed, angry, self-absorbed, power hungry, greedy, stricken with disease. Further, casual cruelty is the norm, as is – in the case of Rick Deckard, *Blade Runner's* nominal hero – social isolation. And by *Blade Runner's* climax, all of the film's most charismatic characters – its replicants – are dead. Deckard himself? This cynical, burnt-out alcoholic killer, who shoots women in the back, ultimately finds himself on the run, soon to be pursued by the very police force that employed him, leaving Deckard emotionally tied to a doomed artificial woman who has only a few years left to live.

Is it any wonder, then, that my memory obsessively returns to the moment Ridley Scott mentioned he took on *Blade Runner* to distract himself from his brother's death? If that was indeed the case, and there is every indication that it was, it seems obvious that *Blade Runner* became, at bottom, a very intense form of personal therapy for its celebrated designer and director, a knotty way of both working out the private feelings he was experiencing regarding his brother's untimely passing and Scott's public statement concerning the eventual extinction that awaits us all.

Death lurks everywhere in *Blade Runner*, as does our inevitable mortality. This is a film stuffed to bursting with all things entropic; the demise of culture, kindness, people, places, animals, things. Of optimism, there is none. In fact, *Blade Runner's* brightest lights, its only true innocents, are its replicants (I intentionally exclude the character of J.F. Sebastian from this group, who, despite his childlike character, professionally colludes with and is therefore amorally attached to Eldon Tyrell, *Blade Runner's* reptilian corporate czar). The replicants have had no say in their genesis or growth. They are genetically engineered victims, whose artificially implanted memories and extremely short life spans imply beings essentially living from moment to moment, like accelerated children. Yet the replicants are also brutally homicidal...as well as members of a newly-minted slave caste.

So for every argument that *Blade Runner* offers viewers glimmers of hope, I would counter by pointing out that those feeble lights are smothered by the film's all-encroaching darkness. Roy Batty's dying speech about "things you people wouldn't believe" is admittedly moving, but it is delivered upon a filthy, rain-soaked rooftop. And Deckard? He may have been slightly nudged towards a certain spiritual reawakening by his understanding of the replicants' fierce lust for life, yet, as previously noted, that insight turns him into a societal fugitive. And his new-found romantic relationship with Rachael will be very, very short.

What then, ultimately, does *Blade Runner* tell us? That beloved family members can die at any moment, and they won't be coming back. That animals will disappear to become impossibly rare luxuries, not even affordable by the ultra-rich. That man's tampering with the environment will turn the very weather against him. That buildings will crumble, and the mighty will fall. And that while those with the power, or the money, may be able to escape the living hell of Los Angeles 2019 to the supposedly beautiful "off-world colonies," *Blade Runner* never offers any evidence of that paradise except through relentless, overbearing advertisements.

It's not a pretty picture, *Blade Runner*, on any level. This, I think – in addition to its justly celebrated graphic design, mesmerizing editorial rhythms, moving music, and subtextual ideations – is why Ridley Scott's best film continues to strike such a resonant emotional chord. A film which, by its director's own admission, is also his most personal. And we feel that. We feel Scott's sorrow, and alarm, and cynicism, and despair. Death lurks everywhere in *Blade Runner*, whether overtly delivered through the massive firepower of Deckard's blaster or the more subtle depiction of its decaying, dying streets.

All of which, if you will only listen, continue to be haunted by those distant drums of doom.

There's Some of Me in You: Revisiting *Do Androids Dream of Electric Sheep?*

by Lou Tambone

Talking About Memories

In 1968, prolific writer Philip K. Dick published a novel called *Do Androids Dream of Electric Sheep?* that, at first, appeared to be just another story in a long list of the author's repertoire. Interest in adapting the book for film happened relatively quickly, although the project would exchange hands and writers for years until eventually landing in Ridley Scott's lap.

The first time I was exposed to the novel was shortly after seeing the film *Blade Runner* in 1982. When I saw the film, I was a curious 12-year-old, a sponge for new ideas. The film affected me in a way that's hard to explain, mostly because I can't conjure up those same thoughts and feelings the way I could with a film like *Star Wars* which I saw when I was seven. That juggernaut brought us to another universe, but *Blade Runner,* much like *Star Trek*, took place in *our* future, and *Blade Runner* not only looked like it was around the corner, but offered a much bleaker vision of the future than something like *Star Trek*.

The movie tie-in version of Philip K. Dick's *Do Androids Dream of Electric Sheep?*, which was retitled *Blade Runner* for the occasion.

The curious 12-year-old previously mentioned was killing time between *The Empire Strikes Back* and *Return of the Jedi* by learning as much as he could about *Blade Runner*. At that point in my life, it was all about music and film. *Starlog* magazine was required reading and I followed the production of the film through that publication almost exclusively. When the film was released, it was the *Official Blade Runner Souvenir Magazine* that led to my extended interest in the film.[1] If I recall correctly, I purchased this magazine the day I saw the film, right at the theater. Sometimes, when films were released back then, theaters would sell souvenir magazines at the counter where you bought your ticket – which you had to do *in person* (imagine that!) From those two sources, I learned about Philip K. Dick and the inspiration for *Blade Runner*, his novel called *Do Androids Dream of Electric Sheep?*

So naturally, I *had* to have that book.

When I saw *Star Wars* as a kid, I remember owning the novel, which was released well before the film. (I don't remember if I had the book first, but I don't think I did.) The film blew me away, so of course I wanted the book. The great thing about it was that it was different from the film in many ways. Lots of scenes that were ultimately deleted from the film were still in there. Many of the lines were different. It was like an alternate version and you had to connect the dots to create a cohesive story in your head. Most of all, it was *fun*.

So when I learned that *Blade Runner* was based on a book, I felt I absolutely had to read it immediately. I thought it would be a similar feeling, but *wow* was I off the mark. When I read Dick's book, I felt like I needed to read it again. I remember thinking, right from chapter one, *do I have the right book?* The cover was rebranded by then to be more marketable and sported the film's poster, so yeah, I had the right book, but it was *so* different from the film that I wasn't prepared for what I was reading. I was also young and naïve, so I'm positive that many of the book's deeper aspects flew over my head like a police spinner.

What I do remember, though, was that I *liked* it. I liked it almost much as I liked the film. The big difference was that it wasn't as tangible to me as a kid. I couldn't see it like I could see the film moving before me. The book was more abstract and forced me to think, re-reading passages over again trying to extrapolate mental imagery.

Every few years, I'd re-read it and every few years it would make a little more sense to me as I grew older and learned more about life. The book seemed to change as I did. It grew up and matured along with my personality.

---

[1] http://www.cinephiliabeyond.org/blade-runner-souvenir-magazine-fascinating-blast-past-heart-ridley-scotts-masterpiece/

Even re-reading it again umpteen years later, it feels like it's changed yet again, and I along with it. Neither of us appears to be the same.

Looking back, I feel it was an artistic rite of passage, in a way; a nostalgic reminder of a simpler, more curious time. Because of the film, the book became something quite special to me. They're an odd pairing of artistic bookends that complement each other well. If not for the film, I might never have read the book or given it a chance, and that's an experience I'm grateful for to this day.

We've Got a Lot in Common

When talking about *Do Androids Dream of Electric Sheep?*, *Blade Runner* always seems to overshadow any real discussion. Folks know and love the film so much that the book tends to fall by the wayside.

If you're one of the uninitiated who hasn't read the book, then there are a few things you should probably be aware of. It's different, it's dustier, it's darker (you probably thought that wasn't possible), and it's definitely trippy. Many of the heady plot lines were stripped out for the film, which for better or worse, resulted in a more streamlined story. Elements of back-story have been totally wiped out with very subtle nods to the source material peppered throughout. The film isn't a strict adaptation at all, but more of a reimagining. If you go into the book with this in mind, you'll find it a lot of fun. If you go into it expecting the film's carbon copy with some dialogue changes and additional scenes, then you're going to be let down, or at least very confused.

Dick drops you directly into a futuristic 1992 (this was later changed to 2021, and is 2019 in the film) where World War Terminus has ravaged the planet so horribly that the United Nations is trying to relocate the human race "Off-World," ostensibly to save it. That itself is a good example of the approach that the filmmakers took in adapting the book to film. The talking blimp that flies all over Los Angeles above Deckard's head is always going on about the Off-World colonies. So the reference is there, just without the full context. There's no talking about a world war (if it happened at all in the film version) or the United Nations. The concept appears in the film simply as a thing people can do in the future, should they choose.

A popular quote from the film's screenplay comes from Eldon Tyrell as he proudly announces his company's motto: *More human than human*. The book most certainly delves into the theme of humanity and what it means to be human, however, running in parallel is the exact opposite theme of *de*humanization, which is much more prevalent in the book's subtext than the film, where it's more on the surface and almost glossed over.

The androids, known as Nexus-6 "andys" (the word "replicant" is only used in the film) still have a short life span, due to their cells basically dying out after a time, but unlike the film, they are not actively seeking a way to correct this intentional design flaw, as far as we're told. They've escaped Mars (where andys exist as personal slave-rewards to migrating humans) and have come to Earth to live out their days, hoping no one will notice they're fugitive androids. The problem is that one of these fugitive Nexus-6 andys shot and nearly killed Deckard's fellow bounty hunter (the term "Blade Runner" is also only used in the film) Dave Holden. After that, the chase is on.

The andys want to fit in. They want to be human, or human-like. They masquerade as humans to get what they want or need, be it work, a place to stay, or even protection, which they find in the form of J. R. Isidore, J.F. Sebastian's literary doppelganger. They would gladly live among humans peacefully if those pesky humans would just let them be.

People like Deckard and Phil Resch (another bounty hunter Deckard meets later in the book) see them as less than human, at least at first. Resch doesn't really bend on this notion, but as the book progresses, Deckard starts to have a change of heart. His experiences in the book drastically change him. That's not a stretch when making a comparison to Deckard in the film, but the book gives us a deeper look into Deckard's psyche as those changes are happening.

In both the film and the book the word "empathy" is employed abundantly; more so in the book. In the film, there's mention of an "empathy" test when referring to the Voight-Kampff test, but not much more. An entire sub-plot in the book revolves around empathy. The survivors of World War Terminus who remain on dystopian Earth have found religion, it seems, and it all revolves around empathy. It's called Mercerism, named after its spiritual leader, Wilbur Mercer. Using special empathy boxes, followers join in consciousness with Mercer in a sort of virtual reality world. In this world, they become one with Mercer, sharing a torturous pilgrimage as he tries to climb a mountain but is relentlessly pummeled by falling rocks.

This is where the notion of dehumanization comes into play. At the very same time that the andys are trying to become like humans, the humans, it seems, are slowly becoming more mechanical, more devoid of emotion, and perhaps *less* human.

Deckard's wife Iris, for example, spends a lot of her time in the book moping around and generally being depressed. In order for her to feel better, she doesn't go to therapy or take some anti-depressants. She doesn't read a book or go out shopping. Deckard suggests that she "dial up" a new mood on the handy-dandy Penfield Mood Organ machine. This is a device that allows humans to *program* their moods for the day. It's not conditioning or training, which one would normally associate with humans, but programming which is something associated with machines or computers. Deckard even notes that he believes the andys have more of a desire to exist than his own wife.

Oddly enough, the humans in the book feel threatened by the few andys that escape to Earth. They're not just threatened out of fear for their lives, but they feel threatened about possibly being replaced by superior beings. They fear extinction. If these andys are allowed to roam free, one day they could wipe everyone out and there won't be any humans left. All this subtext is symbolically relayed via Deckard's boss, Harry Bryant, as he describes Deckard's mission.

This is naturally a metaphor for xenophobia. The roots of many of our negative aspects as humans, like racism and discrimination, lie in xenophobia, which is (loosely) the fear of someone or something we feel is foreign, strange, or different from us.

When the United States was a young country, slave labor was a common practice, especially in the south. Slaves were often regarded as lesser beings, and most-likely less than human. When they were freed, people often hated them and openly discriminated against them, even outright murdering them out of pure hate, but why? Many believe one reason was fear: the fear that they, people of a different color or status, would rise up and take over *their* safe, comfortable world. Fear can often lead to hatred. We fear what we don't understand and therefore hate it when it comes knocking on our door. The andys were literally slaves, albeit on another planet, and they escaped. What was the punishment for a slave who ran away, be it in our past or in Philip K. Dick's future Earth? They were hunted down and destroyed, of course. Could something like that happen again in our near future? Is it happening already? These questions are as valid today as they were in 1968.

Taking that theme one step further is the character of J. R. Isidore. He's what they call a "chickenhead" or a "special" which means he's too poorly equipped mentally to be allowed to migrate off of Earth. Saying that only those who fit into a certain bracket of intelligence are the only ones who are free to leave the planet and live off-world is discrimination at its purest. He's seen as a lesser human than any others who remain behind due to their line of work or some other reason. These specials are treated like second-class citizens, generally abused and made fun of right to their faces, as if their lives don't even matter. Their services are not required to further the human race, thank-you-very-much. Is it any wonder that when andys show up in his building, he feels empathic toward them, going to the extent of breaking the law to try and protect them? These non-humans show him more respect that any human ever has. As you can see, the recurring theme of empathy once again shapes and directs character after character.

There's also a bit of class warfare going on in the book's sub-plotting that has to do with animals, who play a larger role in the book than they do in the film. Because so many animals have become extremely rare or extinct after World War Terminus, people who own *real* animals are seen as upper-class citizens even though no one's ever *really* sure if the animals are real or "electric." Deckard and his wife own a fake sheep, for instance. They used to have a real one but the class warfare was so intense that when it died of tetanus, they immediately purchased an identical fake to replace it so no one would notice. If it were known that they owned a fake animal, they would be viewed as lower class. People are so obsessed with this notion of buying animals (both real and fake) that almost everyone keeps a pocket "Sidney's" catalog with them at all times in case they want to look up how much an animal is going for at the time. In fact, the driving reason behind Deckard's acceptance of the job to hunt down the Nexus-6 refugees is to make enough money to purchase a new, real animal. The concept of "keeping up with the Jones's" is apparently still alive and well in the dusty future.

This particular subplot comes to a head near the end of the book. Deckard, armed with reward money for retiring the android opera singer Luba Luft and hoping to instill some happiness in his depressed wife, buys a real goat to replace his electric sheep, believing it will give them status. This works for a while until Deckard goes home after his mission is over to find that Rachael Rosen, an android identical to Pris and employee of the Rosen Association run by Eldon Rosen, has shown up.

Rachael Rosen of the book is a far more sinister and cunning character than the sympathetic and somewhat clueless Rachael we know from the film. Rosen is a deceiver, not only in the literal sense in that she's an android, but in every other sense of the word also. She tries to bribe Deckard with hush money to protect herself and the Association. She offers to help Deckard with his mission and while Deckard refuses at first, he eventually caves in and calls her, only to wind up sleeping with her and falling in lust with the android woman who then drops an anvil on his heart by telling him she only sleeps with bounty hunters to keep them from doing their jobs. One of the nine she's stopped so far happens to be Phil Resch, who helped Deckard with his efforts in retiring Luba Luft. Everything she did, she did for the company. While Deckard can't bring himself to kill her, he abruptly leaves her and moves on with his plans, faith shattered even more. That's when she decides to kill his goat and ruin him, a devious move for an android, but then again, that's what happens when you lack empathy.

One of the more fun leitmotifs in the book involves an omnipresent media personality named Buster Friendly who stars in nearly non-stop television and radio shows under the banner of *Buster Friendly and his Friendly Friends*. Along with Wilbur Mercer, Buster Friendly is the other popular name known on the planet. Whenever you turn on a television or radio, Buster is there, yet somehow the people left on earth are unable to put two and two together and realize that it's impossible for someone to perform both 23 (he apparently gets an hour off each day) hours of radio and 23 hours of television work at the same time. This goes unquestioned, but perhaps on purpose. To admit that someone you love and respect is nothing but a fake, or as the novel suggests, an andy, would mean that you are worshipping a non-human.

Since we're on the subject of worship, Buster Friendly has an ongoing beef with Wilbur Mercer, the other being who humans openly worship. It's a bit of a one-sided feud, however. Buster goes to great lengths in the book to debunk Mercer as a fraud, which in the end he does with physical proof, exposing Mercer as Al Jarry, a retired Hollywood actor who performed the Mercer experience which runs on a loop for those who "fuse" with Mercer. They're really seeing the same "movie" every time they grab the handles of their empathy boxes, but are blissfully unaware of anything shady.

Let that sink in for a moment as you think about the dehumanization of Earth's populace in the book. Two of the biggest names on Earth are most likely not real people at all. One's a washed up actor and the other is probably an android. False idols, indeed.

One of my favorite characters appearing in the book but not the film is the aforementioned bounty hunter Phil Resch. One could debate that he evolved into Gaff but in my head, they're two completely separate individuals, unlike, say, J.F. Sebastian and J.R. Isidore who I think of as the same person. Phil's a great character although he only appears in earnest for a couple of chapters in the middle of the book. His chapters are some of my favorites for mainly two reasons. First, they're just so weird and seem to come out of nowhere, which I enjoy. Second, they represent a major turning point for Deckard in the book.

In short, Phil Resch is a bounty hunter from another police precinct across town, but one that Deckard has never heard of before. As it turns out, the whole place is a sham designed, staffed, and run by androids – except for Phil Resch, who (as it's determined later by a test Rick gives him) is 100 percent human. Deckard finds himself arrested and brought to the station after tracking down Luba Luft, one of his intended targets. Before he can test her, she calls the police. Deckard allows this, hoping to either call her bluff or simply have the police station confirm his being there, forcing her to cooperate. This all goes south when a cop he doesn't know arrives and takes him to the phony police station after a series of odd deceptions which turn out to be orchestrated by yet more androids. The officer whose name is Crams is an android who is, as it's also implied with Luft, unaware that he isn't actually human.

One of the station's chief inspectors named Garland meets Deckard and accuses him of being an android. He calls in Phil Resch, who is the precinct's version of Deckard, and there's talk of testing not only Deckard but Garland too, at the request of Deckard himself. It's such a paranoid scene that Resch is just about ready to test everyone in the station by the time they're all done talking. Garland eventually admits the sham while Resch is out getting his equipment. He comes back in to find Garland ready to kill them both but Resch employs his bounty hunter reflexes and shoots Garland in the head first. Then the two hunters make their escape.

Working together, they track down Luft, and Resch ruthlessly retires her in a brutal way with little warning. The two are now so full of paranoia that they agree to test each other to make sure they're not androids. Deckard tests Resch only to find that he's a human (at least based on the results). Deckard also comes up human, albeit now a new and improved brand of human complete with empathy for androids.

These scenes of heavy paranoia are some of the most important ones in the book as they start to make Deckard question both humanity and his job for the first time. You can see it when he's so taken aback at Resch's retirement of Luba Luft with such reckless abandon. In the film, these enquiring experiences are different and relate more to his relationship with Rachael than anything else, but the idea is the same. Deckard is questioning humanity itself and what it means to be human, even though in the book he's undoubtedly human while in the film it's very strongly implied that he's a replicant.[2]

In Retirement...

It's fitting that such a thought provoking piece of literature could beget such a thought provoking piece of cinema, albeit well over a decade later. It's always been a wonder to me why it never spawned more direct spin-offs. As far as the original novel, there weren't any companion pieces to go along with it for a long time. Things like a BBC radio drama, audiobooks, and even a stage adaptation eventually reared their heads, but they were all produced well beyond the year 2000. The book lived a lonely life until 1982, when it received newfound popularity with folks like myself, and then retreated back into the shadow of the film adaptation.

Some notable exceptions (albeit latecomers) would be two comic series, which were released around 2010. BOOM! Studios took on the enormous undertaking of producing a 24-issue limited series comic adaptation. This adaptation was remarkable for many reasons, but the main one being that it was an unabridged adaptation of the original novel. Every word in the book was in the comic, eventually resulting in a Bible-sized compendium, which is still in print. This kind of adaptation doesn't happen very often and it's a testament to the novel's strong material that the company thought their adaptation should be unabridged. They could have easily shortened it or changed it in many different ways, much like Ridley Scott did for his film. They decided against this and the results are outstanding. They were so outstanding that a short time later, they published an eight-issue prequel to the novel called *Dust to Dust* which took place right after World War Terminus and, among many other things, documents the rise of Mercerism, but mainly takes us on another bounty hunter's mission. As far as the original novel, that's the closest we have to a spin-off in this rich universe, unfortunately.

As for the film, there were three spin-off novels written by K.W. Jeter (a friend of Dick's) that tried their hardest to capture the magic of the films, but according to many, never quite got there. At times they melded the plots and characters of the film and book, even going so far as to feature both J.F. Sebastian and J.R. Isidore as separate characters in the same book, even though

---

[2] Except in the theatrical version which leaves out Deckard's unicorn dream.

Sebastian's character in the film was based on the novel's Isidore. Reviews were mixed and they never made a lasting impression. Today, they're widely disregarded and with the release of *Blade Runner 2049*, they've been thankfully rendered irrelevant.

As we all know, sequels to classics can be a tricky prospect, even when not everyone agrees that *Blade Runner* is a classic. *Blade Runner 2049* changed our perspectives forcing us to look at the original novel and film in a different light. With any sequel, there will be those who love it and those who don't, plus a few fence-riders. It didn't perform well at the box office but it certainly wasn't as divisive as something like *The Last Jedi*, which almost single-handedly split the *Star Wars* fan base down the middle. Filmmakers like Ridley Scott and Denis Villeneuve seem to care more about their films' integrity and less about their blockbuster statuses.

In any case, there's never a bad time to reacquaint ourselves with not only the original film (and its many versions) but also the wonderful, thought-provoking novel that started it all before we decide if *Blade Runner 2049* passed the Voight-Kampff test or is just another emotionless replicant.

Ethics, Empathy and Reverence for Life: How Philip K. Dick Warns Against the Normalization of Apathy and Violence in *Do Androids Dream of Electric Sheep?*

by Joe Bongiorno

>**Papageno:** "My child, what should we now say?"
>**Pamina:** "The truth. That's what we will say."
> — from Mozart's *The Magic Flute*
>
>For in much wisdom is much grief: and he that increases knowledge increases sorrow.
> — Ecclesiastes 1:18

Although rightly hailed as a thought-provoking, noir, science-fiction opus, in fact, *Blade Runner* – the sumptuous film adaptation of Philip K. Dick's 1968 seminal novel *Do Androids Dream of Electric Sleep?* – barely scratches the surface of the themes played out in the original.

Aware that the majority of American movie audiences, unlike book readers, can handle only so much on a Friday night, director Ridley Scott, along with screenwriters Hampton Fancher and David Peoples, traded in much of the heady material from the novel for a more palatable sci-fi stew. As it turns out, a commitment to the novel and its author's themes was not of great interest to those adapting it, as evidenced by the dim view Fancher expressed of Dick, calling him in one interview a "monster," "egomaniac," and "crazy"! [1] Scott, meanwhile, never even bothered to read the book, saying "he couldn't get into it."[2]

Admittedly, a faithful adaptation would likely not have succeeded at that time, and despite the critical and fan acclaim *Blade Runner* has garnered in 35 years, even it – as flattened, reduced and degraded from the novel as it is – was subjected to scathing reviews and poor box office performance. Test audiences couldn't follow the simple story, and viewers cited the film as depressing and "deadly dull."[3]

Putting aside the fact that different people have different tastes, there is more than a kernel of truth to the sociological idea that many simply don't want their entertainment to challenge them, to ask them to think deeply, or to confront them with unpleasant realities, and a film that requires them to do these things is hardly going to be well received. "The American people are basically anti-intellectual," Dick opined, "They're not interested in novels of idea, and science-fiction is essentially the field of ideas."[4]

To be fair to Americans, the work week is a long and exhausting drudge, and home life is made up of relationships that are difficult and sometimes less than fully-functional. No surprise then that Hollywood – perceiving that most prefer their weekends filled with easy amusements and distractions – overloads the screen with lurid thrills and mindless violence. Forms of art that honestly present social criticism, let alone expose the viewers' inner demons, hardly meets those requirements.

---

[1] *On the Edge of Blade Runner,* documentary by Mark Kermode, UK: Channel, 2000.
[2] http://totaldickhead.blogspot.com/2007/09/ridley-scott-on-blade-runner.html
[3] http://www.tgdaily.com/games-and-entertainment-features/70236-the-disastrous-early-blade-runner-reactions
[4] *On the Edge of Blade Runner,* documentary by Mark Kermode, UK: Channel, 2000.

Thankfully, there are exceptions to every rule. *Blade Runner*, although jettisoning the most salient aspects of the source material, still maintains a deep sense of integrity as a film unto itself, and one which asks audiences to follow Rick Deckard's journey as he comes to see that the synthetically created *replicants* are just as human as we are, and deserving of a life free from enslavement and violence. The underlying moral is clear: society has no right to impose slavery and violence upon one another, regardless of external differences stemming from race, culture, gender, creed, sexual orientation, and/or socioeconomic factors.

The leap may not be a hard one to make, but it still requires audiences to use reason, to draw parallels, to *think*. This, of course, is where many falter. Psychotherapist and author M. Scott Peck noted that "one of the major dilemmas we face both as individuals and as a society is simplistic thinking – or the failure to think at all. It isn't just a problem, it is *the* problem."[5]

Regardless of the openness of its audience, art has as its prerequisite the commission to be truthful, which is what gives it its power to wake people up from the slumber of complacency, misguided thinking, and harmful activities. Yet, it's precisely because art requires active mental and emotional participation that it's been supplanted by mere entertainment, much of which actually reinforces the somnambulant, consumerist, self-centered "lifestyle" so prevalent in the modern age.

The perverse aversion to thinking and truth-seeking, even in art and entertainment, hasn't boded well for society, as witnessed by the rot within the political, cultural, spiritual, and intellectual/academic spectrums. It is beyond the scope of this essay to look at the many serious sociological issues that stem from this dilemma, or to discuss how the propagandistic engineering of a somnambulant citizenry has contributed to civilization's deepening decline. That is the job of the prophets and artists – inclusive of which are our science-fiction and fantasy writers – and that is exactly the mantle that Philip K. Dick wears.

In his novel, *Do Androids Dream of Electric Sleep?* (herein referred to as *Androids*), Dick points out two main problems of the human condition, as well as the means to overcome and transcend them. These problems are strongly tied into the overarching philosophy developed by physician, theologian,

---

[5] *The Road Less Traveled & Beyond: Spiritual Growth in an Age of Anxiety*, by M. Scott Peck, M.D., Simon & Schuster, 1997.

musician, and Pulitzer Prize winning philosopher Albert Schweitzer, who encapsulated it in the phrase *Ehrfurcht vor dem Leben*, or Reverence for Life. Dick was well aware of Albert Schweitzer, and even referenced him in at least three of his novels, *Eye in the Sky*,[6] *The Three Stigmata of Palmer Eldrich*,[7] and *The Man Whose Teeth Were Exactly Alike*.[8]

The idea of ethics, morality, and empathy are crucial themes in *Androids*, and it's helpful to see how Schweitzer defined them within his overarching philosophy: "Ethics," Schweitzer explained, "grow out of the same root as world-and-life-affirmation, for ethics... are nothing but reverence for life. That is what gives me the fundamental principle of morality, namely, that *good consists in maintaining, promoting, and enhancing life, and that destroying, injuring, and limiting life are evil*."[9]

With this greater understanding of good and evil in mind, Schweitzer goes on to demonstrate how the head and heart are tied into living an ethical way of life, which is the encapsulation of the revolutionary Christian teaching found in the Golden Rule: "The fundamental fact of human awareness is this: 'I am life that wills to live in the midst of life that wills to live.' A thinking man feels compelled to approach all life with the same reverence he has for his own. Thus, all life becomes part of his own experience."[10]

In Dick's future-world of *Androids*, "World War Terminus" ended about a few decades prior to the start of the narrative, and resulted in the destruction of countless humans and animal species. No one remembers why the war was started or even who won. A plague followed, killing off even more people and animals. Then came the androids, built to assist in the construction of off-world colonies, foremost of which is Mars. The two main problems that led to this doomsday scenario shroud everything that happens in the story.

The first is that of insufficient or incorrect thinking. It may be surprising to know that well-educated men and women in the high-ranking fields of politics, science, and economics do not think well at all. Dr. Peck notes that "an all-too-common flaw is that most tend to believe they somehow instinctively know how to think and to communicate. In reality, they usually do neither well

---

[6] *Eye in the Sky*, by Philip K. Dick; Ace Books, 1957.
[7] *The Three Stigmata of Palmer Eldrich*, by Philip K. Dick; Doubleday, 1965.
[8] *The Man Whose Teeth Were Exactly Alike, by Philip K. Dick;* Mark V. Ziesing, 1984.
[9] *The Philosophy of Civilization*, by Albert Schweitzer; Prometheus Books, 1948. Italics my own.
[10] "Albert Schweitzer Speaks Out," *World Book Yearbook,* 1964.

because they are either too self-satisfied to examine their assumptions about thinking or too self-absorbed to invest the time and energy to do so... when challenged, they show very little awareness of – or become easily frustrated by – the dynamics involved in truly thinking and communicating well."[11]

In his *The Decay and Restoration of Civilization*, Schweitzer clarifies that thought is "no dry intellectualism, which would suppress all the manifold movements of our inner life, but the *totality of all the functions of our spirit in their living action and interaction*."[12] Clear thinking, therefore, would prevent the kind of compartmentalization that allows the average person to commit "small" acts of cruelty and evil while still considering himself a "just" and "good" person.

Corollary to lack of thinking and foresight, and prominent throughout the book, is the second problem, the utter absence of ethical concern or empathy, what Schweitzer defined as Reverence for Life: "To the man who is truly ethical all life is sacred, including that which from the human point of view seems lower on the scale."[13] Living ethically would, thus, eradicate not only racism and nationalism, but speciesm.

Having failed to think wisely or well, self-satisfied, self-absorbed, without engaging the totality of all the functions of their spirit, and failing to hold the sacredness of life above power and wealth, mankind's ruling elite destroyed much of its own kind along with a large swath of the creatures they shared the planet with. The blame, however, does not rest solely with the politicians who sought greater power, nor even the corporations who sought greater wealth, the scientists who built bigger bombs, or the military leaders who demanded more war, but with the ruled majority who, year after year, decade after decade, century after century, tolerated (and in many cases, supported) the actions of such men. Schweitzer writes:

> We tolerate mass-killing in wartime – about 20 million people died in the Second World War – just as we tolerate the destruction by atomic bombing of whole towns and the populations... When we admit to ourselves that they were the direct results of an act of inhumanity, our admission is qualified by the reflection that "war is war" and there is nothing to be done about it. In so resigning ourselves, without any further

---

[11] *The Road Less Traveled & Beyond: Spiritual Growth in an Age of Anxiety*, by M. Scott Peck, M.D., Simon & Schuster, 1997.
[12] *The Decay and the Restoration of Civilization*, by Albert Schweitzer. A. & C. Black, ltd., 1929. Italics my own.
[13] *Out of My Life and Thought*, by Albert Schweitzer; H. Holt, 1949.

resistance, we ourselves become guilty of inhumanity. The important thing is that we should one and all acknowledge that we have been guilty of this inhumanity. The horror of that avowal must needs arouse every one of us from our torpor, and compel us to hope and work with all our strength for the coming of an age when war will no longer exist.[14]

In other words, the recognition of our guilt coupled with the horror of the fact that we have been inhumane, should awaken us from our moral slumber and urge us to fight against war and its warmongers without using their weapons. In recognition of this uncomfortable truth, *Android's* world is guilt-ridden, existentialist, and depressed. A deep sense of melancholy pervades its characters and the book itself, as if to suggest that this is not the stylistic artefact of an author's story, but the prophetic exemplification of a doomed race already fallen, faded and cursed. Yet, it's within this scenario that a paradox arises: humans are, perhaps for the first time since *the fall*, learning to think and value life.

Neither *Androids* nor *Blade Runner* offer easy answers, requiring instead that audiences think and feel as they embark on the same journey of consciousness awakening that the acutely damaged protagonists embark upon, characters who will, by story's end, find there is much more going on beneath the surface than they realized.

In *Androids,* society makes a much more concentrated effort to be (or at least appear to be) ethical, compassionate, and less like those who led them into mass annihilation. This is best embodied by the internal musings and dialogue of the three main protagonists still living on a post-Apocalyptic Earth at a time when many of the survivors have left for colony worlds. There is the disenchanted bounty hunter Rick Deckard, his depressed wife Iran, and a lonely artificial animal repair van driver named John R. Isidore. All three of these begin their journeys as if they're the dying remnant of a once-great people in the twilight of its years, soon to be nothing more than the radioactive ash and detritus that fill their forlorn buildings, what *Androids* refers to as *kipple*. In the film adaptation, this deep sense of melancholy is present in the music and noir aesthetic elements, the incessant rain, the dim lighting, the haunting cityscape, a futuristic panoply of high-tech neon and plasma, offset by a multitude of jabbering beings and flying vehicles, a darker, dirtier *Jetsons*, a world gone very wrong. The perpetually forlorn Deckard coupled with Vangelis' evocative score hint at the despair that suffuses the characters' lives in the novel.

---

[14] *On Nuclear War and Peace*, by Albert Schweitzer; Brethren Press, 1988.

The film's Deckard is world-weary and hard, but there's no reason given as to why he should return to work as a bounty hunter, save for a nebulous threat from his former employer Captain Bryant. By contrast, the book's Rick Deckard is motivated by a desire to make enough money to afford a living, breathing animal. That might seem odd to those who've never read the novel, but it's demonstrated that in their society, not only are real animals extremely rare – and expensive – as a result of the war, but are considered sacred. They're also valued for the sense of worth they bestow upon their caretakers. Having an animal (or even a rare insect) to take care of is a chief indicator of one's empathy, a trait prized above all else due to the realization that the absence of it is what led to the near-extermination of all life. Not taking care of an animal is considered immoral and anti-empathetic. It was even a crime in the days immediately following the war.

Yet, due to the high cost of animals, the most the average worker can hope to afford is a synthetic version. A synthetic ostrich, for example, costs $800.00. By comparison, the real thing costs $30,000.00. Synthetics are constructed so as to seem identical to the real thing, and the same work is required in caring for one. Yet, for Rick and others, there is a deep sense of shame in not caring for a real animal. He and his wife Iran have an electric sheep that they tend to, and although his few neighbors don't even suspect that it's synthetic, Rick resents it, seeing in this fake sheep a constant reminder of the quality of his life: artificial, empty, and sad.

It's not just the sense of pretense that bothers Rick. He genuinely wants to care for a creature, to be part of the solution – which is to effectively restore life to a dead world – to take pride in knowing that he and his wife are the kinds of people who do that. Rick knows that altruism will give their lives the meaning, purpose and joy that they're otherwise lacking. Thus, he feels he's wasting time on an electric sheep that can't appreciate his efforts or love him in return; it can only simulate appreciation and love.

Rick's career path presents a sharp conflict of interest. As a bounty hunter, he's an agent of death, a hunter of rogue androids. Although his wife questions the morality of this, society views androids as nothing more than machines that've become broken and dangerous. The new Nexus-6 models that he's sent to hunt might be more intelligent and deadly than previous models, but they still lack human empathy. Iran suspects there's more to them than meets the eye, but Rick can't allow himself to consider such possibilities, otherwise he'd be forced to quit, which would effectively end any aspirations he has to afford a real animal and lead a fulfilling life.[15]

Apart from their role as caretakers, people function within this society with the aid of three external factors. The first is an upbeat television show hosted by the colorful, loud (and decidedly irritating) Buster Friendly and His Friendly Friends, which plays on the television and radio 23 hours a day, and reports on all matter of news and entertainment. Those who watch his program generally do so because his buffoonery temporarily drowns out the emptiness of their world and lives. The parallels to the entertainment and infotainment of our world are clear.

The second is a device called a Penfield Mood Organ, which generates user-programmed moods for whatever state of mind one wishes to feel at a given time. There are emotions for every occasion. Conveniently, for those lonely souls who don't want to watch Buster Friendly, there's even a setting that makes you want to! Though not explicitly stated, this digital mind/mood altering device is a high-tech substitute for drugs and alcohol.

The third factor, which along with the prior two, is also absent from the film, is a spiritual/psychological program called Mercerism. This will be discussed in depth later, but it's clearly an analogue to our monotheistic religions.

It's not hard to see why the filmmakers would center their story on the action-y bounty-hunting aspects of the troubled lead character Rick Deckard, played so well by Harrison Ford, and his romantic entanglement with the replicant Rachael, embodied in the beautiful Sean Young. In the film, the bounty hunting employment is portrayed as exciting, giving Deckard the same kind of masculine glamor that the heroes and antiheroes of action films generally possessed, but Scott later subverts that, so that both Deckards develop along the course of their journey until they arrive at greater empathic awareness and transcendence.

The film eliminates Rick's wife entirely. A crucial character in the novel, Iran and Rick present a realistic, dejected couple who've become estranged as the pressures of the world take their toll on them. Both are seeking authenticity,

---

[15] Rick and Iran's self-sacrificing nature can be discerned from the fact that they choose to not have children, that they sublimate that desire for a greater good, both to assist in helping repopulate the world with animal life, and because they don't want to subject a child to the misery that plagues their world.

love, and meaning, but each is going about it in different ways. For example, after hearing the sounds of emptiness in their building, Iran decides to program her Penfield Mood Organ to make her feel depressed six hours a day, twice a month, followed by a more uplifting mood setting. She's not crazy, as some readers might conclude. Rick has heard it too and understands what it portends. Silence is emblematic of death, of loss beyond measure, of the daily encroachment of human extinction. But for Rick, the answer is to use the Mood Organ to feel better, not worse. As earlier noted, the Penfield Mood Organ is a kind of drug that allows users to escape feelings of sorrow and pain. But it's for this very reason that Iran needs to feel depressed. Depression is the only *authentic* response to the fact of a dying world that they (the human race) helped create. Everything else is just escapism.

Rick isn't far behind Iran in the depression department, yet his wife's approach frightens him, fearing it will only lead to deeper despair from which she'll never climb out. The novel doesn't suggest that either is at fault for thinking the way they do, or that the tool itself is evil; it simply reflects two opposite responses to the world they're in. Rick doesn't understand his wife, and sourly concludes that "most androids... have more vitality and desire to live than my wife," and this frustration and inability to connect with her is a catalyst for his later act of adultery with the very vital and desirous Rachael.

As in the film, Rick meets Rachael when he's sent to talk with the creators of the Nexus-6 model and ascertain if the Voigt-Kampff Empathy Test will be able to distinguish androids from humans. Based on the idea that empathy only exists within the human community, the test has, thus far, been their most effective tool, which functions by analyzing the involuntary responses that arise to questions or scenarios that would cause empathetic individuals to react. Rick is asked to use the Voigt-Kampff Test on a high-level representative of the Rosen Association (changed in the film to the Tyrell Corporation), Rachael, who is also said to be the niece of Eldon Rosen, head of the corporation. Among the scenarios the test presents its subjects with are: a gift of a leather wallet, a dead butterfly collection, a picture of a bearskin rug, people eating a lobster, a cabin with a deer's head mounted on the wall, and an abortion.

What's interesting is that these scenarios are deemed so horrific that the average human in that culture would react with revulsion. Even Rachael – who's later revealed to be an android – either knows enough to simulate such a response, or actually does. She decries the boiling alive of a lobster as "depraved." In our world, such base depravity is commonplace and considered culturally acceptable by all but a minority. *Androids,* thus, presents an interesting, if tragic observation. The near annihilation of animal life has finally gotten people to value animals for *who* they are – not as gratification for taste buds, or as fashion items, decorations, or entertainment – but as living, feeling creatures with their own intrinsic worth. Schweitzer predicted "The time will come when public opinion will no longer tolerate amusements based on the mistreatment and killing of animals. The time will come, but when? When will we reach the point that hunting, the pleasure in killing animals for sport, will be regarded as a mental aberration?"[16]

The film version has Ford flatly asking some of the same questions, but without the context of the novel, the audience doesn't understand their significance. More egregiously, the film leaves out the lobster question – and Rachael's response to it – substituting instead the "boiled dog" question (which in the book was asked later on to the android Luba Luft). This safer approach reveals an unwillingness on the part of the filmmakers to present or deal with the book's challenge to carnism – the belief system that claims it's fine to eat some animals (e.g., cows, chickens, pigs) but not others (dogs, cats) – and humanocentrism (or anthropocentrism) – the belief that because humans are the most significant entities in the universe, they have the right to exploit other species for their own benefit. Schweitzer addressed these two entrenched views, noting that the former is nothing more than unethical egoism, while the latter is subjective and arbitrary: "In the past we have tried to make a distinction between animals which we acknowledge have some value and others which, having none, can be liquidated when and as we wish. This standard must be abandoned. Everything that lives has value simply as a living thing, as one manifestation of the mystery that is life."[17]

In eliminating one of *Android's* most provocative themes – that our selfishness and apathy towards the exploitation of animals are a catalyst for the torture, suffering, and death of countless creatures slaughtered for food, clothing, and accessories – the film, thus, takes the easy road. That it also leaves out the idea that a future society has condemned the abortion of a fetus as a lifestyle choice reflects, as well, a cowardly unwillingness to court controversy.[18]

---

[16] *Animals, Nature & Albert Schweitzer*, editing and commentary by Ann Cottrell Free; The Flying Fox Press, AWI Special Edition, 1988.
[17] *The Schweitzer Album*, by Albert Schweitzer; Harper & Row, 1965.
[18] The book does not touch on the extreme case of risk to the mother's life.

Contrary to its advocates who cite *Blade Runner* as "hard science fiction," by comparison to the book, the movie is actually light sci-fi.

In stark contrast, *Androids* doesn't shy away from asking tough questions; it doesn't preach, politicize, or drive home any agenda. It simply does what good literature (and subsequently good science fiction, fantasy, and horror) is supposed to do: hold up a mirror to the true and oftentimes grotesque face of our society.

To that end, *Androids* is harshly critical of the corporation, specifically the kind of transnational corporations that the Rosen Association represents. Rachael is routinely sacrificed by this corporation, first as a test subject to try and discredit the Voigt-Kampff Test, but even more egregiously, as a whore to get empathic bounty hunters who sleep with her to stop hunting androids.

Both tactics generally work. Rick initially accepts the false story that Rachael failed the test because she has underdeveloped empathy due to being only 18 years old and raised on an interstellar ship most of her life. The owl seen in the film is more than just set dressing in this crucial scene. Explaining that owls are extinct save for this specimen and one other, Rachael uses Rick's love of the bird as a lure, offering it to him in exchange for his acceptance of the test's failure in distinguishing humans and androids. He proves to be more diligent than they realize, and discovers that both Rachael and the owl are synthetic.

When Rick confronts Eldon Rosen with the accusation that they knowingly created a killing machine that cannot be detected by any known test, Eldon deflects with the usual corporate justification that he's merely providing a service and giving the people want they want, and that if he didn't, another company would. "It's just business" is as tired, thoughtless, and immoral a cliché as "I was just following orders," but it's one that real-life corporations continue to get away with as they rampantly pollute, poison, and destroy.

Employing truth mixed with a lie, Eldon then blames the police for using a test that doesn't work and potentially murdering humans with underdeveloped empathy. Dick actually doesn't discount this possibility. The corporations, government, and police force are the least changed from our world and thus the most recognizable. Dick will turn his attention to law enforcement and the police state in his book *Flow My Tears, the Policeman Said*, but here, as if channeling his thoughts through Rick, he focuses on the evils of corporate power: "A mammoth corporation like this – it embodies too much experience. It possesses in fact a sort of group mind. And Eldon and Rachael Rosen consisted as spokesmen for that corporate entity. His mistake, evidently, had been in viewing them as individuals. It was a mistake he would not make again." Ironically, he does exactly that in regards to Rachael who he comes to see as an individual, and it nearly proves his undoing, not because she's a replicant and incapable of being an individual, but because she's so deeply embedded in corporate culture.

This aspect of embedded evil and groupthink, of "meet the new boss, same as the old boss" is part of the dystopian genre that the novel and film are often placed within. *Androids,* however, subverts dystopia to look at positive change, not in the world's institutions, which remain exploitative, destructive, and duplicitous, but for the individuals who make up those institutions. Rick, Rachael, and the escaped Nexus-6 models, all engage in the expected cycles of their respective types, inclusive of which is deceit and violence, but they also begin to escape those prisons, as if recognizing in them their ultimate futility, immorality, and stupidity.

One of the prisons employed by the governments and corporations is the unremitting push to get people off-world. The other is the anxiety over social and cultural standing. Together, they provide the carrot and stick; the former includes the incentive of getting a free android; the latter is the fear of becoming second class, embodied in the incessant television propaganda: "Emigrate or degenerate! The choice is yours!"

Given that the Nexus-6 models feel so negatively towards their former employment on Mars that they killed and stole a ship to get back to Earth, it seems clear to the reader, if not the citizen, that the State is using propaganda to lure people to work as slaves on their colony worlds. The perpetual fearmongering adds yet another layer of stress to an already stressed-out citizenry, worried that they too will become affected by radiation, and denigrated from being considered "regular" to subhuman: "special," "degenerate," and "biologically unacceptable," which would leave them sterile and unable to emigrate: "Loitering on Earth potentially meant finding oneself abruptly classed as biologically unacceptable, a menace to the pristine heredity of the race."

John R. Isidore (replaced by a rather different J.F. Sebastian in the film) – likely named after Jack Isidore, another misunderstood but valiant character from Dick's earlier novella *Confessions of a Crap Artist* – is one whose been deemed "biologically unacceptable" and "special." As if this wasn't enough to utterly humiliate and ostracize him, his failure to pass a minimum mental faculties test leaves him characterized as a "chickenhead." As it turns out, Isidore is one of the most intelligent and empathetic characters in the story.

Dick's misfits are his most beloved characters. John Isidore *is* "special," but not in the ways that society has determined. Isidore is a man of deep thought and intuition, a paragon of compassion who seeks out the welfare of others at his own cost. This is first made explicit when the androids Irmgard, Roy, and Pris come to hide out in John's building after Rick begins finding and retiring their associates.

Isidore is also the best thinking character in the book. After first meeting Pris, he explains to her the profoundly deep concept of "kipple," which on the surface refers to garbage and useless things, but which has a more existential meaning as something that will one day take over everything: "No one can win against kipple… except temporarily and maybe in one spot, like in my apartment I've sort of created a stasis between the pressure of kipple and nonkipple, for the time being. But eventually I'll die or go away, and then the kipple will again take over. It's a universal principle operating throughout the universe; the entire universe is moving toward a final state of total, absolute kippleization… except of course for the upward climb of Wilbur Mercer."

Hardly the thoughts of a simpleminded man!

These same ideas are echoed by Rick when at the opera house to find his next bounty, Luba Luft, whose been hiding in plain sight as an opera singer, he thinks to himself while listening to a rehearsal of Mozart: "This rehearsal will end, the performance will end, the singers will die, eventually the last score of the music will be destroyed in one way or another; finally the name 'Mozart' will vanish, the dust will have won… We can evade it awhile. As the andys can evade me and exist a finite stretch longer. But I get them or some other bounty hunter gets them. In a way, he realized, I'm part of the form-destroying process of entropy."

Rick reasons that empathy likely only exists amongst herbivores and omnivores, as empathetic carnivores would otherwise starve. Androids, who are in some ways greater than humans, stronger, faster, and smarter, must therefore be akin to solitary predators. One of the primary doctrines of Mercerism is "kill only the killers." This gives him a moral out. But not entirely, and he asks himself that if androids are predators, is it not their nature to kill in order to survive?

As in the film, his inner conflict is brought to the fore when he comes to see that they're sentient – in the true sense of that word, as beings capable of

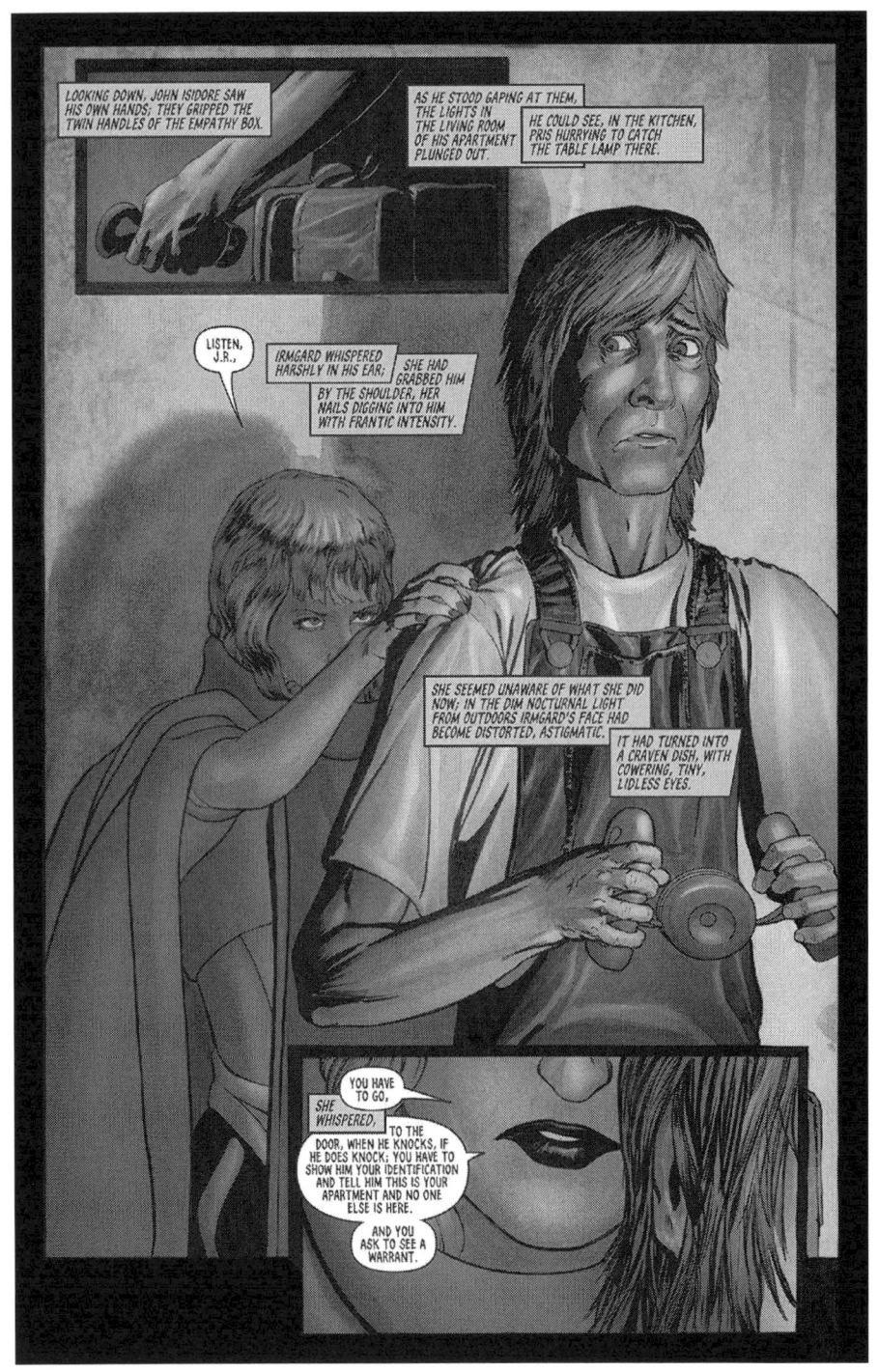

J.R. Isidore as seen in the *Do Androids Dream of Electric Sheep?* comic adaptation.

feeling – in much the same way that animals are.[19] This means that his work as a bounty hunter, which requires his murder of these beings, betrays the very ethical standards to which he and his wife hold themselves to.

A large part of what is so fascinating and enjoyable about *Androids* is the fact that its protagonists are thinking, feeling people. Isidore, for example, correctly ascertains things that the average person would miss. He intuits very quickly that there's something different about Pris Stratton: "Now that her initial fear had diminished, something else had begun to emerge from her. Something more strange. And, he thought, deplorable. A coldness. Like, he thought, a breath from the vacuum between inhabited worlds, in fact from nowhere: it was not what she did or said but what she did *not* do and say."

When Isidore later meets Pris' companions, he perceives: "they're all strange. He sensed it without being able to finger it. As if a peculiar and malign *abstractness* pervaded their mental processes." Seeing Roy Baty, he has a "strange hallucination" and thinks: "he saw briefly a frame of metal, a platform of pullies and circuits and batteries and turrets and gears – and then the slovenly shape of Roy Baty faded back into view."

Rick, who in many ways serves as Isidore's less-actualized spiritual double, picks up on the very same thing about Luft when he first meets her, and even uses the same words to describe her: "Her tone held cold reserve – and that other cold, which he had encountered in so many androids. Always the same: great intellect, ability to accomplish much, but also this. He deplored it."

Isidore also figures out that there's something off about Buster Friendly and his regular cadre of media celebrities, who never seem to grow tired or old, despite broadcasting both a streaming television show and an audio show 23 hours a day each! His employer Hannibal Sloat concludes that Buster, like Mercer, is an immortal, superior being from another system, but Sloat is nowhere near as intuitive or insightful as Isidore, who finally concludes that Buster's derision of Mercerism is a result of the comedian's jealousy and competition for the soul of the people. The narrative seems to confirm Isidore's conclusion, strongly hinting that Buster and his friends are frauds, androids tools of the state providing a never-ending circus designed to keep the people

---

[19] By and large, *Star Trek* influenced science fiction to erroneously repurpose the word "sentient," which refers to the ability to feel (and suffer), to mean "sapient," capable of using knowledge, experience, and reason in one's actions (as humans are capable of), which devalues animals (who are sentient) into mechanical, non-sentient entities.

perpetually distracted.

Isidore instead devotes himself to Mercerism. An important aspect of the novel, Mercerism teaches empathy and is staunchly against war and violence to any and all living creatures. Mercerism is named after Wilbur Mercer, a spiritual guide who can be accessed through a kind of virtual reality machine called an Empathy Box. Once "fused" through the machine, Mercer leads people up a mountain, where along the way stones are thrown at him and those he guides from unseen persons. The bruises are real, as evidenced by users after they've shut off the Empathy Box. Their persecution creates a shared experience of suffering and community as they overcome trials along the arduous journey with Mercer. Once they reach the mountaintop, they fall into a realm called Tomb World, which as the name suggests, is the common grave of man and beast, akin to the Hebrew word *sheol* used in the Old Testament. There, Mercer dies and comes to life again, along with the dead beasts and those who are fused with him.

That participants continually return to fuse and make this journey with Mercer, knowing the subsequent punishment that it will deliver demonstrates not only a deep sense of relief from their personal sufferings and societal guilt, but also the psychological healing that comes of community, hope, and transcendence. Individuals who are fused can also impart their joys and alleviate their suffering with one another. Schweitzer spoke on the value of such community, noting that "At times our own light goes out and is rekindled by a spark from another person. Each of us has cause to think with deep gratitude of those who have lighted the flame within us."[20]

Mercerism is, essentially, a post-apocalyptic metaphor for Christianity; there are principles meant to guide and help people grow, doctrines intended to offer big-picture answers and hope, tenets against violence, and a congregational community where individuals can help and be helped by others. There is also that religion's downside: the ignorance and idolatry of its practitioners. Mercer has been elevated by some from mere prophet into a god. This isn't a teaching of Mercer, but rather a by-product of human frailty that leaves Mercerism vulnerable to attack. Buster seeks to discredit Mercerism and succeeds in doing so, exposing Mercer as a former alcoholic and fraud. But the

---

[20] *Reverence for Life: Sermons 1900-1919*, by Albert Schweitzer; Irvington Publishers, 1993 (originally published in German, 1966).

narrative reveals this to itself be fraudulent, not only because Buster is probably an android shill of the state, but because Mercerism was never about a man.

Rick hasn't fused in some time because he feels he's betrayed the principles of Mercer. Although he continues to try to justify his actions, after his encounter with Luba Luft, his worldview and choices are profoundly altered. Luft and her crucial scenes are excised from the film and replaced instead with a sexualized character named Zhora, an exotic dancer, who's considerably more violent than her book counterpart. Deckard kills her in the film, but the only reason we know he feels any remorse is due once again to Vangelis' sorrowful score and Harrison Ford's reaction, but the viewer is left to infer that either he feels bad because he had to kill such a beautiful woman or because he shot her in the back. Needless to say, this is a far flatter, shallower scene than the one in the novel.

Luft in *Androids* is talented and smart; she even turns the tables on Rick, accusing him of being a pervert, and having him arrested. Luft is the first person to question Rick's status as human, calling him "peculiar, hard and strange," and suggesting that his memories might be false and implanted. The policeman who arrests him suggests he might have the memories of a human bounty hunter. These turn out to be little more than a clever ruse to trip him up, and not intended to be the big mystery it is in the Director's Cut of *Blade Runner*; they're there to create a role reversal and to help the reader to see that there's actually little difference between humans and androids. Yet it's from this scene, and the identity of Phil Resch, that Fancher likely conceived the idea of Deckard potentially being a replicant.

Phil Resch is a fellow bounty hunter, whom Rick meets when he's carted off to a mysterious stationhouse that he never knew existed run by senior police officer Garland. They, in turn, have never heard of him or his superior Bryant. As it turns out, Garland is on Rick's list of targets! Before Resch retires him, Garland tells Rick: "we're not even considered animals... every worm and wood louse is considered more desirable than all of us put together." He then tells him that Resch is actually a Nexus-6 model with false memories. Confronted with the possibility of being an android, Resch argues that androids are cold-blooded machines only interested in self-preservation and unable to feel for any living creature. How then can he – a caregiver for a real squirrel that he loves – be one?

Unfortunately for Luba Luft, this introspection comes too late, as it's Resch who kills her, but her final moments have a profoundly chilling effect on Rick.

Rather than try to escape or do harm to them, she makes an unusual request, and asks Rick to buy her a book containing the Edward Munch painting *Puberty*. The image is that of a wide-eyed young girl, nude on her bed, with a looming black shadow to the right of her. The shadow represents sexual anxiety as the girl's body and mind changes during maturity. In asking him to buy it for her, Luft is, in effect, asking him to try and understand who she is, and how androids could mature if given the chance. Knowing that she's going to soon be killed, this very act is one of empathy that reflects her successful passage through a metaphoric state of puberty, which she'd accomplished by imitating humans, who she finds "strange and touching," and considers a superior life form.

Interestingly, Isidore considers the androids he befriends to be "very superior" to humans, believing that because of their high intelligence he could learn a lot from them. Rick later challenges this notion, but by that point he's come to see the androids in a wholly new light.

Rick's acceptance of Luft's request is his first step towards becoming empathetic to androids. Rick actually tries to prevent Resch from killing her. When he fails, Rick destroys the art book, confounding Resch who can't fathom why he'd obliterate something of value. Of course, that's Rick very point: to show Resch how he had destroyed something of great value, and he underscores it by asking him if he thinks androids have souls. Resch isn't as psychologically or spiritually aware as Rick, and fails to comprehend the point. Rick then tells him: "I'm getting out of this business... I can't anymore; I've had enough. She was a wonderful singer. The planet could have used her. This is insane."

Resch presents another kind of role reversal when it's revealed that he's not an android after all, but human. Rick, thus, determines that Resch must enjoy killing or have underdeveloped empathy. Shockingly, he concludes that he'd have rather have killed Resch than Luft. "So much for the distinction between authentic living humans and humanoid constructs," he thinks to himself. When he has Resch give him the Voigt-Kampff Empathy test, Rick discovers that he's developed considerable empathy for androids in general. Resch tries to convince him that it's nothing more than sexual attraction, and confirming Rick's poor assessment of him, suggests he should sleep with the female androids first before retiring them. Against his better judgment, this is a theory Rick will actually test.

Following Luft's death, Rick collects on bounties for her, Garland, and another android named Polokov, who'd been posing as a Russian bounty hunter. The money and the grief combined cause him to rashly purchase a real Nubian goat, which he brings home to his wife. Despite their concern over future payments, Rick and Iran's spirits are considerably cheered by the animal. He explains to her that he's had a change in his perspective towards the androids, as well as a greater understanding of her depression and the worthlessness she sometimes feels. His new insight and joy, however, are confounded by the impracticality of his decision. Payments on the goat are going to force him to remain a bounty hunter at a time when he's come to believe it's immoral to do so.

Before he can even consider other career options, Bryant calls him back to work to retire the three remaining androids before they flee their latest hideout. Distraught, he fuses with the Empathy Box, and comes to realize that his suffering is in some ways greater than Mercer, who doesn't have to compromise his integrity. He suddenly receives a vision in which Mercer explains that he's not a god and can't save him, but he's there to show him that he's not alone and that he should carry out the task of retiring the remaining androids. While this goes against the concept of Mercerism, and is essentially wrong, Mercer explains that it yet must be done. This is a paradox. The androids are, for all intents and purposes, people, and it's wrong to harm them; yet, they're also murderers with underdeveloped empathy who will kill again if not stopped. Rick can't comprehend the paradox or understand how it's both wrong and, yet, the right thing to do. Dr. Peck explains that paradox is the reality of life and the developed mind does well to avoid easy answers and oversimplifications: "If you want to think with integrity," he writes, "and are willing to bear the pain involved, you will inevitably encounter paradox."[21]

Mercer tries to explain that the violation of one's identity is something every creature at one time or another is forced to do. "It is the ultimate shadow, the defeat of creation; this is the curse at work, the curse that feeds on all life." Although failing to grasp his larger meaning and concluding that Mercer is just an old man climbing to his death, Rick moves on to the final part of his own overarching empathy test, which he doesn't yet realize he's taking. Because Rick doesn't allow his self-doubt and dissonance to stop him from challenging his preconceived notions, he's the opposite of the clichéd hero and antihero overflowing with testosterone and confidence in his power and

---

[21] *The Road Less Traveled & Beyond: Spiritual Growth in an Age of Anxiety*, by M. Scott Peck, M.D., Simon & Schuster, 1997.

violence. He's not infallible and isn't even the book's most moral character (a distinction that falls to Isidore), but he soon comes to see and acknowledge that "the only one who was right is Mercer."

Rick's infallibility is brought to the fore when he takes Rachael up on her offer to help him defeat the remaining Nexus-6 models. He commits adultery with her, in violation of his marriage and the law, both of which he's begun to feel are hollow. Rachael is the most complex of all the androids in the book, and much closer to the femme fatale of the noir genre than her portrayal in the film, which pits her as the characteristic mysterious woman, who Deckard falls in love with. In *Androids*, Rick falls in love with her, as well, but this has disastrous consequences. After he tells her about his goat, she reveals that she was sent to evaluate the androids for flaws so that the Nexus-7 models will be even more indistinguishable from humans. She tells Rick not to go after the remaining Nexus-6 models, particularly Pris Stratton, who is the same model she is, fearing that he'll retire her by mistake. She even promises to kill Pris for him.

The next day, he tells her that he'd marry her if he could, and says that she's alive: "Legally, you're not. But really you are. Biologically. You're not made out of transistorized circuits like a false animal; you're an organic entity." Rachael, however, turns on him, acknowledging that she's been playing him in order to get him to stop killing androids, a tactic that's worked on every bounty hunter before him, except Resch. Feeling betrayed, he begins to understand how Resch became so warped. For her part, Rachael's glad her mission succeeded, but she then says something odd: "That goat... You love the goat more than me. More than you love your wife, probably. First the goat, then your wife, then last of all –"

Rick isn't dissuaded from his mission, not because he wants to do it, or because he still believes they're just rogue machines. He does it because it has to be done. This is borne out by what occurs next.

Having lived for years in a large, empty apartment complex by himself, Isidore is understandably glum. He's not hampered by undue guilt, torn by cognitive dissonance, or part of the "form-destroying process of entropy" that Rick believes he is. He simply wants a different career because the "synthetic suffering of false animals" ties his stomach in knots. When he later discovers that his new friends are hunted Nexus-6 androids, he doesn't hold it against them. He even agrees to take a leave of absence to protect Pris.

Pris is a fascinating character study; moody and petulant, her tempers run from elation to depression in a matter of seconds. She openly weeps, acknowledges feeling lonely, and has a passion for space opera novels and films! She's also snobbish, as her android friend Irmgard calls her when she openly mocks Isidore – her benefactor – as a chickenhead. Pris is also cruel, first hinted at when she reveals to her companions that Isidore has a crush on her. Irmgard appears to be the most empathetic of the bunch, and takes the time to thank John and proclaim him the first friend they found on Earth. True to her mercurial nature, Pris agrees and calls Isidore "a great man" and a credit to his race.

Pris's cruelty comes to the fore when she tortures and kills a spider. After expressing horror at this, Isidore points out that insects are "especially sacrosanct." Pris bristles at this, and echoing Garland's earlier statement, says that by contrast, "everything organic that wriggles or squirms or burrows or flies or swarms or lays eggs..." is protected. But not them.

As with the lobster example in the Voigt-Kampff Empathy Test, the depravity of Pris pulling the legs off a spider might be considered no big deal to the average reader, most of whom have probably given no thought to smashing a spider found in their homes. The act, however, is portrayed horrifically in *Androids*, pushing its readers to think and feel greater than they previously have, to intellectually, emotionally, and spiritually acknowledge what Schweitzer argues is each creature's inherent right to life without being injured or impeded by us, except in cases of absolute need: "We must fight against the spirit of unconscious cruelty with which we treat the animals. Animals suffer as much as we do. True humanity does not allow us to impose such sufferings on them. It is our duty to make the whole world recognize it. Until we extend our circle of compassion to all living things, humanity will not find peace."[22]

Yet, despite all this, and despite Roy's suggestion that they kill him and depart, Isidore's loyalty remains firm. This might seem naïve to many, but Isidore's love for his android friends is built on hope, empathy, and forgiveness, even as it's initially motivated by loneliness. Very little of this is present in his film counterpart, J.F. Sebastian – a genius who makes robotic toys for himself and gets to play chess with the uber-wealthy Eldon Tyrell, head of the Tyrell Corporation. Fancher's screenplay isn't as insightful or understanding of Isidore

---

[22] *The Philosophy of Civilization*, Parts 1-2, by Albert Schweitzer; Prometheus Books, 1987.

as Dick is, and the film writes Sebastian off as an inexperienced man-child who foolishly trusts and loses his life to Roy Batty.[23]

While there is a childlike quality to John Isidore, it's endearing and noble; similarly, there is a *childish* quality to the Nexus-6 androids. Selfishness and cruelty are inherent in some small children that good parents work hard to help them overcome. The androids, however, cannot go through the normal process of emotional and spiritual maturation, certainly not as slaves or fugitives, and it's this that ultimately retards their ability to transcend their selfish desires and become fully empathetic.

It's ironically in their cruelty that it becomes apparent that the androids of *Androids* are more than machines, and like us are imperfectly functioning "living things." After Rick succeeds in killing Pris, Irmgard, and Roy, Rachael steals into Rick's building and kills his beloved goat, a reaction that's clearly precipitated by the very human emotions of anger, revenge, and jealousy. She seeks to hurt him by killing the creature she believes he loves best. Rick is proved correct in his assessment. She's an organic entity, biologically different from humans, but no less capable of thought and feeling. It's more prominent in Rachael because she's not been on the run, but as Luft earlier suggested, the potential for emotional and psychological maturation is there in all the Nexus-6 models.

This is the reason the novel's title isn't *Do Androids Dream?*, but rather *Do Androids Dream of Electric Sheep?*. Rick asks and answers the former in the affirmative: "Evidently: that's why they occasionally kill their employers and flee here. A better life, without servitude. Like Luba Luft, singing Don Giovanni... instead of toiling across the face of a barren rock-strewn field. On a fundamentally uninhabitable colony world." The dream of electric sheep represents a deep longing for empathy and connection to something – expressed in Rick's own longing for a live sheep, for something outside of himself to show love and compassion to. Because of the animals' calming nature, many children were told to think of sheep when they're trying to fall asleep. The sheep, in the Christian tradition, is symbolic "of innocence, gentleness, peacefulness, and patience under suffering and typifies the gentle qualities associated with Jesus."[24] Rick's dream of having a real sheep to care

---

[23] Presumably. We never see a body, and the K.W. Jeter sequels show him alive and well.

[24] http://www.think-differently-about-sheep.com/Sheep%20_In_Religion_and_mythology.htm

for is a dream about a world in which these qualities of innocence, gentleness, peace and patience under suffering are exemplified. If the Nexus-6 android – created in man's image – can long for a similar level of empathy, then how much more so should we – created in God's image – strive to extend our circle of compassion to all living creatures?

There is undoubtedly a cost to living empathetically, and that is suffering, paramount of which is the pain that comes at the death of a loved one: "Owners who get to love their animals... go to pieces," opines Hannibal Sloat in *Androids*. C.S. Lewis in his book *The Four Loves* remarks on this state of love as inclusive of suffering:

> There is no safe investment. To love at all is to be vulnerable. Love anything, and your heart will certainly be wrung and possibly be broken. If you want to make sure of keeping it intact, you must give your heart to no one, not even to an animal. Wrap it carefully round with hobbies and little luxuries; avoid all entanglements; lock it up safe in the casket or coffin of your selfishness. But in that casket – safe, dark, motionless, airless – it will change. It will not be broken; it will become unbreakable, impenetrable, irredeemable. The alternative to tragedy, or at least to the risk of tragedy, is damnation. The only place outside Heaven where you can be perfectly safe from all the dangers and perturbations of love is Hell.[25]

Isidore suffers from his depth of feeling and moral character, and is pained by his loneliness and losses, of the spider, of his new friends – who although empathetically underdeveloped – were still beloved of him. This unstinting depth of love is ultimately why Mercer comes to him; firstly, to give him back the spider, now restored to life and limb, but also to reassure him that he's a highly moral person and that despite Buster Friendly's exposé, Mercerism is real and won't go away.

This is underscored by Rick's second fusion with Mercer, this time without the Empathy Box. The implications of what Mercer says to him are clear: prophets are not gods; they're flawed human beings, sometimes deeply so. And that fact is less important than the truth of their message. Those who wrongly viewed him as a god will lose their faith in not only him, but the principles, doctrines, and community that Mercerism provided, leaving them only Buster Friendly to turn to. Yet, guilty of the sin of idolatry, they missed the whole point of the message, which is: reverence for life, transcendence of suffering, and the knowledge that life continues after death. Dick champions Mercer because, in a sense, he is living out that example. Through his books, he conveys a measure

---

[25] *The Four Loves*, by C.S. Lewis; Geoffrey Bles, 1960.

of wisdom and truth that he, as an individual, can't live up to. But it's his art and what it conveys that matters, not his personal failings as an imperfect man.

Rick suffers from having to commit violence against what he now knows are living beings, and who he understands can't be expected to be more than what they are given their circumstances. Although he must violate Mercer's greatest precept, he does so while gaining greater empathy for the androids who are tragically too far gone, having killed in their escape from Mars, are willing to kill again, and display a grossly indifferent attitude towards life. His confrontation with Pris, Irmgard, and Roy lacks the power of the visual counterpart, and there is no moving "Tears in Rain" speech by Roy Batty, which is the outstanding climax of the film. Rick simply kills them because they brandish weapons and try to kill him. He acknowledges to Roy that he knows he loved Irmgard, just as John loved Pris, and he loved Rachael. Even though forced to kill him, Rick acknowledges Roy's humanity, and, by extension, the humanity that all androids possess.

Rick then goes a step further, inviting Isidore to live in his building. Isidore isn't able to accept this invitation to friendship, but he does say that he's going to move to a more populated part of the city. At last, he understands that he has to nurture himself and not unduly suffer because of what society has foisted upon him. But Isidore's grief moves Rick to deeper guilt: "I'm a scourge, like famine or plague. Where I go the ancient curse follows. As Mercer said, I am required to do wrong. Everything I've done has been wrong from the start." But this isn't true, and out of the darkness comes light.

When Rick returns home, he discovers the murder of his goat. Now emotionally devastated, he departs for Oregon, where the narrative hints that he may intend suicide. Yet, like Mercer's hike upon the mountain, Rick reaches a metaphoric and literal place of death, and then comes back to life. This is signified by his final and permanent fusion with Mercer and the discovery of the toad, an animal long thought extinct, and Mercer's most precious animal.

With this, Rick comes to see that there's something greater in life, there *is* meaning, there *is* hope, and all of it is built on other-centered love, the Golden Rule, *Ehrfurcht vor dem Leben,* Reverence for Life, "If I'm Mercer... I can never die, not in ten thousand years. Mercer is immortal." The point of fusion has been to grow in empathy with Mercer – not the man – but the concept. The spiritual connection between Rick and Isidore is made manifest when Rick finds the toad, and says to himself: "I'm a special... Something has happened to me. Like the chickenhead Isidore and his spider; what happened to him is happening to me. Did Mercer arrange it? But I'm Mercer. I arranged it; I found the toad. Found it because I see through Mercer's eyes." Empathy is the key to immortality. Rick returns home the happiest he's ever been, elevating Iran, to whom he reveals what's transpired.

Isidore represented what an ethical and empathetic person can be; Rick surpasses him because he's required to do so much more. He must work at an unpleasant task, take responsibility for it, suffer the consequences of that responsibility, and all the while grow more deeply empathetic. That he does so is why he becomes – in essence – Mercer. Mercer is a cosmic, prophetic ideal for compassion and transcendence. When told that Buster Friendly exposed Mercer as a fake, Rick responds: "Mercer isn't a fake. Unless reality is a fake." And when the toad is later revealed to be electric, Rick arrives at a far more enlightened conclusion that he would have even just a day earlier: "It doesn't matter," he says to his wife. "The electric things have their lives, too. Paltry as those lives are." Whereas before he resented his electric sheep, he can now extend love even to an electric toad. Whether or not the toad can reciprocate no longer matters; it's enough to know that he's doing good for this tiny life.

His enlightened state is matched by Iran's, who has also grown through her suffering. Iran – who may have appeared (particularly to male readers) selfish at first – is shown to be willing to exchange her joy for the pain of another who's suffering, mature in the awareness that if she holds onto her joy, she can retain part of it. She also genuinely loves her husband, who, in her sorrow, she took for granted. Although her depression wasn't an affectation, but an attempt to live emotionally honest, she comes to see that there are other ways to live honestly. She says that to live is to live under a curse that forces us to sometimes do things that are wrong. She explains to Rick that this curse was brought about by those who seek to destroy life, clarifying for him that the killers are the destroyers of life and liars. "The killers throw the rocks; it's they who are doing it. Still pursuing [Mercer]. And all of us, actually." In effect she's admitting that it's not just the androids who are hunted, but everyone. Some succumb to their wounds and die; some become killers themselves; and some – like John, Rick, and Iran, grow and rise above it.

In all this, *Androids* reveals the potential for transcendence despite suffering. Society will likely not grow, but individuals can, and individuals make up society. Rick chooses to become a promoter of life rather than a destroyer. It's a decision – to suffer and yet remain empathetic – that every human being can make. This, of course, implies that there's something morally and

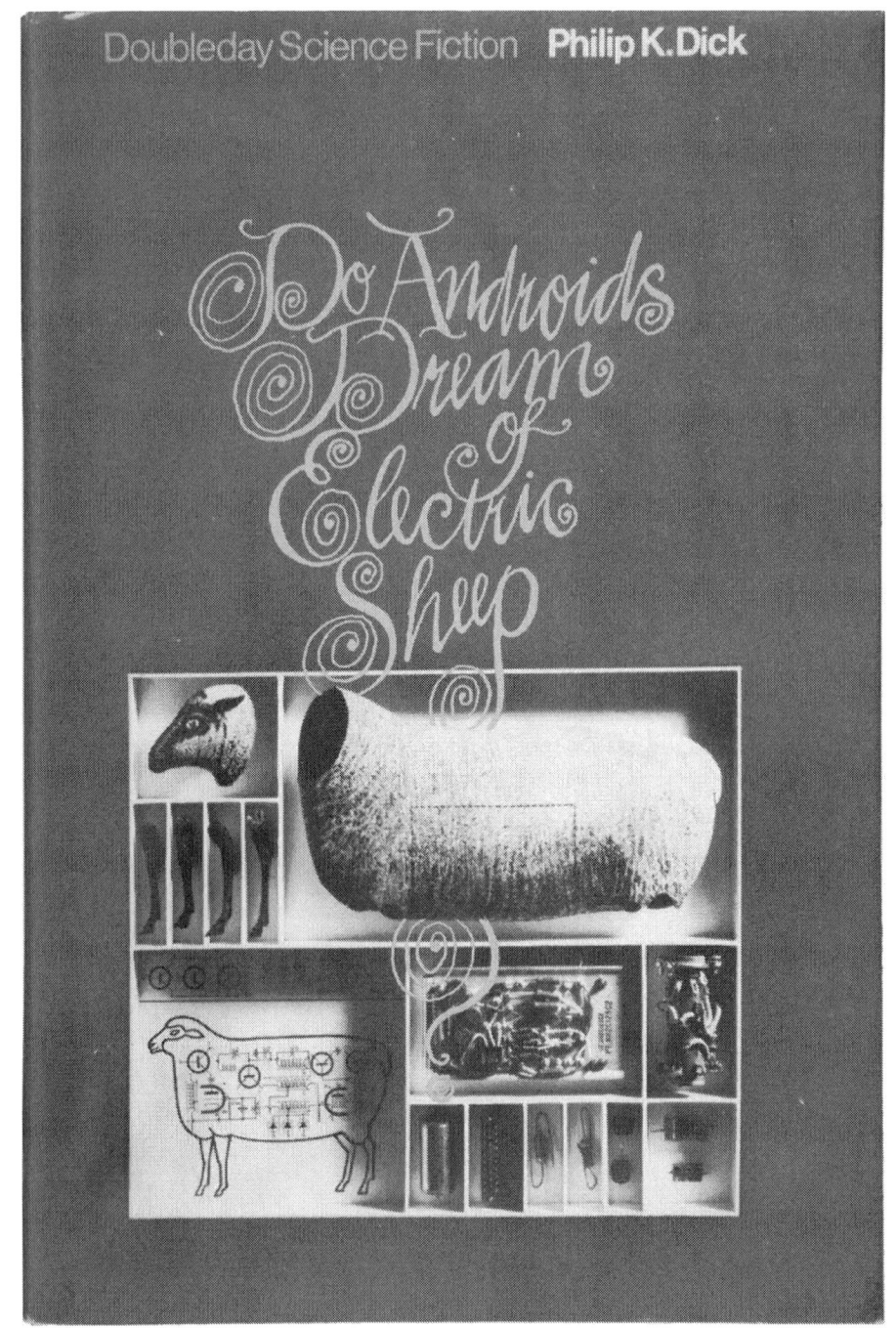

The cover to Philip K. Dick's *Do Androids Dream Electric Sheep?*

psychologically wrong with those who are not empathetic, and the story points a finger at the reader as if to say that we are as underdeveloped as the androids. We, who are emblematic of the modern world, are the real chickenheads and degenerates. We, who may not have had the trials of these characters, and who haven't even come to extend our circle of compassion to our fellow human beings, let alone the animals, are the destroyers, as we continue to make excuses for our tribalism, racism, exploitation, destruction, and war.

The narrative approaches what J.R.R. Tolkien referred to as a *eutopian* ending, which is the opposite of dystopian, not only for the protagonists, who get the happy ending they deserve, but for life and humanity as a whole. At its heart, *Do Androids Dream of Electric Sheep?* looks squarely at the heartlessness and thoughtlessness of man, and helps us to see what it means to wake up from that condition to develop a heart and mind in the hopes that it won't take a World War Terminus for that to happen.

For Rick Deckard, it's a painful awakening, but a worthwhile one that enabled him to not only reconnect to his wife, but achieve authenticity, insight, purpose, and joy. Meaning comes from the willingness to think ethically, and happiness from the willingness to empathize and revere life, *all* life, in whatever multifarious forms it might take.

The Noir of *Blade Runner*: The Dark Heart of Cinema

by Brian Robinson

It states the time and the place clearly: Los Angeles, 2019.

But this is no flashy future. No bright, optimistic architecture. We see nothing in the darkness. A darkness split only by the violence of fire and lightning. Hades. Fire spews upwards from the spires of an alternative architecture, an industrial cityscape reflected in the eye of an observer who takes in the countless city lights scattered across the endless dark. Monolithic buildings, a testament to goliaths of industry, project up through the gloom, no less welcoming than the fiery spires. Within, a smoking man waits, well dressed in a suit that seems more appropriate in one of those old movies from the 1940s. The bright but brief fires outside reflected in an eye; is it our man in the suit? Ceiling fans cut through the hazy room as he waits beneath a window he cannot see out of, almost a prisoner. The walls are high and yet do not reach the ceiling, imprisoning and yet not private. Nor can we see his face as he stands facing away from us, silhouetted in the austere room where a meeting is about to take place.

The opening to *Blade Runner* wears its influence and intentions firmly on its grimly beautiful sleeve. There is simply no mistaking it. This is *noir*. Ridley Scott and Jordan Cronenweth's vision of Philip K. Dick's future was unlike anything audiences had seen before. Well, that is not entirely true. They had seen something like it before but not in any science-fiction film (although a notable exception will be mentioned). The design of science-fiction films had been revolutionized in the eight or so years preceding *Blade Runner*'s release. Scott had himself been wowed by the more realistic approach taken by George Lucas and his designers on the original *Star Wars* (1977) and began to take seriously how this could affect both an audience's engagement with a genre previously open to ridicule for its designs and also how a film can express its intent artistically.

Scott himself took the next step in developing Lucas' used universe aesthetic with his grubby, working class starship in *Alien* (1979). This was an even more realistic world than *Star Wars*' dented droids and battered starships that sat amongst a vast space opera that also included magic, laser guns, and grandiose dialogue. In Scott's vision of the future, starship engineers occupied cramped, steam filled cabins, smeared with oil and sweat, chewing rolled up cigarettes, not unlike their present counterparts afloat in the Earth's oceans. Captains and officers bicker on voyage decisions, dressed in utilitarian but personalized clothes. It's a working environment, where the conversations range from wage disputes to the quality of the coffee. Scott took the used universe and made it more contemporary, creating verisimilitude out of tight spaces, canted angles, cigarette smoke, steam and, importantly, low key lighting to capture the audience before pulling out the rug from beneath their collective feet and turning the cramped workaday environment into a cathedral-like, sinister, and dimly lit place of death and horror. Of course, there is far more to the look of *Alien* than this simple and short list of stylistic choices, but the groundwork for the look of *Blade Runner* was certainly laid in 1979 with a fusion of style and genre that set its own standard. It could be argued (successfully) that *Alien* owed more of its look to German expressionism, but the style established in the film undoubtedly carried over and developed further with Scott's next project. Yet with *Alien*, the genre was clear (with the obvious mix of horror), but the noir style, as applied to science fiction? These cinematic techniques were more at home in the 1940s and 50s.

If we look at what are regarded as the film noir elements of *Blade Runner*, then it's reasonable to ask: what is film noir itself, both as a style and as a genre? And, as we'll see, this is a question not only of design but of narrative and theme. For so many years, film noir was regarded as a lesser kind of movie, a genre comprised of what were mostly seen as B pictures, but there was something more going on than just potboiler plots and repeated character types. There was a darkness in human behavior that was finding an outlet through the genre. Deeper analysis would prove that existential themes bubbled away under the surface, surely the mark of an art form. And what is it under the surface that makes a Noir what it is? What is its dirty heart? What is it saying and how much of this DNA does *Blade Runner* truly share, beyond surface detail?

As a style, film noir emerged as a result of the diaspora of filmmakers from Central and Eastern Europe involved in and influenced by the expressionist film style in Germany in the years leading up to the Second World War, born from the chaos in Germany after the First World War. As an art form, expressionism had emerged alongside other forms of modernism in the first few decades of the 20th century, finding a place in theatre, poetry, and painted art. It sought to show what was inside the human mind, to place less emphasis on realism and more on subjective experience. Part of what can be called formalism, it dealt more with the form of expression in the art, where technique was as important, if not more important, than the story being told. Weird, angular sets, low key lighting with high contrast, outrageous makeup, and contrasting costumes on actors, all intended to connect more with the inner experience than attempts to show "reality" as it was "meant" to be. In other words, it was art, and it didn't take long to transfer to the cinema.

At the time, the German film industry was in rude health, despite the financial mayhem that had gripped the country as a result of the First World War. The weakened mark had enabled the German film industry, headed by UFA (a production entity made up of many production companies), to make huge and ambitious movies at a fraction of the budget Hollywood was spending at that time. Combined with an appetite for artistic expression, absent in their American competitors, this enabled the birth of the German expressionist film movement, demonstrated at the time most notably by *The Cabinet of Doctor Caligari*. Written by Hans Janowitz and Carl Mayer, and directed by Robert Weine in 1920, it told the tale of the inmate of an insane asylum who had been incarcerated after his experiences with the evil Dr. Caligari, a hypnotist who travels the land with his permanently asleep "somnambulist," Cesare, who exists in a state of living death. Caligari uses Cesare to commit a series of grisly murders across the town. Almost theatrical in its design, whenever the film moves to the inmate's description of past events, the look of the film changes drastically; sets are angular, full of harsh lines, strong shadows, costumes and makeup become exaggerated. Also the look of the town as seen from afar is nightmarish, its hilltops, streets, and houses are jagged, terrifying, and indicative of danger. *Caligari* is widely regarded as one of the first true horror films and its design is squarely aimed at creating a particular unease in the audience that is also meant to represent the mental and emotional state of the main character. Soon, more films – taking advantage of a style suited to their darker narratives – went into production, notably F.W. Murnau's *Nosferatu*, a vampire film that strikes more than a resemblance to Bram Stoker's classic tale of vampirism. Murnau's use of shadow to create menace and suggest the presence of the evil Count Orlock, without actually seeing him, planted the film firmly in the cultural consciousness, arguably to this day. Expressionism was finding its way to regular audiences and becoming established as a cinematic style.

This new visual style was bringing new voices to the table. Accompanying Weine and Murnau, Fritz Lang produced the highly influential science-fiction film *Metropolis* and the murder drama *M*, but the brief light that was the expressionist school of filmmaking was to burn out all too soon.

As with many aspects of cinema, the techniques of expressionism found their way into other types of films. Across the Atlantic, the effects of *Caligari* and *Nosferatu* were becoming felt in Hollywood, leading to a surge in horror movies, most notably from Universal Studios, which incorporated the strong shadows and low-key lighting pioneered in Germany. Todd Browning's *Dracula* and James Whale's *Frankenstein* and *Bride of Frankenstein* were huge hits with audiences. They flocked to see Bela Lugosi's charming Count lure the innocent to their undead fate in his gothic castle where he lurked in the shadows, and Colin Clive defying nature in his castle laboratory. Whale was unafraid to tilt his camera to convey Henry Frankenstein's insane determination to recreate life or to show the terrible consequences of playing god, surely something Eldon Tyrell himself could empathize with. What was apparent was that not just that the lighting techniques of expressionism were spreading, but so too was the design aesthetic. Filmmakers now saw the opportunities laid before them to combine light and shadow with exaggerated set design in order to tell stories that dealt with the darker aspects of life and fiction. The creators in Hollywood, however, were about to have some company.

The Germany of the 1930s began to change politically and socially. The rise of the Nazis presented major difficulties for the creative communities there. Firstly, art and intellectualism were seen as threats to the new totalitarian regime that was tightening its grip on all matters communication. Propaganda was the new art, so horrendously perfected by Joseph Goebbels, and a large element of that propaganda affected many artists, not simply because of their occupation but because of their ethnicity. Jews, intellectuals, and anyone who opposed the new Reich were now targets, and survival became the order of the day for many. As gangs and soldiers targeted shops and businesses, numerous artists and intellectuals went missing without a trace. Understandably, many fled, for the prospect of continuing their lives and careers in the free countries of Europe and the United States proved tempting. Among this creative diaspora, the names Fritz Lang, Billy Wilder, Otto Preminger, and Robert Siodmak, would all become synonymous with the new genre about to break out in the United States.

Their arrival brought new voices to American cinema, a type of filmmaking rooted firmly in commercialism but not afraid to use whatever film techniques it took to engage the audience. This was the era of the big studios: MGM and their musicals, Warner Brothers' crime and gangster epics, Twentieth Century Fox's morality tales, and Universal Studios' horror series. The crime genre was incredibly successful, giving birth to some of the most famous movie names of all time, including Humphrey Bogart, James Cagney, Pat O'Brien, and Edward G. Robinson, all of whom had a willingness to confront the darker aspects of human behaviour, both before and after the introduction of the Production Code.[1] Stories of crime sold. How those stories developed in their telling was of importance to the establishment of the genre that came to be known as film noir.

The iconography and tropes of film noir are well known. You take the visual style of the expressionists, as mentioned above, and marry it with the literary genre of early 20th century crime fiction. The characters themselves sprang from the books of Dashiell Hammett and Raymond Chandler, loaded with hardboiled detectives, glamorous women whose motivations could never be taken for granted, unlucky sidekicks, shady underworld characters, assassins, gunsels, and criminal kingpins. In this new genre, the dark narratives of the crime paperbacks flourished, and each literary character type found a visual counterpart, from *The Maltese Falcon* to *Touch of Evil*, generally regarded as the beginning and end of the classic form of film noir.

---

[1] An act of censorship that many filmmakers saw as a challenge to be defeated in visual terms. It unwittingly played a role in the development of cinema language.

The movie poster for *Touch of Evil*.

But it didn't end with *Touch of Evil*. It couldn't. With the rise of the counterculture in the 1960s, the questioning of authority was becoming more popular. There was so much more to be said and movies were one of the most popular ways to say it. A new generation of filmmakers, with a love for the old styles but with far different attitudes, stepped up. Older genres had their revisionist takes, a prominent example being the revisionist westerns, featuring the voices of Sam Peckinpah, Monte Hellman, and Sergio Corbucci telling different, and sometimes more realistic and violent stories of the old west. The happier endings of John Ford and Howard Hawks made way for the dark climaxes of *The Wild Bunch* and *The Great Silence*. So it was with crime and detective movies, also. The themes of the old noirs grew and developed, but spoke with more contemporary tongues. This was the era of the neo-noir. Jack Smight's *Harper*, John Boorman's *Point Blank*, and even Jean-Luc Godard's *Alphaville* (itself a science-fiction neo-noir) explored the narrative and cinematographic shades of the old noirs, arguably culminating in Roman Polanski and Robert Towne's *Chinatown*, where the classic image of the P.I. involved with a glamorous and mysterious woman played into the more downbeat endings of the time.

The 1960s and 1970s were more about reality than ever before, and the voices in film were out to prove it. Jack Nicholson's Jake Gittes, with his own shady past, wandered back into the darkness of human failings and found the same tragic answer, the bad guy often wins. The look on Gittes' face at the film's violent ending shows a man shaken in his sense of self and of who and what he actually is in the world, something Rick Deckard himself would later be confronted with. There were no easy answers for the hero, only shades of grey with bursts of sudden, realistic violence. It could be argued that popular film genres change and evolve with the times, some more effectively than others, as the downfall of the western proved. The characteristics of film noir endured, finding their way into more mature and sophisticated stories. With the use of expressionist techniques in horror films clearly influencing *Alien*, the mix would make its way into Ridley Scott's own dark vision of the future, as combined with Philip K. Dick's narrative and Hampton Fancher's original take on it.

After reading Dick's novel *Do Androids Dream of Electric Sheep?*, about a bureaucratic detective mired by paranoia and his own wife's disapproval, screenwriter Hampton Fancher saw something in the tale that he thought could make the transition from science-fiction literature to commercial film: "I immediately saw a chase movie, with a detective after androids in a dystopic world."[2] There was the first hint at the approach the film would ultimately take – the central character of a detective in a dark world. The very term "dystopia" instantly conjures images of a world gone wrong, of human achievement being flung into question and our detective existing in a dark, oppressive world. Not a million miles away from the dark, rain lashed streets where Philip Marlowe and Sam Spade plied their trade, the story of a detective hunting down prey in this environment and time had clear parallels. Early storyboards and designs created during Fancher's writing period on the film featured Deckard in a fedora and long raincoat, recalling Humphrey Bogart's costume from *The Maltese Falcon*, a design which itself has become shorthand for film noir and private detectives, although the hat was later dropped at Harrison Ford's insistence after spending months wearing the same hat on his previous job as Indiana Jones in *Raiders of the Lost Ark*. But this initial look for the central character clearly showed the route the film was going to take: a science-fiction film influenced by the look and iconography of film noir. The course was set. Scott was clear about this in the documentary *Dangerous Days: Making Blade Runner* when he said, "It's very Marlowe-esque. And very dark."[3]

One need only view *Blade Runner* with the merest knowledge of film noir tropes to see that the characters, design, cinematography, narrative and, significantly, the themes in the film have much in common with the old thrillers of years gone by. And yet, it uses this to say something very much in the vein of science fiction.

When thinking of film noir, what immediately springs to mind is the look and style of the genre, all to create another world that portrayed the darkness that exists within the urban world. The setting of the film is the same as the old noirs, night time in a constantly rainy Los Angeles. The architecture of the film is of old times, featuring the famous Bradbury Building and Frank Lloyd Wright's designs in Deckard's apartment. It's no accident that the film was shot on the old Warner Brothers backlot, the very place where so many gangster and film noirs were brought to life decades prior, resulting in a shared history with the original noirs. One wonders just how many of those buildings, redressed by

---

[2] Sammon, P. (1996). *Future Noir - The Making of Blade Runner*. Page 26.
[3] Ridley Scott, *Dangerous Days: Making Blade Runner*, Documentary, directed by Charles de Lauzirika (2007; Los Angeles: Blade Runner Partnership, Lauzirika Motion Picture Company, and Warner Home Video), Film.

designer Syd Mead, drenched in rain and neon lighting, also played host to the classic noirs of the past.

But ultimately, in terms of style, the relationship between the directors and the cinematographers of film noir was vital to the look of the films, possibly more so than any other type of film up to that point. Ridley Scott's desire to invoke the look and feel of the 1940s and 1950s meant that his collaboration with cinematographer Jordan Cronenweth was key. Scott wanted it dark and that meant reducing and altering key sources of light. Cronenweth lit much of his subjects in *Blade Runner* with large sources very close to the actors. The result was what appeared to be hard key light, but it was also diffused across the subject, providing less contrast between the deep shadows, yet still preserving them. John Alton, the old master of film noir cinematography, would have been proud. There are times when the lighting in *Blade Runner* plays directly from his lighting bible, *Painting with Light*. The lights were also diegetic – part of the world of the film. Neon would dominate the sets and would also serve as an on-set lighting source, unusual for a noir-influenced film. This lighting design choice created many opportunities to use available light to illuminate scenes. Searchlights scanned the city constantly, pointing out advertisements while offering a sense of claustrophobia and relentless observation. During the scene in Deckard's apartment after Rachael rescues Deckard from Leon, such lighting is featured, sweeping in and out of the window over Rachael's shoulder. It's both intrusive (Rachael is a fugitive now) and expressive of the rollercoaster ride of emotions both Deckard and Rachael are experiencing, like an illuminated adrenaline rush.

Light also plays an important part during the sequence where Deckard enters the Bradbury Building. The ruined walls and shuttered windows allow light into the smoky and dim space, silhouetting the characters and placing them in a weird otherworld. Deckard's hunt for Batty doesn't seem to take place in the same world we've witnessed in the preceding scenes. Cronenweth's lighting creates a far more frightening world in this sequence, where we are not sure of our location or who is around the corner. Cronenweth's work bathes the film in an almost surrealistic glory, taking film noir as its cue and moving us onto somewhere else, creating far more dangerous environs for our characters.

After the fire and violence of the opening sequence, Scott takes us to a rain-soaked street lit entirely by neon, bustling with a variety of people: a mix of cultures mostly European and Asian. Like a rolling sea, moving umbrellas with glowing handles navigate past each other. Neon dragons crackle over the sound of the rain and the steam of an open diner. There, patrons shovel noodles and dumplings into their mouths without hesitation, lined up in the cold neon glow and drifting vapors. We're pushing through the crowd toward a man leaning against a wall, in refuge from the downpour. He's dressed in a drab, long raincoat, holding out a large newspaper and scanning it, unimpressed. Above, a floating billboard blimp tempts promises of a new life in the Off-World Colonies. The man looks up, still unimpressed. He's world weary, cynical. The owner of the Japanese diner calls him over and he rushes forward, folding up his newspaper as a substitute umbrella. He places a food order and sits, ready to eat, but before he can, the long arm of the law taps him on the shoulder. They're police officers in rain overalls. Grunts. A dapper chap in a bow tie informs Deckard, and us, that he's a cop, and that he's wanted by the powers that be.

It could be argued that what made film noir truly appealing was its characters. A world can only be as dark as the people who inhabit it, and the characters on the page and screen are so often vessels for us to pour our own fears and anxieties into. Film noir provided people with an outlet at a time when open discussion of the darker aspects of life was taboo.

Regarded by many as the first proper film noir feature, *The Maltese Falcon* was directed by John Huston in 1942. Taking a pulp detective novel as its starting point (as many noirs would), it adapted Dashiell Hammett's story of the hunt for the rare statue of a bird, led by a character who would form part of one of the most common character types in film, Sam Spade. He represented a staple of the genre, the hardboiled private investigator. In *Blade Runner*, Deckard is our hardboiled detective, private or otherwise, but there is always more to a character than just their look. As a character, Deckard shares much with his literary and cinematic predecessors. He's a cop whose particular line of work deals with some very blurred lines when questions of morality come into play.

When we first meet Deckard, he's no longer on the force. We're not told what particular line of work he's in at the moment (if any), but as with Jake Gittes, his past is not something he can escape from. In fact, as with many pulp detectives, we know very little about Rick Deckard at all. We know he used to be a cop whose primary job was assassination and it might be fair to assume that he grew tired of professional murder, leading to him quitting the force. We know he's a drinker. It's his first port of comfort when examining evidence at his home or cleaning himself up after Leon's assault, which contains a wonderfully memorable close up of Deckard shakily sipping from a shot glass of liquor, his blood mixing in and staining the drink like a scarlet cloud. He lives alone, unlike his literary, bureaucratic counterpart who is married. His apartment is messy but comfortable.

Deckard starts out as an almost two-dimensional film noir archetype. It's only the events of the film, ultimately his relationship with Rachael and his final confrontation with Roy Batty, that begin to reveal much if anything about him. With his typical pulp detective appearance, Rick Deckard is Bogart's Spade, Powell's Marlowe, and Nicholson's Gittes, lifted out of their respective times and thrust into a world of a different time but just as dark as their own.

Whatever it is from Deckard's past that lingers like the dirty city rain, it comes calling in the form of Edward James Olmos' dandy brownnose, Gaff. His dialect is a mishmash of languages called "cityspeak" according to the theatrical version's voiceover. He's well-heeled in a sharp hat and suit, all wrapped up in a bow tie. There is something impenetrable about Gaff. At first he comes off as some kind of strong-armed messenger, akin to Polanski's dapper thug in *Chinatown*, who slits Jake Gittes' nose for sticking it where some would rather he didn't, but there is always something else bubbling under the surface of Gaff's actions, mostly unseen by the other characters. While we don't understand his dialogue until the end of the film, it's fair to assume that he has some kind of knowledge of Deckard and the dark world they inhabit. There is something at the core of the film that he seems to represent, which we'll look at further. But his appearance and stance reveal him as some kind of dark herald, both within the surface narrative and also thematically.

Gaff's initial job is to bring Deckard in, and Deckard's response is typically laconic of the noir characters that precede him. Feigning ignorance, Deckard is not for budging from his stool at the noodle bar. Even the mention of his previous occupation, translated for both he and us by the noodle chef, "He say you Blade Runner," fails to stir him. It's only the mention of a name that brings him around: "Bryant, huh?" He smiles at some memory that exposes his attitude toward Bryant. Reluctantly, he acquiesces and runs through the rain to Gaff's spinner.

We meet M. Emmet Walsh's Captain Bryant in a massive police station, dimly lit and full of perps. Obviously Deckard's superior, his appearance and attitude recall countless authority figure cops, some corrupt. As with Gaff, there is something else going on with Bryant, albeit not as deep. His relationship with

Deckard is one of classic noir detectives. He wants his old comrade to come back to the fold. There's one more job to do and he needs "the old magic." Their exchange of dialogue is quick, the lines short and almost staccato and clearly feeding from the noirs of the past. It almost veers into parody. Like so many other pulp detectives, Deckard turns him down. He's left that world now. "I was quit when I walked in here. I'm twice as quit now," he tells Bryant, who then drops the façade and openly threatens Deckard. This whole scene could have been lifted straight out of the pages of the pulp magazine *Black Mask*, which initially serialised many of Raymond Chandler's books. Bryant owes much to the cynical, tough police authority figures of those literary tales and even bears a resemblance to a specific character from film noir. Orson Welles gave us one of the greatest and most memorable corrupt cops in film history in the grotesque shape of Captain Hank Quinlan from Welles' noir masterpiece, *Touch of Evil* (1958). Obese (almost morbidly so), unshaven, and an alcoholic, Quinlan is utterly corrupt, although like the best bad guys, he thinks he's doing the right thing. His exterior appearance symbolizes his inner failings. However, the resemblance between the two policemen ends there. While Bryant shares a resemblance to Welles' Quinlan, he serves no more use than Bernard Lee's M did in the early James Bond films, as a faint authoritarian father figure who issues orders.

Bryant's second scene with Deckard reinforces the film noir look of *Blade Runner*. Once Deckard reluctantly agrees to the job, Bryant shows him the files of their android quarry. As they view the video profiles of the replicants, we are drawn into a darker room, filled with cigarette smoke which is illuminated by the glare of the video screens, much like the projection room in Welles' American expressionist masterpiece, *Citizen Kane*. In fact, Jordan Cronenweth's lighting goes as far as to emulate this, with an unseen source of light coming from behind Deckard and Bryant, like a cinema projector, even though the characters are watching television screens.

Obeying Bryant's order, Deckard goes out into what seems to be an eternal night, beginning in Gaff's spinner. The night is filthy, the air thick with pollution and exhaust. The spinner swims through the smog among the other airborne cars, up above the city streets, into the open air towards an intimidating edifice in the distance; the headquarters of the Tyrell Corporation. The room Deckard enters is vast and luxurious, the primary luxury being that of open space, entirely at odds with the dirty, claustrophobic streets where we first met Deckard. Many classic movies in the film noir tradition would switch location often from the dark, broody streets to luxurious hotel rooms and suites where the upper echelons of the criminal and high societies often mingled – the icing on top of the rotten cake. Sam Spade's initial and memorable encounter with Sydney Greenstreet's corpulent and wealthy Kasper Gutman in *The Maltese Falcon* took place in a suite that reeked of cash and luxury and yet it was a relatively bright affair compared to the space where Deckard first encounters billionaire genetic industrialist Eldon Tyrell and his replicant assistant, Rachael. Tyrell is well dressed, in a black dinner suit and ostentatious bow tie, several times larger than Gaff's. We know he is the creator of human machines that are now regarded as dangerous, but there doesn't seem to be an air of menace about the man. In a film where one of the key themes is about the consequences of playing god, Tyrell seems altruistic, or at least someone not working to oppress others. His offices and apartments clearly display his incredible wealth. This is a man who has benefitted hugely from the manipulation of life and that surely is enough to paint Eldon Tyrell in a morally grey light. His relationship with J.F. Sebastian, with their on-going chess game, suggests one of mentorship, both professionally and in areas of mental prowess, not to mention friendly rivalry. Sebastian, while clearly possessing some sort of genius in his creations, demonstrates a childlike quality when he's interacting with his boss, which makes Tyrell seem like a father figure. He is indeed a father to the replicants and yet he has forgotten about them as a parent, until they return forcing him to reap the consequences of his godlike decision to imbue a mere four-year lifespan upon them.

A similar fate awaits Sebastian, whose innocence is preyed upon by Roy and Pris to gain access to Tyrell's sanctum sanctorum. Sebastian's childlike qualities, offset by his aging illness (Methuselah Syndrome) reflect his own loneliness and desire for friendship outside of his personal creations. His fate seems written by his illness, a potential factor in his own desire to help create new life in the face of nature, although it is this naiveté towards human nature that ends up being his downfall. Like similar characters from noir, he is preyed upon by others. He's a counterpart to characters such as Dennis Weaver's hotel night manager from *Touch of Evil*, for in every film noir, the strong always prey on the weak. Sebastian is a victim, not only of Roy Batty, but of a part of nature that he is complicit in playing around with. His meeting with Pris shows his lack of guile and awkward loneliness, and Pris plays him from the very beginning like the *femme fatale* she is.

The movie poster for *The Maltese Falcon*.

The femme fatale is one of the most iconic and indelible character types of film noir. The plots of just about all of them hinge on the machinations of a dangerous woman, whether the hero knows she's dangerous or not, as in the case of Mary Astor's duplicitous Ruth Wonderly (or is it Bridgit O'Shaunessy?) in *The Maltese Falcon*. But the most common type is the woman who deliberately uses her femininity to lure the unwitting hero or anti-hero to his doom. Some examples that come to mind are Barbara Stanwyck in *Double Indemnity*, Rita Hayworth in *Gilda,* and Ava Gardner in *The Killers*. Not all femme fatales are given away by their appearance, however. When we first meet Pris, she's a complete mess. She's been on the run, her clothes are tattered, her stockings ripped, her mascara running, and her hair is a messy blonde mushroom. Wrapping herself in newspapers, she transforms herself into the homeless urchin, the soul of the street, just one more of the "little people" Bryant mentions earlier while taunting Deckard.

The movie poster for *Double Indemnity.*

There is often a tragedy associated with the femme fatale in noir. Mary Astor pleads for her life after her ruse is uncovered, Faye Dunaway's Evelyn Mulwray in *Chinatown* loses hers after only trying to look after her daughter. In

Blade Runner, all the replicants want to do is survive. Their enhanced strength and intelligence combine with the strongest survival instincts to create desperate beings whom we and society fear. This tragic form of femme fatale is evident in Joanna Cassidy's Zhora. Blending in as an exotic dancer in Taffy Lewis' highly stylized nightclub (another location often seen in film noir), it seems she is just trying to get by, and not on any kind of mission from Roy Batty. In noir, she is the stripper, the whore who might provide some useful information like Marlene Deitrich's Tanya in *Touch of Evil*. Zhora isn't a source, but Deckard's target. His ruse as a union delegate is simply to get her alone where he can eliminate her with minimal fuss and that's when the unexpected happens. She acts against Deckard's masculinity. Unafraid to show force, even when naked, what could be seen as the male antagonist preying upon the apparently vulnerable, sexualized female, is turned on its head as Zhora proceeds to nearly kill Deckard with her bare hands before fleeing. The fact that she doesn't kill him gives her an air of sympathy and it's hard to choose who to root for when Deckard is hunting her in the overcrowded streets a minute later. Her end is glorious, as she smashes past the faceless mannequins in the shop windows, becoming one of them as police officers turn her body over to reveal her dead eyes. Her tragedy is that no one ever saw her as truly being alive. Deckard gazes down at the being he has just legally murdered, and through her death we see something start to change in him.

If any of the female characters of *Blade Runner* most resemble the classic femme fatale, it's Rachael. She looks like she stepped right out of a 1940s film, or even a pinup, with her Betty Grable "peek-a-boo" hairstyle, huge raised collar/hood, and shoulders that Joan Crawford would have been proud of. Rachael is designed to emulate that classic look so well that, lighting aside, she is possibly the most film noir visual in the entire film.

Scott plays with our expectations of her. We know she's a replicant, as does Deckard, and this information immediately places her under suspicion. We are told that replicants are outlawed and dangerous, and so she poses a danger to Deckard, but for one thing: she doesn't *know* she's a replicant. She possesses a child-like innocence similar to J.F. Sebastian. It's both Zhora's death and Rachael's realization about her true nature that Deckard's own awakening (regardless of whether or not he himself is a replicant) is brought about. In a way, Rachael can be seen as the downfall of the Blade Runner cop, the man who "retires" replicants. In her own initial examination of Deckard, she asks him, "Have you ever retired a human by mistake?" She seems to be testing him here, or possibly even subconsciously (if replicants have a subconscious) examining her own sense of whether she is human or not.

So Scott, Fancher, and Peoples created a character who was both sides of the coin – on the surface, your classic femme fatale, but underneath, the (mostly) fragile but ultimately resourceful girl from out of town who is looking for herself and finds more than she bargains for. A character analogy might be found in Deanna Durbin's Jackie Lamont in Robert Siodmak's *Christmas Holiday* (1944), a noir set during the festive period, seemingly unusual, but surely setting the precedent for many of Shane Black's own thrillers, often set at Christmas. Durbin's Lamont begins, plot-wise, as a singer in a nightclub, femme fatale territory if there ever was any. But through Siodmak's non-linear narrative and flashback structure, she starts in her own story as a wide-eyed innocent who meets the wrong man. The outcomes of Rachael and Jackie's stories are not the same, but they do both mark the journey from innocence to femme fatale. Rachael's new knowledge causes her to make a decision which places her firmly on Deckard's side – she takes the life of another replicant, Leon, in order to save Deckard. The experience clearly shakes her. She already came to Deckard with questions about her own existence but the denial of her true nature does not shift until she murders one of her own kind.

Leon also seems childlike, but brutally so. Assigned to lift heavy cargo loads, he is the least intelligent of the group, not quite a simpleton but seemingly close to it. At times, he functions as Batty's thug as they roam the darkened streets searching for their creator. Latest in a long line of noir thugs, there is something sympathetic in Leon. He may be a brute but his goal is the same as anyone else's – he is looking for answers to his existence, albeit following the intellectually superior Batty's lead. He is Batty's right hand man in their quest and Roy appears visibly distressed when informing Pris of Leon's demise. This isn't something often seen in crime films. A villain displaying emotion regarding his minion's fate seems quite unusual. This gives us our first inkling that perhaps Batty and the others aren't mindless bio-mechanisms bent on destruction. Rather, we and Deckard ought to be looking for something else, perhaps a shared humanity in those who didn't ask to be created.

Leon's "muscle" is more than, say, Elisha Cook Jr.'s hired gunsel for Sidney Greenstreet in *The Maltese Falcon*. He's more than a narrative convenience created to impede the hero. Leon's true purpose seems invisible to us until his own death, serving to portray one of the film's themes: what is it to be human. Leon, with all his violence and apparent dimwittery, is a friend to someone. His passing marks Batty emotionally, pushing the film's existential questions past the simple ambiguity of its noir predecessors and giving value to the lives of those we judge as having been the enemy. Leon's death has value.

While he sees himself as the hero in his own story, Batty plays the role of antagonist in the film, but his story has little to do with the villains of film noir. In retrospect Roy appears more like the hero in Rudolph Mate's *D.O.A.* (1955). Edmund O'Brien plays a detective investigating his own murder. He is dying from a slow acting poison and is up against the clock. Batty is clearly against the clock, along with his comrades, but it's not until the end of the film that we discover just how close he is. Before this, we meet a lone man in black, accompanied by his muscle, wandering through an underworld. Forced down into the dark corners of the city, Batty needs the darkness and secrecy of the shadows in order to carry out his quest. Like the villains of old, he moves in the shadows, but does he ultimately want to be a part of them?

Blade Runner can be perceived as the character of Rick Deckard coming to terms with or questioning his own humanity through a series of deaths. Ultimately, it's Batty's story and death that nail the film's focus. For a film that has been accused of lacking humanity by some critics,[4] it might be worth noting that the perceived villain of the film appears to be the most emotional character within it, a real departure from the tropes of film noir. Batty mourns for the loss of his friends, almost unable to speak about Leon to Pris, and then grieves over Pris like an alpha wolf howling at the night in the face of his own end. He takes it upon himself to challenge Deckard, this little man who has gunned down his family. The question that remains is whether Batty really wanted to kill Deckard or if he only wanted the human to know the value of his own life. While the film portrays Batty in the final hunt as a predator, loping through the slatted lighting of the shuttered windows of the Bradbury Building, do we ever truly know his intent, or does he have a moment of clarity when he sees what Deckard has been reduced to, hanging from the edge of a building, whimpering like an injured animal? This could be the moment where Batty realized his potential, limited as his life was, to show this man what matters and

---

[4] As noted in Paul M. Sammon's *Future Noir*, critical giant Pauline Kael wrote that "If anybody comes around with a test to detect humanoids; maybe Ridley Scott and his associates should hide." Sammon, Paul. M. (1996). *Future Noir - The Making of Blade Runner*, p. 314.

what it means to truly live. "Quite an experience to live in fear, isn't it?" he states to a rescued and utterly confused Deckard.

A film noir delivers a message about existence to its protagonist. They are, after all, existential pieces at heart. The perceived villain delivers truth to the hero, but not as an ultimatum or threat. In *Chinatown*, the hero learns a truth from the death of a potential innocent. Roy Batty is not innocent but he also never asked to be created with such a finite lifespan. The simple delivery of memories, imparted in a rare moment of calm in the rain, alters Deckard's perception of whom he has been hunting (and has been hunted by). This huge android has not only spared his life in a demonstration of his immense genetically engineered strength but now finds himself accepting of his own fate. His expiration date is upon him and instead of continuing his murderous spree he opts to share not only what he has experienced as a unique being, but his vast sadness that these experiences are about to be lost forever. It's a fate shared by all, but made all the more immediate through his actual "youth" and the primal nature of the chase he has just chosen to end in order to make Deckard see what he has been missing.

It would be remiss not to look a little more at *Blade Runner*'s infamous voiceover. Imposed by the completion bond company, they sought to clarify certain plot points. After all, it was a hardboiled detective movie; surely they should have voiceovers, right? Many did in the past, but voiceover is a tricky thing to use effectively. David Landau suggests, "The pull of the first-person voiceover narration works on the audience because they are in the main character's shoes…rather than having an omniscient view, seeing things that happen in various locations at the same times or different times that the main character has no knowledge. The audience is as surprised, confused, disappointed, scared and humoured as the lead character."[5]

Blade Runner's split narrative, one branch following Deckard and the other following Batty and Pris, is a source of conflict here. Why put us in the shoes of the main character and then send us somewhere else to follow the villain? This causes a sense of separation from Deckard and also interferes with any sense of dramatic irony as we follow the replicants' quest while Deckard hunts them.

Ford and Scott are both on record regarding their joint displeasure at having to record the voiceover. Cinema is a mostly visual medium (although sound is just as important) and what we *see* should really be informing us.

---

[5] Landau, David. (2017) *Film Noir Production*. Routledge, p. 133.

Voiceover can hammer things home, repeating what we see so there is a danger of insulting the audience's intelligence.

So, where are the great voiceovers? They can be done well, in service of the story, as a dramatic device that functions in its own way. A good example can be found in Wilder's *Double Indemnity*. Fred MacMurray's insurance salesman, Walter Neff, is recounting his story into a voice recorder. When we meet Neff he has already experienced the events of the story; he is injured and what he is recording is clearly a confession. He drip-feeds us information throughout the film and it works in keeping the audience's attention. As he speaks there is still the question of his survival. There is urgency to it.

The voiceover in *Blade Runner* doesn't help fill in information gaps, nor does it really help us get inside Deckard's mind. It merely points out what we already see, tells us what we already know, or gets in the way of what our eyes are experiencing. *Blade Runner* is a film that loves faces; the number of close ups of expressions is considerable. It can be argued that much of the information that we need can be sought in the faces of the characters we are seeing. The voiceover is, in my estimation, clumsy and unnecessary, ruining the final moments of the original cut by expanding on the unnecessary happy ending that was tacked on. In a film concerned with the genre as an influence, not every element of film noir is required.

Stripped of the original voiceover, Deckard's look as Batty expires with dignity in the rain indicates enlightenment for Deckard. Here, the constant rain, also associated with film noir, seems to be lit differently. There is a quality of brightness to it. It's no longer oppressive but seems to wash away Deckard's already wavering prejudice towards his prey. He sees life: Batty's ending, his own now revitalized, and Rachael's in question. His return home and to Rachael opens with him lifting a sheet from her face. Is she dead? Has she suffered the same fate as Batty and the others? The answer relieves him, and Gaff's final origami gift in the lobby echoes his words on the rooftop: "You've done a man's job, sir," offering the question, is it truly a man's job to kill those who are created? Was the purpose of this "man's job" for Deckard to truly see his own humanity in the deaths of those who so wanted to live, and in the woman he appears to love, whose own fate is unknown but predicted? His humanity is examined. He is no longer the "little people" Bryant spoke of. Whatever it was that drove Deckard away from his job before the film, it planted a seed in him that Rachael's circumstance brought to fruition: what it is to be human. But is simply being *labelled* a human enough?

After all of this, the question of *Blade Runner*'s film noir influences are clear, but it is more than just the layered style of the film that ties it to the grey morality and existentialism of those older films. Its connection and soul are brought out in its characters. First appearing as tropes and types, *Blade Runner* lets them move beyond those old influences in order to do what science fiction does so well – ask questions about who we are, why we exist, and what it means to be a human.

Any question of *Blade Runner* having a heart of noir must surely result in a resounding yes. *Blade Runner* clearly has noir influence in spades, but what raises it above a mere copycat is its own views of the world and humanity rooted firmly in the camps of both noir and science fiction. It does more than look cool, it probes our basic nature, as science fiction must, and as noir did. A true hybrid, the techniques and tropes of both genres work together in a manner that means they rely on and complement each other. Any film can look beautiful, but without a certain regard for its characters, a film can and probably will fail. *Blade Runner* openly lifts characters and visual styles from noir *to its benefit*.

"It's too bad she won't live. But then again, who does?"

Gaff's words echo in Deckard's mind. Indeed, who truly does live? Roy Batty did, against the odds and society's fear of him. His final act was one of nobility and humanity. It's almost irrelevant to ask whether Deckard was a replicant (an argument the film makes no real use of anyway). What matters is that he recognizes the commonality held between those created in the womb and those in a lab.

Replicant or not, Deckard rejects his old life. In the true tradition of the pulp detective, he'll grab the girl and take his chances.

Another life awaits in the night.

Metal Machine Movies: The Lasting Influence of *Heavy Metal* and *Métal Hurlant* on *Blade Runner* and the Science-Fiction Cinema of Ridley Scott

by Tom Lennon

Blade Runner is rightly considered to be one of the most visually stunning films in the history of cinema. As screenwriting guru Robert McKee once said, "If we were to take a single frame from *Blade Runner* and ask the world's finest prose stylist to create the verbal equivalent of that composition, he or she would fill pages and pages with words and never capture its essence."[1] Many factors helped shape the conception, design, and realization of the film's cinematically game-changing depiction of a dark, perpetually rain-soaked, neon-saturated Los Angeles of 2019. First and foremost was the vision of the film's director, Ridley Scott, one of cinema's greatest visual stylists. Yet Scott's compelling portrayal of a nightmare near-future did not occur in isolation. It

---

[1] McKee, Robert. "Story". Methuen, 1998. P366.

was shaped by his various influences, which ranged from Edward Hopper's moody 1947 painting *Nighthawks* to Fritz Lang's classic 1927 silent science-fiction film, *Metropolis*.

However, one of the biggest influences on *Blade Runner*'s look came from a most unlikely source, not a painting or a film, but the pages of a sexy science-fiction/fantasy comic magazine known for its bold, sometimes avant-garde approach to art and storytelling, as well as for its often unbelievably risqué front covers. That comic was called *Heavy Metal*, and it not only influenced *Blade Runner* – one of the most influential films ever made – but its creative DNA can be detected in every single one of Ridley Scott's science-fiction movies. Scott recalled his admiration for the publication back in 1982:

> I'd always been a fan of that magazine, which dealt with what I term 'half-fantasy'. In fact, I first encountered it in its original French appearance, which is called *Métal Hurlant*. And I particularly enjoyed the work of the French artist known as Moebius, whose real name is Jean Giraud. He was one of the best *Heavy Metal* illustrators, without question. I'm still knocked out by the stuff he does. And yet, I can't put my finger on why, or what it is about the way he handles himself. Perhaps it's the way that Moebius juxtaposes familiar elements with the fantastic, to make some sort of architectural or fashion statement. Or it could be simply his graphic insolence.[2]

When filmmakers namecheck *Heavy Metal* magazine, they're referring to two separate publications that have become bundled together over time. There's *Heavy Metal* itself, an X-rated American science-fiction and fantasy comic magazine that first appeared in 1977, that *annus mirabilis* for science-fiction movies, and which remains in publication to this day. Then there's its French publishing primogenitor *Métal Hurlant* (which translates into English as *Screaming* or *Howling* Metal, but definitely not *Heavy* Metal), the pioneering French adult comic with a similar theme that was published from 1975 to 1987.

A name that has been synonymous with both magazines since their early days is Jean Giraud (1938-2012), the legendary French comic illustrator who became better known by his somewhat enigmatic artistic pseudonym, Moebius. Giraud was born in the eastern suburbs of Paris. As a comics artist he first made his name working in the Western genre under the sobriquet *Gir* and in 1963 co-created the anti-hero Lieutenant Mike S. Blueberry with veteran comic writer

---

[2] Lightman, Herb A. and Patterson, Richard. "Blade Runner: Production Design and Photography." *American Cinemaphotographer*, July 1982. Quoted in Sammon, Paul M., *Future Noir*. Dey St 2017 edition. p 82-3.

Jean-Michel Charlier. The Blueberry stories were massively popular in France (and remain so to this day), but during the early 1970s Giraud became increasingly restless as an artist. He felt trapped by the stylistic and thematic conventions of the Western genre, so he dusted off an old pseudonym that he hadn't used since the early 1960s, and under this name he would create a more personal, unique, and experimental body of work within the science-fiction and fantasy genre.

The first issue of *Métal Hurlant* was published in January 1975 by the self-styled Les Humanoïdes Associés (The Associated Humanoids), a rag tag group of veteran comic book visionaries that included Moebius, his fellow comic artist Philippe Druillet, and the writer, editor, and occasional raconteur Jean-Pierre Dionnet. Right from the start *Métal Hurlant* was quite unlike anything else that was appearing in comic books or anywhere else for that matter. Not only was it aimed squarely at adults at a time when comic books were still thought of as just for kids, but it was printed on high grade, glossy paper stock at a time when cheap newsprint was still the medium's norm. Looking more like *Paris Match* than *Tintin* or *Asterix the Gaul*, it made the magazine's already lavishly painted artwork look sharper, brighter, and so eye-poppingly vivid to contemporary readers that it must have been a bit like watching a 4K Ultra HD Blu-ray copy of *Blade Runner* back in the days of VHS.

Early issues featured Moebius strips like *Arzach* and *The Airtight Garage* which quickly became classics of the genre. In *Arzach*, a grumpy warrior travelled across a weird and desolate, yet beautifully rendered, wasteland on the back of a pterodactyl-like creature.[3] *The Airtight Garage*, if anything, was even weirder. Its hero, Major Grubert – an anachronistic space adventurer who dressed like a Victorian big game hunter – found himself embroiled in an increasingly bizarre and seemingly random series of events as he performed his duties as the custodian and protector of a three-level pocket universe that's encased within an asteroid.

This was bold, visually innovative, avant-garde stuff, but Moebius wasn't the only artist creating ground-breaking material in *Métal Hurlant*. His fellow Humanoids Druillet and Dionnet were also producing classic work that eventually would prove to be influential both within and beyond the comic

---

[3] The stunning "Taarna" segment of the film *Heavy Metal* borrowed directly from this aesthetic, while the cityscape of the "Harry Canyon" segment borrows from *The Long Tomorrow*, as did *Blade Runner*.

The cover to *Métal Hurlant* #1.

book medium. Dionnet wrote the heroic fantasy epic *Conquering Armies* with painstakingly detailed art by Jean-Claude Gal; later, he would publish the gritty future war saga *Exterminator 17,* illustrated by Enki Bilal. Meanwhile, Druillet consolidated his reputation as, literally, the poster boy of 1970s fantasy art with stories like *La Nuit* (1976), *Gail* (1975-76), and an utterly deranged adaptation of Gustave Flaubert's historical novel *Salammbô* (1980).

Métal Hurlant's list of contributors would soon begin to resemble a "who's who" of international comic book excellence. Within its pages, Franco-Belgian artists like Jacques Tardi and Alain Voss would rub elbows with Italian counterparts like Milo Manara and Hugo Pratt. Its talent pool wasn't confined to mainland Europe: the American artist Richard Corben was a prolific contributor, as was the British illustrator Angus McKee.

The French magazine quickly became known for its bold vision and iconoclastic swagger, with editor Dionnet encouraging artists to take risks and experiment with the medium. It published early work by pioneers of the influential "Atom Style" like Joost Swarte and Serge Clerc, who – in contrast to *Blade Runner*'s grim aesthetic – delivered retro-future dystopias with a distinct 1950s vibe. Given Dionnet's anything-goes agenda, it's inevitable that some ideas wouldn't work. As with any art laboratory sometimes an experiment would backfire, producing material that might now seem pretentious, self-indulgent, and toe-curlingly "of its time." Strips like American artist Richard Corben's fleshy swords and sorcery epic *Den*, for instance, have not aged particularly well. However, it revolutionized comics and helped give the medium a respectability that had previously eluded it.

As the magazine became more popular and influential, *Métal Hurlant*'s publication frequency went from quarterly to bi-monthly with issue six, and then monthly with issue nine. Rival adult comic titles started appearing in the European market, and the Humanoids themselves even produced a short-lived sister publication called *Ah! Nana*, which mainly featured work by female comics creators like Chantal Montellier. By 1976, Dionnet was frequently travelling to the United States looking to expand into the lucrative American market. "*Métal Hurlant* came to Marvel seeking an American publisher," remembers former Marvel Comics Editor in Chief, Jim Shooter. "After they did their presentation, we had a talk and [Stan Lee] thought that the stuff was too violent, too sexy and that good old sanitized Marvel couldn't do that. We thought he was crazy, but he was afraid that Marvel would get bad headlines."[4]

Dionnet had a similar experience with Marvel's Distinguished Competition, DC Comics: "I had seen [DC's Publisher Carmine Infantino], and I sent him an issue [but] he was not enthusiastic." He even tried reaching a deal with soft porn magnate, Bob Guccione, but the *Penthouse* publisher "scared me to death,

---

[4] https://www.cbr.com/jim-shooter-interview-part-1/

because he was living in a very big house with Christs everywhere, and naked ladies."[5]

Métal Hurlant eventually found an American home with the publishers of *National Lampoon*, the satirical magazine that by the late 1970s had become a successful multimedia masthead for comedy books, radio shows, and movies like *Animal House* (1978). In early 1977, Dionnet signed a licensing deal with the magazine's publisher Leonard Mogel, and the March 1977 issue of *National Lampoon* featured a 10 page preview of a "forthcoming illustrated fantasy magazine" that would go by the name of *Heavy Metal*.

The first issue of *Heavy Metal* appeared in April 1977, just a month before *Star Wars* was released. Initially the magazine was largely made up of English translations of *Métal Hurlant* content, although the translators were sometimes known to take liberties with the source material. "They made the stories funnier than they were," recalls Dionnet. He claimed that low-brow gags were added to the often cerebral comic strips because many of the stories were "translated by the team who were still at the Lampoon at the time," and that visiting *Animal House* star John Belushi would sometimes "find a joke where there was no joke."[6]

In time *Heavy Metal* began to attract more homegrown talent. Some were young American artists who got early career breaks with the title, like Steve Bissette and John Totleben, who would subsequently collaborate with the acclaimed English writer Alan Moore on classic runs of the comic titles *Swamp Thing* and *Miracleman*. Others were veteran creators like horror illustrator Bernie Wrightson, pop-art innovator Jim Steranko, and the writer-artist who would later revitalize Marvel's *Thor*, Walt Simonson. For these creators, *Heavy Metal* offered the opportunity to create innovative work and tackle adult themes in ways that mainstream publishers like Marvel and DC would never have permitted.

Besides comic strips and interviews with industry legends like Will Eisner, *Heavy Metal* broadened its appeal by branching out into other art forms. It championed the work of illustrators from outside of the comic book field, like H. R. Giger, Olivia De Berardinis, and Terrance Lindall. The magazine also featured strong editorial content. There were text pieces and short stories by new wave

---

[5] http://www.tcj.com/because-ive-already-forgot-what-i-said-to-you-but-i-know-its-the-truth-the-testimony-of-jean-pierre-dionnet/
[6] Ibid.

science-fiction authors like Harlan Ellison and interviews with pop culture fringe icons like David Lynch and William Burroughs (whose 1979 unused film treatment *Blade Runner: a Movie* provided a somewhat marquee-friendlier title to Ridley Scott's seminal Philip K. Dick adaptation than *Do Androids Dream of Electric Sheep?*). There were also hard-hitting and often impassioned album reviews from the respected American music journalist Lou Stathis, as well as articles and reviews about movies and the visual arts. This was the kind of stuff you'd expect to find in a hip, literary lifestyle magazine, albeit one with lavishly illustrated comic strips and an abundance of airbrushed nudity.

Heavy Metal soon became a huge and influential hit, and by 1981 had spawned an R-rated animated feature film that adapted several of its strips including Richard Corben's *Den* and Angus McKie's *So Beautiful and So Dangerous*. Tellingly, the promotional campaign for *National Lampoon's Vacation* featured a deliberately incongruous and unmistakably *Heavy Metal*-esque theatrical release poster by Boris Vallejo.

Just like *Métal Hurlant* in Europe, its American sister publication's success would give rise to adult fantasy comic imitators of varying degrees of quality, such as Warren Publishing's *1984*, which was launched in 1978 and, in a cruel twist of fate, cancelled in 1983. Despite Stan Lee's earlier prudishness, even Marvel Comics got in on the act. In 1980 they launched their adult-orientated *Epic Illustrated* magazine, which – while toning down the excessive sex and violence often found in *Heavy Metal* – was nevertheless targeting the same demographic.

Heavy Metal and *Métal·Hurlant* were more than just great comic books. They revolutionized comic art, rejuvenated the comics medium, and – in the parlance of modern business speak – disrupted the comics industry model.

But all of that was nothing compared to the impact that they were about to have on movies.

Ridley Scott first encountered *Métal Hurlant* while filming his debut picture, the historical drama *The Duellists*, in the Dordogne region of France. He was introduced to the magazine – and to its most famous artist, Moebius – by his long-time associate (and later *Blade Runner* associate producer) Ivor Powell:

> Moebius always designs everything from the ground up in his science fiction stories. Wardrobes, buildings, weapons, transportation systems, everything. So, since I knew Ridley was interested in all types of art, I felt he'd probably like this, too. That's why I showed him a copy of [*Métal Hurlant*] when we were in the Dordogne doing *The Duellists*. Ridley apparently hadn't been aware of the magazine before this, but he took

one look at it and said something like, 'Bloody Hell! Why don't they make films like this?'[7]

Scott planned to follow up *The Duellists* with an adaptation of the medieval romantic epic *Tristan and Isolde*. As he prepped his next move, the director was also devouring back issues of *Métal Hurlant* and *Heavy Metal*, trying to find a way to integrate their innovative visuals and design aesthetics into his new film:

> *Heavy Metal*, like Kubrick's 2001, which I thought was brilliant, made me realize how the environment of a fantasy or science fiction piece could be raised to a much higher level. That insight made me aim for a very exotic, 'no time, no place' look for *Tristan*. Something that was historical, but in a gritty, stylized, *Heavy Metal* kind of way. Where the heroes would more closely resemble down-on-their-luck cowboys than traditional knights in shining armor.[8]

A script had been written and pre-production was well underway when Scott found himself "completely waylaid by another film that came out in 1977."[9] *Star Wars* was more than just a box office smash, it was a global pop cultural phenomenon, and studio executives were desperate to cash in on its success, greenlighting big budget science-fiction movies as if there was no tomorrow. After all, this was the era when even Roger Moore's James Bond felt obliged to swap his Walther PPK for a ray gun and have an adventure in space. In commercial terms, this meant it wasn't the right time for a movie about a doomed medieval romance. Scott's *Tristan and Isolde* went into long term hiatus.[10]

A director with as precise an eye for detail as Scott's must have noticed that George Lucas's epic from a galaxy far, far away was already incorporating visual elements from *Heavy Metal*, albeit in a far subtler way than he had planned. The grungy, lived-in look of the *Star Wars* universe may have marked a stylistic break from traditional movie depictions of slick science-fiction environments, but to readers of *Heavy Metal* it was nothing new. The arid desert wasteland of Tatooine, with its giant skeletons of mysterious creatures half buried in the sand, looked a lot like Moebius' imaginary environments in strips like *Arzach* and *The Airtight Garage*, while the evil Intergalactic Empire, with its penchant

---

[7] Sammon, Paul M., *Ridley Scott: Close Up - The Making of His Movies*. Thunder's Mouth Press, 1999.
[8] Ibid.
[9] Ibid.
[10] Ridley and his brother Tony Scott would eventually produce an adaptation of the story in 2006.

for theatrical armor and massive but impractical weaponry, evoked the work of Philippe Druillet. Lucas, like Scott, was a fan of *Heavy Metal* and an admirer of both Moebius and Druillet. He mentioned the two of them in a 1979 interview and wrote introductions to collections of their work.

Star Wars proved to Ridley Scott that there was an appetite amongst moviegoers for the *Heavy Metal* aesthetic, even in a somewhat diluted form. While he wasn't able to make a *Heavy Metal* infused *Tristan and Isolde* in 1977, he saw an opportunity to get *Heavy Metal* up on the screen when he was offered a science-fiction film to direct later that year:

> I stepped into *Alien*, in a way, almost by accident. I hadn't or would never set out to do that kind of movie, really. But when the script was sent to me, I had been burying myself in the area of *Heavy Metal* comics and graphic novels and other similar things, and *Alien* seemed well suited for those types of design possibilities. In fact, *Alien* really was the first film I did with a *Heavy Metal* sensibility. I think that's pretty obvious to anyone who saw the film and is also familiar with the magazine.[11]

It was an instance of cinematic synchronicity that Scott probably wasn't aware of at the time, but the script that was sent to him was written by a former *Heavy Metal* writer. Dan O'Bannon's original script for *Alien* was entitled *Starbeast*, which he originally conceived as a low budget science-fiction slasher film that he planned to direct himself. After the success of *Star Wars*, however, all that changed. Twentieth Century Fox bought the script, seeing it as a potentially lucrative mash-up of two of Hollywood's recent biggest hits. To put it in the language of an elevator pitch, it was *Star Wars* meets *Jaws*.

O'Bannon played a key role in helping Scott make his first *Heavy Metal* movie. He provided a personal link to Moebius, his friend and former collaborator, who Scott then hired to design costumes and spacesuits for the doomed crew of the spaceship Nostromo. He was also instrumental in making Scott aware of another artist in his Rolodex who was destined to become forever linked to the terrifying world of face-huggers, chest-bursters and xenomorphs:

> After Dan O'Bannon gave me a book of Giger's art one day I started flipping through it and nearly fell off my desk. Because I'd hit upon a particular painting [Necronomicon IV] with this frightening, truly unique creature in it. I took one look at the thing and said 'Good God! This is it!

---

[11] Ibid.

This is our Beast!' That was that. I've never been so sure of anything in my life.[12]

To this day, H. R. Giger's Alien design remains one of cinema's most horrifying and memorable creatures. Although the Swiss artist wasn't a *Heavy Metal* comic artist per se, he was in tune with the Humanoids' spirit of outrageous, uncompromising artistic innovation, and his work had been championed by both magazines. For instance, his *Necronomicon* book was the cover story for the September 1977 issue of *Métal Hurlant*.

Another non-comic artist whose work had appeared in *Métal Hurlant* was British science-fiction illustrator Chris Foss, who was hired by Scott to design spaceships for the film. O'Bannon, Moebius, Giger, and Foss had all previously worked together on the Chilean surrealist director Alejandro Jodorowsky's ill-fated attempt at producing a movie adaptation of Frank Herbert's *Dune*. It could be argued that *Dune* was the first real attempt at translating the *Heavy Metal* aesthetic to the big screen. Although Jodorowsky's massively ambitious film never went into production, many of its design elements would later find their way into Ridley Scott's films. What's more, it's fair to speculate that *Alien* would probably have been a very different looking film if Jodorowsky hadn't assembled such an eclectic team of artists in the first place. Would Dan O'Bannon have introduced Ridley Scott to Giger and Moebius if they hadn't already known each other? We'll never know.

Speculation aside, Jodorowsky and Moebius would later go on to produce the classic comic book series *The Incal*, which incorporated many of Jodorowsky's more outlandish concepts and plot elements from his *Dune* adaptation. *The Incal* made its debut in the Christmas 1980 issue of *Métal Hurlant*, while *Blade Runner*'s extensive pre-production phase was underway. Its memorable opening page features the book's anti-hero John DiFool hurtling to what looks like certain death in an immense and intricately detailed futuristic city. It's a great Moebius image, very cinematic, and there must have been times during the filming of *Blade Runner* when Ridley Scott was able to identify very closely with the protagonist's dilemma. He was, after all, building a city inspired by Moebius drawings.

When *Alien* was released it was a commercial and critical success. Ridley Scott had finally made his first *Heavy Metal* movie, but it wouldn't be his last. During the making of *Alien*, Dan O'Bannon showed Scott a comic strip that he

---

[12] Ibid.

had written for Moebius that was entitled *The Long Tomorrow*. According to *Alien*'s associate producer, Ivor Powell, this story would have a lasting impact on Ridley Scott: "It seeded something in Ridley's mind for the future, for *Blade Runner*."[13]

There are many reasons why *Blade Runner* remains a benchmark of quality science-fiction moviemaking. For one thing, it's a sumptuous piece of pure cinema, and even after all these years, and all the exponential advances in movie making technology, it remains absolutely breathtaking. Much of the film's visual richness is due to Scott and his crew's remarkable feat of world building. Their Los Angeles of 2019 ranks alongside Fritz Lang's *Metropolis* and Stanley Kubrick's *2001: A Space Odyssey* as a classic, fully-realized, fictional environment. In a film with no shortage of memorable, iconic characters, the city itself was perhaps the most memorable and iconic of them all. Its impact on science-fiction movie making can't be underestimated. After 1982, every science-fiction film that was set in a future city would find itself compared to *Blade Runner*, and usually unfavorably. However much they tried to avoid it, the dystopian town planners of Hollywood invariably found themselves influenced by, or reacting against, the design aesthetics of the film. The home of Deckard, Rachael, Batty, and Pris became a watershed moment for the genre, and was quite unlike anything that had been seen before.

Well, in movies, at least.

The Long Tomorrow was created by O'Bannon and Moebius while the two were working on Jodorowsky's ill-fated *Dune* project. Like *Blade Runner*, *The Long Tomorrow* was an innovative mash-up of science fiction and classic film noir, containing all the tropes you'd expect to find in the latter. Its hero, Pete Club, is a hard-boiled Private Eye – or in the colorful parlance of the story, a "confidential nose" – with a weakness for world-weary voiceover narration, duplicitous femme fatales, and taking on cases that turn out to be a lot more complicated than they first appear. In terms of characterization, he wouldn't have looked out of place in a 1940s black and white crime flick starring Humphrey Bogart or Edward G. Robinson.

While Pete Club might have been a good thematic fit for a classic film noir flick, he'd probably have been turned away at the door for not meeting the dress code. "Because it was a very strong story, I felt right away that it would enable me to do some really crazy and wonderful things [with the art]," said

---

[13] *Dangerous Days: Making Blade Runner* (2007), dir. Charles de Lauzirika.

From *The Long Tomorrow*, illustrated by Moebius.

Moebius in an afterword to Marvel Comic's 1987 English language edition of the story. "Instead of going back to the classical, dark look of the private eye – the Bogart-style of trenchcoat – I chose to give Club a very colorful and fancy costume." He certainly did that. When we first meet the shaven headed Club, he's sporting a technicolored coat, three-quarter length pants, and a rather ornate policeman's helmet. Later in the story, he slips into a rather fetching but somewhat impractical all-white ensemble. In terms of fashion choices, he was a far cry from Harrison Ford's Rick Deckard, although Edward James Olmos's more eclectically-attired Gaff would have probably approved.

Even if the protagonists of *Blade Runner* and *The Long Tomorrow* may have had little in common in terms of appearance, the same can't be said for their respective cities. The first page of the comic consists of a sequence of panels that establishes the environment in much the same way the "Hades Landscape" opening scene did for *Blade Runner*. In the first panel, we can see that the story takes place in what would become a staple Moebius imaginary environment – and one that he would later revisit in *The Incal* – namely, the subterranean city shaft. As we zoom into this immense crack on the planetary surface, we can see a vast, vertiginous, underground metropolis. There are flying vehicles, mile-high elevated highways, and towering, monolithic buildings, each a seemingly unique mash-up of contradictory architectural styles.

Later in the story, as we hit the streets with Pete Club, we find a world far removed from the white plastic paneled utopias that are so common in the science-fiction movies of the era. This place looks overcrowded, seedy, lived-in, and overloaded with neon. The resemblance to Scott's film is unmistakable. It's almost impossible to imagine that anyone who first discovered the story after 1982 didn't immediately think of *Blade Runner*.

Scott had hoped that Moebius would be able to provide production designs for *Blade Runner* much in the same way as he had for *Alien*, but this wasn't possible due to a scheduling conflict:

> Later, Ridley asked me to work on *Blade Runner*, but at the time I was going to work on another film, *The Time Masters*, so I could not. Now, I'm a bit sorry that I did not, because I love *Blade Runner*. But I am very happy, touched even, that my collaboration with Dan [O'Bannon] became one of the visual references of the film.[14]

While the "visual futurist" Syd Mead and the film's cast and crew played a vital role in *Blade Runner*'s unprecedented feats of world building, it's fair to say that Moebius' influence on the filmmakers was profound. The cityscapes from *The Long Tomorrow* and *The Incal* permeate the architecture of its fictional Los Angeles. According to *Blade Runner* production illustrator Tom Southwell, during meetings with Ridley Scott the director would urge him to "have more and more variety, take more and more chances, be more like *Heavy Metal*."[15]

---

[14] Giraud, Jean. *Moebius 4: The Long Tomorrow and Other Science Fiction Stories*, Marvel, 1987.
[15] *Dangerous Days: Making Blade Runner* (2007), dir. Charles de Lauzirika.

Scott himself was a talented illustrator with a background in art and design. "I was a designer, trained as a painter, then an art director, and then from art direction drifted into graphic design," he said in 1982.[16] While making *Blade Runner*, he extensively storyboarded the film and produced an abundance of detailed sketches that the crew nicknamed "Ridleygrams" to convey his vision of the film's city. In one of these sketches, we see a distinctly *Blade Runner*-esque street scene featuring a giant, futuristic-looking truck with a fictional logo that reads "Zevon" (presumably a nod to the acclaimed American singer-songwriter Warren Zevon, whose 1989 album *Transverse City* would, ironically enough, be heavily influenced by *Blade Runner*). It's not only remarkable how close these "Ridleygrams" resemble the final look of the film, but also how clearly they're influenced by *The Long Tomorrow*.

Moebius wasn't the only *Heavy Metal* artist to have influenced the film. While Moebius's dystopias tend to be well-lit and colorful, the moody and atmospheric ambience of *Blade Runner* owes more to the saturated darkness of Philippe Druillet's art, as well as the work of Franco-Serbian illustrator Enki Bilal. Born in Belgrade in the former Yugoslavia in 1951, Bilal's stories ranged from mature, political thrillers like *The Black Order Brigade* to science-fiction tales with a magical realist twist, such as his award-winning *Nikopol Trilogy*. The latter, which featured a cast of pale, haunted characters living in an ornate yet dilapidated dystopian world, were a likely influence on *Blade Runner*'s replicant characters. Rutger Hauer, who played Roy Batty, certainly had the artist in mind when it came to defining his character's appearance. During his initial meeting with Ridley Scott, Hauer asked, "Ridley, what about this *Blade Runner*? What does it look like?" to which Scott replied, "Well, one of the major influences for me is Bilal, who is a cartoonist in France." Hauer was taken aback, noting, "I happened to know that cartoonist, and I went, 'Whoa!'"[17]

As has been well documented in this book and elsewhere, *Blade Runner* was anything but the commercial and critical success that Scott and the studio had hoped for. It seems that mainstream audiences in 1982 weren't quite ready for such a concentrated dose of the *Heavy Metal* aesthetic – at least, not yet:

> So I figured I'm going to apply what I know about *Heavy Metal* comics to *Blade Runner*, which is fundamentally doing Philip Marlowe. So it's Philip

---

[16] Lightman, Herb A. and Patterson, Richard. "Blade Runner: Production Design and Photography." *American Cinemaphotographer*, July 1982., quoted in Sammon, Paul M., *Future Noir*. Dey St 2017 edition.

[17] Dangerous Days: Making Blade Runner (2007), dir. Charles de Lauzirika.

Marlowe meets *Heavy Metal* meets Hampton Fancher's screenplay, which was originally called *Dangerous Days*. And it didn't strike a chord. People didn't get it, because people didn't know what *Heavy Metal* comics were, then. They hadn't a clue.[18]

Undeterred, Scott once again found inspiration in the work of one of the greats of French comic book art, albeit in a less overt manner, for his next project, 1985's dark fantasy film, *Legend*. The award-winning make-up design of Tim Curry's bright red, phallic-horned Lord of Darkness owes a debt to the baroque, nightmarish illustrations of Phillippe Druillet, in particular his aforementioned adaptation of Gustave Flaubert's *Salammbô*.

Druillet's art had a far stronger influence on George Miller's *Mad Max* film series, the first of which was released the same year as *Alien*. Miller, like Scott, was a huge fan of *Heavy Metal*, so much so that the logo for the original *Mad Max* film, with its strong font and distinct double lightning bolt backdrop, was an unmistakable homage to *Métal Hurlant*. The wildly kinetic and visually-stunning latest instalment of the series, 2015's *Mad Max: Fury Road*, continues this tradition, and is even more overtly influenced by Druillet.

The mid-1980s were not kind to Ridley Scott or *Métal Hurlant*. The contributions of its star artist Moebius declined in quantity as he became increasingly disillusioned with the pressures of his *Métal Hurlant* workload and the Parisian comics scene. He moved to Los Angeles to work on the 1982 film *Tron*, and then to Tahiti where he joined a commune, founded a pair of publishing houses dedicated to his own work, and focused on his most ambitious project to date, the *Edena* cycle of stories. Sales of the magazine were on the decline. This was partly due to increased competition in the marketplace, and partly because a title that had started out with such a bold, idealistic mission statement had seemed to lose its way.

To make matters worse, *Métal Hurlant* had been hemorrhaging money for years. "We had to pay these banks," recalls Dionnet, "so we would go to another bank, and the hole was growing slowly, but regularly, because we had more to pay to the banks than we had profits. So I knew very early, around the third and the fifth years of [*Métal Hurlant*], that we were doomed." Dionnet left the magazine in 1986 and by August of 1987 it had ceased publication. An attempt was made to relaunch the title as a Franco-American publication in 2002, but this second incarnation only lasted 14 issues before folding. *Heavy*

---

[18] http://www.hollywood.com/general/after-25-years-ridley-scott-at-last-has-final-cut-on-blade-runner-57173816/

Metal, on the other hand, continues to be published to this day. Although the magazine has had its ups and downs over the intervening years, it has recently undergone something of a creative resurgence with the 2016 appointment of A-list comics author Grant Morrison as its editor in chief.

After Ridley Scott's *Legend* flopped at the box office in 1985, the director retreated from science-fiction and fantasy filmmaking and kept his distance from the genre for more than a quarter of a century. When he finally made a comeback with 2012's *Alien* prequel, *Prometheus*, he brought his old *Heavy Metal* influences back with him. The tall, bald, humanity-creating Engineer introduced in the film's opening minutes bears a strong resemblance to the Master Burg character that appears as a spirit guide in Moebius' aforementioned *Edena* cycle of stories. A presumably well-thumbed copy of Marvel Comics' 1987 Moebius collection is clearly visible during the behind-the-scenes documentary film *The Furious Gods: Making Prometheus*. The scene in the film where the Engineer is attacked by a hideous, tentacled creature carries a strong visual similarity to a memorable scene in *The Long Tomorrow*, where a naked Pete Club is engaged in a similar tussle. Scott's follow-up to *Prometheus*, 2017's *Alien: Covenant*, also contained a strong Moebius flavor.

Even when Ridley Scott lets other people play in his sandbox, the *Heavy Metal* influence is inescapable. The acclaimed French-Canadian film-maker Denis Villeneuve, who Scott hand-picked to direct *Blade Runner*'s sequel *Blade Runner 2049*, had his own personal history with the magazine. When he was a boy, an eccentric aunt sent him boxes containing back issues of *Métal Hurlant*. Even today, he says, "I think the best sci-fi has been designed by those guys,"[19] and it's no coincidence that Agent K's apartment building is called "Moebius 21." His younger brother, the film director Martin Villeneuve, is also a fan. His 2012 science-fiction romance, *Mars and April*, is very much a homage to *Métal Hurlant* and features production design by the Belgian comic book artist François Schuiten, who was a regular contributor to the title.

Jean "Moebius" Giraud died in March 2012 after a long illness but he continues to exert an influence on science-fiction movies. Everything that's been influenced by *Blade Runner* or *Alien* over the years – not just science-fiction films, but books, music, clothes, and even buildings – are, directly or indirectly channeling the visual frequencies first broadcast by Moebius and his fellow *Heavy Metal* Humanoids back in the early 1970s.

---

[19] http://www.wired.co.uk/article/blade-runner-2049-denis-villeneuve

An issue of *Métal Hurlant* featuring *Blade Runner*.

While promoting the 2007 Final Cut of *Blade Runner*, Scott remarked, "Moebius had designed my space suits for *Alien*. I've still got his drawings."[20] One of those spacesuits, an unused design, featured a distinctive orange color

---

[20] http://www.hollywood.com/general/after-25-years-ridley-scott-at-last-has-final-cut-on-blade-runner-57173816

scheme. In 2015, three years after Moebius's death, Ridley Scott's film *The Martian* was released. The film starred Matt Damon as a stranded astronaut and was a huge critical and commercial hit. However, unlike his previous forays into the science-fiction genre, this one didn't look like a love letter to Moebius and his fellow *Heavy Metal* artists; nor was it set in the pre-existing environments of *Alien* or *Blade Runner*. It was a much more grounded and relatable piece of speculative fiction. There were no hyper-stylized future noir dystopias, no angst-ridden replicants, no self-doubting robot-killers, or acid-gushing xenomorphs.

It was just Matt Damon trapped on Mars, wearing Moebius's orange space suit.

I Dreamt Music: Replicating *Blade Runner*

by Bentley Ousley

Few soundtracks have contributed as much to the atmosphere of a film as the score to *Blade Runner*. It would be difficult, if not impossible to imagine a score that more perfectly matches the vibe of this motion picture. However, if you are only familiar with the officially released soundtrack versions, you may be victim to as much of a revisionist past as the movie's replicant, Rachael.

Even the music released directly by Vangelis for his "official" soundtrack version is deceptive. I find it interesting that just as the film played with one's concept of what we perceive as real, the Vangelis soundtrack releases follow suit with a score played over dialogue that never happened, segues that never existed, and cues that were never in the film (some of which weren't even composed in the same decade or even the same century). Even the soundtracks demand: Question reality! Phillip K. Dick would be so proud.

Here is an interesting question: What is the "*Blade Runner* Soundtrack"? It sounds like a preposterous inquiry at first glance. Upon closer scrutiny, however, the question becomes more germane. It seems that even the filmmaker and composer can't agree on a simple definition.

Including all the bootleg releases, there are more than 60 versions of the soundtrack. By comparison, there are five different "official" versions of the film. This means that there are at least 60 different opinions of what makes up this work.

The official *Blade Runner* soundtrack by Vangelis.

Why all the bootlegs? Why is the soundtrack so hard to define? It started as the film release approached in 1982. Per producer Michael Deeley, composer Vangelis decided not to sign his contract, which would have allowed the studio to release the original Vangelis soundtrack cues as a soundtrack album. Much speculation has occurred regarding this move by Vangelis. Some say he was dissatisfied with the changes to his score in the final film, or that he was hesitant to hand over control of the soundtrack to the financial guarantors who had assumed ownership of the project due to the film running over budget, which seems to make some sense purely as a business decision.

It is not uncommon for a composer to surrender all rights to a composition and recording when composing a score for a Hollywood studio film. Vangelis' previous film score *Chariots of Fire* was a monster hit, with Vangelis retaining the publishing and making out handsomely with his royalties from the sales and radio play. Had he signed over the *Blade Runner* score rights to Warner Brothers, there is little doubt that even if the film had been a big hit, Vangelis wouldn't have made out nearly as well as he did with *Chariots of Fire*. He was hardly a starving artist at this point, so time was a luxury he could afford.

This had to come as a surprise to Warner Brothers, because the Vangelis soundtrack release was touted in the credits of the film. This meant that at the time when the final credits were being created, Warner Brothers still thought that the Vangelis soundtrack would be released. Another interesting fact that seems to indicate confidence in an imminent Vangelis release: Warner Brothers sent out press kits, including a cassette containing the original Vangelis score tracks, which were arguably pretty close to the intended content of the stymied soundtrack. So, what do you do when you need a releasable soundtrack and the original is unavailable? You make a sound-alike. Using a studio orchestra, Warner Brothers created and released a version of the soundtrack using none of the Vangelis score but closely emulating it.

This was no small feat considering that no written score existed for the Vangelis film cues. Vangelis doesn't write or read standard musical notation, working instead improvisationally, reacting to the screen images while playing and recording layer upon layer onto a multi-track recorder. Nothing is written down, which is a far cry from the "Hollywood" method where a composer notates all the parts of an orchestra within the score, and the orchestra is recorded in one pass with all the instruments captured simultaneously.

This meant that the creators of the "New American Orchestra" version of the soundtrack had to listen carefully to the fully produced Vangelis tracks, decide on what available instruments would best emulate the feel, texture, and content of the score, transcribe the musical parts into orchestral notation, assemble an orchestra, and then record it. All this took place while presumably under severe pressure and time constraints.

It is fascinating to listen to the Vangelis cues next to the orchestral tracks. They used some of the best studio musicians in L.A. at the time (which meant, of course, they used some of the best studio musicians in the world), and it shows. The work is pristinely executed and remarkable, considering what must have been a herculean task within a short time period. The places where the orchestral version falls short are the places where Vangelis' unique talent and approach can't be reduced to musical notation, and where synthesizers are used in a manner that transcends what is possible with orchestral instruments (or even synthesizers in less capable hands.)

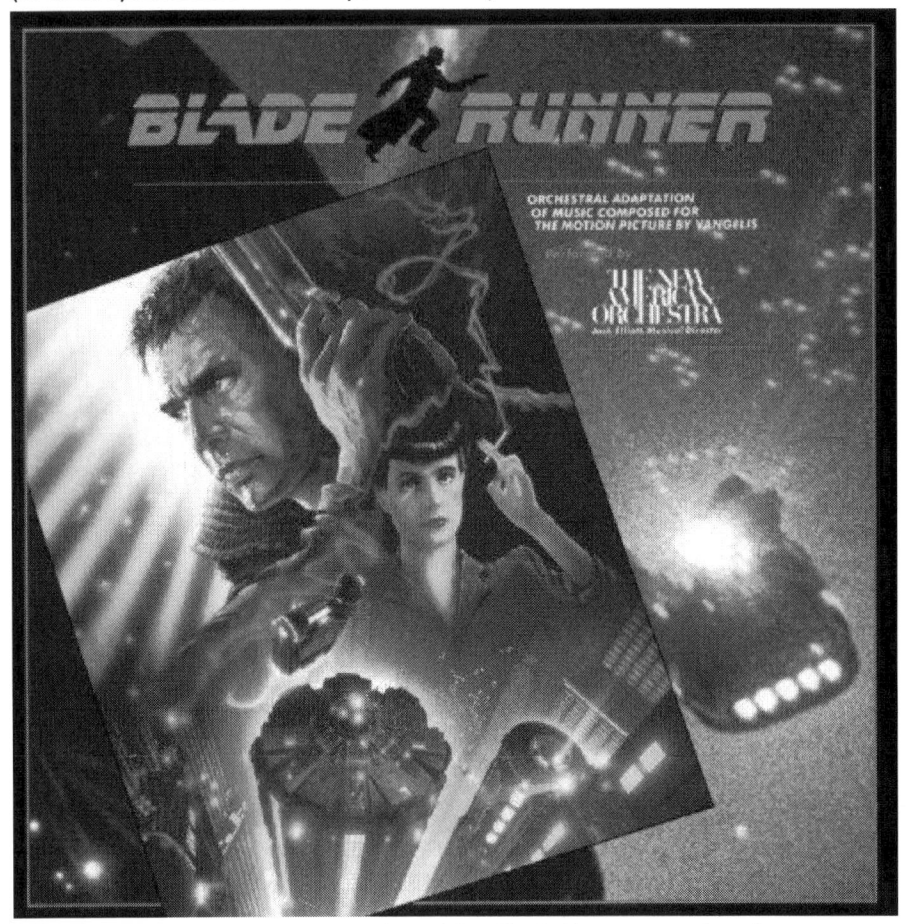

The New American Orchsetra version of the *Blade Runner* soundtrack.

Many fans found the sound-alike score unsatisfying. This started an underground hunger for the original Vangelis-performed score, and that, in turn, resulted in what is arguably one of the most bootlegged film scores ever.

The first bootlegs weren't really bootlegs at all. They were copies of Warner Brothers' promotional package cassette. I've heard it argued that this is the purest soundtrack version. It only contains isolated score performed by Vangelis. This, of course, disregards the idea that much of the atmosphere of the film is contained, not just in the Vangelis score, but also in the non-score sound effects and textures. Imagine the sound of *Blade Runner* without the rain, the traffic, the crowds, the electronic buzzes, beeps and burps, the humming neon, or the distant sound of sirens. The joining of the Vangelis tracks with this dense cacophony of sounds is quite transcendent in this film and absolutely brilliant in my estimation.

I can't help but wonder what role the existing Vangelis track "Memories of Green" had in shaping the sonic texture of *Blade Runner*. "Memories of Green" is a haunting solo piano composition released before Vangelis' work on *Blade Runner,* on the 1981 Vangelis album *See You Later*. It's been argued that Terry Rawlings' (film editor for *Blade Runner* and *Chariots of Fire*) introduction of Ridley Scott to this track was one of the main motivations for hiring Vangelis as the composer for *Blade Runner*. This would seem to mirror how Rawlings' use of Vangelis tracks to temporarily score *Chariots of Fire* led to Vangelis' involvement in that film.

If you listen to "Memories of Green" now, it is impossible to *not* think about *Blade Runner*. The synthesizers gently invoke distant sirens and wind. The lazy, random beeps and boops sound like a partially sedated R2-D2, chattering subtly in the background. The nostalgic melody played on a slightly out of tune piano evokes a sense of loss. How can you not think about Deckard's cocoon-like apartment? Couldn't this be something you would expect to come oozing from Deckard's piano, if he had just enough (or maybe too much) Johnnie Walker Black? Oddly enough, the New American Orchestra version of "Memories of Green" found new life when it made an appearance in Ridley Scott's subsequent film *Someone to Watch Over Me*.

That brings us to our next bootleg source: The entire audio of the film *Blade Runner* with all dialogue removed. You want buzzes and burps? Traffic and crowds? Neon and sirens? Well, here we have it all in spades; a truly immersive audio experience with no distracting dialogue. How can such a thing exist, you ask? Wouldn't it be impossible to completely remove the dialogue without the original multi-track audio masters?

This version exists because Warner Brothers produced the content from the original audio masters, but *not* for the purpose of creating an alternate soundtrack. Allow me to explain. It is common to dub films released in foreign countries into their native languages. This requires an audio dub of the complete film. Everything is left intact except all dialogue, which is removed and then replaced with new dialogue in another language. Even though the full version of this bootleg was produced in very limited quantities, the effect on the second generation of bootlegs produced with this content was immense. The material in this release, combined with the material from the Warner Brothers promotional cassette, along with the non-Vangelis composed tracks used in the film, would keep the bootleggers busy up until (and way beyond) the "official" Vangelis soundtrack release in 1994.

Something happened in 1990 that changed the fortunes of the film and its soundtrack. An accidental screening of a 70mm version of one of the screening print versions caused an unexpected revival of interest in *Blade Runner*. This eventually led to a new Director's Cut of the film being assembled, and in 1994 (12 years after the film's release) an official Vangelis *Blade Runner* Soundtrack release was finally realized. We had, for the first time, in pristine digital format, Vangelis' vision for *Blade Runner*.

All the soundtrack fans had to be completely satisfied now, right? This must have been the end of the bootleg soundtracks, right?

Well, not exactly. Considering that this was a Vangelis "album" called *Blade Runner*, there was none of the non-Vangelis composed material presented. "Fair enough," one might say, "those other tracks are available from the original sources." Yet, one does miss the atmosphere they added.

Then there are tracks that never appeared in the film. "Cool, rare bonus material!" one could say, except that the production on some of those tracks seems a little modern for what was available in 1982.

Finally, people began to realize those dialogue bits didn't match the original film's underscore. What was going on here?

The 1994 Vangelis score contains multiple examples of on-screen dialogue over what purports to be film score. The problem is, with the exception of the Roy Batty soliloquy, none of the dialogue matches the corresponding score used in the film. This was a curious decision on someone's part. Could it be that these were the cues that Vangelis had intended to use in those scenes? Wasn't there a rumor regarding Vangelis being dissatisfied with the way his score appeared in the film?

I had visions of the man compiling the score 12 years after the fact, watching a synchronized cut of the film and deciding to give his fans a taste of what might have been, extracting bits of the dialogue to orient the listener to this alternate reality and preparing them for his original vision. Ah, sweet reverie. Then, upon careful listening, another more realistic theory intruded upon my sweet daydream: the *revisionist* theory.

This theory involves Vangelis in his studio in 1994 watching the new Director's Cut DVD and improvising on top of the existing score, picking the best bits to use as transitions or, in some cases, creating completely new tracks and re-imagining the score as he would have approached it in 1994.

What ended my daydream and caused my suspicion? Listen carefully to the dialogue sections used on the 1994 soundtrack release. The Director's Cut score is still there, although at a low level and mostly drowned-out by the new "imagining" of the cue. This dialogue wasn't taken from a scoring cut of the film. It was taken from the Director's Cut and overdubbed with new music, (mostly) masking the original score. This is most evident in the "Do you like our owl?" dialogue used as an intro to the soundtrack cut "Blush Response." Right after the line "I'm Rachael," you can hear the original score peeking out. This seems even more relevant, considering that the track "Blush Response" is not heard in the film at all. It seems a bit out of step with the production value of the tracks that are actually audible in the film.

There are four tracks that don't appear in the original film. My first guess was that all of them were composed after the fact, probably around the time of the release compilation in 1994. Then I discovered an interesting fact that I chalk up to the power of the internet and the fans' obsessive natures. The vocalist on the track "Rachael's Song" was Mary Hopkin. She scored a big hit in the 1970s with "Those Were the Days." A fan of hers maintained a website which contained a complete listing of all her live dates and studio session dates throughout the 1970s and 1980s. I started looking through her session dates for early 1982 and found a Vangelis session! She most likely recorded the vocals for the track in 1982. This is a genuine "recorded for the score but not used" track. Color me surprised!

One thing is certain though. Most of the transitions between the tracks were created after the fact to make the cues more cohesive, which worked very well. Another minor niggle is that the track titled "Main Titles" is not actually the music heard during the main title sequence. This track is an amalgamation of: 1) a newly created intro with dialogue, 2) the music immediately following the main titles sequence, and 3) an unrelated piece of score that occurs underneath the scene when Deckard and Gaff fly to Police headquarters.

I've often wondered about the music under the Director's Cut unicorn scene. This scene doesn't appear in the theatrical version, or even the early screening print (in contradiction to Ridley Scott's insistence that it was removed from the screening print for the shortened theatrical release). Was it actually scored by Vangelis for the film? If not, where did the music come from? I discovered that the film *Antarctica*, a film Vangelis scored immediately after *Blade Runner*, uses this same cue as underscore. Consequently, it existed in roughly the same time frame as the composition of the *Blade Runner* soundtrack. The track seems to consist of a sampled choir droning a complex chord swelling to the onscreen action. Vangelis had an early sampling synthesizer (Emulator) in his studio, which he used for other *Blade Runner* score cues. Was this track recycled by Vangelis when he thought it wasn't going to be used in *Blade Runner*? Was it originally composed for *Antarctica* and then lent to Warner Brothers for the Director's Cut? Inquiring minds want to know.

The *Blade Runner* Director's Cut release and positive reception marked *Blade Runner's* acknowledgment as a cult classic. With home computers attaining the ability to process (for the time) fairly advanced graphics and interactive game play, Westwood Studios took on the task of adapting *Blade Runner* into a "real-time, 3-D adventure game."

What would the *Blade Runner* experience be without the score and ambient sound effects? Unfortunately, Westwood was unable to license the original score, so it was time for another sound-alike. This time, Westwood's staff composer Frank Klepacki would rise to the challenge. And rise he did, creating some near perfect emulations of some of the most note-worthy cues in the film, and also some very competent original tracks that work very well within the context of the game. Klepacki's score was never officially released, but there was a bootleg release that made the rounds and it's quite good. Even if you don't have the game, you can still hear some of Klepacki's score on his website.[1] Interestingly, he covers Vangelis' "Wait for Me," a track that wasn't in the film and almost certainly was composed as a re-imagining of the score in 1994. Thus, we have Klepacki emulating 1994 Vangelis emulating 1982 Vangelis. Triple score!

The atmospheric sounds in this game deserve a mention. They are very well executed and really put you right in that dirty, crowded, neon-drenched city. The atmospheric tracks are cleverly and inconspicuously looped in order to create a continuous sonic atmosphere as long as one lingers in a specific game location. Some folks liked the looped atmospheres enough to record hours of the audio and put them on YouTube, where you can still find them.

Have you heard the music from the *Blade Runner* television series? In 1999, Showtime imagined a series that had ambitions of bringing *Blade Runner* to television. Unable to secure the rights to the *Blade Runner* name, they licensed another Phillip K. Dick property and called the series *Total Recall: 2070*. Make no mistake, regardless of the title, they were channeling pure *Blade Runner*.

---

[1] http://www.frankklepacki.com/portfolio/game-BR.html

Promotional poster for the TV series *Total Recall 2070*.

The creator, Art Monterastelli, makes no bones about it in interviews about the series. The score is also very much in the vein of *Blade Runner*. It's nicely executed with an accent on dense, dark atmospheric cues. The series split the scoring work between two very competent composers: Jack Lenz and Zoran Borisavljevic. Both do a very credible job of invoking the style of the original score. The series was released on DVD in Canada only. Although a bit hard to find, it is worth the effort.[2]

In 2007, the film and soundtrack took another turn as Ridley Scott became involved in creating what he considered the ultimate version of *Blade Runner*. Dubbed the "Final Cut," it corrected many of the "mistakes" that fans found in the film. These were mostly minor: removing wires, correcting a bit of dialogue, and so forth, but some required considerable CGI magic to accomplish. It is a testament to the work of producer Charles de Lauzirika that the changes seem so fan driven. The end result is spot on.

The most noticeable improvement is the way the film looks. The restoration work on this version is truly remarkable. Details that were lost in the background in the somewhat dark and flat Director's Cut come bursting out, giving fans a whole new appreciation for the quality of the production design and cinematography of this film.

With a new release came rumors that Vangelis might also revisit the score. There were many Vangelis-composed tracks that were present in the film but left out of the 1994 release, and there was hope that Vangelis, at minimum, would release those cues. Some fans held out hope that there might be a comprehensive, retrospective boxed set that celebrated all the versions and answered some of the many questions surrounding the production.

What was released was a three-disc set entitled *Blade Runner - Trilogy*. The content of the first disc is the 1994 release, no more no less. This is exactly the same content as in the original 1994 Vangelis release. The second disc was purported to include all tracks associated with the film that weren't included in the 1994 release. The Wikipedia page for the score lists more than a dozen instances where this is not the case.[3] The third disc contains new compositions from Vangelis described as "inspired" by the film. I have a hard time listening through this disc. It's not that the compositions are bad or poorly performed. It just seems so tepid compared to the actual soundtrack cues. I have trouble

---

[2] As of this writing, it can currently be found on Youtube.com.
[3] https://en.wikipedia.org/wiki/Blade_Runner_(soundtrack)

understanding how this enhances the work. (And what's the deal with the muffled voices coming in at seemingly random intervals in the middle of the tracks?) Sorry, I just don't get it.

This collection was billed as a *complete* release, but they didn't even include the real *Main Titles*! Another interesting omission is the cue for the "Deckard meets Rachael" scene. This cue was included on both the original promotional cassette and the New American Orchestra release. It has been available on bootlegs since bootlegs existed for this score. The only source I've heard for this cue performed by Vangelis comes from the promotional cassette, and the quality leaves something to be desired. This would have been an obvious choice for inclusion for anyone compiling a comprehensive version of the soundtrack, except (obviously) Vangelis. I think it is an interesting juxtaposition, comparing the fan-driven nature of the DVD/blu-ray releases and the fan-tone-deaf nature of those in charge of the official soundtrack releases.

With the explosion of Electronica and the ability to cheaply produce recordings opening up the possibility of becoming a recording artist for anyone with a laptop and a dream, there has been an avalanche of new artists influenced by *Blade Runner* and Vangelis. There could be thousands of "replicants" out there at any given time creating their own re-imaginings of the score.

Don't believe me? Just surf to SoundCloud.com and search. Most of what you hear will be mediocre, some will be merely terrible, but once in a while you'll find something that you really connect with and appreciate. Support those artists! Welcome to the new democratization of music. Don't like what you hear? Roll your own.

Why the Theatrical Cut is the Truest Version of *Blade Runner*

by Paul J. Salamoff

As many of you might know, there are no less than five different versions of *Blade Runner*. The three most notable ones are the Original Theatrical Cut (1982), The Director's Cut (1991), and The Final Cut (2007). Because I'm a huge cinephile, and *Blade Runner* is my favorite film, I'm invariably asked, "What's your favorite version?"

"That's easy," I say. "The Theatrical Cut."

As much as I admire the improvements, especially in The Final Cut, I will always prefer the Theatrical Cut.

Those uninitiated with the different versions typically give me a head-scratching look, so I add, "The version with the voiceover." Those who *are* aware of the different versions typically give me the same head-scratching look and then reply with, "You know they forced Harrison Ford to do that voiceover, so he phoned it in on purpose," and/or "The footage at the end is just outtakes from Kubrick's *The Shining*."

As true as these facts may or may not be, I stand my ground. As far as I'm concerned the truest version of *Blade Runner* is still the Theatrical Cut. Fortunately, I have a forum to explain why!

The four main elements that differentiate the Theatrical Cut from the Director's Cut (or all subsequent cuts of the film) are the voiceover, the lack of the unicorn dream, the "happy" ending, and the underlying question of whether or not Deckard is a replicant.

Let's start with the most obvious.

The Voiceover

A reason why many people seem to dislike the Theatrical Cut is Harrison Ford's lackluster performance of the voiceover narration that runs throughout the film. Popular urban legend dictates that both Ridley Scott and Harrison Ford were against it, but the studio insisted and so Ford purposely did a poor job in the hope it would get scrapped, which it didn't.[1]

I honestly believe that many who were introduced to *Blade Runner* via the Theatrical Cut are incapable of watching the other versions (sans narration) without filling in the blanks. I know I personally can't help myself from mentally adding those distinctive lines back in when I watch the other cuts. Every time I see Deckard's introduction sequence, the words "They don't advertise for killers in a newspaper. That was my profession. Ex-cop, ex-blade runner, ex-killer," are spoken drolly in my head followed soon after by "Sushi, that's what my ex-wife called me. Cold fish."

A hallmark of the hardboiled detective genre is the inner dialogue of the protagonist which provides us with their point of view of the story. There's a mystery or problem to be solved and the detective is our guide. This commentary is sometimes a mere framing device at the beginning and the end, other times it's a running commentary that pops up every now and then to remind us that what we're watching has already occurred. It has been employed with cinematic skill in such film noir classics as *Double Indemnity*, *Mildred Pierce*, and *Out of the Past*, as well as more contemporary movies as *The Postman Always Rings Twice*, *The Usual Suspects*, and the science-fiction/noir film *Gattaca*.

Historically speaking, most voiceovers suggest that the story we're watching takes place in the past and what we're really witnessing is a memory; a recounting of events by our main protagonist. But Rick Deckard's narration is

---

[1] The actual story of the voiceover recordings is fascinating and is slavishly recounted in Paul M. Sammon's *Future Noir: The Making of Blade Runner* (Harper Prism, 1996).

clearly present tense. We see things as he see things. We learn as he learns. He is reacting to events as they unfold in *real time* and the narration works as an aside to the audience – a breaking of the fourth wall, you might say. Deckard holds our hand along this journey and he wants us to know what's on his mind.

Another reason people seem to dislike Deckard's voiceover is that they feel it's unnecessary; that it doesn't add anything to the film and we're better off without it.

I don't agree.

> The charmer's name was Gaff. I'd seen him around. Bryant must have upped him to the Blade Runner unit. That gibberish he talked was cityspeak, guttertalk, a mishmash of Japanese, Spanish, German, what have you. I didn't really need a translator. I knew the lingo, every good cop did. But I wasn't going to make it easier for him.

I defy you to convince me that you could extrapolate any of this information about Gaff from a voiceover-less introduction. Yes, we can easily figure out Gaff's name via the film's dialogue, but how would we know Gaff had recently been promoted? Why does this matter? It certainly speaks to Gaff's motivations when dealing with Deckard. If he's new to the Blade Runner unit then he has something to prove. Does he see Deckard as a mentor or does he see him as washed-up? Is Deckard what's left of the old guard and Gaff the new blood?

We certainly know how Deckard feels. He's a loner. He doesn't want Gaff's help and he's not going to go easy on him. The audible shorthand of his thoughts playing out on top of the scene adds a rich layer to their relationship that may have been too subtle to conclude based solely on their behavior toward each other. We can see that Deckard isn't thrilled with Gaff by his demeanor and body language, but thanks to the voiceover, we know why and that opens up the narrative. It gives us much more than just the adversarial cop cliché. That said, we ultimately get a better understanding of Gaff's motivation in creating his origami figures, but we'll discuss that later.

The voiceover also provides us with a clear explanation of what the "gibberish" that Gaff speaks is. I'm not a linguist, so I would have naturally assumed he was speaking an Asian language that I was unfamiliar with. The fact that it's some kind of cityspeak ("a mishmash of Japanese, Spanish, German, what have you.") that has emerged from the streets is a far more intriguing aspect to the future of 2019 and would have been lost "like tears in rain" without Deckard's explanation.

> I'd quit because I'd had a belly full of killing. But then I'd rather be a killer than a victim. And that's exactly what Bryant's threat about little people meant. So I hooked in once more, thinking that if I couldn't take it, I'd split later. I didn't have to worry about Gaff. He was brown-nosing for a promotion, so he didn't want me back anyway.

The above speaks volumes about Rick Deckard. We fully understand that he has done his share of killing and that weighs on his soul. This part of the voiceover prepares us for the ultimate decision he makes regarding Rachael, and later on, Roy Batty. The seeds of his character arc are firmly planted. He says he'd rather be a killer than a victim, yet he ultimately sheds this truism about himself for an uncertain future. He recognizes that he has always been the victim of a system designed to inure him to killing. So he rejects the system.

Deckard, in the film's final moments, informs us: "Gaff had been there, and let her live. Four years, he figured. He was wrong. Tyrell had told me Rachael was special: no termination date. I didn't know how long we had together, who does?"

Love ultimately conquers all. It redeems Rick Deckard. Even armed with the knowledge that it might be short-lived, he strives to be more than just a hired gun; a tool for a system that has, for a time, turned him into the very thing he sought to destroy – an automaton, brainwashed by an uncaring world.

While I prefer the Theatrical Cut, I concede that some parts of the voiceover can come off as perfunctory:

> Skin jobs. That's what Bryant called replicants. In history books he's the kind of cop that used to call black men niggers.

> I didn't know whether Leon gave Holden a legit address. But it was the only lead I had, so I checked it out. [pause] Whatever was in the bathtub was not human. Replicants don't have scales. [pause] And family photos? Replicants didn't have families either.

> The report would be routine retirement of a replicant, which didn't make me feel any better about shooting a woman in the back. There it was again. Feeling, in myself. For her, for Rachael.

We may not need to be told these things, but they add flavor, color, and a bit of contrast to the dark and oppressive images on the screen.

Look, *Blade Runner* is a complex movie and expects a lot from its audience. It's not such a bad idea for the film to hit you over the head every once in a while to make sure you're not spending too much valuable time trying to figure things out. Also, the fact that we're reinforcing Deckard's feelings helps us to understand the inner turmoil he's wrestling with. He's trying to act like a cold machine but those pesky feelings keep getting in the way; his feelings for Rachael in particular. This only strengthens Deckard's character arc and reinforces the film's human element.

This brings us to the two final key pieces of narration:

> Tyrell really did a job on Rachael. Right down to a snapshot of a mother she never had, a daughter she never was. Replicants weren't supposed to have feelings. Neither were blade runners. What the hell was happening to me? [pause] Leon's pictures had to be as phony as Rachael's. I didn't know why a replicant would collect photos. Maybe they were like Rachael. They needed memories.

> I don't know why he saved my life. Maybe in those last moments he loved life more than he ever had before. Not just his life, anybody's life, my life. All he'd wanted were the same answers the rest of us want. Where did I come from? Where am I going? How long have I got? All I could do was sit there and watch him die.

You want to know why *Blade Runner* is so special to me? It's the lines, "They needed memories," and "Maybe in those last moments he loved life more than he ever had before. Not just his life, anybody's life, my life."

This is poetry pure and simple – A glimpse into the human condition. A stone-cold killer trained to be entirely unsympathetic to his prey, yet unable to shake that empathy. It's Deckard's own humanity that ultimately allows him to recognize humanity in the last place he expects to find it: in non-human beings. These lines epitomize the power of science fiction and the ability to tell stories that are on one hand fantastical, and on the other, painfully human.

Deckard's words give us a better understanding of his personal tragedy, one of a killer in search of some kind of redemption in a cold dark world, which comes in the form of a simulacrum in the shape of a woman and his perceived enemy. When Rachel bluntly replies to Deckard's comments about "the business" of retiring replicants with, *"I'm not in the business... I am the business,"* he recognizes the humanity in these machines and the now apparent lack of it in himself.

Regardless of how you feel about the quality of Ford's voiceover performance, the words themselves are quite wonderful and – as demonstrated – add another dimension to the film that was not there previously.

The Unicorn Dream

Since its first appearance in The Director's Cut, there has been much speculation about what exactly the "Unicorn Dream" sequence represents. Of course, this scene is *not* included in the Theatrical Cut and thus we have yet another reason why it's my preferred version of *Blade Runner*.

For those that don't know, the minute-long scene is rather simple. The camera slowly pans across Deckard's apartment where we find him hunched over his piano tapping out a languid melody on the keys. As if in the midst of a daydream, the shot dissolves to a lush green forest where a unicorn gallops in slow motion over a series of four shots before dissolving back to Deckard. The scene continues with him looking over the photographs scattered on top of the piano and choosing the one he found in Leon's apartment.

Many people believe that the insertion of the unicorn scene is a clear suggestion that Deckard is a replicant. The connection being that Deckard has a dream about a unicorn and then, at the end of the film, we see that Gaff has left an origami unicorn for Deckard to find. This implies that Gaff knows what's inside Deckard's head. Is he a mind-reader? There's certainly no evidence of that, so people assume that since he somehow knows Deckard's memories are implanted, Deckard *must* be a replicant.

On the surface, this is a very sound argument as we are certainly conditioned to believe that a replicant can be fooled into thinking it's a human being (like Rachael, for example.) But this logic is flawed and there's another suitable explanation for the unicorn motif.

First, let's discuss the flaw: if Deckard is indeed a replicant, why all the subterfuge?

Why would it be necessary to convince Deckard he was a human to be able to do his job properly as a cold and efficient killing machine? The last thing you'd want was a Blade Runner having any semblance of empathy. Making him believe he was human would have logically included convincing him he had a conscience and a soul. If he were to actually start caring about these replicants, he might think twice before retiring them.

Deckard being a replicant also serves up the question of his incept date. When, exactly, was he created? He seems to have a very clear history with Bryant. Are we to believe that Bryant is in on this? Does he know what Deckard is? Is he forced to put on a charade every time Deckard is around reinforcing that they are old buddies and that Deckard is the *best of the best*? Is Gaff in on it too, acting as Deckard's watchdog, making sure he sticks to the script? If this is all true, it defies common sense. Besides, isn't it illegal for replicants to be on Earth? Bryant wouldn't allow it. He has clear contempt for replicants. Bryant even insists that Rachael, the most "human" of the replicants, be retired.

One could make the counter-argument that Tyrell somehow has his hands in law enforcement and that Bryant is forced to do this, but that gives rise to its own set of problems.

First off, we are led to believe that Rachel is the first of her kind – a replicant who doesn't know she's a replicant because of implanted memories. This is reinforced by the idea that Tyrell keeps her on a tight leash and under close observation. He clearly wants to study her. Look how curious he is about how Rachel responds to the Voight-Kampff test. If replicants with implanted memories were a dime a dozen then it would be hard to believe that Tyrell would be so excited by this little game of his.

Deckard and the Voight-Kampff machine.

We are given no other reason to believe that Rachel is anything but unique as it's an important plot detail that culminates with Deckard's decision to go away with her. But let's say she is not unique. Let's say that there are other replicants like her. Okay, then the assumption would be that there are a number of them already out there doing important jobs. It's a tad absurd to think that Tyrell would've previously created only one other special replicant (Deckard) and then let him loose in the world to work as a lowly Blade Runner – a job that would require Deckard to hunt down and destroy Tyrell's own creations.

Why would Tyrell want this?

Tyrell seems to get off on the idea that his "children" are becoming more sapient. It's certainly not a leap in logic to believe he's upset that his creations have been banned on Earth. So, if that is the case, what does he gain from helping the police destroy his creations? If we're talking commerce, it makes more sense to create a replicant lobbyist to petition the government to allow replicants back on Earth than to create a single replicant whose sole purpose is to make sure that all replicants are *persona non grata*.

But what about the damn unicorn, you say?

You might want to sit down for this one. Let's chat about Gaff's propensity for making comments about Deckard through origami. The three origami we see in the film are the chicken, the matchstick man with the erection and, of course, the unicorn. Because there is a one-to-one correlation between the unicorn and the Deckard's daydream from the other versions of the film, viewers tend to fixate on a subtextual meaning that may not be there.

But Gaff's origami figurines serve two important purposes in the film. The first is that Gaff seems to be one step ahead of Deckard at all times and ultimately gifts him with not killing Rachael when he clearly has the opportunity. Gaff represents a sense of dread and inevitability; a constant reminder that Deckard is a cog in the wheel of a much larger machine and that the divide between Deckard's station in life and the "little people" is more tenuous than he wants to believe.

The other has to do with Gaff's thoughts about Deckard. This is another reason why the voiceover is so important. I admit that this is a bit of a stretch and probably doesn't hold as much water as I'd like it to, but think about this. The viewer hears Deckard's inner thoughts via narration. We glean Gaff's inner thoughts via visual representation. It's a nice juxtaposition of the two characters. Deckard tends to be loud, sloppy, and all over the place, telling the viewer directly what's on his mind. Gaff is quiet, insular, and far more refined. He gives us insight into what makes him tick with his purposely-vague bon mots and "gifts" that require a certain level of interpretation.

Take the origami chicken, for example. Is this what Gaff thinks of Deckard? Does he think that he's a washed up Blade Runner, afraid to do his job? What about the matchstick man with the erection? Does he mean to imply that Deckard is a simpleton who only thinks about sex? Is he saying that Deckard is crude and unrefined? Does it mean Deckard's not even a man at all?

And then there's the unicorn, the mythical beast that epitomizes the unattainable virginal beauty. Is Gaff commenting on Rachael? Is he saying that she is the unicorn in Deckard's life? Gaff clearly has the opportunity and motive to kill her, but he doesn't. Instead he tells Deckard that he's done a "man's job" and then pointedly comments, "It's too bad she won't live. But then again, who does?" in direct reference to the pair's future together. Maybe the unicorn represents the complete opposite of what viewers ultimately embraced. Maybe it means that Deckard has proven that he is indeed a *man* and has earned Gaff's respect, thus making him deserving of the unicorn that he has been seeking.

Occam's Razor, where the simplest explanation is usually the correct one, can be applied here. Deckard being a human, not a replicant, makes the most sense. Deckard being a replicant leaves us with questions.

The "Happy" Ending

Deckard and Rachael step into the elevator and it slams shut.

Cut to black.

Does this bleak ending of the unknown future for our two protagonists work? Definitely! It's very strong and certainly powerful. But does the journey away from the hell that is the city of Los Angeles included in the Theatrical Version also work? Definitely!

Maybe I'm a softie, but I like the hopefulness that it gives us. Dystopian narratives don't always have to give us the *"You Maniacs! You blew it up! Ah, damn you! God damn you all to hell!"* ending to be successful as dystopian fiction. A perfect example is *Logan's Run*, a watershed movie of the science-fiction genre. In its climax, Logan takes down the system and frees all the dome dwellers from the tyranny of a computer-run society. It leaves us with the hope that things can get better.

Given that *Blade Runner* essentially takes place in the ninth circle of Hell (Los Angeles, 2019), it's a nice change of pace to discover that having completed his quest, our hero escapes from Hell into a somewhat brighter and more hopeful future. He's been scathed by the experience and there is some ambiguity to his victory, but there is the plausibility of happiness with Rachael, even if it's short-lived.

A complaint that I often hear when defending the ending of the Theatrical Version is that the producers used outtakes from Stanley Kubrick's film *The Shining*. Also, if there's such beautiful countryside to be had, why are so many people living such miserable lives in the trash heap that is Los Angeles? Well, dear reader, for the same reason that people do it today! There are city folk and there are country folk. People choose to live where they want. It's a weak argument to say just because something is available that you should take advantage of it. If you believe that then pack up and move to the country right now. Just do me a favor if you do and check and see how Deckard and Rachael are doing. I still worry about those two lovebirds.

Humanity in Question

On the surface, *Blade Runner* is an action-based science-fiction noir but what makes it such a masterwork is the multilayered exploration of its themes, such as the dangers of playing God, hubris, slavery, technology, surveillance, and how we perceive the world around us. But one major theme that gets muddled by the tinkering that resulted in the various versions of the film is the theme of humanity and what it really means to be human.

Excluding the Theatrical Cut, all the subsequent versions of *Blade Runner* suggest that Deckard may be a replicant himself, the idea being that it takes one to hunt one down. Philip K. Dick, the author of *Do Androids Dream of Electric Sheep?*, the source material for the film, wrote Deckard as undeniably human. Hampton Fancher, the screenwriter of the original draft, wrote Deckard as human. Even Harrison Ford has been quoted as saying Deckard was human. Ridley Scott, on the other hand, has made it very clear that he feels Deckard is a replicant. So there is definitely a spattering of opinions.[2]

With all due respect to Ridley Scott, I feel that Deckard being a replicant completely destroys everything that makes *Blade Runner* so special to me. To me the most important theme of the film is that you have, for lack of a better word, "machines" acting like human beings and a human being acting like a machine. I find that concept a truly haunting and tragic element that plays out in *Blade Runner* with exceptional skill with regards to the visual storytelling as well as the lyrical writing.

Yes, Tyrell espouses that his creations are *"more human than human,"* but what does that truly mean? That not only are they psychically more enhanced but they are far more enlightened as well? Are we seriously required to dig so deep into a quagmire of contradictions to find some kind of rational explanation

---

[2] These assertions have been most recently re-comfirmed in "Reborn to Run – Exclusive First Look at *Blade Runner 2049*" (Entertainment Weekly, Futuristic Double-Issue #1147 and #1448, 30 Dec 2016 and 6 Jan 2017).

to fit an already shoddy theory about the nature of Rick Deckard's existence? If anything Tyrell's catchphrase strengthens my argument. It's clear that Deckard has had some kind of an epiphany by the film's end due to his time spent with the replicants. He concludes that life has more meaning than he initially considered. If he was a replicant than he would already be enlightened, and don't get me started on his lack of physical stamina! *"More human than human"* certainly does *not* describe Rick Deckard in any way, shape, or form.

Many will insist that I am completely crazy and that it's cooler if Deckard is a replicant because who doesn't like the unicorn scene? But what does the film gain from this?

Nothing.

I feel that it actually weakens the themes and confuses the narrative, leaving major plot holes which require additional explaining.

The Candle that Burns Twice as Bright...

I know the Theatrical Version subtly suggests that Deckard may be a replicant, but I find no problem with that. It's just a mere suggestion; one more thing to ponder among all the other things to ponder in the story. It's not a major plot point like it is in the subsequent versions. There's an air of mystery and ambiguity to it all that compels the viewer to revisit and re-watch it over and over again.

Ultimately, the Theatrical Version of *Blade Runner* is a masterpiece of science-fiction cinema that hasn't lost an ounce of its luster even as the real 2019 rapidly approaches and the film's long anticipated sequel *Blade Runner 2049* passes us by. It's a movie that demands your attention – a film of ideas that raises questions as it views humanity through the lens of a man struggling with his morality in a murky world of grey that lacks empathy.

Strip away that humanity by reducing Deckard to a machine (as in the subsequent versions of the film) and all you're left with is something that visually *burns twice as bright* but ultimately *burns half as long*.

The Theatrical Version, like its version of Rachel, has no termination date.

Deckard: B26354 – Coming to Terms with Deckard Being a Replicant

by Lou Tambone

Before there was an Internet, movies were made without a lot of the baggage that comes with them today. You followed the news of the making of a film by reading newspapers and magazines, watching television, and discussing things with your friends or other people who were also following the exploits of the filmmaking industry. I consider myself lucky enough to be one of those people who grew up in the pre-cyberpunk era and saw it all come to pass. Technology overtook everything slowly and to be honest, I loved every minute of it.

Today, when filmmakers are trying to do their jobs, they have to take all kinds of other things into account. Movie fans have joined forces with the Internet to create a sub-culture all their own. Not one iota of information about a film goes unnoticed and commented upon daily by these cyber-cinemaphiles. There are articles with headlines like "[Film Name] Run Time Revealed!" or "[Film Name] trailer synopsis leaked!" When did we start needing to know exactly how long a movie or its trailer was?

There are bootleg scripts and image leaks from movie sets on a very regular basis, with sites dedicated exclusively to them. These things lead to all kinds of speculation by fans (many times correct) which ultimately lead to the dreaded S-word: Spoilers, and that's a big hot button issue on its own. In fact, many of the debates about films that are released in today's age happen *before* the film is actually released. Just check out any movie site's comments section, if you have the stomach for that sort of thing. Once a film is out, one side of the online community is silenced while the other side gloats and revels in a hollow "told you so" victory.

One thing's for certain in all this: Filmmakers are not as free to do their jobs as they once were. They can't simply enjoy the creative process anymore. They have to deal with everyone knowing everything about the film – or wanting to know everything about the film – long before it's even complete. They have to worry about people taking photos on set and instantly sharing them with the world. They have to carefully watch what they say and to whom they say it, always running the risk of ending up quoted out of context within an hour. They have to employ CIA levels of secrecy that would make James Bond look like Fred Flintstone. Thankfully, Ridley Scott didn't have that problem with *Blade Runner*, but why does this even matter?

To answer that question, you have to travel back in time to the year 1981 when *Blade Runner* was being shot. Outside of magazines, newspapers, television interviews, and occasional segments on the news, there weren't many sources for information about the film or any others, for that matter. If you wanted to openly discuss the film, you might try the schoolyard or the water cooler at work. There weren't a hundred clips of footage released to various sources, nor were there any ways to release them outside of television, which was usually given the same few clips (usually on tape) to choose from. Trailers were usually limited to theater viewings and you had to be lucky enough to see one you really wanted to see, unlike modern times where it's announced in advance what trailers will be showing before what films in order to drive sales. Do you believe a film like *The Waterboy* would have made as much money as it did had it not been for the fact that the trailer for *The Phantom Menace* was playing before it? You might not believe me when I say this but I know people who paid for a ticket, watched the trailer, and left as soon as it was over.

That said, we really didn't know about all the issues that plagued the making of the film until many years later. After all the trials of adapting Philip K. Dick's story *Do Androids Dream of Electric Sheep?* into what would become *Blade Runner*, certain corners were cut both financially and artistically. One of those issues was Ridley Scott's decision to make detective Rick Deckard, the hero of the story, a replicant himself.

For years after the film was released, no one really talked about this, including Scott. Everyone simply assumed Deckard was human. Then Scott threw everyone a curve ball by releasing his Director's Cut of the film in 1992, which included (amid other minor changes) a scene he had always wanted to include of Deckard daydreaming about a unicorn. This would, of course, tie in with the origami unicorn he finds on the floor at the end of the film while making his escape with Rachael, therefore implying he is indeed a replicant, since Gaff presumably knows about his memories.

That one scene alters the way you think about *every other* scene in the film, which is an amazing feat when you think about it.

Many people thought this addition was a tacked-on exercise in self-indulgence, but if you're a fan of Ridley Scott, you know that self-indulgence is not really on his filmmaking radar. Everything he does when making a film has a definite purpose and in this case, the unicorn scene was meant to drive home the idea that Deckard is a replicant while trying not to hit you over the head with it using clunky dialogue or some other ham-fisted method.

I had mixed feelings about this at the time.

I can honestly say that never once, from the moment I first saw the film until the moment I first saw the Director's Cut, did it ever cross my mind that Rick Deckard could be a replicant. I can also say that no one ever brought the idea up to me when discussing the film. I think that most people were sold on the fact that Deckard was the main representative of humanity in that bleak world of 2019. Unlike someone like Tyrell or Bryant, we could relate to Deckard. He was just a guy trying to do his job, and getting beat up pretty badly in the process. I thought all that stuff about him looking at old pictures was only there to parallel Rachael's phony pictures and memories. I thought that perhaps Ridley Scott was trying to show us that Deckard had things that she didn't, and that's what made them different. That's what gave him that feeling of superiority which starts to diminish later in the film. Perhaps he even took those photos and memories for granted and felt guilty as he sat there at his piano thinking about this crazy case he was working. Are we defined by our past? Can something be considered alive if it has no past? Do my memories and photos validate me as a real human being? Is Rachael not really alive because she has implanted memories in her replicant brain?

Deckard at the Tyrell Corporation.

So for years I was blissfully unaware that Scott had fully intended Deckard to be a replicant the whole time, whether it was apparent in the theatrical release or not. Perhaps he mentioned it, but I don't remember reading any interviews with him where he made it known until after the Director's Cut was released. Even if he did state his intention back then, I'm thinking people wouldn't have bought it.

Even Harrison Ford wasn't on board with it as late as 2013 when he commented to an interviewer at an AFI (American Film Institute) event. "I was moved to ask Ridley whether or not he thought that the character I was playing was a replicant," he said. "Well, I never got a straight answer. Which is okay, I guess. But I thought it was important that the audience be able to have a human representative on screen, somebody that they could have an emotional understanding of. Ridley didn't think that was all that important."[1]

I didn't buy it at first either. Deep down, I didn't want to it to be true. He was Harrison Ford. He was my hero. He was Han Solo and Indiana Jones and I had already added Rick Deckard to that list of heroes long before this big revelation. I didn't want to have to remove him because he wasn't what I wanted him to be. It was tough to come to terms with the whole thing because I really felt for the guy as he was gumshoeing his way through a dark and rainy Los Angeles of the not-so-distant future. I was rooting for the guy and now, here he was, reduced to another one of *them*. It was a punch in the throat.

There were rumors that the unicorn dream scene consisted of footage from Scott's film *Legend,* but that turned out to be untrue. The turning point for me

---

[1] http://comicbook.com/2014/12/18/ridley-scott-answers-whether-deckard-is-a-replicant-in-blade-run/

was when I learned that the scene was filmed during the film's initial production and it was originally *intended* to be in the film. The idea was there at the onset.

So I ultimately converted, and here's why. Never before had I experienced a situation where I looked at a film one way for a long time and then, after some kind of alteration, looked at a film in a completely new way. Everything was flipped upside down and I started wondering about things like the question of who knew about Deckard if he was a replicant? Did Bryant and Gaff know? Did Holden? Did Roy Batty know somehow? Did he see a file? Was he able to sense it somehow? Is *that* why he saved Deckard at the end?

After you resign yourself to the fact that Deckard is indeed a replicant, you can watch the film again and *every scene* is different. It's like a whole new film, really.

For instance, when Deckard goes to the Tyrell building, he comes across Rachael, whose last name is never revealed although we know she has the memories of Tyrell's niece implanted in her mind. Of course, that doesn't mean she's Rachael Tyrell. They could have given her any last name, really. In *Do Androids Dream of Electric Sheep?* her last name is Rosen, which is also the last name of Tyrell's doppelganger in the book, Eldon Rosen (the corporation is naturally called the Rosen Association as opposed to the Tyrell Corporation), but this is all academic.

Watching the film before knowing Deckard is a replicant, you see a cop doing his job. He's supposed to follow Bryant's orders, go over to the Tyrell Corporation, find the Nexus-6 in question and "put the machine on it." It's one of a number of scenes intended to get Deckard from point A to point B in the film. He meets Tyrell, performs the Voight-Kampff test on Rachael, they discuss her failure of the test, and we move along.

Coming to terms with Deckard's true identity as a replicant, this scene becomes *much* more entertaining. Now we're witnessing two replicants who don't know they're replicants talking about replicants being a benefit or a hazard, among other things. They're talking about themselves without knowing it and all the while, there's Tyrell watching in amusement. Was he secretly enjoying the dark comedy playing out before him as one replicant, unaware of what he is, tries to suss out another, also unaware of what she is?

"Have you ever retired a human by mistake?" Rachael asks Deckard before Tyrell makes himself known. After Deckard replies with a negative, she responds, "But in your position that is a risk." Then Tyrell interrupts. His deviously analytical brain was probably watching this exchange from the shadows, noting every nuance and every reaction.

Tyrell's God complex really comes into play here. He must know that Deckard is a replicant yet he toys with him, strings him along, even helps him with his detective work by (we assume based on later dialogue) letting him see confidential files about the Nexus-based replicants. He must get off on watching his creations interact. He's researching. He's mentally taking notes. "How can it not know what it is?" Deckard asks him after Rachael leaves the room. That line must have given Tyrell a mental chuckle.

I like to think that when this scene was over, Tyrell want back to his room or office and just sat there thinking for a long time about what he just experienced, silently praising himself. Deckard certainly seems to be "more human than human," or at least more human than Rachael, who shows very little emotion throughout the entire film.

So if he's a replicant, is Deckard a new model or some kind of prototype? While there's no real documented evidence to support this claim, Ridley Scott alludes to the fact that Deckard could possibly be part of the next generation of replicant: a Nexus 7 or even Nexus 8.[2] He's also mentioned this fact in various interviews, stating that if this were so, we really don't know what kind of life span he would have. This is a convenient set up for *Blade Runner 2049*, of course, but an interesting thing to think about.

The only part that bothers me about this is that I often wonder why he didn't have more prowess. The fight between him and Roy shouldn't have really been so one-sided. Then again, if Deckard really was "more human than human" then perhaps he was defined by his own limitations. If you know you're a replicant and you're told you can do amazing things, you probably believe in your own abilities without resignation. If you don't know you have these abilities and you believe (or you're made to believe) that you're just a human and therefore inferior to a super-human replicant, then you'll pale in comparison. Better yet, perhaps in Tyrell's quest to create humans that blend in better, he refrained from giving certain models certain powers so they wouldn't stand out. Being a replicant doesn't have to equal being Superman. The possibilities are endless.

"Did you ever take that test yourself?" Rachael asks Deckard in his apartment. He never answers, but it raises another interesting question and

---

[2] *Blade Runner* Final Cut director commentary.

(again) changes our perspective. What if he did take the test? Would he pass? Are the new models designed in such a way that they can pass the test? If I were Tyrell and I knew that the police had such a test, I'd be trying to invent a way to circumvent it. Perhaps Deckard is a new model with the capability to not only pass the test, but administer it as well. Deckard's empathy increases as the film goes on, eventually peaking on the rooftop at the end. Perhaps Tyrell found a way to finally give his replicants empathy, which in turn would allow them to pass an empathy test like the Voight-Kampff.

Deckard on the L.A. streets.

If he's been given empathy, is he also capable of love? Does he know what love is or remember being in love, be those memories real or implanted? This leads us to the uncomfortable discussion of Deckard and Rachael's awkward love scene, for lack of a better term. Deckard is clearly more advanced than Rachael, taking on the role of the teacher in the relationship, literally telling her what to say and do as if they were putting together a piece of furniture from Ikea.

That seems to support the theory that Deckard is a next-gen replicant and not a Nexus-6. He has empathy (or at least a primitive, developing version of it) and he knows what love is. Rachael doesn't know what's happening to her or what to feel. At first it appears that Deckard is taking advantage of her, slamming the door on her as she tries to leave, slamming her against the window, and so on. He looks angry and impatient, like a wife-abusing husband about to lay a smack-down on his wife for serving his dinner to him cold. At one point he even puts his hands up as if to say, "Okay, I'm not going to hit you."

It's an awkward scene no matter what your perspective is. For years, I took it as Deckard teaching Rachael how to love, kiss, and make love (off screen, I assumed). But looking at it from the perspective of Deckard as a replicant, things get a little skewed. You have to dig into his subconscious a little, phony as it may be. He's still giving her a love lesson, but at the same time he's also teaching himself how to handle a woman. Maybe his programming or conditioning seeded him with the traits of an abuser and this was that behavior manifesting itself for the first time. If (as the original voiceover suggests) he really did have an ex-wife, or the memory of an ex-wife, they are obviously no longer together. Was this due to some kind of abusive relationship, implanted or not? Maybe Deckard was going through a learning curve without knowing it.

As a human, you see a man giving into desire. He's saying, "I know you're not human, but I'm in love with you and we're going to make this happen, dammit." He has human desires and he knows she doesn't so he's going to use that as an excuse to make her do what he wants under the guise of educating her. She's not as developed emotionally so she stays put and cooperates unlike a human who might perhaps fight back or try to escape with more effort than she did. She's clearly scared but is not really sure what to do.

As a replicant, this could feasibly be his first attempt at love as well, since we don't know how long he's been around or where he was before. His first time, however, is based on memories given to him by Tyrell, we assume. He thinks he knows what he's doing but does he really? Maybe that's why he's so rough and domineering. He never really had those experiences, just memories of them. This is his first time actually performing these actions and they're coming out in the way his memories are instructing him.

Something else I've always noticed, and you might have also, is that near the end of the film, Roy Batty calls Deckard out by name. I always found it odd that he knew Deckard's name since they hadn't interacted in the film until after the death of Pris. I had previously attributed this to a simple script oversight but now I'm not so sure. In an early version of the script, it's stated that Roy may have tapped into the police's ESPER computer network in order to monitor police behavior and make sure he and the other replicants were safe. If this is true, Roy calling Deckard out by name may be an echo of this concept that bled over into the filmed version. Perhaps Roy found mention in the ESPER network that a detective named Rick Deckard was assigned to the case to find the rogue replicants, probably along with a photo of Deckard to boot, which leads me to yet another interesting perspective change.

Let's say for a moment that Bryant and Gaff knew about Deckard. It's very heavily implied in the film that Gaff knows about him, so that's not a stretch. In fact, Ridley Scott has stated in a few interviews that Gaff is a bit more important than we're led to believe. "That's the whole point of Gaff, the guy who makes origami and leaves little matchstick figures around," he told *Wired* magazine in 2007. "He doesn't like Deckard, and we don't really know why. If you accept for a moment that Deckard is a Nexus 7, he probably has an unknown life span and therefore is becoming human. Gaff, at the very end, leaves an origami, which is a piece of silver paper you might find in a cigarette packet, and it's a unicorn. Now, the unicorn in Deckard's daydream tells me that Deckard wouldn't normally talk about such a thing to anyone. If Gaff knew about that, it's Gaff's message to say, 'I've read your file, mate.'"[3] He goes on to clarify that when Deckard finds the origami unicorn at the end of the film, Deckard nods to himself, therefore confirming his status as a replicant, affirmed by Gaff's little paper gift.

So if Gaff knew, then surely his boss knew as well, right? Could Gaff have been working independently? I hardly think so. I like to believe Bryant was in on the whole thing. In my mind, it all leads to the top of the pyramid – the Tyrell Corporation. My theory implies simply that the police department where Bryant and Gaff operate is what we call in street parlance "on the take." It could go all the way to the top, with Bryant and Gaff just doing what they're told from some unknown boss above them, or it could be that Tyrell contacted Bryant individually and he roped Gaff in for support. If there was enough money involved, both Bryant and Gaff seem dirty enough to take on such a covert operation in order for Tyrell to test out his latest model. It certainly ties in with the "dirty cop" trope of those old film noir movies.

This deal works out for Bryant and the department in another way as well. It's convenient for him to employ the services of a machine to handle this type of dangerous job than to risk the life of a human like Gaff (if he's even human!) or some other cop. Remember when Bryant tasks Deckard with heading to the Tyrell Corporation to "put the machine" on the replicant there? Deckard asks, "And if the machine doesn't work?" Bryant just looks away and never answers the question. Replicants are expendable, not to mention illegal, on Earth. Should Rick Deckard expire in the line of duty, Bryant could just call someone upstairs or at the Tyrell corporation (depending on how deep this conspiracy

---

[3] http://www.wired.com/2007/09/ff-bladerunner/

goes) and get himself another Blade Runner, complete with memories and some kind of back story. It might even be another Deckard. Maybe the Deckard we see in the film isn't even the first Deckard, just the first one who succeeded. Maybe that's why Roy Batty knows Deckard's name? He's seen him before. Aren't these wonderful theories? It's great fun to think about what could be going on under the cover of the L.A. darkness.

As I stated earlier, many of these theories were the result of that *one* unicorn scene added to the Director's Cut, turning my perspectives upside down. It makes me wonder what kinds of discussions we'd be having today if it were included in the original film. In the *Wired* interview from 2007, Ridley explains why it didn't make the original cut: "[There] was too much discussion in the room. I wanted it. They didn't want it. I said, 'Well, it's a fundamental part of the story.' And they said, 'Well, isn't it obvious that he's a replicant?' And I said, 'No more obvious than that he's not a replicant at the end.' So, it's a matter of choice, isn't it?"[4]

When I realized that was the initial intent and the idea was always part of the narrative, then I found it easier to swallow. My thoughts were less conflicted. The question for me stopped being, "Is Deckard a replicant?" and became instead "Why didn't I want him to be a replicant?"

Was there some selfish motivation? Did I love the character of Rick Deckard (played by Harrision Ford, one of my favorite actors) so much that it hurt me to find out he was some sort of artificial hero? What heroes were left then? Surely, I couldn't look up to someone like Roy Batty as a hero, or could I? Everyone loves a good villain but what do you do when you find out the villain might not be a villain at all?

On a deeper level, maybe I didn't want Deckard to be a replicant because if he turned out to be artificial, then perhaps anyone could be artificial. Can we take what happened to Deckard and overlay it on top of our existences? Could there be a Tyrell out there right now experimenting with replicants while we go on with our busy lives? Was that cashier at Wendy's no more human than the register she used to ring me up?

For a long time, *Blade Runner* was like an old friend that I had a falling out with. I still loved the film but we hadn't really talked about our deeper issues for about 20 years or so. Then, after those issues were resolved, we were both able to move on and enjoy each other's company. We cherished the old days,

---

[4] Ibid.

enjoyed the current ones, and look forward to the future knowing that our perspectives were in line with each other and everything made sense.

The release of *Blade Runner 2049* did a wonderful job of keeping Deckard's status vague. Deep down, I had hoped they would answer the question definitively, and on screen, perhaps making it a bigger part of the story. That never happened, but the film worked so well that it didn't bother me. I did, however, watch it with two different perspectives this time, and that made the experience twice as enjoyable.

All Those Moments Lost in Time: Deleted and Alternate Scenes

by Joeseph Dilworth, Jr.

For as long as there have been movies, there have been deleted scenes. Just about every film has them; scenes that, for whatever reason, were trimmed. Those reasons can range from a subplot that just didn't work, a character whose actor either died or became ill, or, more commonly, a running time that was simply too long and needed to be shortened. For decades, audiences in general either didn't know or didn't care that there were moments cut from a given narrative. The movie that was seen in the theater was all that mattered. The advent of repeating films on television and, later, home video, is what brought deleted scenes into the public conscious.

Superman – The Movie was one of the first to make use of deleted and extended scenes to lure an audience into a re-watch on television. The broadcast television premiere was a two-night event that added around 40 minutes to its original runtime. The first two *Star Trek* films also made use of added content. This was a great reward for fervent fans, but an even bigger enticement for those who may have seen a film once in the theater or perhaps had missed it altogether. Additionally, in the early 1980s, HBO had finally caught on and began airing movies commercial free. Television networks needed something extra to draw in audiences, and additional scenes did the trick. Of course, the home video market would change all that.

Renting VHS tapes to watch a film at home had become ubiquitous by the mid-1980s, but the market really came into its own as tapes became available for home purchase. Films on VHS that were rented could be purchased for approximately $70-80 (sometimes more), which relegated owning a film to rabid enthusiasts only. Eventually stores started selling their surplus of used tapes for substantially less and prices on new tapes eventually dropped to the point where it became reasonable for general consumers to make those purchases. Now, of course, owning a film is as easy as a mouse click. Again, much like restored scenes made television broadcasts appealing, they also made owning a film extra special.

"Director's Cuts" of films helped give a boost to the early home video market. You may be asking what this has to do with *Blade Runner*. The answer is twofold. First, it was one of the first films to release a Director's Cut on home video. A lot of what has been referred to as a Director's Cut was often the studio owning the film rights, re-adding deleted and/or extended scenes to a film, and slapping a special label on the packaging. Occasionally these have been called "Extended Cuts" generally when the original director strongly pointed out that it is, in fact, *not* a version that they cut together. Increasingly, the directors got involved, as in the case of the first non-theatrical version of *Blade Runner* officially released to the public.

Secondly, after the release of the film in theaters, there was a work print version of *Blade Runner* that made the rounds for many years containing scenes that were unseen by the public. These extra scenes had been hotly talked about and debated for years, and still are to this day. There are as many people who argue that they belong in the film as there are those who believe they merit being discarded. Both sides contain those who have only read about these mythical lost scenes.

It wasn't until 2007 that most fans could make an informed opinion, however. In 2007, *Blade Runner – The Final Cut* was released on DVD and Blu-ray. This impressive set contained every version of the film released to date, plus a plethora of new extras. Among those extras was, at long last, a collection of deleted and extended scenes, but with a *Blade Runner* twist. Rather than presenting them as stand-alone clips, Warner Home Video instead assembled them into what amounts to a 45-minute abridged version of the movie. This was an unusual, yet highly creative move, and gives the long-lost scenes their own narrative, even if it results in a somewhat disjointed flow.

It starts off with different opening credits, this time next to a blue bar showing slow motion water droplets. This is obviously a nod to not only the rain that is prevalent throughout the film, but the Roy Batty's famous "tears in rain" monologue. That, or someone just thought it looked sufficiently sci-fi or art-housey enough to tack on to the film. Other than that, it's not worth pining over.

The credits lead into a shot of the city from up high, with one of the advertising dirigibles slowly passing by. We hear the now-famous ad-line "A new life awaits you in the Off-world colonies. The chance to begin again in a golden land of opportunity and adventure..." The shot of the city seems to be a matte painting and somewhat unremarkable, but I like it. It gives us more of the scope of the future we are entering and feels like a fuller and more rounded vision of the future.

Then we are introduced to Rick Deckard. As in the finished film, he is waiting around for his turn at the noodle bar. The voiceover narration is there, only it isn't the one that everyone either loves or loathes. Featured throughout the deleted and alternate scenes are alternate takes of the narration. These lines are even more revealing than what we first heard in the theatrical version and Harrison Ford sounds as bored as ever. The narration has always been a heated point of contention among *Blade Runner* fans. Some feel it is essential while others view it as a scourge on a masterpiece. Usually, there isn't any middle ground, but as it happens, I am of two minds about it. On one hand, it really isn't necessary to the artistic, science-fiction masterpiece that *Blade Runner* has become over the years. On the other hand, deadpan narration has always been an integral piece of the film noir genre that this movie has always wanted to be. I can, and often, watch it either way, but if I had to weigh in, I would say I prefer the film without the voiceover.

Next, we see Gaff picking up Deckard and taking him to police headquarters along with a brief alternate scene involving Captain Bryant. Gaff escorts Deckard into the Police Station, this time in a wider shot instead of obscured by Deckard walking into Bryant's office. This has the benefit of showing Gaff affectionately touching the shoulder of a female office, and even smiling at her, as Deckard's narration mentions Gaff's girlfriend. This one brief little segment helps develop the Gaff character and perhaps helps to explain his motivation in letting Deckard and Rachael escape at the end. Is it possible that Gaff is an old softy and believes in love?

The narration here is really off, not in the information that it conveys, but in the tone. The only other interesting part of this whole sequence is the odd, pointed looks that Bryant gives Deckard as the two take a look at Roy Batty's files. Deckard is tired and uncomfortable and Bryant is watching the Blade Runner like a hawk. For those who subscribe to the theory that Deckard is a replicant, there is plenty to add to their argument.

Next we arrive at one of the most popular, and possibly even legendary deleted scenes from *Blade Runner*, one breathlessly described by those who had seen it in reverent tones to those that had not: the "Holden hospital" scene. By the time I bought the 2007 set and finally watched it, I experienced a weird sense of déjà vu. A couple of stills from this particular scene had been featured in various media publications and all of it had been meticulously reconstructed in newsletters and magazines over the years.

This shooting of this scene was described in detail in Paul M. Sammon's book *Future Noir: The Making of Blade Runner* and some unreliable sources had claimed to have seen it in early work print versions of the film. Yet it had been talked about and pulled apart almost as much as the film itself. It's a fairly short scene, heavy on the dialogue, but there is a lot there for those who take the time to look.

Holden, having been shot by Leon, is in an enclosed hospital bed that resembles an iron lung. When Deckard enters, Holden is reading *Treasure Island*.[1] The two talk about Holden's interview with Leon and some of the possible ramifications. The scene is short, sweet, and seemingly incongruous, but is that really all that is going on?

I have often wondered if *Blade Runner* is essentially one big Voight-Kampff test for not only Deckard, but the audience as well. The Voight-Kampff machine is what the Blade Runners use to determine if an individual is human or a replicant. It involves a series of questions designed to elicit an emotional response to determine empathy, something the replicants are deficient in. One of the questions includes: "…the tortoise lays on its back, its belly baking in the hot sun, beating its legs trying to turn itself over, but it can't, not without your help. But you're not helping. Why is that?"

---

[1] Interestingly enough, Deckard's first lines of dialogue in *Blade Runner 2049* are quotes from *Treasure Island*. Coincidence?

Interestingly, when Deckard enters the room, Holden is in his hospital tube on his back. He isn't literally trying to turn himself over, and he isn't baking in the hot sun, though the room décor is white and brightly lit in stark contrast to the rest of the film. Yet, he's clearly in pain, and at one point, Holden asks Deckard to help him, which he does. He also asks Deckard to find the replicant that did this to him. We know that Deckard eventually does come across Leon who is then retired by Rachael. The real question is: did Deckard pass this part of the test?

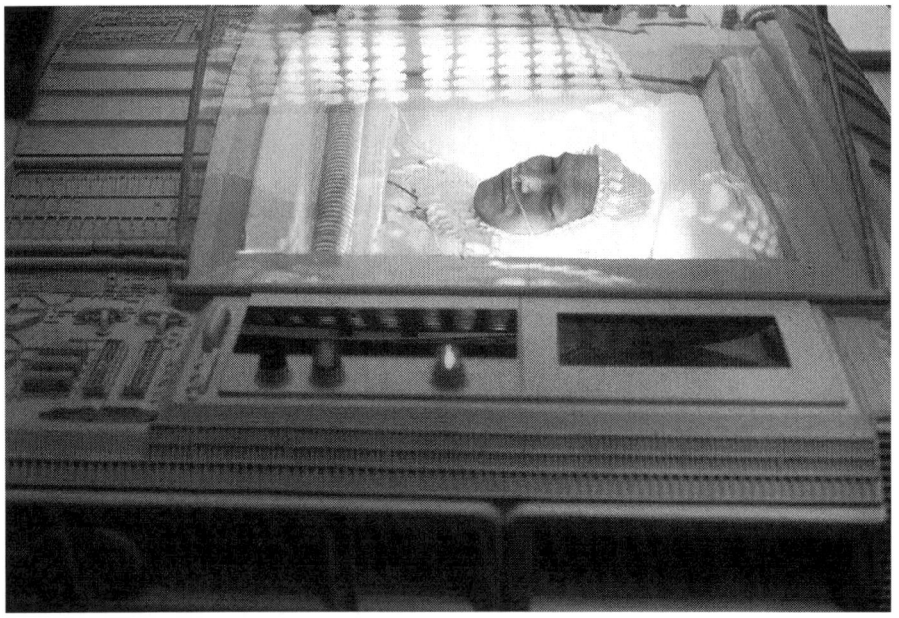

Holden in the hospital (deleted scene).

Deckard doesn't seem empathetic in his conversation with Holden, remaining even-keeled through the whole thing. The closest he gets to showing even a little emotion is to reprimand Holden for doing a bad job outing Leon. That could simply be banter between rival colleagues, but it doesn't seem so to me. Holden doesn't hold back his frustration and anger at all, but Deckard doesn't seem to share it. Admittedly, Deckard doesn't really show much emotion in the film at all until he encounters Rachael at Tyrell's office, so this could just be his regular demeanor. However, if we're grading Deckard in our hypothetical Voight-Kampff test, I'd say he failed.

As renowned as this deleted scene is, I'm glad it was left out. It just doesn't fit. It's too bright and runs counter to the color palette of the rest of the film. Harrison Ford's performance is pretty flat, whether intentional or not, and there is zero chemistry between Deckard and Holden, two colleagues who are supposed to be friends. With all the hype over the years, I was expecting something quite riveting, but instead the scene comes across as a forgettable one. We revisit this location later in this mini-movie, but more on that in a bit.

After this, we are treated to Gaff and Deckard flying in a spinner to the Tyrell Corporation. It's one long and narrated expositional scene that gives the viewer some background on each of the replicants. Once again, there's some rather unremarkable dialogue, but it does contain one valuable nugget. While perusing the replicants' files, Deckard notes that Zhora's psychological profile reads like a cross between "a porno tape and a road accident." If any version of the narration had been as colorful as this, it might have been better regarded.

A small snippet of an alternate version, with narration, of Rachael's Voight-Kampff test follows. This reveals nothing new except for the made-up levels of the test, another not-so-great loss. Following this, however, is another much talked about deleted scene, perhaps less popular than the Holden hospital scene. It starts with Deckard and Gaff investigating Leon's apartment. It should be noted that one of the hidden gifts of these deleted and extended scenes is that we see a lot more of Gaff. He doesn't necessarily have more dialogue, but it's clearer that he and Deckard are supposed to be partners. It makes more sense that you'd buddy up with someone to investigate the stone-cold killers the replicants are made out to be instead of stumbling along solo. Gaff is one of Edward James Olmos' most unusual roles, so seeing more of him is a treat.

Tossing Leon's place is a bit more involved here than in the original, but more or less the same. It has the added unnerving revelation that Leon was hiding in the bathroom ceiling the entire time. I like this bit and wish it had remained in the final product as it adds cunning and guile to Leon, who otherwise comes across as a childish oaf, which may have been the intention.

Pris meeting J.F. Sebastian for the first time involves less glass breaking and is, to me, inferior. It comes off as a rehearsal take. Likewise, the ESPER scene and Deckard's investigation of the snake scale which leads to Taffy Lewis' bar are not as good as what we saw in the finished product. Taffy Lewis is more cooperative, at least. Both the vid-phone call to Rachael and the scene in Zhora's dressing room, along with her death, are brief and over-narrated, as is Deckard taking Rachael to his apartment. The compressed timeframe makes it seem that Rachael is upset over Zhora's death rather than having just killed Leon, but it still works.

Deckard cleaning himself up in his apartment includes a bit more blood and the narration, for the first time, explains Deckard's growing conflict over falling for the thing he is supposed to kill, namely Rachael. This leads to a tenderer and less violent love scene between the two that includes a bit of nudity previously absent. This is another take that I think works better than the original. The "love" scene in the finished film always bothers me and I find it very uncomfortable to watch. That may have been the point, and I think I understand why it may have been shot and edited that way, but having a moment of sweetness between two characters that recently enacted violence upon two others fits better narratively in my mind.

A second hospital visit to Holden has the foul-mouthed, injured Blade Runner guessing what Deckard has done, at least obliquely. The two are observed by Bryant and Gaff, the latter of which has a great line: "I spit on metaphysics." While he eschews metaphysics, it's possible that Gaff relies more on instinct and emotion, which would make him a very effective Blade Runner. More to the point, it also ties in with the mention of his girlfriend in the police station scene and his decision to allow Blade Runner and replicant to run away together in the end.

This second hospital visit, while extremely brief, feels much more natural and real than the previous one. Deckard is more relaxed and casual, and the banter between him and Holden is more nuanced, like the way two friends and colleagues would talk to each other. While a lot of it is relegated to the conversation between Bryant and Gaff, I can't help but wonder if there's a longer and unedited scene of just Deckard and Holden talking. I'd love to know what they're saying.

The death of Tyrell is handled off-screen in this compilation with some of the dialogue heard over an aerial shot of the Tyrell Corporation's pyramid. Afterwards, we see a distraught Batty getting in the elevator hugging Sebastian's coat (he was killed too, although we don't see it in this version either.) Upon hearing the elevator's automated voice, he cries out, "Mom?" It is most likely that Batty is just experiencing a minor breakdown, having murdered the man he believed to be his father. Obviously, Batty doesn't think the machine is truly his mother, but maybe Tyrell was playing around with implanted memories and that is what Batty "remembers" his mother's voice to be. There is nothing at all to indicate that this is the case, but it's a fun theory.

In another scene, we see Deckard proving his identity to another spinner cop. In the background, the wires and crane used to lift the other spinner off the ground are completely visible.

Eventually, we approach the big ending that includes part of Batty's soliloquy and death, along with the release of the dove. This time, the bird flies off into an appropriately dark sky, instead of dawn's first light. That particular error was fixed in the Final Cut, but is still present in all the previously released versions. In these final scenes, the narration becomes poignant as we fade between Deckard and Batty. Before Gaff arrives, Deckard's voiceover tells us, "I watched him die all night. It was a long, slow thing. He never whimpered and he never quit. He took all the time he had as though he loved life very much, every second of it. Even the pain. Then he was dead." This is heartbreakingly poetic and segues perfectly into Deckard's decision about what to do with Rachael in the end.

Gaff's final lines to Deckard revisit the theory that Deckard is also a replicant. "You've done a man's job, sir, but are you sure you are a man? It's hard to tell who's who around here." If that had been included in the final version, it would have probably been the definitive bit of proof that Deckard was indeed a machine who, up to that point in time, believed himself to be a broken man trying to regain his humanity. If you are of the opinion that Deckard is a replicant, this could be the moment where he himself realized that was case, hence his running away with Rachel at the end. It would also imply that Gaff knows this as well, yet still chooses to let them live. The question remains purposely ambiguous in *Blade Runner 2049*.

This mini-version of the film ends with not one, but two versions of the "happy" ending. Both feature Deckard and Rachael driving through the countryside. The first one has a somewhat somber, yet open-ended narration, pretty bland in tone but still works within the noir detective aesthetic that the film borrows from. Overall, it ties in well with the rest of the story, particularly Batty's death. The second version features a conversation between Rachael and Deckard and contains no narration. It ends with Rachael declaring that she feels the two of them "were made for each other." And the Deckard-is-a-replicant crowd goes wild! This ending could have worked as well, but ultimately I think the ending that Ridley Scott chose is the one to go with.

A wise man once opined that Chinese mysticism is much like a salad bar. The practitioners take what they want and leave the rest. I find this metaphor applicable to *Blade Runner*. There are so many versions of the film (at least six, counting this mini-version) that it's easy to pick and choose the narrative an individual wants it to follow. Whether you think Deckard is a replicant or not, you can pull scenes from here and there that form a cohesive story to back up that opinion. But there is so much more to mine from this story. Even after watching all the versions multiple times, I can still notice things I haven't seen before.

A shot of Rachael and Deckard from the "happy" ending (deleted scene).

In that context, the deleted and alternate scenes may be the most important version of *Blade Runner*. While several parts might seem to sway things in the direction of Deckard being a replicant, it can also be argued that most of what is presented here simply further highlights a man who, beaten down by life and circumstance, and has become, in essence, a machine. It is only through his interactions with these androids that cling to every iota of life that he returns to love, and his love of life.

It is completely up to the viewer to determine which way the movie plays out, and neither side is wrong. *Blade Runner 2049* didn't give us a definitive answer, but check out the deleted and alternate scenes from the original film and you might view *Blade Runner* in a whole new way.

The Creation of *Blade Runner*'s Unique 70mm Prints

by Steven Slaughter Head

The first screening of *Blade Runner* at New York's Criterion Center was a disaster.

Either the film or the projector, or both, broke. If it was the film, it wasn't one of the more than 3,000 standard 35mm release prints duplicated by Warner Brothers and shipped to theaters. It was a rare bird: a hand-made 70mm Technicolor special, of which likely fewer than a dozen were created. The breaking of a print isn't unprecedented, of course, but this instance could certainly represent the state of film projection at that time.

The Criterion, which was located in Times Square – and is clearly visible, along with *Blade Runner* on its marquee, in Martin Scorsese's *King of Comedy* – had fallen from its glory days. By 1982, like other often semi-vacant cinema palaces, its owners divided the theater into six smaller venues. Its main theater, however, with its 70mm projector, remained intact, despite the decline of the once palatial venue amid Times Square's most sordid era.

New York Times critic Vincent Canby, in a July 1982 article entitled "Film View; 'Going to the Movies, II,'" recalled that first showing. "This is a true story," he wrote. "Read it, Ridley Scott, and weep."[1]

It was the 12:30 PM show on Friday, 25 June 1982. The audience, "Having stood in line outside the theater waiting to purchase their tickets," wrote Canby, was "prepared to adore the film even before seeing a frame of it."

A ticket for one of the 70mm showings.

After the lights went down, the trailer for *The Road Warrior*, one of Warner Brothers' May 1982 releases, began and was cut short when the print broke, "or, possibly, it's the projector," Canby noted. After a minute of darkness the trailer resumed, and after that, the feature.

During the opening shots, "The names of almost everyone connected with the film" were applauded; and in Harrison Ford and Ridley Scott's cases, cheered. "The initial scenes," wrote Canby, were "as spectacular as anyone in that opening day's audience could have wished." Then, one hour into the film, the frame horizontally split. The image jumped "two-thirds of the way up the screen" sending character's feet to the top of the frame and heads and torsos to the bottom. The issue wasn't immediately corrected and the audience turned "increasingly angry." Eventually the framing was fixed. "This was simply a trailer for the disasters to come," wrote Canby. "In the next hour the film broke down three times in rapid succession."

Interruption number 1: The film stopped. The theater's lights remained down, and the film restarted. Interruption number 2: The film stopped. The theater's lights came one. It was a lengthy delay, with management playing

---

[1] http://www.nytimes.com/1982/07/04/movies/film-view-going-to-the-moviesii.html
All Canby quotes are from this article.

music over the sound system as the audience waited. The music, wrote Canby, "continued to be played even when the film started again." Interruption number 3: This was an extended exercise in impatience that led one front-and-center audience member to yell, "This place doesn't deserve 70 millimeter and Dolby sound!"

After a technician "with a briefcase" entered the projection booth, one final attempt was made to restart the screening, but it failed. Again the film stopped, the lights came up, and that was it. Management announced that the theater would give refunds or passes for another screening. The experience led Canby to ask, among other questions, "Is it the poor quality of the prints that causes the trouble?"

"Screening a print when it's projected properly does not put it to any risk," said Rob Hummel when I asked him about this in preparation for this essay, and he would know. He was one of the creators of *Blade Runner*'s 70mm prints. "And the key phrase is 'when projected properly.'"

Working at Technicolor, Hummel's job involved handling a film's dailies, often for more than one film at one time. "I'm the first guy to see the film after it comes back from the developer," he told me. Ultimately, this is how he got involved with *Blade Runner*. "I was the liaison with Jordan Cronenweth, the cinematographer." Hummel would later move on in *Blade Runner*'s production to work with Douglas Trumbull at his Entertainment Effects Group (EEG).

Blade Runner is a film that begs to be seen in the best possible way. Within its beauty, its details are worthy of close inspection. The film was built that way. Its visual effects are intended to be finely scrutinized. Fans of *Blade Runner* are particularly ardent, even boastful, of their admiration. They've always wanted the best possible viewing of *Blade Runner*.

Nevertheless, it's fair to say few have seen *Blade Runner* in its most excellent, most visually optimal form. "I tell you though," Hummel said, "4K projection is going to give a 70mm print a run for its money, and they did do a 4K restoration of *Blade Runner*." Still, 4K can't best the resolution and sound quality of a 70mm print. There are those who believe, regardless of advancements in projection technology, that a 70mm film print with 6-track magnetic stereo sound remains the best way to watch a film. That's what Ridley Scott wanted to deliver, but with something extra; something no other 70mm print had ever offered.

How the "Extra-Special-Effort" 70mm Prints Came to Be

As *Blade Runner* was nearing the end of principal photography, Ridley Scott was presented with one of the production's many perplexing problems. It wasn't a production problem, it was a presentation problem. Scott was greatly concerned by the fact that for *Blade Runner's* 70mm prints, its special effects would be greatly reduced in clarity from their 65mm quality. Hummel recalled Scott saying, "We've got all the spectacular visual effects shots, shot in-camera composites. First generation kick-ass visual effects. And in the 70mm prints, they're going to be six generations away!" If the shots didn't look as good as they truly were, it would be a travesty.

To explain, *Blade Runner's* principal photography was shot in 35mm. Its visual effects, photographed by Douglas Trumbull using a large format VistaVision camera were shot in 70mm (technically 65mm).[2] A 70mm release print of a 35mm film is typically created by striking the prints from a 35mm *interpositive* – the same one that's used to create the 35mm prints. That being the case, *Blade Runner's* visual effects, having already been considerably reduced in clarity in the 35mm interpositive, would be further reduced, and its muddiness massively magnified, in 70mm.

The late 1970s and early 1980s were also an era of blue screen effects shots which, by the time they ended up in a film's release print, were many generations away from an original negative. Nevertheless, Scott wanted 70mm screenings. Furthermore, being sure *Blade Runner's* visual effects shots looked great in this grand format wasn't just to wow moviegoers, but to honor the work of every visual effects person employed by the production. So how then could the 70mm prints best showcase the production's accomplishments?

Rob Hummel came up with an idea. He recalls, "They were wringing their hands like there was nothing they could do. I used to work at Technicolor, so I said, 'Guys, there's a solution. I know Donah Bassett, the negative cutter, really well. Why don't we get her? What we'll do is we'll cut in the 65mm shots, the original camera negative for the visual effects, into the 70mm printing negative. We're only going to be making no more than 12 prints, so that's not subjecting the original visual effects negative to very much risk.'"

---

[2] At the time, Trumbull was the only visual effects artist shooting in 65mm – the purpose of which was to offset eventual grain from reprints. After his company, Effects Entertainment Group, folded in the wake of *Brainstorm* and star Natalie Wood's death, Richard Edlund and his company Boss Film bought Trumbull's equipment and continued using the VistaVision camera and lenses.

It was possible. There was time before the June 25th release date and Ridley Scott loved the idea. So that was it. The production decided to do what no other had done before with a 70mm release print: cut first generation copies of the camera's 65mm visual effects negative directly into the 70mm printing negative.

Hummel called Donah Bassett, who he affectionately called Mother Cutter. Highly regarded within the Hollywood community, Bassett had, by 1980, an unmatched filmography spanning over 200 films, and a list of directors who trusted her with their gold: the film's negative.[3] "She said, 'Sure, no problem at all.' And so we did it." Hummel and Bassett set to work at Technicolor creating *Blade Runner*'s hand-made 65mm interpositive for the 70mm prints.

After all was done, the 65mm printing negative for *Blade Runner* was a couple generations away from the principal photography original negative. Its visual effects were first generation. That being the case, anyone who saw a 70mm print of *Blade Runner* when it first opened got to see its visual effects in a manner better than any subsequent presentation of any version of *Blade Runner* to date.

On the whole, 70mm film prints are treated entirely differently. Back then, a 70mm print cost around $10,000 to $12,000. This is because, to make the print, the lab must make a 70mm printing negative. There is an extensive process of checking and rechecking the quality of the print.

"It's a very hand-manufacturing process," said Hummel. "There's quality control up the ying-yang." The process is, "You make the 65mm printing negative and check it to make sure it's okay. Then, you send it out to get striked, mag-striked." It's screened again after 24 hours "to check for damage. Then you record the audio onto the tracks and screen it again to make sure it's okay and there aren't any dropouts."

Sound and 70mm is a whole subject unto itself. In fact, in the late 1970s and through the 1980s, when 70mm projection enjoyed a boost in popularity, sound quality was the primary reason distributors loved it. The format offered 6-channel magnetic track sound, as opposed to optical sound, where noise, pops, and clicks were evident. This was the great advantage to 70mm prints, but it didn't last forever. Digital sound, particularly Dolby SR (sound reduction) was introduced to 35mm prints. It improved the sound, filtering noise, and

---

[3] She cut the negative on Kubrick's *2001: A Space Odyssey* and Warren Beatty flew her to London to cut the negative on *Reds*.

eliminating pops and clicks. However, it still couldn't match the fidelity offered by 70mm.

70mm printing also required its own audio mix. For *Blade Runner* purists, this means that the sound for the prints is, in certain ways, different from the 35mm prints. "They always did a different mix of the film because 70mm has discrete channels," Hummel explained. "You have five channels up front, and one version with the single surround channel behind you. Sometimes they have three channels up front: left, center, right, and then three channels in the back: center, left, and right. So it surrounds and goes behind the audience. So, if they were doing it correctly they would often do a separate pass on the mix for the 70mm version."

Fans would be interested to know that there are differences in the audio, but this doesn't mean there's a difference in dialogue. The difference is likely a matter of where the dialogue and sound effects emanate from the screen. Hummel explained: "In 70mm, typically dialogue is always coming out of the center channel, but sometimes the mixers would start to get fancy. It would be only for the 70mm release that they would have the dialogue, if the characters were on the right side of the screen, over in the right channel. It was very distinctive that they had the dialogue mixed in multiple channels."

Individual film prints, of course, aren't signed off on with regard to quality. In the early 1980s, Technicolor's lab manufactured release prints via high speed printers at 3,000 feet per minute. It was also routine that print runs for theaters wouldn't be completed until less than a week before the film's release date. Quality control for each new 35mm print wasn't humanly impossible.

The answer print, or the printing negative, is signed off on by the director and the cinematographer. This was the case for *Blade Runner*'s 70mm printing negative and subsequent restorations. "They called Ridley and got his thumbs up for the restoration in 2006," said Hummel.

Were the 70mm prints perfect? Almost, but not quite. According to Douglas Trumbull, in spite of the visual quality 70mm offers, there was a flaw in *Blade Runner*'s blow-up process. He explained the flaw to me personally the last time we spoke:

> What happened on *Blade Runner* was a big tragedy, because right towards the end of the completion of the movie, Ridley Scott was fired by the studio, and the movie was taken over by the studio and the other producers. And they made a really bad job of reducing our 65mm to the anamorphic 35mm negative to put into the final negative cut, whereas we had already spent $100,000 building this super-lens to do the very same

thing with much higher quality. But the entire project was taken away from us and given to a lab [Technicolor] to do the conversions. And so they did it, and what happened was there was a white line at the top and bottom of every effects shot in the release prints. Someone stupid at the lab didn't catch that when they made the blow-up, and so, if the gate on the projector was a little bit too open you would see a line at the top and bottom of the shot. And I don't know if subsequently they've ever gone back and done them properly, or replaced them. I do know that in the Director's Cut we gave them the 65mm originals and they re-scanned those at Fotokem, 8K scans of the original effects shots and then cut those into the digital intermediate. That resulted in a really big leap in quality.

How Many 70mm Prints Were There?

There is some discrepancy as to how many 70mm prints of *Blade Runner* were created. *Weekly Variety*, in an article dated 28 July 1982, noted there were 10 prints. Michael Coate at TheDigitalBits.com, in an article entitled "Return to 2019: Remembering *Blade Runner*" on its 35th Anniversary, published on 26 June 2017, noted that there were 11 prints.

Hummel recalls differently: "I remember they said they were going to make 12. But by the time the prints were made I'd left EEG and because of Natalie Wood's accident on *Brainstorm* the place shut down, but that's a whole other story. It was only going to be a dozen prints. I'm not surprised that [reports are] there were only 10."

Today, the original 70mm prints would look pretty in pink. Fans would certainly love to see one, but the unfortunate truth is, if any still exist, they would be quite pink, or even a deep, dark magenta red. In 1982, Kodak had yet to change the chemical process of film prints which would allow them to better retain their color. It would be a couple years before the company was able to add stable dyes to their film.

Also, release prints weren't meant to be archival. They were meant to be disposable. A film's negative was, or is, the archival element. Duplicate negatives were sometimes made for archiving. However, around 1980, Martin Scorsese, who had by that time accumulated a large library of film prints, saw that his prints were fading. They were never designed *not* to fade. They were meant to be shipped to a theater, run through projectors, and eventually trashed after being thrashed. There weren't different film stocks. There wasn't one for the theater and one for the studio archive. It was all the same print stock. That being the case, even studio copies of prints would fade. The negatives, however, would be fine.

Kodak eventually produced a print stock called LP – a variant on their release print stock that was intended for long-term film preservation. It was a little more expensive, perhaps a half cent a foot more expensive, but the dyes were stable. And for a short period you could order a different, more stable type of print stock. Then Kodak soon incorporated it into all print stocks. All of this happened around 1983 to 1984, with *Blade Runner* having just missed the print stock revolution.

As for the actual existence of these 70mm prints, Trumbull said, "I have no idea," and added the reminder that "prints don't age well." Hummel posited, "The movie had so many versions. Somebody might've cut them up to try to reformat them into a different version. There's a good chance that there might be a few in existence."

The Hades Landscape – an Example of Why *Blade Runner*'s Visual Effects Should Be Seen in 70mm

One particular special effects shot exemplifies why *Blade Runner*'s filmmakers wanted the film's effects to be seen in all their high-definition glory. They wanted to show the audience what they were really seeing and what they accomplished. It's a shot the filmmakers dubbed "The Hades Landscape" from the opening sequence. There is a depth, beauty, and clarity to it that truly amazes.

The Hades Landscape isn't an optical composite. It's one piece of film rewound and run through the camera again and again. For the effect, the camera glides over a 2019 industrial Los Angeles; a dystopian vision of vast glittering industrial structures overshadowing urban blight. One pass for the landscape, one pass for the towers, one pass for the lights, and one pass for the incredible skyrocketing flames. There's no CGI or animation. They were actual flames. The filmmakers interspersed tiny cards amid the Hades models and projected the flames onto the cards. It was a double exposure. They added passes for the ambient light, the smoke, and the Tyrell Pyramids, which were giant photographs illuminated from behind.

The addition of the flames in the Hades landscape was in fact the result of good fortune. After Stanley Kubrick's *2001: A Space Odyssey*, Trumbull was hired by director Michelangelo Antonioni to film some visual effects for *Zabriskie Point*. The ending of the film featured an apocalyptic carpet bombing of Los Angles, and Antonioni had never done any visual effects before.

"I was just fresh off of *2001* so I was really ready to do something wild," Trumbull said. "So we went out to the California desert. There's a place out in California you can book legally and make any explosion you want. And we did."

Trumbull, wanting "the biggest explosion short of a thermonuclear bomb," hired a crew of "pyrotechnic maniacs" from MGM. He recalled, "The team brought in 30-foot wide steel cauldrons and filled them with dynamite, methylene, gasoline, and phosphor. They shot a number of earth-shaking explosions with towering flames."

Upon showing the footage to Antonioni, however, Trumbull said, "He didn't get it. He didn't understand what we were doing and I got fired off the job." Nevertheless, Trumbull saved the *Zabriskie Point* footage.

Ten years later, when Ridley Scott described *Blade Runner*'s opening scene to Trumbull as an "apocalyptic landscape" with "flames cracking like all of Los Angeles was turned into a chemical cracking plant," he remembered saving the explosion footage he shot for Antonioni. Trumbull recalled asking Scott if he wanted to use the explosions. Scott said yes, and got all those fiery shots for free.

The Future of Movies (is Higher Frame Rates)

Although Quentin Tarantino, Paul Thomas Anderson, and Christopher Nolan pulled 70mm photography and projection from the past into the present, rare is the movie theater that still projects the format. It is now mainly the domain of independent theaters, such as the Loft Cinema in Tuscan, the Somerville Theater in Massachusetts, the Music Box in Chicago, or the Seattle Cinerama. 70mm is no longer mainstream, and the main reason, of course, is cost.

Trumbull never lost his considerable concern for the future of high-resolution cinema. He absolutely believes theaters can offer a presentation that equals, if not surpasses, the Cinerama and 70mm spectacles of *How the West Was Won*, *It's a Mad Mad Mad Mad World*, and *2001: A Space Odyssey*. "I've been experimenting with higher frame rates for over 35 years and not getting much traction," he said. "Higher frame rates in the world of film meant more film, more raw stock, more processing, more print size. Everything got worse. The industry did not embrace anything that would profoundly increase costs."

When theatrical exhibition switched to digital photography and projection, with the cost of data having phenomenally decreased, Trumbull decided it was time to again devote his efforts to film production, and to solving the modern movie theater's most pressing problem: presentation.

In 2014, Trumbull produced, wrote, and directed a short demonstration film *UFOTOG*. Its story of a UFO hunter who's pursued by a secret government agency is used as a narrative thread to showcase interiors, exteriors, close-ups, sound effects, and special effects. "It's extremely vivid. It's ultra-high frame rate, 120 frames per-second, 4K 3D with high brightness," he described.

While bringing *UFOTOG* to Los Angeles to show the film to studios, Trumbull found it was impossible to actually screen the film the way it was meant to be seen. Screening rooms were unacceptable. "There's no place to show it. The theaters were all narrow, with a little rectangular screen at the end of the room, like a shoebox. I said, 'Well, the magic isn't happening.'" That was when he realized that when it came to the most superior presentation of a film, "It's actually the theaters themselves that are the limiting factor. It's the design and the shape of the theater that's wrong."

Trumbull believes movie theaters have "been largely left behind," as they continue using antiquated projection in less than optimal venues. "The standard of movies of 24 frames per second was established for *The Jazz Singer* in 1927 and it hasn't changed since; hardly at all."

In 2017, at his studio in New Marlborough, Massachusetts, Trumbull built the first of what he hopes will be many more supremely optimal movie theaters. He calls it the MagiPod – a modular theater with a 60-foot-high curved (top and bottom) widescreen, seat vibration, and a powerful multi-directional sound system. He describes:

> With curving the rows of seats so they face the center of the screen, it becomes more comfortable to view. The more deeply you curve the screen, like we did with Cinerama many, many years ago, it tends to become immersive; which is what led to some of the factors that informed the design of this MagiPod and trying to get this kind of immersive experience in a theater. [...] One of the inadvertent discoveries of this is to find out that we can have what I would call a Giant Screen Experience in a Small Theater. You get the feeling that you're in the movie in some way. It's not just that you're looking at a rectangular screen or a television set or something. It's more participatory. And it's something I've been after all my life.

Trumbull also believes watching movies via streaming, downloading, and on demand has put "the art form of presenting movies in theaters" under threat. "You can have any movie you want, any time you want, anywhere you want, on your smart phone, or your tablet, or your computer, or your laptop, or your TV.

It's totally changing the dynamic of how people experience media. My feeling is if people are going to go out of the house to have some movie experience, it had better be better than it presently is."

Doug Trumbull and Steven Slaughter Head in front of Trumbull's MagiPod cinema.

With perhaps the exception of *2001: A Space Odyssey*, Trumbull is rarely completely satisfied with the images he's filmed.[4] He always believes he can create a better shot. He's a problem solver. He can figure it out, somehow. That said, with the sequels, restorations, and re-releases of his films, he's bewildered that the studios don't generally consult with him.

"It's interesting that they would make a sequel to *Blade Runner* and not give me a call," Trumbull said. "They're releasing a 4K re-release of *Close Encounters* and they didn't give me a call. They made a restoration of *Blade Runner*, the director's cut, a few years ago and they didn't give me a call except to find out what I thought about it. I said, 'Well, I just happened to have all of the 65mm original shots.' They said, 'Oh! Well, could we use them?' They forgot they had them. And the same thing is happening with *Close Encounters* right

---

[4] His favorite visual effects shot in *Blade Runner* is that of the off-world advertising blimp gliding over the roof of the Bradbury Building.

now. We did all the visual effects in 65mm. And so, generally, there's a loss of institutional memory."

Having been asked to comment on *Blade Runner 2049*, Trumbull believes it wouldn't be fair of him to do so. "*Blade Runner* is a very hard movie to follow. I mean, it's a very hard movie to better. I'm really proud of *Blade Runner*. I'm really proud of all the movies I've worked on."

Trumbull does admit he isn't against the idea of sequels and remakes, however: "I see directors and producers and actors coming at it from a different angle and saying, 'We're gonna do our take on it' and 'We're gonna re-boot it' or do whatever. And I say, 'Fine, do it. Take your best shot.'"

Mirrors for the Human Condition

by Timothy Shanahan

Blade Runner is justifiably celebrated as a seminal cinematic achievement due to its remarkable visual density, haunting soundtrack, and novel melding of *film noir*, science fiction, and cyberpunk genres and motifs. It is also a deeply thought-provoking film. How did Los Angeles circa 2019 descend into such a sorry state of urban decay? What's up with those amazing artificial animals? Why does Roy Batty save Deckard in that famous rooftop scene? What will become of Deckard and Rachael as fugitives from the law? Is Deckard himself really a replicant, as many viewers believe? As Roy Batty says to Chew at one point, "Yes, questions…"

All of these questions and many more besides are eminently worth pondering.[1] Still, there is one question that nearly all commentators agree is central to the film, namely, "What does it mean to be human?" It is on the answer to this classic *philosophical* question that the fate of the replicants, and the humanity of the human beings who attempt to control them, ultimately depends. Part of what makes the film's treatment of this question so intriguing is that it hints at an answer but refuses to definitively settle it. Nonetheless, there are sundry clues throughout the film suggesting that understanding the

---

[1] Shanahan, T. (2014), *Philosophy and Blade Runner* (Houndmills: Palgrave Macmillan).

nature and seemingly special plight of the *replicants* illuminates the nature of *being human*. Indeed, one might say that ultimately the replicants in *Blade Runner* serve as *mirrors for the human condition*. As viewers thoughtfully gazing into these mirrors, we can perhaps accomplish part of what philosophy has always set out to do, namely, to provide an insightful perspective on *our* nature, thereby helping us to live more wisely. With that lofty ambition before us, let's get started.

"It's Artificial?"

The scene is the cavernous office of Dr. Eldon Tyrell, the brilliant, eponymous CEO of the Tyrell Corporation and the replicants' creator. Rick Deckard had just administered the Voight-Kampff test to Rachael – ostensibly Tyrell's niece. After Rachael is brusquely dismissed by Tyrell, the two men talk. Tyrell confirms that Rachael is a replicant that does not *know* that it is a replicant. Deckard is stunned: "How can it not know what it is?!" As Tyrell proceeds to explain, his company has created a new experimental model that is even more humanlike than previous models. Not only is Rachael, like previous models, physically almost indistinguishable from a human, but she also has memory implants that lead her to *believe* that she is human. As Tyrell explains, "Commerce is our goal here at Tyrell. 'More Human than Human' is our motto." Tyrell's boast notwithstanding, Deckard now knows that Rachael is merely a replicant, not a human being. Of course, at that point *she* still believes herself to be human; but as she later learns, that belief is deeply, heartbreakingly, mistaken.

Or is it? The answer depends on the conditions that must be satisfied for any being to qualify as genuinely "human" and on whether Rachael satisfies those conditions. Neither issue is simple. Even within the film there are contrary views. At the beginning of the film, at least, Deckard considers the replicants to be *less than human*. He brushes off Rachael's question about whether he feels that the Tyrell Corporation's work is a benefit to the public by retorting: "Replicants are like any other machine. They're either a benefit or a hazard. If they're a benefit, it's not my problem." By contrast, Eldon Tyrell boasts that his replicants are *"more* human than human." Certainly the replicants themselves *aspire* to be acknowledged as something greater than mere commodities. When J.F. Sebastian implores his strange new houseguests to "Show me something," Roy Batty indignantly retorts, "We're not computers, Sebastian!"

Dr. Eldon Tyrell.

So what, exactly, *are* the replicants? Are they human? Less than human? "More human than human?" To answer these questions, we can begin by revisiting Tyrell's dimly-lit office, the scene of Deckard and Rachael's first encounter. Deckard is startled by an owl fluttering past his head and gracefully alighting on the other side of the room. He is clearly impressed and keenly interested, prompting Rachael to ask him whether he likes their owl. Deckard's response indicates that his answer to *that* question turns on the answer to another one: "It's artificial?" Once Rachael confirms that it is, Deckard immediately loses interest. Apparently, for Deckard only a *real* owl would be a suitable object of interest. Virtually the same scene is repeated later in Zhora's dressing room when he asks whether her snake is real. Again, once he learns that it is artificial, he loses all interest. Deckard, of course, does not pause in either scene to explain how he makes the real/artificial distinction, or why it matters so much to him. He has more pressing concerns, namely, to find out whether the Voight-Kampff test works on Nexus-6 replicants, in the former scene, and whether Zhora is one of the dangerous rogue replicants, in the latter one. Fortunately, centuries before Rick Deckard began retiring rogue replicants, the brilliant mathematician and natural philosopher René Descartes (1596–1650) *did* have the leisure to explore that distinction, and thereupon drew some remarkable conclusions that are still worth considering as we ponder the replicants' human, less-than-human, or more-than-human status.

According to Descartes, human beings are unique among all living things because they alone *think*. He conceded that animals may convey the *appearance* of thinking, but maintained that they are simply unthinking automata that respond to events in a purely mechanical fashion just as if they were composed of ropes, pulleys, levers, tubes, fluids, and so on – standard components of the rudimentary mechanical creatures in his day. In his view there is no thinking connected with real animals' behavior, nor even any physical sensations for that matter, because these are ultimately mental phenomena as well. Thus, he concluded that, "if there were such machines having the organs and the shape of a monkey or of some other animal that lacked reason, we would have no way of recognizing that they were not entirely of the same nature as these [real] animals."[2]

---

[2] Descartes, R. (1998), *Discourse on Method, and Meditations on First Philosophy*, 4th edition (Indianapolis, IN: Hackett).

This is, of course, just what we see in *Blade Runner*. By 2019 the art and science of manufacturing animoids (artificial animals) has reached such an advanced stage that it can be exceedingly difficult to tell the difference between real and artificial animals. Descartes would say that this is because there *is* no essential difference, and that the artificial/real distinction as applied to animoids/animals is, metaphysically at least, insignificant. Artificial animals may be made by us, exercising our intelligence, whereas real animals are made by God, exercising his, but that merely concerns *who* made them, not their essential nature as *machines*. In his view, the distinction commonly drawn between *living animals*, on the one hand, and *mere machines*, on the other, disappears: real animals no less than artificial ones just *are* machines, albeit the former are of much greater complexity and beyond the abilities of humans to make.

Human beings, on the other hand, are metaphysically in a class of their own that sets them apart from animals. He was well aware of the ingenious mechanical animals some of the artisans of his day had already constructed, and even imagined someone someday creating mechanical "humans" that exactly resembled human beings in outward appearance. But he concluded that even if God himself were to produce "the body of a man exactly like one of ours," and composed of the very same materials that constitute a human body, yet "without putting into it, at the start, any rational mind," it would still fail to be human. No matter how physically indistinguishable from a human being such a creature might be, it would necessarily fail to be human because it would lack an essential element that *we* have but that mere machines necessarily lack, namely, a *soul* or *mind* endowed with *consciousness*.

Descartes thought that there were two diagnostic features that would permit us to reliably distinguish artificial humans (without minds) from real human beings (with minds).[3] The first tell-tale difference would be that artificial humans "could never use words or other signs, or put them together as we do in order to declare our thoughts to others." Even if an artificial human could produce sounds that made sense in relation to its bodily actions – for example, crying out *as if* in pain when its body is damaged, or responding to questions *as if* it understood the questions posed to it – it would soon be exposed as a mere simulacrum of a human being because it could never "arrange its words differently so as to respond to the sense of all that will be said in its presence,

---

[3] Ibid.

as even the dullest men can do." Its patent inability to demonstrate the linguistic flexibility that humans effortlessly enjoy would reveal its true nature.

The second telltale sign that would expose such artificial humans as less-than-human is that, "although they might perform many tasks very well or perhaps better than any of us, one would discover that they were acting not through knowledge but only through the disposition of their organs."[4] The image of the mechanical clock, which loomed so large in the imaginations of 17th century natural philosophers, is put to use here. Animals might perform some tasks better than us, yet without any *understanding* of what they do, "just as we see that a clock composed exclusively of wheels and springs can count the hours and measure time more accurately than we can with all our carefulness." Ironically, however, "the fact that they do something *better* than we do does not prove that they have any intelligence... rather it proves that they have no intelligence at all."[5] The same conclusion would follow for any artificial humans.

It surely will not have gone unnoticed that the replicants appear to satisfy Descartes' two criteria for being *genuinely human* with flying colors. Not only is Roy Batty as linguistically gifted as any human being in the film, but he is even given to reciting poetry, as his exuberantly playful self-introduction to Chew demonstrates. The replicants also exhibit great behavioral flexibility in adjusting to novel situations and problems. Leon infiltrates the Tyrell Corporation as an employee in order to gain access to Tyrell – presumably not an easy task. Eventually he along with other low-level Tyrell Corporation employees is subjected to a Voight-Kampff test. So long as his interrogation is going well, he plays along. But when it becomes clear that he is about to be exposed as a replicant, he shoots Holden and escapes unscathed. Likewise, Zhora patiently bides her time before attempting to kill Deckard and fleeing. Pris employs a clever ruse to successfully manipulate Sebastian. When his first two attempts to gain access to Tyrell fail, Roy discovers an ingenious way to finally succeed in his quest; and so on.

Given the fact that the replicants appear to easily satisfy his two diagnostic criteria for having minds, and thus for being human, Descartes faces a stark dilemma. Either he has to conclude that the replicants are *artificial humans with minds* – a conclusion that would implode his distinction between artificial

---

[4] Ibid.
[5] Ibid.

and real humans – or he has to *deny* that the replicants are *conscious, thinking beings* – which seems desperate given how easily they pass his two tests. We have about as much reason to doubt that the replicants are conscious, sapient beings as we do to doubt that other specimens of *Homo sapiens* are – which is to say, no reason at all. In short, there seems to be no good reason to deny that the replicants think and feel much as we do. But if so, Descartes is wrong to assume that artificially created beings would necessarily lack minds. By itself, however, this would only show that the replicants satisfy *Descartes'* specific criteria for being human. It would not settle the issue of whether they *are* human. In order to make *that* judgment with confidence we need to consider additional facts about them.

"You Nexus, Huh?"

From the film's opening crawl we learn that, "Early in the 21st Century, THE TYRELL CORPORATION advanced Robot evolution into the NEXUS phase – a being virtually identical to a human – known as a replicant." We also learn that replicants are superior in strength and agility, and at least equal in intelligence, to the genetic engineers who created them. We can probably assume that although these genetic engineers have at best average human strength and agility, they are nonetheless more intelligent than most other people. This would make the four rogue replicants superior in one respect or another to most people. Indeed, all of them appear to be phenomenally strong and/or agile, and even the relatively modest mental capabilities of Leon are at least equal to those of an average human being, making them extremely dangerous and formidable adversaries even for an exceptionally skilled ex-blade runner like Rick Deckard.

During Deckard's briefing by Capt. Bryant we are given more detailed information about the functions and capabilities of the four replicants that Deckard is (initially) tasked with retiring:

Replicant (M) Des: LEON
NEXUS 6 N6MAC41717
Incept Date: 10 APRIL, 2017
Func: Combat/Loader (Nuc. Fiss.)

Phys: LEV. A Mental: LEV. C

Replicant (F) Des: ZHORA
NEXUS 6 N6FAB61216
Incept Date: 12 JUNE, 2016
Func: Retrained (9 FEB., 2018) Polit. Homicide

Phys: LEV. A Mental: LEV. B

Replicant (M) Des: BATTY (Roy)
NEXUS 6 N6MAA10816

Replicant (F) Des: PRIS
NEXUS 6 N6FAB21416

Incept Date: 8 JAN., 2016   Incept Date: 14 FEB., 2016
Func: Combat, Colonization Defense Prog   Func: Military/Leisure
Phys: LEV. A Mental: LEV. A   Phys: LEV. A Mental: LEV. B

The individual identification code on the second line of each description is a compressed summary of the key properties of each replicant. "N6FAB61216" indicates that Zhora is a Nexus-6 Female, with A-level physical capabilities, B-level mental capabilities, and an incept date of 6/12/16. Leon is a Nexus-6 Male, with A-level physical capabilities, C-level mental capabilities, and an incept date of 4/17/17. (Oddly, a different incept date is provided on the next line; it is this latter date that Leon hurls at Deckard in the alley, calling it his "birthday.") Fittingly for a "leisure" model, Pris's incept date is Valentine's Day. We learn that Roy Batty, the oldest of the replicants, is a couple of months shy of four years old – a fact that soon becomes very important.

The Workprint version of the film includes a somewhat different definition of "replicant" that provides additional information worth considering:

> **REPLICANT**\rep'-li-cant\n. See also ROBOT (*antique*):
>
> ANDROID (*obsolete*): NEXUS (*generic*): Synthetic human with paraphysical capabilities, having skin/flesh culture.
>
> Also: Rep, skin job (*slang*): Off-world uses: Combat, high risk industrial, deep-space probe. On-world use prohibited.
>
> Specifications and quantities – information classified.
>
> NEW AMERICAN DICTIONARY.

This is the only time in any version of the film that the word 'android' appears, and it does so only to inform us that this term has become obsolete. This semantic decision reflects Ridley Scott's belief that the term had acquired too many clichéd associations to be suitable for his film. The new word 'replicant,' by contrast, naturally prompts the viewer to reflect on how closely the synthetic humans in the film replicate the qualities of human beings. We are also informed that the replicants have "paraphysical capabilities." Because they have been designed to perform specific tasks Off-world (combat, nuclear loading, political homicide, recreational sex, and so on) they have enhanced physical capabilities for these tasks. We are told little about how the replicants were created. According to Scott, this was deliberate in order to bring other issues to the foreground.[6] As suggested by the scenes in the Eye Works

---

[6] Kennedy, H. (1982), "Twenty-First Century Nervous Breakdown," in L. F. Knapp and A. F. Kulas (eds.), *Ridley Scott: Interviews* (Jackson, MS: University Press of Mississippi, 2005), pp. 32–41.

laboratory, however, we can surmise that they are assembled with the production of specific organs farmed out to subcontractors like Chew, rather than being grown sequentially through a process of embryonic development, as clones would be. Accordingly, they may each begin to exist as one-of-a-kind, adult organisms. They have no childhoods and, of course, no parents – a point of some sensitivity whose implicit acknowledgment in one of the film's early scenes becomes the "trigger" for Leon to blast Blade Runner Dave Holden through a wall and into the next room.

Interestingly and, initially at least, somewhat incongruously, both versions of the opening crawl – the one in the Workprint as well as the one that appears in all subsequent versions – identify the replicants as "robots." In his essay, "Crashing the Gates of Insight," Jack Boozer judges this epithet to be misleading because the replicants are "biogenetic creations" rather than "an electro-mechanical machine made of inorganic materials, controlled by [a] computer and electronic programming ... that performs routine tasks automatically without consciousness or autonomy."[7] The description of the replicants as "robots" might also strike one as incongruous inasmuch as the replicants seem so "un-robotic" in their *behavior*. Think of the impressive athleticism displayed by Pris when she is playfully showing off for Sebastian, and later when she is violently applying her gymnastic skills on Deckard. Likewise, Roy Batty and Zhora seem anything but "robotic" in their respective demeanors and behaviors. So, *are* they robots?

The answer, I think, is "it depends." Robots are conventionally thought of as having a suite of physical and behavioral characteristics including materiality, rigidity, predictability, subservience, compliance, and so on. Of course, a standard plot device in much science fiction involves subverting these conventional associations by making robots look and behave just like human beings and by making them act in ways that their creators don't anticipate (even if readers and viewers can predict from a mile away that the supposedly "obedient" robots will at some point go berserk and rebel against their inexplicably shocked creators). Even to list some of the characteristics conventionally associated with robots, as above, is to invite counter-examples.

---

[7] Boozer, J. Jr. (1997), "Crashing the Gates of Insight," in J. B. Kerman (ed.), *Retrofitting Blade Runner: Issues in Ridley Scott's Blade Runner and Philip K. Dick's Do Androids Dream of Electric Sheep?*, 2nd edition (Bowling Green, Ohio: Bowling Green University Press), pp. 212–28.

But that is the point. Science fiction that has robots appearing and behaving just like humans succeeds (to the extent that it does) because it can confidently *presuppose* such conventional associations – before subverting them.

Indeed, this venerable narrative strategy descends from the very first "robots." The English *word* 'robot' comes from the Czech word *robota*, meaning "servitude," "drudgery," or "forced labor." 'Robota,' in turn, is derived from the Slavic root *rab*, meaning "slave."[8] Robots are thus slaves. They first appear as such in Karel Čapek's play, *R.U.R.: Rossum's Universal Robots* (1921). In the play, robot servants that are virtually indistinguishable from humans revolt against their human masters. Key issues in the play are whether the robots are being exploited and the moral consequences of their forced servitude – the very same issues that reappear 61 years later in *Blade Runner*. By explicitly identifying the replicants as *robots* at the very *beginning* of the film, *Blade Runner* draws upon stereotypical associations to first establish and then progressively destabilize the viewer's understanding of their nature and moral status.

Boozer is thus correct that the replicants are not "robots" in the conventional sense in which he defines that term, but they *are* robots in the original sense of that term. Are they (or could they be) *human* as well? In the Workprint they are described as "synthetic humans," which suggests that they are a *kind* of human whose distinguishing feature is that they are made in a way other than through the normal biological processes associated with human reproduction. The alternative adjective "artificial" is never applied to the replicants, although it *is* used, as noted above, in the sense of being *fake*, to distinguish Tyrell's owl and Zhora's snake from their real counterparts. As synthetic humans, the replicants are thus not quite "fake humans." Whether they are *genuinely human*, however, and what that might *mean*, requires additional examination.

"You're So Different"

The fact that the replicants differ in significant respects from the humans in the film provides some *prima facie* reasons for concluding that the replicants are something other than genuinely human. The scene in Sebastian's apartment when he suspects that his guests are Nexus-6 replicants highlights some of these differences. His new friends seem so superior to the typical human beings

---

[8] Zunt, D. (2006), "Who Did Actually Invent the Word 'Robot' and What Does it Mean?" http://capek.misto.cz/english/robot.html

that remain on earth that he is led to exclaim, "You're so different. You're so perfect." Not one to humbly demur, Roy simply answers, "Yes." Yet despite their physical superiority in other respects, the replicants have been created as adults with a maximum four-year life span, resulting in a mismatch between their levels of physical and emotional maturity. Leon, the most physically powerful of the replicants, pouts over his confiscated photographs. Roy Batty, the oldest of the replicants, seems emotionally immature compared to adult humans, as when he gushes to Sebastian like a nine-year old boy visiting a friend's playroom for the first time: "Gosh. You've really got some nice toys here." When Pris is shot by Deckard, she looks like an adolescent girl throwing an *epic* temper tantrum. Despite being an advanced model "gifted" with memories from Tyrell's niece, even Rachael's emotional reactions to dramatic events tend to stay within fairly narrow limits.

Roy Batty shares a playful moment with Sebastian and Pris.

It's not only to the human beings in the film and to us as viewers that the replicants appear to be different. The replicants themselves sometimes acknowledge and even draw attention to their otherness. While attempting to manipulate Sebastian, Pris remarks, "I don't think there's another *human being* in the whole world who would have helped us" (emphasis added). In response to Roy's question to Leon about whether the latter was able to retrieve his "precious photos" from his room, Leon says flatly, "Someone was there." Roy then presses him farther: "*Men*? Police-*men*?" – both times stressing "men" with perhaps a tinge of contempt for his human adversaries. The replicants' recognition of their status as *other* is emphasized even more noticeably as Roy begins to relate to Deckard what it means to him that his life is about to end:

"I've seen things you *people* wouldn't believe" (emphasis in original). Given his design as an Off-world combat model, Roy has experienced amazing things that "people" – a category still co-extensive with human beings for Deckard – could never experience.

"We Have a Lot in Common"

There are, then, reasons to view the replicants as, if not less-than-human, then at least as other-than-human. But the film *also* encourages us to reach the opposite conclusion, namely, that the replicants are fully human or even "more human than human." It does this by endowing them with many characteristic features of humans, and by depicting human beings as sorely lacking characteristics often considered to be uniquely human, thereby blurring the supposed distinction.

As Roy Batty remarks to J.F. Sebastian, "We have a lot in common." Although he is referring specifically to their shared problem of accelerated decrepitude, it is equally true in a more inclusive sense. Most obviously, the replicants resemble human beings so closely in their physical appearance that an elaborate psycho-physiological test is required to distinguish them from human beings. It is true that the replicants are "superior in strength and agility" to most human beings – an attribution that is amply confirmed when we see Pris' hyper-athletic agility, Roy's almost effortless ability to overcome physical obstacles by thrusting his hand and head through solid walls, and Leon's seeming invulnerability to extreme cold when he retrieves an eye from a vat of liquid nitrogen with his bare hand. Such impressive abilities highlight the physical differences between the replicants and human beings; but it is possible to exaggerate their importance. The replicants' unusual physical capabilities fall just beyond the range of normal human capacities. Although Ridley Scott once described the replicants as "supermen who couldn't fly,"[9] none of the replicants is faster than a speeding bullet, more powerful than a locomotive, or able to leap over (and not between the rooftops of) tall buildings in a single bound. They are not invulnerable to bullets, blessed with x-ray vision, or able to reverse the direction of time. Despite their impressive physical capabilities they are more like *us* than like the Man of Steel (who, of course, is not a *man* at all).

---

[9] Sammon, P. M. (1996), *Future Noir: The Making of* Blade Runner (New York: HarperCollins).

Much the same could be said for the replicants' *psychological* characteristics. A high level of intelligence is routinely thought to be *the* distinctive human characteristic – that which sets us apart from and above all other living things. Yet the replicants' own high level of intelligence is demonstrated repeatedly. Pris skillfully contrives a false identity and carries out her ruse well enough to persuade Sebastian to invite her in. Zhora quickly sees through Deckard's (admittedly lame) attempt to pass himself off as a representative of the "American Federation of Variety Artists" concerned about her exploitation. Roy's impressive *tête à tête* with Tyrell over the molecular chemistry of life-extension reveals him to be on an intellectual par with his creator, someone whom Sebastian had previously declared to be "a genius." Although Tyrell has more *knowledge* than Roy, there is no evidence that he is more *intelligent* than Roy.

By contrast, the replicants are considered to be devoid of the supposedly distinctive human capacity for *empathy*. The Voight-Kampff test, we are told, works by detecting minute physiological changes elicited by the subject's emotional responses to a series of carefully designed questions involving human or animal suffering. The logic behind the test is that it takes years to develop an empathic capacity – longer (it is supposed) than the meager four years allotted to the replicants. Because humans are assumed to be naturally empathic, the Voight-Kampff test can be used as a diagnostic tool to distinguish replicants from humans – if, that is, one can be certain that all humans have at least some empathic response to others' suffering, and that all replicants necessarily lack one. As the film progresses, these assumptions are at first challenged and then finally refuted. Rachael comes very close to passing the test, thereby deeply unsettling Deckard. As he explains to Tyrell, it usually requires "20, 30 [questions], cross-referenced" to identify a subject as a replicant; but in Rachael's case it required more than 100 questions, suggesting that she may be approaching humans in her capacity for empathy. In a few more years she might do as well on the test as the average human, thereby making her, according the standard presupposed in the test, human.

Leon, Zhora, and Pris show no obvious or unequivocal signs of empathy, and thus would be unlikely to do as well on the test as Rachael. Indeed, Leon was on the verge of failing the test when he took matters into his own hands and shot Holden. There are hints that Roy *may* be developing empathy, although the evidence is ambiguous. On the one hand, he seems to lack any trace of empathy in his treatment of Chew, Sebastian, and Tyrell, each of whom he treats simply as a means to achieving his goal of "more life," murdering each when he is no longer of use to him. His treatment of Sebastian is especially cruel. Sebastian is at first enthralled by Roy and Pris, proudly seeing in them some of his genetic handwork. Although he is terrified of them, he is also sympathetic to their plight, recognizing that they, like him, suffer from accelerated decrepitude. Moreover, he is the one human being in the whole world (to echo Pris' observation) to befriend them, even introducing Roy to Tyrell as "a friend." He feels a bond with Pris and Roy and does what he can (granted, under some duress) to help them. Consequently, after witnessing Batty's brutal murder of Tyrell, Sebastian might have hoped that Roy would spare him, given the invaluable assistance he has provided. But Batty kills Sebastian as well, even though he has nothing to gain by doing so. The fact that Batty speaks to Sebastian as one might to a dog ("Stay," "Come") further underscores his chilling lack of empathy for someone with whom he has, by his own admission, "a lot in common." On the other hand, Roy's behavior towards the other replicants suggests that he may not be *entirely* lacking in empathy. He seems to express almost brotherly care for Leon when he inquires, "Did you get your precious photos?" Likewise, he shows tender concern for Pris, telling Sebastian, "If we don't find help soon, Pris hasn't got long to live. We can't allow that." It is also true, of course, that Roy himself hasn't got long to live; so it is significant that his concern here is, ostensibly at least, for Pris' well-being.

"Did You Ever Take That Test Yourself?"

Just as the film narrows the presumed gap between humans and replicants from one direction by depicting replicants as possessing a suite of human characteristics, it also narrows the gap from the opposite direction by depicting humans as *lacking* some supposedly distinctive human characteristics. Some humans appear even more rigid, immature, and emotionless than the replicants. Leon asks Holden, "Do you make up these questions, Mr. Holden, or do they write them down for you?" Holden, apparently oblivious to the sarcasm in Leon's question, responds as if it were a straightforward request for information: "In answer to your query, they're written down for me. It's a test, designed to provoke an emotional response." Despite his undeniable brilliance, Tyrell is still quite naïve, a fact that Roy skillfully exploits through Sebastian's chess game with him. For much of the film, Deckard comes across as cold (according to his own testimony, his ex-wife used to call him "sushi… cold fish"), predictable (Gaff knows just where and when to find him at the noodle bar), compliant (Bryant has little difficulty getting him to comply with his demands), narrowly logical (as evidenced by his methodical analysis of evidence in tracking down Zhora), emotionally dead (as Bryant laconically observes after he retires Zhora), and grimly serious (as he appears throughout most of the film.)

Leon is interviewed by Holden at the Tyrell Corporation.

Significantly, the humans in the film show little or no empathy toward one another. Bryant couldn't care less about Deckard's desire to remain "quit." He coerces him into reprising his role as a blade runner merely to serve his own interests. Gaff's only interest is kissing up to Bryant to get a promotion. Tyrell treats Sebastian as if he were a child. After assuring Rachael that he would not come after her because "I owe you one" – as if their developing relationship was nothing more than a business transaction – Rachael is led to ask him: "You know that Voight-Kampff test of yours? Did you ever take that test yourself?" The ironic implication is that Deckard himself lacks the very quality whose absence he must rely on to identify replicants. But if so, then the supposedly clear line between humans and replicants is questionable, and perhaps even fictitious.

What Does it Mean to Be Human?

We have been considering the specific question of whether the *replicants* are human, and by implication the broader question of what it might *mean* to be human. The film initially offers us two contrary perspectives. Cops like Dave Holden, Rick Deckard, and Harry Bryant have been taught to think of replicants as less than human – as mere machines or as "skin jobs," in fact. By contrast, Eldon Tyrell boasts that the newest replicants are "more human than human." As the film's story slowly unfolds, it progressively becomes clearer to viewers that the differences between replicants and humans, although real, are not as great one might initially have supposed, and perhaps ultimately that there are no truly significant differences. But if that is so, why do the human characters in the film refuse to see this? What basic assumptions about what it means to be human prevent them from seeing this?

Broadly speaking, there are three ways of thinking about what it means to be human. One way attempts to identify some objective characteristic or set of characteristics that uniquely distinguish human beings from all other living things. This is the approach taken by the police in *Blade Runner*. As they no doubt realized, not just any uniquely-possessed objective characteristic or set of characteristics would do. Humans might be the only living things to have exactly 23 pairs of chromosomes, but this aspect of our biology would fail to signify anything thought to be *essentially human*. If a species of lizard were discovered to have exactly 23 pairs of chromosomes, we would hardly welcome it into the human race, nor would we deduce from this empirical discovery that we are no longer human. We, no less than the cops in *Blade Runner*, realize that whatever it is that makes us distinctively human, it must be something that confers *significance* on us in a way that some random fact about us cannot.

Over the centuries various candidates for this special characteristic have been proposed, including reason, morality, language, tool use, belief in a God or gods, free will, possession of an immortal soul, and/or empathy. All have been defended, and challenged, in one way or another. Reason, morality, language, and tool use to some degree can be detected in some non-human primates.[10] Belief in a God or gods is hardly universal. Whether humans possess free will and immortal souls are matters of perennial debate. We have already seen how problematic *empathy* can be as a demarcation criterion. Why not then simply insist that "what it means to be human" is just to be a member of our biological species, *Homo sapiens*? Unfortunately, this stipulation invites further difficult questions about the conditions for species membership. Although there is no chance of mistaking an alligator for a human being, legitimate questions arise when one considers more ambiguous cases such as a fertilized human ovum that has just begun cell division, and the prospect of human clones. Are these beings fully human, quasi-human, or not-yet-human? Reasonable people disagree, and it is unclear how facts *alone* could decisively answer this question. We have plenty of *facts*; it is their *interpretation* that engenders impassioned

---

[10] de Waal, F. (2013), *The Bonobo and the Atheist: In Search of Humanism Among the Primates* (New York: W. W. Norton).

disagreement.

Perhaps, then, we should think of "what it means to be human" purely as a social construct. According to this view, the failure to agree upon an essentialist definition teaches us that objective facts are simply irrelevant. At various times and in various places, children, women, slaves, and barbarians were not considered (fully) human. But from an enlightened perspective, of course, they are. Hence, "what it means to be human" is simply a matter of historically-situated social convention. There is no deeper fact of the matter beyond the dominant belief system of any given society. Consequently, if in Los Angeles circa 2019 replicants are not considered to be human by the dominant social group, they aren't, and there is nothing more that can or should be said about it.

Despite the air of academic sophistication with which the foregoing view is sometimes advanced, it is worthy of deep skepticism. Is being human (or not) really just a matter of social consensus? Could it really be true that children, women, slaves, and foreigners are *not human* just because the majority of the people in a given society at a given time refuse to acknowledge them as such? Could a social consensus that muskrats *are*, but that women *are not*, "human" ever *make* it so? It is difficult not to conclude that the unadulterated constructivist approach is in danger of overreacting to the perceived failures of essentialist approaches to the question of what it means to be human to the point of spouting absurdities.

Recognition of the foregoing problems suggests a *via media* between purely essentialist and constructivist approaches. Facts are relevant for deciding what it means to be human, as the essentialist assumes, but so are social systems of meaning, as the constructivist insists. The key is to realize that facts don't speak for themselves; they always require interpretation within a larger framework of meaning that gives those facts significance. In deciding what it means to be human, therefore, we need to consider not just objective characteristics, but also the *importance* that should be attached to those characteristics. If we are concerned with the question of what it means to be human in the context of evolution, for example, we might well consider the presence of certain objective attributes (e.g., large cranial capacity, upright posture, evidence of tool or language use, etc.) as significant in a way that we might not for the presence of other less consequential physical or behavioral characteristics (e.g., eye color, straight or curly hair, right- or left-handedness, etc.). Similar remarks would pertain in other contexts in which the question of what it means to be human arises. Facts are not irrelevant to answering such questions, but they are not sufficient, either. Accordingly, "what it means to be human" crucially depends on the significance placed on certain facts. Insofar as the significance of those facts is decided by us, but *only* that far, *we* decide what it means to be human. The question of "what it means to be human" is thus irreducibly, but not exclusively, a *moral* question that reflects our deepest values.

Conclusions

Arguably, this is one of the main lessons of *Blade Runner*, a film that adroitly leads viewers to question the presumption that the replicants are less-than-human by persuading us that they may be indistinguishable from humans in the ways that matter most. Merely *having* many of the same characteristics that we identify humans as having, however, is not sufficient to guarantee that the replicants will be *acknowledged* as such by the humans in the film on whom their fate depends – a point that can be appreciated by reflecting on Deckard's slowly evolving perspective. From Capt. Bryant we learn that formerly Deckard was the preeminent blade runner for the LAPD. Part of Deckard's prowess no doubt derived from his unconflicted view of the replicants as mere machines to be "retired" should they malfunction. When we first meet Deckard there is no reason to think that his attitude toward them is any different. But over the course of the film we see his perspective undergo a dramatic transformation as he comes to view them as not so very different from himself. His growing romantic attraction to Rachael is undoubtedly a primary factor, but the final step is not taken until he witnesses Roy's moving soliloquy in his final moments and thereby perhaps for the first time is able to see the replicants as beset by the same existential concerns as himself. As he narrates in the Theatrical Release, "All he'd wanted were the same answers the rest of us want. Where did I come from? Where am I going? How long have I got?" By including Roy among "the rest of us," and referring to the replicant as *he* rather than *it*, Deckard finally acknowledges that in relation to the most important matters, there is no significant difference between the replicants and himself. Ironically, as Deckard comes to see the replicants as worthy of the same consideration due to other humans, he thereby becomes "humanized." The viewer is thus subtly reminded once again of Roy's simple yet profound observation to Sebastian: "We've got a lot in common." That important insight is Roy's parting gift to Deckard, and to us.

On Death and Dying in *Blade Runner*

by Ian Dawe

One apt description of *Blade Runner* is, "It's a beautiful film about death." Death is at the heart of what Rick Deckard does, and at the heart of what motivates the replicant protagonists in this film. But it isn't death as much as how we deal with death and loss that the film ultimately explores. Death and change are realities of life that can't be overcome, not for "non-living" replicants, nor even for replicants who try to cheat it, get around it, or push it back out of reach. Ultimately, it's replicant Roy Batty who comes the closest to really grappling with death, loss, change, and what it all means, ultimately achieving a graceful state of acceptance. But he and all the other characters, including Deckard, are moving through what psychology recognizes as the Five Stages of Grief, or the Kübler-Ross model. Even though modern psychology has moved beyond this rather simplistic model of how humans process loss, it provides a useful and interesting way to understand at least part of what makes *Blade Runner* the stunning artistic achievement it is.

Introduced in 1969 by Swiss psychiatrist Elisabeth Kübler-Ross in 1969, the stages of grief represent one common way in which humans react to losing someone or thing, and although Kübler-Ross developed this cognitive tool for those suffering from terminal cancer, the stages are variously deployed to assist in the cognition of many types of loss, such as loss of a job, or even loss of a favorite sports team or band.

The five stages, in order, are described as Denial, in which the individual simply refuses to admit that the loss has occurred; Anger, in which the person admits that the loss has occurred but reacts by lashing out; Bargaining, where the individual seeks to make a deal with the forces of fate and nature to mollify a portion of the loss; Depression, in which the individual internalizes the loss and surrenders to feelings of self-pity and woe; and finally Acceptance, where the individual comes to peace with the loss and moves on. Modern psychology asserts that the process does not have to proceed in that order, and some people may not experience all the stages, but characters and situations from *Blade Runner* can be used to illustrate what a person in any given stage looks like, and how they can help us as viewers recognize how they are represented on the continuum of human activity.

In terms of narrative structure, one presumption we shall make for this discussion is that the protagonist of this film is emphatically *not* Rick Deckard, played by Harrison Ford. One way to understand the literary concept of a protagonist is that this is the character with the freedom to act, who drives the narrative forward and overcomes obstacles. The character who most clearly fits that description here is Roy Batty, played by Rutger Hauer. It's Batty who jumps ship in the Off-World colonies and leads his rag tag group of replicants back to earth in search of their creator. It's Batty who instigates all of the action here, and it's Batty who finally has the most complete character arc (although Deckard begins to parallel him towards the end in his own search for identity and meaning).

A key question to be asked of any story is a simple one: What does the protagonist actually *want*? And Batty, fortunately for those performing an analysis, tells us. "I want more life. Fucker!"[1] he says to his maker, Eldon Tyrell. As the film explains, replicants have a limited, four-year lifespan. Batty, the advanced Nexus-6 model, has become aware of this limited lifespan and moreover, that he has a potential to discover new things and develop new memories and understanding that are uniquely his. He seems to consider this arbitrary four-year lifespan a waste of that potential, and as the film starts, we see Batty deep into both the Anger and Bargaining stages of grief. He's grieving fundamentally for himself, which makes the whole situation that much more

---

[1] This is the line from the original sound mix of the film and the 1992 Director's Cut. The 2007 Final Cut changes the "Fucker" to "Father," which one could say implies the same thing, but less bluntly.

emotionally charged, because in essence, every replicant lives like a cancer patient with a terminal diagnosis. They *know* they're going to die and they know they should live much longer. Still, they have to live somehow with that knowledge. Batty is trying to change the rules of the game of life, a classic case of Bargaining.[2]

Batty's bargaining first takes him to Hannibal Chew, the eye manufacturer for the Tyrell Corporation, and Batty starts leaning into the scientist menacingly. He questions Chew about the nature of his programming and the limitations of his biological reality. He wants, most of all, for Chew to tell him that everything is going to be okay and with a simple switch he can provide Batty with longer life. But it simply isn't to be. Chew leads them to J.F. Sebastian, and once again, Batty tries to bargain with him, this time offering friendship to this lonely person in exchange for knowledge about how to prolong his life. But Batty really isn't interested in friendship. He uses Sebastian to get to his true goal – his maker.

The scene between Roy Batty and Eldon Tyrell (played by Joe Turkel) is rightly regarded as one of the most tense and effective scenes in the film. Batty is not violent at first, but rather sits down on a bed with his father with whom he has a long, technical discussion about all of the theories Batty has either developed himself or discovered through independent research about how to prolong the life of a replicant. One by one, Tyrell calmly addresses and then discounts these theories for numerous technical reasons. He is not without sympathy, as evidenced by the fact that he and his team have looked into the issue and explored it to the best of their abilities. There's simply nothing to be done. It's a bargaining scene, and one can imagine any number of cancer patients playing out the same scene with their physicians, discussing treatment options until there are none left to explore. When Batty is told, in no uncertain terms, that there is no help available for him, he switches from Bargaining into Anger, kills his father and spends the rest of the film in a rage against the forces of time and nature. That is, until his final scene.

After the climactic action sequence at the end of the film, in which Batty and Deckard go head-to-head in Sebastian's mostly deserted apartment

---

[2] It is well known that Ridley Scott's brother, Fred, passed away from cancer just before production started on *Blade Runner*, and this may contribute to why this metaphor of raging against the dying of the light is so potently rendered in the film, but the story elements were in place regardless of Scott's personal experience.

building, Batty is finally spent. He can feel himself dying as he sits, cradling a dove in the rain as the sun comes up. He muses on the arbitrariness of his fate and mourns the life he could have had and the loss of all the knowledge he's managed to gain over the course of his short time. But there's no anger about it at this point, only sadness. And his final words, "Time to die," ring of the truth of someone who passed through anger and bargaining into acceptance. Deckard, viewing the whole scene having been viciously attacked by this man, looks astounded at the depth of his capacity for emotional growth, and is perhaps inspired by that capacity to enter into his own process of grief.

For Rick Deckard, the journey through *Blade Runner* is almost a process of trying to do as little as possible, very uncharacteristic behavior from a nominal protagonist. Right from the start, Deckard fancies himself completely retired from the life of a Blade Runner. "I was quit when I came in here, and I'm twice as quit now," he says to his supervisor, Bryant, near the start of the film. Deckard appears to be in Denial, but we don't see the precipitating incident that has led him into the five stages of grief. There is a hint of a recent tragedy, and although dialogue in the film establishes that this isn't the most obvious tragedy (killing a human instead of a replicant), we're not given anything more specific. If anything, Deckard is in a general state denial of his own nature, both as a replicant[3] and as a hunter of replicants. He eventually bargains with Bryant that he kill only the outstanding replicants who are running wild, although Bryant changes the bargain mid-stream when it is revealed that Rachael, Tyrell's associate and the film's supposed love interest, is also a replicant.

Deckard also exhibits some classic symptoms of depression, drinking alone in his apartment and comforting himself however he can, but he ultimately feels powerless in the face of his responsibilities and nature and responds to that by going internal. His clumsy courtship of Rachael is another classic case of depression, as Deckard reaches out for some connection to another human that is not based on violence or responsibility.

So, here we have a very confused character, psychologically speaking, showing symptoms of denial, bargaining, depression and anger all at once,

---

[3] The question of Deckard being a replicant is beyond the scope of this essay, but for the purposes of this discussion, and because it enhances our thesis, we will go with director Ridley Scott's interpretation that he emphatically is some sort of replicant. However, even if Deckard is fully human, many of our points still stand. For example, he may be grieving for what he perceives as the loss of his own humanity due to the death-dealing nature of his work.

which is not unheard of in grief analysis. What makes Deckard different is that he has some external guides through the grieving process, most notably Roy Batty, who constantly externalizes what Deckard internalizes. Although it might seem as if the two are locked in mortal combat to the death, and the level of violence between them is brutal and ugly, Deckard does more watching than he does shooting, and in the end doesn't actually "defeat" Batty at all, but becomes a witness to Batty's profound realizations about the meaning of his own life and death.

Roy Batty prepares to take flight.

One great gift that Batty gives Deckard in this sequence, although it doesn't appear that way at the time, is that he forces Deckard to fight for his life. At the beginning of the film, and throughout the film, Deckard doesn't appear to be someone with a great passion for life, but hanging on that steel girder in the rain, Deckard still doesn't want to let go. It's significant that Batty saves Deckard from death here, because Batty knows that he's teaching Deckard something, and that lesson won't be clear until Batty himself finally expires. Once Batty dies, and particularly in the way he chooses to end his existence, Deckard finally appears to find peace with himself and his identity. He moves from that complex mixture of all the stages of grief to accept things the way they are. "It's too bad she won't live," as Gaff puts it, "but then again, who does?" By the end of the film, Deckard will not be the same as he was before. He moves more confidently, nods his head, and stands at ease with who (or what) he is. He no longer looks back, but forward, a classic evocation of the power of acceptance.

The stages of grief in *Blade Runner* appear in characters beyond the central dyad of Deckard and Batty, most notably, and perhaps most profoundly, in the character of J.F. Sebastian, played by William Sanderson. Sebastian, as portrayed in the film, suffers from a disorder ("Methuselah Syndrome") that causes him to age rapidly. This rapid aging puts him in a similar situation as the replicants, but there is a stark difference between how he faces the inevitability of his death and how the replicants react.

Sebastian is lonely, but not particularly sad, having created many artificial "friends" using his skills as a genetic designer. This advanced scientific knowledge gives him an ability to face what is going to happen with more resolve, and in fact Sebastian might be the only character (with the possible exception of Gaff) who begins the film in the spirit of acceptance. Sebastian's southern cordiality (probably something to do with Sanderson's performance) and easy manner set him apart from other characters in the film. He isn't seeking anything except to mind his own business and let death take him in the fullness of time. But he also lacks the assertiveness that might lead him to oppose Batty and Pris who are obviously using him for their own purposes.

Sebastian provides mainly an example for other characters to follow, and although his trusting nature leads to his personal demise, one cannot help but imagine that Batty thought a little bit about this strange little man who accepted his place in the world as he died. For Sebastian has done his mourning, and his mourning is not for himself, but for the world that surrounds him. And that world is the one in most need of finding its way through the five stages of grief.

From the first shot of *Blade Runner*, we're unequivocally introduced to a world that has clearly fallen from grace. The constant darkness, rain and atmospheric pollution (all used, it appears, by director Ridley Scott to create visual effects on a modest budget), combined with notable calls for people to abandon earth for one of the Off-World colonies, drives home the point that the planet itself has run its course. Philip K. Dick's original novel, *Do Androids Dream of Electric Sheep?* makes it even clearer, describing in detail that humanity now lives in the aftermath of a nuclear conflict and the planet is a biological wasteland. Hence, for example, the market for artificial animals, ostensibly to be kept as pets. There is a hint of this connection in an early *Blade Runner* scene in which Rachael asks Deckard if he likes the owl they keep at the headquarters of the Tyrell Corporation. "It's artificial?" Deckard asks, to which Rachael responds, "Of course it is." The novel makes it clear that the owls were the first animals to die in the newly polluted world, making this exchange a key moment of insight into the ruined nature of earth, at least in terms of the environment. Therefore, all of the characters in the story are somehow in grief over the loss of the planet and the diversity of life that once characterized it. Their reactions not only illustrate an interesting parallel with how some real-world figures today deal with environmental challenges, but how a society in mourning becomes profoundly dysfunctional.

In the face of environmental collapse, one common response is Denial, and we need look no further than the reaction of certain ones to climate change for evidence of that. It's much easier to simply say, "No, it isn't happening," than to seek solutions and remedies, so denial becomes a useful tool for those who yearn for business as usual. In *Blade Runner*, Tyrell himself seems to be living in a state of denial, living high above the world in his temple, surrounded by the accouterments of past civilizations, living as if the world will continue as it always has. Like many in a position of socioeconomic privilege, Tyrell will be the last to feel the effects of an environmental catastrophe and thus has the luxury of smiling and playing chess while the streets accumulate filth and struggle. But Tyrell is also living in the Bargaining stage, and in fact has made his fortune by catering to those who wish to simply replace what they have lost (nature) with an artificial approximation of it (replicant animals), a trade that allows the customer to reinforce their belief that nothing has changed, and allows the producer to maintain the status quo.

Other members of society that we are introduced to in the film, such as Taffy Lewis, seem either oblivious to the decay that surrounds them or somehow welcome it in a nihilistic display of end-of-times cynicism. Assuming he's aware of who Zhora really is, the fact that Lewis is willing to employ a replicant to dance in his nightclub, and that he allows her to use a clearly artificial snake in a supposedly lascivious way, is an act of defiance not only against the law (replicants are outlawed on earth) but against the reality of his environment. The world is falling into chaos, and Taffy Lewis is almost stoking the fire of environmental and societal degradation. If this kind of behavior fits anywhere in the five stages, it's in the Denial stage, just as it is for Tyrell.

When Deckard, in his investigation, finally speaks to Taffy Lewis, he fails to show very much interest in Lewis himself, but rather enjoys a large drink and the snake show before calling Rachael to see if she would like to join him (another example, as mentioned above, of Deckard as the inert protagonist). It seems that here, as in other parts of the film, Deckard is very sensitive to the attitudes of the people around him and tends to take on their attitudes. When around Batty, Deckard learns the value of anger and acceptance, but as Taffy Lewis is less useful as a teacher, Deckard merely indulges his baser nature.

This raises a question. At what point does Deckard move from Denial to the rest of the stages of grief? It seems that the best answer is that he moves back and forth between the stages, pushed and pulled by the circumstances of his journey through the narrative as well as by what various characters around him do. For people with a weak sense of self-worth, like Deckard, the film seems to be suggesting that grief can make them extremely vulnerable. What's needed for those in grief to make better choices is a counselor or therapist, and as it happens, *Blade Runner* provides Deckard with one: the character of Gaff, played by Edward James Olmos.

Gaff seems, at face value, to have little relevance to the story structure of *Blade Runner*. Ostensibly Deckard's partner, he leaves Deckard when danger arises and only follows him around when he's going through the mundane process of detective investigation. But through his origami figures, Gaff provides a vital stabilizing influence on Deckard that gently pushes him through the stages of grief until he finally arrives, at the end, at acceptance. Gaff's first origami figure is a chicken, delivered to Deckard in Bryant's office when he expresses reluctance to take on his assignment. It's the equivalent of saying, "I know you don't want to do this, but what else are you doing with your life right now? It's time to be proactive." Deckard takes the case. Later, when Deckard is searching Leon's apartment for evidence that could lead him to the other replicants, Gaff makes an origami man sporting a heroic erection, perhaps suggesting that something sexual occurred in this space, or even more simply, that Deckard needs to search for something erotic in order to take him to the next step. (This turns out to be good advice, as it leads Deckard to Zhora.) Finally, Gaff's infamous origami unicorn echoes Deckard's waking dream about unicorns, poetically related to his memories of childhood and of a time when the world was better, before the environment collapsed.[4]

On a psychological level, however, Gaff is reminding Deckard that there is a life to be lived once one accepts what has been lost, and peace is made with one's own identity and purpose. Gaff, one could say, is even informing Deckard with some subtlety that denying his skills as a hunter of replicants is a denial of

---

[4] Vangelis' score cue for this section is titled "Memories of Green," which is very apt and underscores the point.

his own nature and skill set, which is not necessarily something to discard without some contemplation. In any case, without Gaff, Deckard would never have been emotionally available to Batty's ultimately positive influence on his emotional state. In working through the stages of grief (which Deckard may not have even been consciously aware of), Gaff serves as his therapist, and Batty his triggering event. Together, they help push Deckard towards acceptance.

Rachael also moves through some of the stages of grief in learning that she is a replicant and not, as she has always been told, a human. She denies it until Deckard provides proof, goes through a period of anger as she storms out of Deckard's apartment, and passes through depression, but her character remains frustratingly incomplete at the film's end. With little dialogue or action to go on – Rachael simply waits at Deckard's apartment in the final sequence for him to return – we must presume that her journey towards acceptance of her nature continues.

Our final question then asks what, precisely, is Rick Deckard accepting? We have established that Batty is learning to accept death; that the world at large is struggling with accepting its degraded environmental state and the idea of moving off the planet; that J.F. Sebastian has accepted his own mortality; and that Tyrell is in deep denial of anything but his own power and privilege. Deckard, by contrast, is energized, positive, focused and awake by the end of the film, whatever version we choose to watch.[5] He has accepted something that he was denying at the outset.

Certainly one thing Deckard seems to have accepted is his identity and skills as a police detective. When Bryant scolds Deckard for not accepting his assignment early on in the film, saying, "If you're not cop – you're *little* people," Deckard is wondering which category he prefers. He appears, with his lonely little rituals in the street of reading the newspaper and visiting the noodle bar, to be embracing his identity as "little people." It's only through Gaff's gentle nudging and a path that leads Deckard (almost despite himself) to a successful conclusion to his assignment, that he must admit to himself that, yes, he *is* a good Blade Runner. But, significantly, he also realizes that this is only one part of his larger identity. His spiritual life, his memories, his experiences that go

---

[5] Though the original theatrical cut offers us a "happy ending" of Deckard and Rachael driving off into an unspoiled wilderness, there is no dialogue and the relationship between the characters appears consistent with the endings to the Director's Cut and the Final Cut, where Deckard offers a short, decisive nod and then exits.

beyond the cold logic of hunting down illegal androids – this is what Roy Batty teaches him not to lose like so many "tears in rain." Deckard realizes that he doesn't have to choose between "cop" and "little people," but instead can carve out a path less travelled, write a new life script with Rachael and open up unimagined possibilities.

Deckard is also struggling with his identity not just as a Blade Runner but as a human being. Whether he is a replicant or human, Deckard is struggling to identify what that actually means in the here and now. Can a replicant also be a good person? Can someone who hunts replicants also be a good person? These questions are unanswered by the end of the film, but the clear impression is that Deckard is determined to find out the answers through experience, rather than accepting the received racist wisdom of someone like Bryant, or the fatalistic depression of Rachael, who mourns the loss of her perceived humanity.

Deckard, perhaps being the next iteration of replicant or perhaps being just a human in a very unique psychological situation, is determined to reconcile what value authentic memory has to one's life in the practical sense. If someone whose memories are programmed, as replicants are, and whose life is determined by outside forces, as replicants' lives are, can still be a good person and live a rich and full existence, then it raises the interesting question of what meaning the distinction has at all.

Perhaps what Deckard really mourns is his own preconceived notion of what his life can or should be. At the beginning of the film, Deckard has chosen to be a "little person," but by the end, he chooses simply to be a "person." That's what he learned by going through the stages of grief with Batty, with the help of his therapist, Gaff, and by simply opening himself up to a new way of seeing the world. For all its darkness, *Blade Runner*, regardless of the cut, ends on a note of healing and hope, as anyone who has dealt with the stages of grief hopes to attain by the end of the process.

The Humanity of *Blade Runner*

by Nelson W. Pyles

One of the challenges of any science-fiction film is making sure that the characters are likable enough to carry the audience through the entire story. As the viewer of these films, we the audience experience the events through the prism of the characters, hero or otherwise, based on a certain level of basic humanity.

The multiple *Star Trek* TV series, films, and literature, endure mainly due to the beloved and sometimes hated characters that carry the storyline. *Alien* and its relentless sequel *Aliens* deliver the goods because they have characters the audience can rally behind and worry about even after the end credits. *Star Wars* has a rich cast of likeable characters to choose from, such as Luke Skywalker and Han Solo.

It is no small accident that Harrison Ford was cast in the role of Rick Deckard for Ridley's Scott's adaptation of Phillip K. Dick's *Do Androids Dream of Electric Sheep?* (replacing the original choice, Dustin Hoffman.) Renamed *Blade Runner*, the film seemed to be set up to become one of the most iconic science-fiction films ever made, and although a commercial flop at the time (explored elsewhere in this book[1]), it did eventually succeed. But why did a film about

---

[1] See "Awe, Wonder, and Disappointment - The Summer of 1982 and the Box-Office of *Blade Runner*" by Robert Meyer Burnett.

killer androids being hunted by Harrison Ford tank so badly in the first place?

Sheila Benson, film reviewer from the *Los Angeles Times* called the film, "Blade Crawler"[2] in reference to its slow, deliberate pace. *New Yorker* reviewer Pauline Kael, mentioned that the film "...hasn't been thought out in human terms."[3] This suggests a shallow look at a film that requires more in-depth consideration. There are parts that contain *much more humanity* when you take a closer look.

From the very opening sequence with the replicant Leon being given the Voight-Kampff test (which measures emotional responses) and being absolutely petrified during the entire process, you can discern that he *knows* he's going to fail. So does the test's administrator Dave Holden. The test proves beyond a shadow of a doubt that Leon is a replicant. But, the sequence is full of tension because he's trying so hard to *not* be a replicant. If only for a few moments, his emotional reactions aren't of stealth or subterfuge, but fear: fear of what he is, fear of what he isn't, and fear of being found out. How fitting it is that the question that finally breaks him is in reference to his mother.

If you can recall a time when you've told a serious lie and were on the cusp of being found out, that sick knot that churns and grinds in the pit of your soul was Leon's experience, and is one that many watching can at least identify with for that moment.

The look on his face when he shoots Holden for the first time isn't malice. It's a defensive look borne out of an artificial survival instinct based on a genuine fear. He wears the same look when he shoots Holden the second time as well. Leon displays considerable malice later on in the film, but that scene reflects a combination of fear and success. Maybe it's for the first time, maybe even for the last. But it's human in any case.

We then meet Deckard, the human hero the audience is expected to identify with, *our* human, *our* identifier, played by Harrison Ford (for all intents and purposes, both Han Solo and Indiana Jones), the embodiment of bravado, iron will, and guts. Yet, the film subverts our expectations. Deckard doesn't carry the traits we anticipate. Ford plays him perfectly as a flawed character with some less than noble qualities, yet still relatable with arguably the most humanity of anyone in the film.

---

[2] http://articles.latimes.com/2010/jan/24/entertainment/la-ca-philip-k-dick24-2010jan24/3
[3] http://scrapsfromtheloft.com/2016/12/28/blade-runner-review-pauline-kael/

But he's not alone in having this quality.

Deckard is forced back into the violent career he walked away from, a Blade Runner and one of some note, as reflected in the variety of cold sounding nicknames, like "Mr. Nighttime" and "Boogeyman" according to some earlier versions of the script (but we'll stick to the version I am basing this upon: the Director's Cut.)

Deckard is one of the best (if not *the* best) at tracking down replicants and the toll it has taken on him is apparent. He's already worn out when he meets with Bryant, who coerces him back into "retiring" some "skin-jobs" who have smuggled themselves to Earth. Here we get our official introduction to the main thrust of the film – the hunt for our four villains, and in particular, their leader Roy Batty.

This whole exchange is delivered coldly. After all, it's not actual *people* the heroes are talking about killing, but machines, and Bryant does nothing to hide this fact. Deckard's response is one of weary reluctance, although he accepts the job pretty quickly, albeit under duress.

We hear why these four fugitives are wanted so badly; hijacking an off-world shuttle and killing everyone on board. We also see the footage of Leon again, "airing out" Holden for talking about his mom, and here we see it in a different light. Now, we have perspective.

Bryant sets Deckard on his path, and for all of his hesitation, Deckard dives right in and goes straight to the birthplace of the replicants: the Tyrell Corporation. We immediately meet Rachael; a beautiful if not a trifle cold woman who introduces us to Dr. Eldon Tyrell. Tyrell has Deckard administer the Voight-Kampff test on Rachael resulting in somewhat predictable results, but with one exception.

Rachael doesn't know she's a replicant.

Now, here is a scene worth breaking down a bit as there seems to be a surprising lack of humanity. To hear Tyrell explain Rachael to Deckard is akin to the way someone describes how a machine works. He's very proud of his work to be sure, explaining why the Nexus-6 models only have a four year life span. The slogan of his company, "More Human than Human," comes across more sinister and sad than clever.

The film, at its heart, is a detective story. It's not about solving a mystery, per se, but about *detection*. It's a very deceptive one at that, because while Deckard is out looking for skin-jobs, the skin-jobs are looking for something else entirely: a way to stay alive.

Part of the problem with finding humanity in the characters of this film is that the focus is *not* on the magnificence of the human spirit (at least not for the bulk of the film.) There's tremendous humanity all throughout it, but it's not the kind of humanity we as casual viewers are used to seeing. Up until this point, we have a very real problem in that the human element and the replicant element are both self-serving. They aren't very likable thus far, and there isn't much of a sign that anyone is going to do anything to change that opinion.

That is, until Roy and Leon go to Chew's.

After a brief (but important) exchange between Leon and Roy at the hotel where Leon lives, they go to Chew's Eye Works, a designer shop that specializes in making replicant eyes. The reason that the brief exchange between Roy and Leon is important is because although it appears that Roy honestly doesn't care about Leon's pictures, he understands why he went back for his "precious photos" in the first place. The replicants are all too aware that their memories are artificial. Leon may be insufferable, but he's not *insensitive*. The memories are false, but they're *his*, and as we learn later, not all the pictures are a sham of his memory banks. Also, Roy's exchange about the "police men" isn't to besmirch Leon's photos, it's to keep Leon focused on what they're trying to accomplish: the all-important mission of extending their lives.

Chew is questioned by Roy and Leon.

Upon seeing Roy and Leon, Chew knows he is in trouble. The following exchange is one of the best and oddest in the film, but it's absolutely compelling because of what is *not* being said while it's occurring.

Roy looks directly through *everyone* and drops the line that I've heard recited by many people since this movie's release: "Fiery the angels fell, deep thunder roll'd around their shores, burning with the fires of Orc." Chew's facial expression tells all. He reacts appropriately by delivering the best "I am so screwed face" since Ned Beatty in *Deliverance*. He knows these are replicants. He made their eyes. And those eyes are firmly upon him.

They want answers, and to his credit, Chew really knows exactly *when* to cave in amidst vague threats of violence. Roy, to *his* credit, doesn't overtly convey these threatening actions, unlike Leon, who lords over the room, randomly placing eyeballs on Chew's person. Chew tries the old "I made your eyes" routine, which deliciously backfires when Roy retorts "If only you could see what I've seen with your eyes." As it's the first time we've met Roy for more than a glance, we get to know quite a bit about him. The biggest thing that we learn is that he's *not* impatient (at least not yet.) He's quite methodical and systematic. Cold? Absolutely, but what is he trying to do after all? He's trying to live. This is a recurring issue, and each time the theme is readdressed in the film, it does so with a bite.

Deckard, meanwhile, makes it home to find Rachael in his elevator. She is a bit concerned at the things Tyrell has told him about her. She opens up to, essentially, a total stranger and what he does next is simply awful.

He tells her the *truth*.

Up until this point, Rachael's demeanor has been nothing short of intellectual flirting with a slight edge. Now, she's damn near beside herself in that she may be something that perhaps she's secretly feared. After her attempts to prove herself human fail, it appears as if Deckard begins to see her in a different light, through *his own* humanity, and he feels suddenly bad. He tries to casually wave it off to her as sort of a "Hey, just kidding" moment, but the damage is already done. Here is where Deckard begins in earnest to be the detective he is but more out of a real desire to no longer be a Blade Runner. He's hurt someone he's starting to have feelings for, and she is, for all intents and purposes, the enemy.

Deckard enhances one of Leon's pictures and finds a clue to go along with the artificial snake scale he's found. This leads him to the replicant named Zhora, who's been living in hiding as an exotic dancer. Oddly enough, his initial approach isn't full guns blazing. He pretends (poorly) to be an inspector.

This seems to work long enough for Zhora to take a shower and for Deckard to look around her dressing room. It's when Zhora gets semi-dressed that Deckard begins to receive the series of beatings that will plague him for the rest of the film. In fact, she displays a certain amount of pleasure in trying to strangle Deckard before another dancer comes into the room and pushes her to leave at a rapid hike. Deckard manages to pull himself together enough to pursue the half-naked replicant.

In one of the film's most intense sequences, Deckard chases a clearly terrified Zhora through the cyberpunk L.A. streets. This is a far cry from the confident, almost gleeful way she nearly attempted to kill him moments before. Pure survival instinct drives Zhora to run as fast as she can, which is considerable. Deckard is waving his gun around and even firing it a few times with little regard for the actual humans he's trying to protect.

If there is any recurring theme with regards to humanity, it is a consistent reinforcement of the raging will to live regardless of the consequences. Deckard wants to live too, but at the same time he wants this replicant dead; not only because it's his job, but also because she just tried to "retire" him.

Two things happen next that are of some importance. First, Deckard kills Zhora after an exhausting chase, concluding with her being shot and crashing through plate glass windows. The look on Deckard's face says it all. Yeah, he's exacted some small revenge, but he's also done his job. This is where his earlier weariness returns. Replicant or not, he's just retired someone (or something) in grand fashion and in front of a *lot* of people. It doesn't seem to sit well with him at all.

Second is the reappearance of Gaff accompanied by Captain Bryant. Bryant congratulates Deckard on his work calling him a "Goddamn one man slaughterhouse." Then adding, coldly, "Four more to go." Deckard frowns, already knowing what this means, but corrects him anyway. It's now four because of Rachael, Bryant explains. The look on Deckard's face is a mixed expression of fear, anger and quiet resignation. This is not what he needed to hear. Part of this has to do with Bryant's delivery. Bryant isn't inhuman. He's *inhumane*. Here, he represents the not-so-magnificent side of humanity. He even gloats about how Rachael didn't even know she was a replicant before leaving Deckard with this disturbing change in his mission.

He never gets time to let this properly sink in because Leon, who has witnessed the murder of Zhora, finds him first, and he isn't interested in consoling Deckard.

Leon enters the scene in a rage, catching Deckard off-guard. Deckard (who hasn't been punched in at least five minutes) begins to make up for lost time. Leon opens his festival of violence by asking Deckard, "How old am I?" You already know this isn't going to go well for Deckard. The beating begins, peppered with banter. This continues until, just when things seem hopeless and Deckard is literally staring death in the eyes, a shot rings out and a spray of Leon's blood splashes his face. A shocked Deckard is even more surprised when his savior is revealed to be Rachael. She has retired one of her own.

After taking her home for a stiff drink, he finds it's never easy to put yourself together when you're surrounded by so much death. Deckard isn't immune to it though, and notices that Rachael isn't either; she's shaking. He tells her its part of the business and her reply is so stunningly apt, it's chilling: "I'm not in the business. I *am* the business."

Again, she's opening herself up to a man who has now been tasked with killing her, but she knows he can't, or rather won't. As he says, he owes her one. She saved his life and he knows why. There's a level of humanity that hasn't been apparent in the film up until this point. Both of these characters are broken. What follows all of this is a widely debated "love" scene.

When I first saw the scene in question, I didn't fully understand it. The reaction I had was that Deckard was trying to force Rachael into having sex. Years later, I found that I may have been mistaken. Looking at it now, I see two damaged people with only the vaguest sense of what it is to be vulnerable, what it is to feel something other than the ugliness that is 2019 Los Angeles, rain and cold and death. Deckard awkwardly shows Rachael how to "desire him" and while it really does look like he's forcing himself on her, in reality it's merely something she has yet to encounter in her short life. It's an actual feeling he's trying to show her and she picks up on it pretty quickly. This is cathartic for her as much as it is for him. He's teaching her how to feel something and in that act alone, he's also teaching himself how to feel.

At this point in the film we've already met Pris and J.F. Sebastian. Their scenes mirror Deckard's and Rachael's in an odd way. When we meet Pris, she's apparently setting herself up to *appeal* to J.F. Sebastian. This works without a hitch, of course, because that's what Pris has been designed to do. However, she gets much more than she bargained for as J.F. isn't seduced by her as much as he is charmed by her childlike demeanor. He doesn't come across as one intellectually armed for what happens to him. He's 25 (in spite of his appearance, due to Methuselah's syndrome) with no friends except the toys he's made for himself. It's nearly heartbreaking to see them greet him at the door with welcoming proclamations like "Home again home again, jigitty jig! Gooooood evening, J.F."

At this particular point in the film, Pris seems to be the replicant we're going to have some, if any, sympathy for other than Rachael. Almost everything we learn about Pris is done in the presence of Sebastian, who is at this point so grateful to have actual friends in Pris and Roy (even though he possibly knows they are using him) that he agrees to help them. *He's* going to get Roy in to see Eldon Tyrell. The scenes with Sebastian and Pris are almost sweet even though there is a thread of tension, if only felt by the audience who knows knows why Pris is there. J.F. certainly does not and is genuinely pleased to have something more akin to a friend than his "toys."

Thus far, *Blade Runner* is the futuristic grand tour of not only the seven deadly sins, but it's highlighted all of the *worst* aspects of the human spirit, which makes it hard to choose sides. As in real life, the choices aren't always black and white. They're not even grey. They're choices that hinge on what you're willing to live with and for how long. In other words, the lesser of two evils. In that aspect, *Blade Runner* becomes a retelling of Lucifer's fall from Heaven, but with *very* different results.

The fall of Lucifer is pretty cut and dry; Lucifer, a favorite of God became obsessed with his own beauty and cleverness which resulted in him wishing to become God. Ultimately, God threw him and the other angels like him out of Heaven for their sin of self-generated pride. In this case, however, it is Tyrell, attempting to play God, who is prideful to an extreme. Roy may be the designated "bad guy" in this story, but his motivations are mostly based on his desire to keep on living. Tyrell is simply far too impressed with himself to be bothered to try and repair something he created and already believes to be perfect. Perfection with an expiration date, as it were, and perfection that is self-aware. When Roy kills Tyrell, it isn't out of pride. Roy is killing the devil as well as his god. Roy hasn't fallen as much as he has simply let his anger for wanting to live take him over.

His anger is such that he stalks and kills Sebastian, thankfully off-screen. Now, it is an extremely human trait to take anger out on those around us and Roy is no exception. He murders the one person who had actually helped him out of a bizarre act of kindness. It can easily be explained away that Roy is a cold-blooded killing *machine*. Roy is looked upon as the main villain in this film and he's doing what villains do. So why doesn't it feel right? Why doesn't this sit well with anyone watching this movie?

At this point in the film, we realize that the replicants really *are* slaves who broke free. They could have blissfully gone elsewhere to live out what was left of their lives, but like Leon said, "Nothing is worse than having an itch you can never scratch." Roy had the means to scratch his itch (or so he thought), but once he learned that his expiration date was irreversible, he took it out on poor Sebastian.

With the deaths of Pris and Sebastian, we come to a climax that isn't so much of a climax as it is a reckoning. Once it gets rolling, it's hard to look away.

Deckard encounters Pris at Sebastian's place and it is one of the more unnerving scenes in the film. Pris attacks him with such savagery, it's almost as if we're seeing another character entirely. There isn't really anything in her personality make-up that prepares the viewer for what she is capable of doing, and it's reflected in Deckard's face. It's not a long scene, but it's agonizing to watch because of the sheer brutality from Pris. But again, this violence is a reflection of the desire to live over everything else. She knows she's dead sooner or later, but it is infinitely better to die later than sooner and on her own terms. Deckard, desperate to live as well, shoots Pris and leaves her in a heap. He is relieved momentarily because he knows there's one left to go.

Roy finds the body of Pris and he breaks down, not so much with uncontrolled rage as with genuine heartbreak. He is now the last one and he is truly alone. He even howls like a lone wolf. This sound hits Deckard like a train and invites untold fear upon him. Deckard's facing the alpha now. This is a fight he doesn't want, but he is resigned that it's going to happen regardless. It's part of the business.

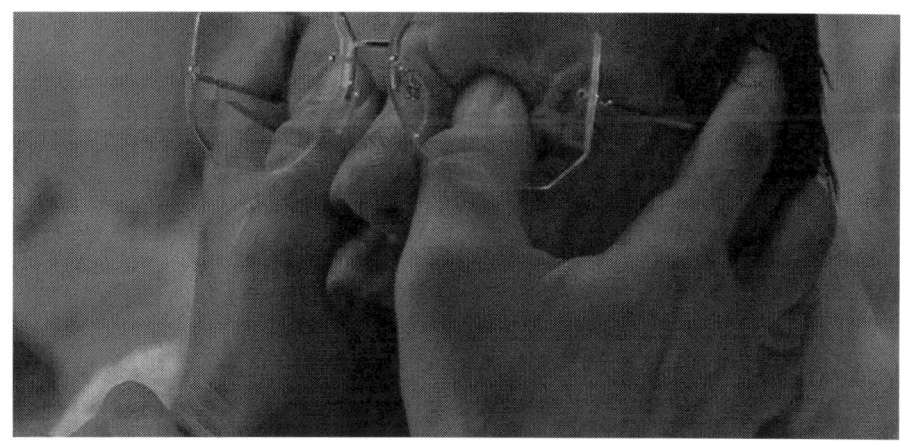

Roy Batty meets (and kills) his maker.

During these final scenes, Batty does something the other replicants were only slightly successful in accomplishing. He becomes truly frightening, and he isn't going to go quietly. He's seen what Deckard has done to Pris. It appears that all is lost, including whatever humanity he had developing inside of him. He's killed his god/father. His beloved Pris is gone, along with Zhora and Leon, so what is left for him?

All throughout the end chase, Deckard is petrified and functioning on pure adrenaline. His survival instinct is taking over. Although Deckard has come out on top, probably by sheer luck, he knows that there just isn't any more luck left in the tank. The hunter has become the hunted.

As Roy begins his countdown in an effort to be sporting and even more intimidating, he also begins the process of expiration, which gives his countdown a double meaning of sorts. He looks not afraid, but angry. His will to live becomes about something other than survival. It's also about living just long enough to see things come to a proper end, and after much ado on a rooftop, they do. Before this morphology, Deckard finds himself dangling from a beam, looking down into the pit of death.

"Quite an experience to live in fear, isn't it?" Roy says, not at all unsympathetically. "That's what it is to be a *slave*." This is the all-important pivotal moment of truth when this cold, sad, relentlessly *inhuman* film delivers a punch so hard it continues to resonate decades later. As Deckard takes this in, his hands slip, and for a nanosecond, he's falling to his certain death until Roy saves him. In perhaps the most unexpected move in this bleak film, Roy sits down and looks at Deckard, who is now in awe of what he is seeing.

Roy begins to deliver the most raw and emotional moment in the film and possibly the most human scene in *any* science-fiction film. "I've seen things you people wouldn't believe. Attack ships on fire off the shoulder of Orion. I watched C-beams glitter in the dark near the Tannhäuser Gate. All those moments will be lost in time, like tears in rain." Deckard is stunned, as are the rest of us. This was the *villain*. There is no villain now. There are just these two more broken pieces of humanity. Replicant or not, Roy in this moment isn't an artificial anything. He looks at Deckard one last time and says, "Time to die." He does just that, letting the bird he's been holding soar away to live out its life.

The film concludes with Deckard getting ready to hit the road with Rachael, but as they leave Deckard's apartment, we realize Gaff had been there and left behind a little origami unicorn. A voiceover reinforces this fact: "It's too bad she won't live...but then again, who does?" Although overshadowed by the righteousness of the rooftop speech, there is considerable humanity (as well as controversy) in that scene.

Blade Runner contains many examples of the worst parts of the human spirit. The characters are compelling enough to make you worry about what happens to them, especially the replicants. When Roy reminds us that for every dark soul, for everyone who lives in fear, for everyone who knows what it is to be a slave, there is, underneath, one unifying potential we all have and sadly, often choose to ignore.

The magnificence of the human spirit.

The Science and Technology of *Blade Runner*

by Sabrina Fried

There's a challenge to writing science fiction: The science doesn't always remain fiction. And the change can happen much faster than expected. If you read Philip K. Dick's original novel *Do Androids Dream of Electric Sheep?* the Earth is a truly desolate place, inhabited by the dregs of humanity. The people of Earth are those that either haven't migrated off-world yet, or have been deemed unworthy of the privilege. And while most of humanity no longer considers the world a good place to live, the replicant servants of the off-world colonies do, risking their very existence to escape to the Earth only to be hunted down and "retired" by bounty hunters known as Blade Runners. When Ridley Scott brought Dick's novel to the screen as *Blade Runner*, he created a moody, flashy aesthetic for the film that has been imitated, but never duplicated. The film glossed over the more subtle world building in Dick's novel, especially the parts that they believed didn't make for compelling cinema, but *Blade Runner* is the kind of film that you are still thinking about long after you have left the theater.

It wasn't enough for *Blade Runner* to simply look convincing; the world of the film had to work to some degree. And this required Scott and his designers to work hard to envision a not-so-distant world of the future. Nearly 50 years after *Do Androids Dream of Electric Sheep?* was published, the world of the future is a very different place. Although not optimistic about the state of the Earth, Dick postulated that in just a few short decades flying cars would be commonplace, there would be android servants so advanced that they surpassed their masters in strength and intelligence, and who would look nothing like the clunky metal robots popular in the science fiction of his day.

I regret to inform, however, that as 2019 approaches (as of this writing), the year in which this story is supposed to take place, my car doesn't fly and the robots in my life don't look anything like me and aren't all that smart. On the bright side, Earth is still habitable, at least for now. So where is the world Dick promised us? How does the technology of our present match up with the future Dick never got to see except in his imagination?

In some ways, we've already surpassed some of the technology in *Blade Runner*. Think of the vidphones that are commonplace in both book and film. Technology in the real world has become so advanced that it is possible to have real-time video conversations on a pocket-sized device with people all around the world – and this is not new technology. The earliest incarnation of Skype is over a decade old and can enable video conferencing on computers, phones, smart televisions, or anything with a camera, microphone, and access to the internet. But not unlike J. R. Isidore, the "chickenhead" in the novel used as a patsy by the escaped replicants, many people today still prefer voice-only calls, being self-conscious about how they appear on screen.

There are, however, additional feats of science and technology in the film and novel that are still the stuff of science fiction to our modern world, and there are three I will explore in detail because so much is happening with them right now.

Let's start with a look at the one gadget we all want: A flying car. We've had the technology to fly for over a century now, but for most people flight is an infrequent thing. Birds and airplanes fly by generating enough lift to overcome the pull of gravity. They do this by creating a differential in the air pressure above and below their wings. Add in some jets to create thrust and "push" the plane through the air, and it's possible to fly fast enough to break the sound barrier.[1]

The flying cars of *Blade Runner* were dubbed "spinners" by their designer,

---

[1] NASA. (2014, June 12). *Dynamics of Flight*. Retrieved from NASA: https://www.grc.nasa.gov/www/k-12/UEET/StudentSite/dynamicsofflight.html

"Visual Futurist" Syd Mead. They became such an integral element of the story that he would later develop his entire design aesthetic for *Blade Runner* around them.[2] The spinner is an example of a Vertical Take Off and Landing (VTOL) aircraft. True to its name, it doesn't require a runway to take off. There's actually nothing all that futuristic about VOTL aircraft either. We call them helicopters. There are also a series of military VTOL aircraft around the world. The most famous and thus far most successful of these is the Harrier jet.

A Police spinner flies over Los Angeles, 2019.

Military VTOL aircraft launch themselves into the air on a big burst of wash from their jet engines. By changing the orientation of the exhaust vent for the jet engine, or just tilting the entire wing of the plane, they can redirect the wash of their jets at the ground directly beneath them. VTOL aircraft like the Harrier require huge amounts of fuel, large, powerful engines that are expensive to build and tricky to maintain, and a great deal of pilot training and skill. Most are large vehicles with tiny cockpits and little, if any, cargo space. They need all the space they can spare for the massive jet engines necessary to get them off the ground, and the fuel tanks to feed them.

The line between flying cars and aircraft is thin and subjective. A true flying car would be a vehicle of some description that a pilot (and passengers) could use to travel to their destination with the same level of ease as a conventional

---

[2] Designing Blade Runner. (1996). In P. M. Sammon, *Future Noir: The Making of Blade Runner* (pp. 71-81). New York: HarperPrism.

ground vehicle. There would be no need to travel to a dedicated airport or launch area to use it. Ideally it would also be mass produced, relatively affordable, and simple enough to be controlled with the same amount of training that drivers receive now. So aircraft that require runways and the technological might of the military-industrial complex to keep them going are not what I would consider flying cars.

The practical considerations of a VTOL aircraft were not lost on Mead when he designed the spinners. Mead began his career designing cars for the Ford Motor Company[3] where he honed the skill of designing visually appealing cars that could take advantage of the best technology and engineering of the day. Scott wanted vehicles for his film that were believable, but not overly flashy. Mead proposed the idea of making the spinners larger and blockier than Scott had originally envisioned specifically so they would be more convincing as VTOL craft.[4] He gave them an obvious source of thrust in the form of jets in the wheel wells and designed the spinners so that the wheels could be moved as needed to allow them to function as ground vehicles as well. But spinners don't have anything we would recognize as wings, or any visually obvious means of maintaining their lift. The jets can be used for navigation and propulsion, but if they were somehow used to maintain lift, then a spinner would destroy anything it flew over with its jet wash.

The problem with the flying car is that it sounds like a great idea until you actually try it. The transportation network in most cities has been meticulously planned and developed, sometimes over millennia, to help people get where they want to go in a safe and efficient way. It has changed over time to keep the peace between different modes of transportation. Think of the sidewalks along a major road that give pedestrians a place to walk where they don't have to worry about being run over by cars. Deviating from this transportation network is strictly discouraged both for reasons of safety and efficiency. The widespread adoption of flying cars would mean expanding this transportation network vertically. Drivers (or perhaps pilots) would not only have to pay attention to what is around them, but also above and below them. Traffic routes for flying cars would have to consider the impact of their propulsion wash on

---

[3] Mead, S. (2015). *Biography*. Retrieved from The Official Website of Syd Mead: http://sydmead.com/v/12/biography/

[4] Designing Blade Runner. (1996). In P. M. Sammon, *Future Noir: The Making of Blade Runner* (pp. 71-81). NewYork: HarperPrism.

neighbouring traffic, much as boat captains have to think about the effect of their wake on other nearby watercraft. Conventional ground vehicles also have no need of dedicated runways, or protected takeoff areas.

There are also important considerations about the appropriate level of training for the people controlling flying cars. Both aircraft pilots and drivers of ground vehicles are required to undergo training and testing. They have to prove that they have a certain minimum level of skill. And while airplane crashes are relatively few and far between, there are still thousands of deaths and injuries every year from car accidents. The flight of contemporary aircraft is also tightly controlled by a network of air traffic controllers that keep aircraft in their approved flight paths. These flight paths are designed to consider not just the safety of the aircraft and allow them to navigate around obstacles, but also noise abatement, political boundaries, and – as with the current generation of unmanned drones – even the privacy of people on the ground. Although technology such as radar has improved the effectiveness of air traffic controllers a great deal, controlling aerial traffic still requires a great deal of fast-paced human decision-making and communication. Adding a fleet of flying cars into the airspace would require the air traffic control network to expand exponentially.

But don't think there aren't companies out there at least trying to make flying cars a reality. Start-up AeroMobil even has a working prototype with dimensions that allow it to use existing roadways for surface travel and requires a runway of only a few hundred meters to take off. It can even fly on the same gasoline used in regular cars. But for the purposes of regulation and training, the AeroMobil is considered an airplane with foldable wings. The people at the controls are trained and licensed aircraft pilots.[5] The amount of instrumentation required for safe flight is simply more than your average driver is ready to handle. And good luck finding enough clear roadway near any major city to achieve takeoff, especially at rush hour. Airbus, one of the largest aircraft manufacturers in the industry, is developing concepts for a project it calls the CityAirbus – a flying taxi/bus type….thing.[6] But the CityAirbus is being conceived as sort of a short-range commuter craft designed to transport travellers from

---

[5] AeroMobil. (2015). *AeroMobil*. Retrieved from AeroMobil: http://www.aeromobil.com/#url-video

[6] Repellin, M. (2016). *Future of Urban Mobility - My Kind of Flyover*. Retrieved from Airbus Group: http://www.airbusgroup.com/int/en/news-media/corporate-magazine/Forum-88/My-Kind-Of-Flyover.html

airports to other important destinations. It can penetrate deeper into a city's transportation network than conventional aircraft, but it still needs the infrastructure of an airport to support it.

We take it for granted that as a species, we have the spare resources to not just dream about things like flying cars, but actually try to make them a reality. Another such dream that we are still trying to make a reality is the colonization of space. We don't really see the off-world colonies in either the novel or the film, but if Buster Friendly and his Friendly Friends are to be believed, they are there, and moving to the off-world colonies is supposed to be preferable to life on Earth. Both film and novel make scant references to space-based colonies and colonies on other world such as Mars. In the novel, their existence is used as a contrast to the current state of Earth. Ravaged by pollution and the after-effects of World War Terminus, Earth is gradually losing its ability to support life. Dick describes the killer of Earth as a mysterious dust of unknown origin that has spread planet wide. By the time the story starts it has already wiped out most non-human life. Owning an animal, no matter how small, has become a status symbol and those of modest means keep up appearances with convincing, lifelike robots.

In modern environmental science, there is an important distinction that is made between changes to the Earth that affect its ability to support any life at all and changes that challenge the status quo to which the humans alive right now have become accustomed. The oldest known fossils of anatomically modern humans are believed by some to be around 195,000 years old. And based on our understanding of the fossil record and other stores of environmental information such as glacial cores and archaeological sites we estimate that even the Earth the first humans saw was vastly different from the one we know today. So the Earth itself does change. Sometimes those changes result in the extinction of a species, either in a specific area, or worldwide. Many scientists have said that like all living creatures, humans have evolved to thrive in their environments. And like other living creatures, if their environment changes to the point where they can no longer thrive in a given place, a human population will either go somewhere else, or die out. The change can happen quickly, say, within the lifespan of a typical human, or over centuries and millennia. In modern times, the city of Pripyat, Ukraine, vanished overnight, evacuated as part of the exclusion zone following the Chernobyl nuclear disaster.[7] In the decades since, the city has been reclaimed by the surrounding forest and now teems with plant and animal life, just not that many humans.[8]

It is entirely possible for events to occur, both natural and human-caused, that could drastically reshape the living map of an area. But the entire planet? Scientists believe they've identified at least five global mass extinctions in the geological history of the Earth. The Permian-Triassic extinction event, for example, is estimated to have wiped out up to 90 percent of all marine species that would have existed on Earth at the time.[9]

With our modern technology, a rapidly increasing population and a civilization that spans the entire planet, humans are in a position where we are capable of triggering a sixth or seventh planet wide mass extinction. Some would argue it is already underway as human-caused habitat destruction drives many species to extinction every day. When the changes become severe enough to overwhelm the ability of local human populations to adapt, individuals may leave the area, but the population can no longer move away to greener pastures. There is no longer any "away" that isn't already colonized by other humans.

Or is there?

Low earth orbit was first colonized back in the 1970s by the Soviet Salyut series of space stations. The current colony, if you will, is the International Space Station (ISS) and it has been continuously inhabited for just over 15 years. Entrance to the ISS is still restricted to an extremely few elite: astronauts from partner nations who have met very stringent physical, psychological, and skill requirements. Most tours of duty on the ISS last about four to six months at a time, for which the astronauts spend years preparing before the mission and many months recovering afterward. Travelling into space is still considered the trip of a lifetime but is not without its risks.

---

[7] Rich, V. (20 Apr 1991). *An ill wind from Chernobyl*. Retrieved from New Scientist: https://www.newscientist.com/article/mg13017655-000-an-ill-wind-from-chernobyl/

[8] Barras, C. (22 Apr 2016). *The Chernobyl exclusion zone is arguably a nature reserve*. Retrieved from BBC Earth: http://www.bbc.com/earth/story/20160421-the-chernobyl-exclusion-zone-is-arguably-a-nature-reserve

[9] Benton, M. J. (2003). *When Life Nearly Died: The Greatest Mass Extinction of All Time*. London: Thames & Hudson Ltd.

Humans are adapted to living on Earth. We breathe a very specific mix of nitrogen, oxygen, and other trace gases only found near the surface of the Earth. Although we are technologically savvy enough to develop clothes and other means of thriving in harsh environments, our bodies function properly at very specific temperatures and pressures found, you guessed it, near the surface of the Earth. Even this planet's typical gravitational pull is required for our cardiovascular system to work at its best. There are a great many challenges to living apart from the Earth. Living in continuous free fall, as one does on the ISS, takes a heavy physical toll on most parts of the body. Astronauts must spend a good portion of each day exercising to slow the deterioration of their bodies. The earth's atmosphere provides a level of shielding from cosmic radiation that we have not been able to fully replicate yet. And on a more psychological level, there are the stressors that come from living in what is essentially a huge tin can for months on end.

Although NASA and other international space agencies have considered the idea of sending manned missions to Mars, those missions are still only in the earliest of planning stages. Unlike the robots that currently roam the red planet, sending humans to Mars requires a large payload that includes food, potable water, and an acceleration system powerful enough to make the journey, but able to ensure that the fragile humans aboard make it there intact. The former two requirements alone put the mission beyond what is practical with current rocket technology. And not unlike the ISS, passengers on the journey to Mars would have to survive the physical and psychological rigours of the trip. We have decades of research now on what happens to humans living in free fall for a few weeks or months at a time, but only a handful of astronauts have lived continuously on the ISS for much longer than that. Getting to Mars with current rocket technology could take the better part of a year. Our technology is still lacking one of those wonderful science-fiction shortcuts that could actually come in handy here: artificial gravity. After all, it's not enough for humans to just survive a trip to Mars, they have to be able to carry out their mission once they get there. Assuming all that was possible, a great deal of resources and energy would have to be expended to create and maintain a habitat to live in. And that is just to maintain the most spartan of lifestyles. It says nothing of creating a life more desirable than that of Earth.

Perhaps that is why the government of Dick's novel assigned every colonist a replicant servant; a way of sweetening the pot to get them to leave the relative comforts of Earth and resettle off-world.

The replicants of both Dick's novel and Scott's film are described as being indistinguishable from a normal human, at least in their physical appearance. They can be made to have enhanced strength and intelligence. Aside from the keen instincts of a Blade Runner, a series of tests are used in the field to identify potential replicants, the most notable of those being the Voight-Kampff test. Further analysis might be done post-mortem to confirm that the retired replicant was not actually a human who does not fit into the psychological norm. Some replicants, such as Rachael, are even programed with false memories and believe that they are human. While this might provide more of a challenge for the Voight-Kampff machine, a good Blade Runner will figure it out in the end.

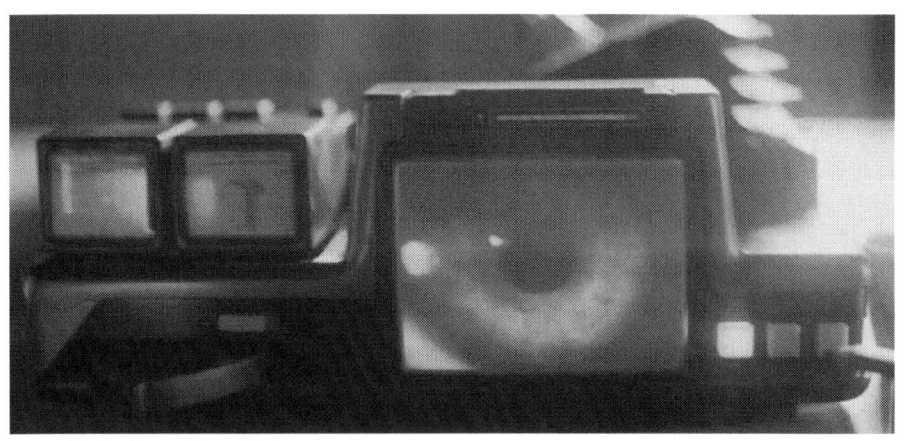

The Voight-Kampff machine.

In the film, it is explained that replicants have been designed to have a four-year lifespan, in part to limit their ability to survive very long should they escape both their masters and the Blade Runners. Roy Batty's entire motivation for his escape is to find a way to beat this time limit for himself and the other replicants. As Nexus-6 models, Pris and Roy struggle with emotional development, or at least the simulation of emotions convincing enough to almost-but-not-quite fool the Voight-Kampff machine. The flaw with this machine is that it assumes that all humans are the same and will have the same reaction to the same stimuli. The Voight-Kampff machine measures involuntary biological responses to stimuli such as pupil dilation and blood flow. The stimuli given is a fictional scenario designed to elicit the involuntary emotional response, something replicants are supposed to be largely incapable of. Generally speaking, the response the machine is expecting is rooted deeply in the prevailing Earth religion of Mercerism, which holds all life sacred. Many of the questions used both in the novel and the film invite the subject to imagine a scenario where an animal has been or will be harmed, something that should be revolting to a normal, Earth human raised by the tenets of Mercerism.

But imagine the same test used in the real world, say on an employee who works at a slaughterhouse or on an animal farm, who faces the mass killing of animals every day, or a person that is a clinical sociopath. The Voight-Kampff test would probably declare a good many of them replicants. They have been raised to interact with animals in a different way, and have been inculcated to think of them differently. This is why, in the real world, psychology is as much of an art as it is a science.

In the novel, in addition to holding all life sacred or "killing only the killers" as Deckard rationalizes it, followers of Mercerism participate in fusion using empathy boxes. These empathy boxes come across as something akin to a shared virtual reality experience so utterly convincing that participants feel physical pain when stones are cast at the representation of Mercer. But the boxes just don't work for replicants, who lack whatever quality allows humans to use them. And here, Dick furthers his exploration of what it means to be human by creating a mystery. Having established that known replicants are not affected by empathy boxes we eventually learn in the story that neither is Deckard. He is even chided by his wife, Iran, at one point for his inability to fully immerse himself in fusion. Although he later fuses with Mercer without the use of the empathy box, this may have been what inspired *Blade Runner* screenplay writer Hampton Fancher to launch one of the great mysteries of modern film:

Is Deckard human?

Deckard, replicant or not, looks like a human. All the replicants in the film and novel look perfectly human, and it goes without saying that in the film they were all portrayed by humans. But the future world of the Blade Runners was perhaps far more optimistic about how quickly artificial beings would advance than in the real world. Although there are roboticists in Japan that are making robots with coverings that are almost convincing,[10] we're still having trouble developing bipedal robots that can actually walk, let alone run, and they would

---

[10] Russon, M.-A. (24 June 2014). *Human or Machine? Life-Like Android Robots from Japan Show Glimpses of the Future*. Retrieved from International Business Times: http://www.ibtimes.co.uk/human-machine-life-like-android-robots-japan-show-glimpses-future-1453992

never be mistaken for a human. The general level of intelligence among our robot population is also, shall we say, not great. Even the humble Roomba is capable of mapping out a room, navigating around obstacles to vacuum your floor in the most efficient way possible, and find its own way back to its charging station. But don't ask it to empty its own dirt bin. It's not programmed to do that, so it wouldn't even understand the question. At the moment, our smartest robots are only capable of completing a limited number of simple tasks on their own. Ultimately they still rely on their programmers to tell them not only what to do, but exactly how to do it.

That's not to say that our robots are not making progress. The Atlas robot, a self-contained bipedal prototype built by Boston Dynamics, is capable of walking and running, including on uneven terrain, and more importantly, righting itself after a fall without any human assistance. If interrupted during a simple task, such as lifting and carrying a box, it will pick up where it left off.[11] The DARPA (Defense Advanced Research Projects Agency) Robotics Challenge featured robots from competing design teams around the world. The goal DARPA gave to the challenge participants was for them to create a robot that could carry out various disaster response tasks in an environment with what they termed "degraded communication." That is to say the robot had to rely on its programming to complete the tasks with little or no help from humans. At the 2015 finals, tasks included things such as driving a standard human vehicle, selecting and using a tool, and clearing rubble away from a doorway. The robot of South Korea's Team Kaist, DRC-HUBO, was declared the winner as one of the few robots able to complete the course at all. Most of its competitors didn't even make it into the car.[12]

In modern robotics, we are creating robots that can already be faster and stronger than the average human. With cosmetic skins of silicone, some can even be given a human-like appearance, but true artificial intelligence in robots is still a long ways away. Prototype industrial robots manufactured by Fanuc in Japan have a limited ability to teach themselves "rules" to complete tasks in ways that were not explicitly programmed into them. For the most part, the

---

[11] Boston Dynamics. (23 Feb 2016). *Atlas: the Next Generation*. Retrieved from YouTube: https://www.youtube.com/watch?v=rVlhMGQgDkY

[12] DARPA. (2015). *DARPA Robotics Challenge Finals 2015*. Retrieved from DARPA: http://archive.darpa.mil/roboticschallenge/index.htm

robots learn by trial and error.[13] But for practical purposes it is still faster for a robot to be programmed to complete a task. We're working diligently to develop all the parts of the replicants of *Blade Runner*. We just haven't come up with a way to get them together in one package yet.

Contemporary robotics is also still largely the domain of the mechanical, part of the reason why it would be impossible to mistake even our smartest, most convincing robots for humans. To be indistinguishable from living humans, the replicants would have to be biological machines. Perhaps they are not even machines at all. They could be a genetically engineered servant caste of humans that are given the more machine-like name of replicants to put the minds of their masters at ease. Pondering what it means to be human is a core theme that runs through Dick's novel and the film, and both are careful to allow the viewer to reach his or her own conclusion on whether the replicants are human or not. In the real world, researchers have made some progress using bacteria as a data storage medium, and the 3D printing of tissue for use in reconstructive surgery is becoming more commonplace. In theory, we have the ability to grow simple organisms and program them. The genetic engineering of plants and non-human animals is almost routine, especially in agriculture.

But, as far as we know, we don't clone humans, and the only genetic engineering of humans going on right now is the same selective breeding we have been doing to ourselves since we first came to be. In many countries the genetic engineering of human embryos is either banned or severely restricted. In countries where such research is permitted at all, genetically engineered embryos can be used for research purposes only, and must be non-viable. It's not that the technology is incapable, it's that our civilization is still grappling with the moral and ethical issues that human genetic engineering poses. For better or worse, lawmakers have sidestepped the issue by suppressing the research for now.

It was never Dick's intent to tell us how to make a flying car, or how to make a replicant, or even to tell us how to save the Earth from its future demise. Yet, one of the purposes of the science-fiction genre is to inspire dreamers to pursue the sciences and technology so that they can figure out if it

---

[13] Alpeyev, P. (3 Dec 2015). *Zero to Expert in Eight Hours: These Robots Can Learn For Themselves*. Retrieved from Bloomberg: http://www.bloomberg.com/news/articles/2015-12-03/zero-to-expert-in-eight-hours-these-robots-can-learn-for-themselves

can even be done, and to inspire thinkers to debate whether it should be done. Dick merely imagined a world where all those things were already possible. For better or worse.

Awe, Wonder, and Disappointment: The Summer of 1982 and the Box Office of *Blade Runner*

by Robert Meyer Burnett

It was 25 June 1982 at 12:15 in the afternoon the first time I saw *Blade Runner* at its debut screening in Seattle's Cinerama Theater. I'd recently turned 15.

The Cinerama proudly presented *Blade Runner* in both 70mm and in Warner Brothers' short-lived Megasound, a deep-bass enhancement system remembered for its "infrasonic" rumble capability, utilizing additional speakers with more subs and horns to provide low-frequency content.

I'd brought along my good friends Mike Shertz and Jolie von Suhr, our excitement over seeing Harrison Ford in another iconic role palpable. The three of us were already raging movie fans, riding both the shockwave of the recent home video explosion and crest of the summer blockbuster wave begun in the mid-1970s with the release of *Jaws*, and continuing on to this very moment.

Mike and I usually spent our weekends with our RCA VFT 650 VHS decks daisy-chained together, whirring away 24/7, copying the stacks of films I'd brought back from my job as a "video consultant" at Videospace, at the time

Starlog #52 offers a sneak preview of *Blade Runner*, billing it as a Harison Ford vehicle and giving little indication of the film's later importance.

one of the nation's premiere video stores.

With *Blade Runner* being rated R, both Mike and I, fearful we'd be denied entry, sent Jolie ahead to buy our tickets. Even then, we all knew girls had a better chance of breaking the rules than guys did, so her odds of securing the tickets to an R-rated movie most certainly were better than ours. Ego never once entered into the equation because we'd all been waiting for the film since first glimpsing production photos in the pages of *Starlog* magazine.

A little over two hours later, the three of us emerged from the theater, filled with wonder, our imaginations awestruck by Ridley Scott's darkly imagined vision of the future, and a society gripped in a perpetual state of technological ennui. Our senses reeled from the film's unparalleled visual and aural phantasmagoria as Vangelis' groundbreaking score echoed in our memories.

However, like so many other members of the movie-going public that summer, the three of us didn't know if we actually liked the film all that much.

We weren't alone. *Blade Runner* grossed $6,150,002 over opening weekend, far behind the second weekend grosses of *E.T.: The Extra-Terrestrial*, which put up $13,729,552 on the way to becoming not only the year's box-office champion with $359,197,037 in domestic grosses, but the most successful film ever released up to that point. It wasn't until *Titanic* came along in 1997 that it finally sunk down to number two (not adjusted for inflation).

Harrison Ford's two previous films, 1980's *The Empire Strikes Back* and 1981's *Raiders of the Lost Ark*, were both celebrated, cinematic pop masterstrokes, pushing the actor front and center in the industry, his charmingly handsome, hangdog persona cementing the star's iconic, leading man status in Hollywood history. Both films were also enormous financial successes, spearheaded by the two most powerful cinematic forces of the day, George Lucas and Steven Spielberg. So Ford's blazing star power seemingly assured *Blade Runner* would follow in those previous films' footsteps.

However, financial success proved elusive, and unfortunately, *Blade Runner* finished the 1982 box-office derby in 27th place for the year, behind films such as *Porky's* (5), *The Best Little Whorehouse in Texas* (9), *The Toy* (14), *The Sword and the Sorcerer* (18), *Friday the 13th Part 3-D* (21) *Young Doctors in Love* (23) and *Victor/Victoria* (26).

So, what happened? Why didn't *Blade Runner* connect with audiences already primed to love everything it represented? Director Ridley Scott's previous effort, the seminal *Alien*, reinvented horrific science fiction just as audaciously as *Star Wars* forever altered space opera. The headlining star was at the height of his career and even Vangelis had won an Academy Award for best score the previous year for his iconic work on *Chariots of Fire*. On paper, everything about the film screamed smash hit.

A New York-area newspaper ad for *Blade Runner*.

And yet, during the summer of 1982, two powerful forces conspired to prevent *Blade Runner*'s box office success. At the time of the film's release, a massive sea change was ongoing in Hollywood, not only rapidly changing the face of the motion picture business, but the very cultural standing of movies themselves.

The late 1970s and early 1980s saw the rapid rise of cable television and the explosive introduction of home video, completely altering the movie-goer's relationship with cinema. Movies were no longer ephemeral experiences, savored only in darkened theaters or perhaps once a year when the big three networks aired perennial favorites. No, motion pictures were now on-demand, aired sometimes even daily on premium cable channels, or perhaps rented on a whim at the local video store if one could afford an expensive video cassette recorder.

The aftershocks of the cable television explosion continued to be felt as the reach of premium channels grew across the land. The demand for Home Box Office and Showtime remained enormous because who wouldn't want the ability to see uncut films in the privacy of their own homes? July of 1981 saw Showtime beat Home Box Office to the punch, and adopt a 24 hour a day schedule. 1982 saw the network produce their first original feature film, *Falcon's Gold*. That year also saw Home Box Office rebrand itself to simply HBO, joining Showtime in finally providing around-the-clock programming, although HBO wouldn't debut their first original feature, *The Terry Fox Story*, until a year later.

The meteoric sales of consumer VCRs and the proliferation of the video rental store allowed favorite films to be rented and even purchased and owned for the first time on a mass scale. The general public now had the ability to collect beloved films, and, through the power of *re-watchability*, develop singular relationships with a film's story and characters to a level never before possible.

Children could now watch Disney classics on endless loops, the studio's famous songs and princesses now as much a part of childhood as visiting Santa or riding a bike for the first time. Pre-recorded tapes, both store-bought and time-shifted, filled houses and apartments like bookshelves full of significant novels, to be taken down and experienced over and over again. Movies provided a new kind of comfort akin to an old friend or a family photo album.

Even *Star Wars* made its way to rental VHS and BETA tapes in May of 1982, dispelling any notion the home video era would somehow signal the end of the theatrical movie-going experience. Indeed, a case could be made that the very opposite occurred; that premium cable channels and home video turned the entire world into movie addicts, creating a voracious hunger within armchair cineastes, everyone now able to curate their own film festival in the privacy of their homes.

This power of choice fundamentally altered the perception of movies in the mind of the public. They now possessed a previously unavailable ability other than simply picking a new release out of the newsprint of Friday's paper. Unless reviewers waxed rhapsodic about the latest potential Hollywood blockbuster, movie aficionados understood they might have better luck at the local video store, finding a previously unseen film or revisiting a classic favorite from

Hollywood's Golden Age. If a movie didn't garner immediate, jubilant, critical praise, or passionate word of mouth, filmgoers knew they could now "wait for the rental."

Yet, the phenomenon of movie-going was changing. This change began in the latter-half of the 1970s and continued into the early 1980s as the summer movie season became increasingly important to Hollywood following the phenomenal successes of the blockbuster genre releases *Jaws*, *Star Wars*, and *Alien*. As much cultural events as movies, these films played for months on end, with audiences lining up and down sidewalks, filling movie houses with unprecedented repeat business. Drive-Ins too were bursting with cars filled with teens eager to dare one another to experience the burgeoning, gore-filled horrors kicked off with John Carpenter's outrageously successful indie slasher *Halloween*.

By the summer of 1982, this new paradigm reached its zenith. Hollywood came out weapons hot, with a blast of robustly-budgeted science-fiction, horror and fantasy films covering a wide spectrum of subject matter, blowing the minds of audiences on an almost weekly basis. For the first time in cinema history, audiences possessed more cinematic choices than ever before. Whether it was a videotape, cable TV, or the cinema itself, audiences were less inclined to take risks, venture into unfamiliar territory, or sample films they might not have otherwise known they liked. Why bother venturing out to the cinema when one can watch a favorite film again and again whenever they choose? Better yet, why not head to the video store and find something you'd previously missed but already believed was great?

The second biggest impediment to *Blade Runner*'s success at the box office wasn't an audience cooling to Harrison Ford, or a tiring of the science-fiction and fantasy genre, or even being lost amongst so many other great releases in the summer of 1982, arguably the best period of genre films in cinema history.

No, *Blade Runner*'s greatest box office enemy was... the film itself.

In his initial review, Roger Ebert wrote, "[Ridley Scott] seems more concerned with creating his film worlds than populating them with plausible characters, and that's the trouble this time. *Blade Runner* is a stunningly interesting visual achievement, but a failure as a story."[1]

In his 15 July 1982 review, *The Christian Science Monitor*'s David Sterritt wrote:

---

[1] https://www.rogerebert.com/reviews/blade-runner-1982-1

Blade Runner was directed by Ridley Scott, who seems determined to outdo the violence of his hit *Alien*. Actually, only a few scenes are marred by sadistic outbursts, but the movie as a whole is so relentlessly grim that the effect is multiplied. The result has already stirred a new round of complaints about Hollywood excesses. And it certainly makes a fierce contrast to *Tron*, with Scott's fearful view of "artificial intelligence" as a savage menace rather than a slippery but ultimately convivial phenomenon.[2]

The great Pauline Kael had this to say in *The New Yorker* on 12 July 1982:

> Ridley Scott may not notice that when Hauer is onscreen the camera seems stalled and time breaks down, because the whole movie gives you a feeling of not getting anywhere. Deckard's mission seems of no particular consequence. Whom is he trying to save? Those sewer-rat people in the city? They're presented as so dehumanized that their life or death hardly matters. Deckard feels no more connection with them than Ridley Scott does. They're just part of the film's bluish-gray, heavy-metal chic—inertia made glamorous.[3]

While even the harshest critics admired the evocation of the most beautiful dystopia ever committed to film, everyone agreed that in a summer which included some of the most revered fantasy films of all time, *Blade Runner* simply wasn't a very good time at the movies. Audiences accustomed to seeing Harrison Ford as either the reluctant hero or the scrappy, seat-of-his-pants adventurer, just weren't in the mood for a genre pastiche which featured "Indiana Solo" gunning down two women in the coldest of blood.

Much has been written about the other cinematic offerings of the summer of 1982, but the breathless excitement found at theaters that summer remains, even three and a half decades later, unparalleled. There was simply no way *Blade Runner* had any hope of satisfying the general audiences in that environment.

May kicked the season off with enfant terrible director John Milius' blood-soaked adaptation of Robert E. Howard's *Conan the Barbarian*, serving up Arnold Schwarzenegger in his breakout role, much like the human stew consumed by Thulsa Doom and his followers. A week later, *Mad Max II*, retitled *The Road Warrior* for its American release, roared into theaters, bringing forth Mel Gibson in his "apocalypse pow" moment. Steve Martin and Sylvester Stallone followed with *Dead Men Don't Wear Plaid* and *Rocky III*, respectively, rounding out the month. Filmgoers rejoiced with laughter, cheers, screams, and

---

[2] https://www.csmonitor.com/1982/0715/071502.html
[3] http://scrapsfromtheloft.com/2016/12/28/blade-runner-review-pauline-kael/

most of all, tremendous satisfaction. Clubber Lang might have predicted "pain" for his fight with the Italian Stallion, but audiences felt exactly the opposite. *Rocky III* opened to a stellar $12,431,486.

The week of June 4th brought the Spielberg-produced, family-friendly *Poltergeist* and the beloved *Star Trek II: The Wrath of Khan* to theaters *on the same day*, creating a *Sophie's Choice* situation for genre film lovers all over the country who had to make the decision of which film to see first.

If that wasn't enough, the following week brought the summer's most highly anticipated film, the latest from the hottest director on the planet, Steven Spielberg. Fresh off the success of his previous hit, *Raiders of the Lost Ark*, released the year before, *E.T.: The Extra-Terrestrial* arrived like the Concorde from France, with a sonic boom of delight, shaking audiences of all ages, from the youngest child to the oldest grandparent, who could all enjoy the titular extraterrestrial's adventures on Earth sitting in a room together. It was four-quadrant entertainment the likes of which Hollywood hadn't seen since the release of *Star Wars*, half a decade earlier.

Grease 2 arrived on the 11th of June, but no one much cared. June 18th saw the release of the film version of the Broadway smash *Annie* and Clint Eastwood's futuristic *Firefox*, but the summer had already been won. However, for anyone reading *Starlog*, *Fantastic Films*, or *Cinefantastique* magazine, June 25th seemed promising with three significant, highly-anticipated, genre offerings opening on the same day. Joining *Blade Runner* were *Megaforce* and John Carpenter's *The Thing*.

Smokey and the Bandit director Hal Needham's first (and only) foray into the science-fiction action realm, *Megaforce*, was truly wretched, with terrible visual effects and an overall tone and storyline better suited to Saturday morning television. It grossed a dismal $2,350,021 for the weekend.

John Carpenter's eagerly awaited *The Thing*, a stately reimaging of the John W. Campbell short story "Who Goes There," with physical monster effects by the celebrated Rob Bottin still referred to with reverence today, was also, like *Blade Runner*, attacked upon its initial release by critics with a similar lack of vision, and failed to find a mass audience. Roger Ebert said of the film, "*The Thing* is basically, then, just a geek show, a gross-out movie in which teenagers can dare one another to watch the screen."[4] *The New York Times'* Vincent Canby said, "*The Thing* is a foolish, depressing, overproduced movie that mixes

---

[4] https://www.rogerebert.com/reviews/the-thing-1982

horror with science fiction to make something that is fun as neither one thing or the other."[5] Faring little better than *Megaforce* at the box office, *The Thing* managed to eke out an opening weekend box office take of $3,107,760.

Although a simplistic assessment, Canby's canny observation about fun cannot be ignored when discussing the box office fate of *Blade Runner* in the summer of 1982. While the film is beautifully atmospheric and evocative in so many ways, general audiences would most likely agree that's simply not enough for them. First and foremost, they want to be entertained, but most of all, they want to have fun. *Blade Runner* remains a film with an almost singular *lack* of fun. Audiences had been sold on, and were expecting, a familiar Harrison Ford characterization, a blustery, new take on a noir detective, which they assuredly did not get. Worse still, it could be argued that Ford's Rick Deckard isn't even a particularly likable character. His now famous disdain for the experience of making the film permeated throughout his performance, which wasn't lost on the critics or the movie-going public.

Even the extreme violence of the R rated *Conan* and *The Road Warrior* was gleefully presented with a huge dollop of uproarious appeal. The anti-heroes were heroes. Audiences left theaters with huge smiles on their faces, a great time had by all. But both *Blade Runner* and *The Thing* worked in a contrary fashion, leaving some scratching their heads, wondering not only why they even bothered, but why anyone would even bother to make such a film?

Filmgoers that summer clearly preferred seeing a reflection of themselves in the accessible, easily-digested and deliciously entertaining suburban science fiction and horror served up by maestro Steven Spielberg, rather than the apocalyptic nihilism of dystopian futures or dire extraterrestrial threats. Newly armed with the choices provided by cable television and VCRs, audiences were quicker than ever to reject theatrical films which failed to live up to their expectations.

In his *Christian Science Monitor* review of *Blade Runner*, David Sterritt says:
> But the plot is ordinary, and the scenarists have undermined it with a narration that even Ford considers foolish, judging from the way he reads it. Too bad the filmmakers didn't try to recapture the modest virtues of the Dick novel, which (despite many flaws of its own) has a humor and humanity that are nowhere felt in *Blade Runner*.

Theatrical feature motion pictures reside in the middle ground

---

[5] http://www.nytimes.com/1982/06/25/movies/the-thing-horror-and-science-fiction.html

between the light of a projector bulb and the shadow of the audience: a twilight zone where art and commerce collide and where Hollywood success, by definition, can only be measured in dollars. Yet artistic success is borne out by history, with generations of audience members who continue to respond to an auteur's vision, year after year, decade after decade.

Blade Runner's lifetime domestic box office gross is $32,868,943, still barely covering its original production costs. Yet the film's legend grows with each passing year, its fans, old and new, returning again and again to its ruminations on what it means to be human. But certainly, for the producers of the film and the studio which made it possible, *Blade Runner* will always be looked upon as a handsome failure.

On 3 November 2007, on the occasion of the release of *Blade Runner: The Final Cut*, Roger Ebert wrote, "I have been assured that my problems in the past with *Blade Runner* represent a failure of my own taste and imagination, but if the film was perfect, why has Sir Ridley continued to tinker with it, and now released his *fifth* version? I guess he's only... human."[6]

And yet, when Mike, Jolie, and I emerged from Seattle's Cinerama theater on that warm June afternoon in 1982, one thing was obvious: while *Blade Runner* certainly wasn't the expansion of the Ford persona we'd come to love, or the stimulating and engrossing narrative we'd anticipated, the first-rate theatrical experience of the film, its transporting, entrancing and utterly hypnotic world-building unlike anything seen on screen before, continued to resonate long after leaving the theater, days, months, and even years later.

Like the fleeting experience of waking up from a dream, the film continued to exist in the subconscious of susceptible members of the audience, never to be entirely forgotten. For those so inclined, the visual profundity of *Blade Runner*'s ruminations on the soul's existence, mortality, and humanity far exceeded any importance paid to any box office grosses.

Since their inception as a mass entertainment medium over a century ago, movies always balanced on the tightrope between art and commerce. They are, after all, a very expensive and risky product to produce, and must, by definition, appeal to the greatest number of consumers to

---

[6] https://www.rogerebert.com/reviews/great-movie-blade-runner-the-final-cut-1982

become successful. This financial success most often stood hand in hand with a movie's relative merits. The better the film, the greater appeal to all members of the audience.

As originally conceived, the studio most certainly did consider *Blade Runner* an extension of *Star Wars* and *Raiders of the Lost Ark*; popcorn-fueled mass entertainment, hopefully reinventing old tropes to reach modern audiences much the same way as those previous Ford outings managed to do so successfully. Certainly, they believed the film was destined for summer box office heights.

Unfortunately for the studio, Ridley Scott's artistic vision for the film overshadowed any financial concerns both during production and certainly upon the film's release. In what can only be considered a dubious financial decision on the part of the financiers, who clearly mistook *Blade Runner's* long-running cult status, respect, and reverence as mass appeal, on 6 October 2017, more than 35 years after the original film's release, Warner Brothers debuted the Denis Villeneuve directed and Ridley Scott produced *Blade Runner 2049* to smashing critical acclaim.

This brilliant, mournful, and beautiful sequel, set 30 years after the original film, not only honored Ridley Scott's original vision, but advanced the first film's narrative and core concerns in grand fashion, deeply enriching the legacy of the now-franchise in the way few sequels could ever hope to achieve.

Reportedly made with a production budget of $185,000,000, the film grossed only $91,524,557 domestically and $166,474,483 internationally, for a total of $257,999,040. By Hollywood arithmetic, *Blade Runner 2049*, like the first film, was an abject failure, needing to earn at least $555,000,000.00 to break even by covering not only its production budget, but all marketing and ancillary costs associated with its release.

So once again, *Blade Runner* disappointed financially. Strangely, why anyone thought a mass audience would respond to an extension of the original film's concerns remains a mystery, since even today, only a small portion of the population would ever want to be reminded of just how fleeting life can be...especially at the prices now charged by theater chains at the multiplex.

Yet to the small but ever-growing worldwide audience who continues to discover and rediscover the two films year after year, decade after decade, all those dollars lost by the *Blade Runner* franchise mean absolutely nothing next to the all those tears shed over Roy Batty dying in the rain.

The *Blade Runner* Sequels You Never Read

by Mike Beidler

INT. TYRELL DEN - NIGHT

Jeter: I'm surprised you didn't read my *Blade Runner* sequels sooner.
Beidler: It's not an easy thing to read your sequels.
Jeter: And what can I do for you?
Beidler: Can the author repair what he wrote?
Jeter: Would you like my *Blade Runner* sequels to be… modified?
Beidler: I had in mind something a little more radical.
Jeter: What – what seems to be the problem?
Beidler: Boredom.
Jeter: Boredom. Well, I'm afraid that's a little out of my jurisdiction, you–
Beidler: I want more Ridley Scott… [expletive deleted]

In 1982, Ridley Scott's *Blade Runner*, written by Hampton Fancher and David Peoples, stunned filmgoers with its neo-noir, dystopian vision of 21st century Los Angeles. Although not a commercial box office success in America, the movie proved more popular internationally. Eventually, however, American audiences came to adore the film's treatment of *simulacrum* and rocketed it to cult classic status; as such, *Blade Runner* became an inspiration for other dystopian stories, such as the reimagined *Battlestar Galactica* and *Ghost in the*

Shell. Although most science-fiction cinephiles know that the cyberpunk film was actually a loose yet thematically faithful adaptation of Philip K. Dick's 1968 novel *Do Androids Dream of Electric Sheep?* (hereafter, *Sheep*), fewer have read Dick's source material, much less its literary sequels. *Wait*, you exclaim, *Dick didn't write any sequels to* Sheep! Technically, you would be right. Let me explain. No, there is too much. Let me sum up. Buttercup is marrying Humperdinck in little less than half an hour. So all we have to do is get in, break up the wedding, steal the princess, make our escape... after I kill Count Rugen.

Er... Sorry. Wrong movie.

In the mid-'90s, as the odds of a cinematic sequel to *Blade Runner* were looking extremely improbable, Dick's estate and the movie rights-holding Blade Runner Partnership (alleged to be Bud Yorkin and Jerry Perenchio) authorized science-fiction author Kevin Wayne Jeter – known professionally as K.W. Jeter – to write official sequels to Scott's movie. A personal friend and colleague of Dick's, Jeter shared with the psychologically troubled author a penchant for writing dark science-fiction and an obsession with questions surrounding the nature of reality. Thus, Jeter was a "natural pick" to carry on the *Blade Runner* flame-spouting tower. Early on, Dick even touted Jeter's controversial cyberpunk novel *Dr. Adder*, which, due to its graphic sex and violence, had a difficult yet ultimately successful publication history (completed in 1972 and finally published in 1984). In all, Jeter wrote three poorly received *Blade Runner* novels: *Blade Runner 2: The Edge of Human (A Novel)* (Bantam Books 1995), *Blade Runner: Replicant Night (A Novel)* (Bantam Books 1996), and *Blade Runner 4: Eye and Talon* (Victor Gollancz 2000).[1]

Do Authors Dream of Electric Sequels?

Unfortunately, entertainment critics like *Entertainment Weekly*'s Michael Glitz expressed concern about Jeter's *The Edge of Human*, calling it "literary necrophilia," a term coined to describe an author writing a sequel to a dead

---

[1] In the U.K., *Blade Runner: Replicant Night (a Novel)* was titled *Blade Runner 3: Replicant Night*, maintaining the numbering convention established with *Blade Runner 2: The Edge of Human*. *Blade Runner 4: Eye and Talon* was never published in the U.S. and was originally titled *Blade Runner 4: Beyond Orion*, but publisher Victor Gollancz presumably changed it (for the better) because it revealed the twist at the novel's conclusion. The four-year publication gap between *Replicant Night* and *Eye and Talon* was the result of Jeter's contract with Bantam Books to write a trilogy of *Star Wars* novels about bounty hunters: *The Mandalorian Armor* (1998), *Slave Ship* (1998), and *Hard Merchandise* (1999).

Blade Runner 2: The Edge of Human.

author's original work without his or her permission.[2] It is not a kindly phrase, but accurate enough in Jeter's case. However, allow me to go one controversial step further. Rather than having served as legitimate sequels to Ridley Scott's masterpiece, Jeter's novels actually followed *Blade Runner* into a dark, rainy Los Angeles alley, beat it unconscious, and rummaged through its pockets looking for all of the visual elements and neo-noir atmosphere that gave Scott's version its ultimate success. Once done with his mugging, Jeter dressed himself up in Rick Deckard's overcoat, strapped on a Ridley Scott mask, went to the home of Dick's original novel, and treated *Sheep* like a female pleasure model replicant.

Jeter accomplished two things with his literary sequels, one of them being bold and interesting, and the other being a simulacrum of plagiarism. The bold and interesting aspect of Jeter's *The Edge of Human* (and his two follow-ups to a lesser extent) was his attempt to creatively bridge the chasm that exists between *Sheep*'s actual storyline and Scott's cinematic incarnation. As with any novel's big screen adaptation, a screenwriter and/or director often chooses not to carry over certain elements of the source material for the purposes of tightening the storyline, thus reducing the movie's length to something more digestible to both box office and moviegoer, or to give the story a setting more familiar to the audience. For example, Scott transformed *Sheep*'s post-apocalyptic, *kipplized*,[3] nuclear dust-covered 1992[4] San Francisco into an overpopulated, monsoonish, smog-ridden 2019 Los Angeles – something closer to what southern Californians might truly come to expect decades in the future.

Screenwriters may also choose to create composite characters that co-opt roles and lines of dialogue from two different characters, or completely transform a character to play a different role. Unexpectedly, Jeter did the opposite. For *Blade Runner*, Fancher and Peoples transformed *Sheep*'s J. R. Isidore, the "chickenhead" Van Nuys Pet Hospital employee who originally

---

[2] Glitz, Michael. Review of *Blade Runner 2: The Edge of Human*. Entertainment Weekly, 17 Nov 1995. http://ew.com/article/1995/11/17/blade-runner-2-edge-human. Accessed 27 Apr 2017.

[3] Dick coined the term "kipple" to describe the rubbish that, without human attempts to remove the debris, builds up over the course of time. In conversation, it is used to describe the principle of the second law of thermodynamics, which states that an isolated system's total entropy can only increase over time: "No one can win against kipple, except temporarily and maybe in one spot."

[4] Coincidental with *Blade Runner*'s release was the publisher's re-release of *Sheep*, which featured subtle revisions that placed the story in 2021, thus coinciding closer with the movie's chronological setting of 2019.

befriended replicants Priscilla "Pris" Stratton and Roy Batty, into the diseased and tragically-fated genetic designer J.F. Sebastian. With *The Edge of Human*, however, Jeter retained *both* characters, preserving Sebastian and, in his *Blade Runner*-verse debut, the stuttering J. R. Isidore, who has (since the end of *Sheep* and, logically, *Blade Runner*) been promoted to the head of the hospital since the "off-screen" death of his former boss, Hannibal Sloat.[5] *Wait,* you ask, *didn't Sebastian die in* Blade Runner? Patience. We'll get to that.

Another clever incorporation of *Sheep* elements into the *Blade Runner*-verse is Jeter's transformation of Rachael Rosen, Eldon Rosen's niece, into Sarah Tyrell, Eldon Tyrell's niece, complete with *real* childhood memories of baby spiders eating their mother.[6] In *Sheep*, Deckard administers the Voigt-Kampff test to Rachael Rosen, concluding rightly that she is a Nexus-6 android. Eldon Rosen, however, attempts to deceive Deckard and discredit the Voigt-Kampff method of differentiating android from human by explaining Rachael's lack of empathy as the result of her isolation from human contact (other than her parents) while aboard the interstellar vessel *Salander 3*, on which she was born. In *The Edge of Human*, Jeter gives Eldon Tyrell's human niece, Sarah, Rachael Rosen's cold and manipulative personality. Jeter also takes Rachael Rosen's alleged *Salander 3* experiences and uses them as the foundation for one particular plot thread in his second sequel, *Replicant Night*.

Clearly, Jeter's weaving of certain elements of *Sheep* into the *Blade Runner*-verse wasn't so much for the purposes of resolving contradictions between the two so much as it was to honor Dick's original work. In fact, I greatly appreciate Jeter's valiant attempt to combine elements of the two without using a heavy hand. Still, as I read through *The Edge of Human* and its successors, I found myself hoping Jeter would incorporate even more *Sheep* elements into his sequel novels, like the quasi-religious Mercerism movement, the "empathy box," social critic TV show *Buster Friendly and His Friendly Friends*, the disposition-altering Penfield Mood Organ, Deckard's (ex-)wife Iran,[7] or *Sidney's*

---

[5] Yes, head of the hospital. You don't need to see his identification. This isn't the chickenhead J. R. Isidore you're looking for. This shrewder and smarter J. R. Isidore can go about his business. Move along.

[6] In *Blade Runner*, Sarah Tyrell is merely mentioned but neither seen on-screen nor given a first name. In addition, the assertion that Rachael's borrowed memories are truly Sarah's, as the reader of Jeter's sequels will discover, may not be true after all.

[7] Although Deckard and Iran are married in *Sheep*, Deckard mentions his unnamed ex-wife in Harrison Ford's much-maligned voiceover featured in *Blade Runner*'s

Catalog. Eliminating elements that outright contradicted Scott's version and subsequently incorporating or modifying these additional elements (along with *Sheep*'s anti-nuclear war theme[8]) to fit the Scott-verse, as Jeter brilliantly did with Isidore/Sebastian and Rachael Rosen/Sarah Tyrell, would have been, in my opinion, a superior method of paying tribute to *Sheep*. Alas, a lost opportunity.

As for my charge that Jeter's derivative work was too derivative, bordering on plagiarism, it is not just my observation. Glitz also observed that Jeter's "habit of echoing dialogue and scenes from the film is annoying and begs comparisons he would do well to avoid."[9] This habit is evidenced throughout Jeter's three sequels and becomes tiring (bordering on obnoxious) from a storytelling point of view. It is almost as if Jeter had written his own fan-fiction *Blade Runner* novelization after the movie came out – yet another example of "literary necrophilia," despite the fact that Fancher and Peoples are still alive! – and found an opportunity in Bantam Books to release favorite excerpts within his larger body of work. Ironically, these mini-novelizations are the most compelling and well-written sections. That being said, I would have no issue with Jeter releasing an official *Blade Runner* novelization. However, as a *Blade Runner* fan, I do not need Jeter revisiting those scenes within the context of his sequels, either in flashback or in some sort of simulacrum (more on the simulacrum aspect later). *Blade Runner* is already etched permanently in my mind; I neither need nor want it retold to me as if I had never seen it.

Before I get into analyzing further the strengths and weaknesses of Jeter's *Blade Runner* trilogy, summaries of these novels are in order. I do this for purely practical reasons. If the reader of this essay hasn't already read Jeter's *Blade Runner* novels, they, in all likelihood, never will, especially after exposure to online reviews of the "Jeter-verse" trilogy, a vast majority of which declare Jeter's ultimate failure to capture the spirit of Scott's cult classic. Besides, Ridley Scott's 35-years-in-the-making sequel, *Blade Runner 2049*, directed by Denis Villeneuve, not only features a still-intact Tyrell Corporation headquarters but

---

1982 domestic and international theatrical releases. Had Jeter incorporated Iran into his novels in some fashion, even if only a mere mention, he would have likely referred to Iran as his ex-wife.

[8] *Blade Runner* never explains why animal life on earth is rare, leaving the audience to imagine that humanity's poor stewardship of the Earth was responsible.

[9] Glitz, Michael. Review of *Blade Runner 2: The Edge of Human*. Entertainment Weekly, 17 Nov 1995. http://ew.com/article/1995/11/17/blade-runner-2-edge-human. Accessed 27 Apr 2017.

also provides the audience with the canonical account of Rachael's death and proves that (at least certain) replicants do not need to be off-world to procreate. These three "historical" facts outright necessitate the Jeter trilogy's de-canonization, giving the prospective reader even less of a reason to read them.

Summary: *The Edge of Human*

A year after the events of *Blade Runner*, we find Deckard living in exile in the Pacific Northwest with Rachael, whom he believes is a Nexus-6 replicant with a four-year life span. Domiciling in a remote shack, Deckard and Rachael have agreed to extend their life together by cryogenically storing Rachael in a stolen Tyrell shipping container — designed to preserve replicant lifespans during lengthy transits to off-world colonies — and releasing her for a single day of blissful interaction with Deckard every two months.

Tyrell's niece and new head of the Tyrell Corporation — the heretofore-unnamed Sarah Tyrell — tracks Deckard down. A confused Deckard believes Sarah is a hallucination, but she explains that she was born during her parents' aborted attempt to leave the solar system aboard the interstellar vessel *Salander 3*, and that she served as Rachael's "templant."[10] Not only does Sarah accuse Deckard of miscounting the number of replicants he was hired to "retire" in the movie, but she also alleges that Pris was not a replicant. Pris was, she claims, human — a replicant-wannabe whose lack of empathy was learned from her replicant cohorts, and whose exhibited superhuman strength (as depicted in *Blade Runner*) found its source solely in the psychological strength of her misguided belief that she was a replicant. Exploiting the fact that he's now wanted for Pris's alleged murder,[11] Sarah offers Deckard a job tracking down a missing *sixth* replicant in return for clemency.[12] Sarah also claims that the United Nations — which wanted the Tyrell Corporation to make slave-labor

---

[10] In Jeter's trilogy, a "templ*ant*" (as opposed to "replic*ant*") is synonymous with "template."

[11] As in *Sheep*, only bone marrow analysis can definitively determine one's identity as a human or a replicant. In the case of *The Edge of Human*, Pris's status as human is merely alleged and never proven.

[12] The claim of a sixth replicant's existence is based on an alternate line of dialogue found in the theatrical and Director's Cut versions of *Blade Runner*, in which Bryant states that of the six replicants who returned to Earth illegally, only one — not two, per the workprint version and the 2007 Final Cut — was killed attempting to infiltrate the Tyrell Corporation.

replicants "more human than human" for the purposes of attracting emigrants for its off-world colonization program – wants to shift blame for the replicant rebellion onto the Tyrell Corporation and is threatening to destroy the company should the LAPD's blade runner unit fail to retire the fugitive replicant.

Forcibly escorted back to Los Angeles (later in the novel, Sarah – now in charge of Tyrell Corporation – orders Rachael's capsule removed and Deckard's shack torched), Deckard is taken to the Van Nuys Pet Hospital. There, he meets J. R. Isidore, who reveals the hospital's real purpose: to "convert" replicants so as to be undetectable by the Voigt-Kampff test and serve as an embarkation point for a replicant "Underground Railroad."

Deckard leaves the pet hospital and returns surreptitiously to Captain Harry Bryant's office to confront him about Pris and the alleged sixth replicant, only to discover his former boss had been recently murdered. Deckard escapes LAPD headquarters and seeks refuge in a blade runner safe house, where he finds two unlikely squatters: Tyrell genetic engineer J.F. Sebastian, who is alive (!) but not well,[13] and a deranged and maniacal Pris, whom Sebastian claims to have (somewhat) repaired after Deckard administered his fatal gunshot wounds in *Blade Runner*.

These two story elements – that Sebastian is alive and that Pris is, Jeter claims, human – constitute two of the most heavily criticized features of *The Edge of Human*, especially in light of the fact that Ridley Scott's movie outright declares that the LAPD discovered Sebastian's dead body in Eldon Tyrell's chambers and that Pris is a replicant. For Jeter's scenario to be the case involves either gross incompetence on the part of LAPD coroners (who I assume would know a dead body when they see one) or a high-level conspiracy to frame a burned-out cop for no apparent reason.[14]

Meanwhile, the human Roy Batty templant for the UN's combat-model replicant infiltrates a guarded hospital to abscond with ventilator-wearing Dave Holden and arranges for biomechanical replacements of Holden's heart and lungs at a secret facility. During Holden's post-operative recovery, Batty tries to convince Holden that *all* blade runners are replicants (to avoid potential ethical

---

[13] To stave off the deleterious effects of his Methuselah Syndrome, Sebastian self-amputated three of his limbs to reduce the workload for which is body core is responsible for sustaining.

[14] One would also think that, of anyone, a genetic designer like Sebastian would be in a position to know whether Pris was a replicant or human. I will side with Sebastian on this one.

problems with humans retiring replicants) and that Deckard is the missing sixth replicant for which he has been hired (by whom we do not know) to "retire." With the introduction of this unlikely duo, Dick's paranoia theme heightens as Holden struggles to determine whether it is Deckard or Batty who needs retirement. Once they track down Deckard, a violent confrontation erupts between Batty and Deckard. After Batty exhibits apparently superhuman strength, Holden is convinced that Batty is the replicant and retires (kills?) Batty.

As Sebastian continues scavenging among the LA ruins, he encounters a group of replicant sympathizers ("rep-symps"), the apparent leader of which gives Sebastian an old first-aid kit salvaged from Sarah Tyrell's former interstellar transport, *Salander 3*.

Deckard returns to Tyrell Corporation headquarters to confront and kill Sarah. He finds her sleeping silently in Eldon Tyrell's bed and moves to shoot her when, just before he pulls the trigger, Sarah contacts Deckard by video communication. Now believing the sleeping woman to be Rachael, Deckard listens to Sarah as she confesses her desire to engineer the destruction of the company out of hatred for her late uncle, who not only sexually abused her as a child but also played out his sick desires with Rachael. Thus, by claiming the sixth replicant could not be found, Sarah contrives the UN's complete destruction of the company's ziggurat-like headquarters. As the massive structure begins to implode, Rachael awakens and Holden arrives on the scene to help the two escape. Of course, Sarah's real-time video communication is later revealed to be a synthetic ruse. Jealous of Deckard's relationship with Rachael, Sarah earlier murdered Rachael and assumed her identity, hoping to become the object of Deckard's love.

Deckard and Rachael/Sarah, using false identities, emigrate from Earth and take up temporary residence on Mars to await follow-on immigration to the off-world colonies. Due to a verbal slipup, Sarah inadvertently reveals her true identity, but Deckard accepts the circumstances as they are and chooses to see how life on Mars with Sarah will play out.

Summary: *Replicant Night*

In Jeter's second sequel novel, we find Sarah Tyrell living a lonely life in a pre-fab hovel, depressed, suicidal, and loathing her relationship (or lack thereof) with Deckard. Deckard, we learn, has found employment off Mars to make ends meet as he and Sarah await follow-on immigration to the off-world

Blade Runner 3: Replicant Night.

colonies, which the UN has delayed indefinitely due to a rumored replicant rebellion. Deckard is now a paid consultant on an off-world-produced movie about his "real-life" experiences retiring the four "skin jobs" (featured in Scott's *Blade Runner*). Disgusted with the movie director's choice to kill actual replicants for the purposes of heightening the movie's realism, Deckard quits.

A fully recovered Holden arrives at Outer Hollywood, seeking to deliver to Deckard a briefcase containing the mental contents of the now-physically deceased Roy Batty templant, whose new mission is to deliver critical information important to the increasingly violent rep-symp movement we briefly encountered in *The Edge of Human*. Unfortunately, while seeking out Deckard, the studio misidentifies Holden as a stand-in actor assigned (ironically) to play his own role in a rehearsal of *Blade Runner*'s opening scene. Unexpectedly, the bullets are real, and an unwitting Leon Kowalski replicant kills Holden for good. The briefcase, however, makes it into Deckard's possession and he begins his trek back to Mars.

Before Deckard returns, Sarah is approached by two surviving members of a shadow element of the Tyrell Corporation tasked with returning the company back to economic power with a Tyrell at the helm. They convince Sarah, the last living Tyrell heir, to leave Mars and return to Earth. They arrive at the Scapa Flow, off the Scottish coast, where older interstellar craft – including her parents' faster-than-light (FTL) interstellar vessel, *Salander 3* – were scuttled to minimize temporal anomalies caused by the unsafe, early-model FTL drives. The two Tyrellites, for reasons unknown, urge her to discover what had caused her father, Anson, to go insane and murder her mother, Ruth, and then turn the knife upon himself, causing the ship's computers to abort the mission and raise Sarah on the return voyage to Earth.

Once aboard the temporal anomaly-ridden *Salander 3*, Sarah finds herself witnessing aspects of her mother's murder and father's suicide. Sarah also meets a 10-year-old girl who looks identical to her and calls herself Rachael. She dismisses both the relived events and the presumably mentally scarred Sarah/Rachael as hallucinations caused by the FTL drive's temporal hiccups. However, as Sarah departs the vessel, the young girl follows! Rachael is quite real, and her inexplicable presence outside the craft causes Sarah to drift deeper into insanity. Wanting nothing to do with the Tyrell Corporation, she murders her two owlish escorts and, with Rachael in hallucinatory tow, pilots their space yacht back to Mars to kill Deckard.

Meanwhile, Briefcase Batty informs Deckard that he works for the rep-symps and that Sebastian, who died in the period between the two sequel novels, arranged for the transformation of his cerebral contents into what is known popularly as a "dehydrated deity," a type of interactive drug. Briefcase Batty convinces Deckard to take the drug to receive Sebastian's important message from the rep-symps. Toward the end of the drug's effectiveness and thus the conclusion of Sebastian and Deckard's conversation, Sebastian hands Deckard his "message" – the *Salander 3* first-aid kit Sebastian had acquired from the rep-symps in *The Edge of Human* – which somehow (scientific explanation be damned) manifests itself in Deckard's hands after the drug wears off!

Soon afterwards, Sarah reunites with Deckard on Mars and attempts to murder him. Deckard, however, knocks Sarah unconscious, escaping with the young Sarah/Rachael, unsure of her true identity. During his escape, a man named Marley confronts Deckard, claiming that both Holden and Briefcase Batty are unwittingly working for the UN, which has infiltrated the rep-symp movement, and that he is the true leader of the replicant rebellion. Marley explains that the Earth generates a "morphogenetic field," the absence of which gradually mutates slave-labor replicants into biomechanical organisms capable of living beyond their programmed four-year life spans, developing empathy, and procreating! Human interstellar travelers, however, eventually lose their ability to empathize and become sterile. In a very real way, the further humans remove themselves from Earth's morphogenetic field, the more they become like replicants; conversely, the further replicants travel from Earth, the more human they become. Of course, this newfound humanity is "repealed" upon their return to Earth, foisting upon replicants once again the limitations Eldon Tyrell built into their genetic code. Should Deckard successfully deliver Briefcase Batty's "mimetic bomb" to the replicant rebellion, it would trigger the fail-safe Tyrell buried deep in the replicants' genetic code in the event replicants became more human: a program that will cause them to kill their own offspring, forestalling replicant population growth.

Sarah manages to track down Deckard and holds him at gunpoint. Deckard who discovered a picture of Anson and Ruth Tyrell – and their *twin* daughters! – in *Salander 3*'s first-aid kit, takes advantage of her mentally fragile state and reveals to Sarah that her parents were not Eldon Tyrell's actual brother and sister-in-law. They were, in fact, replicants Tyrell designed to travel to the Proxima system for the purposes of testing his theory about the relationship between Earth's morphogenetic field and changes in replicant morphology, as well as the fail-safe. During their trek, Anson and Ruth – both of whom believed they were human – had twin girls, Sarah and Rachael, but Anson's fail-safe coding triggered causing him to attempt to murder his children. While Ruth successfully hid Rachael in a sleep transport chamber, she didn't have enough time to hide Sarah. As a result, Anson slit Ruth's throat as she endeavored to protect Sarah. Distraught over murdering his wife, Anson committed suicide, leaving the girls unharmed. When *Salander 3* reached earth, Tyrell adopted Sarah as his niece; Rachael, however, remained hidden in a sleep chamber, emerging only after the Tyrell Corporation scuttled the vessel. As a result of *Salander 3*'s temporal anomalies, Rachael remained relatively young. With Deckard's revelation that Sarah is not human, Sarah's psyche cracks, and she commits suicide.

As the novel concludes, Deckard "adopts" the seemingly 10-year-old Rachael replicant and obtains approval to depart Mars for the off-world colonies, where she will presumably live beyond her four-year life span but where Deckard's capacity for empathy might deteriorate.

Summary: *Eye and Talon*

In the least convoluted of Jeter's three sequel novels, we are introduced to blade runner Iris Knaught, who is considered one of the best in the business. After retiring a replicant disguised as a human replicant impersonator (take a moment to figure that out), Meyer, Bryant's successor, gives her a new assignment: retrieve Eldon Tyrell's missing owl,[15] which is not (as Rachael bragged in *Blade Runner*) actually artificial. Meyer doesn't give Iris any information regarding who hired the LAPD to find the owl.

As Iris begins her search, she meets a man named Vogel, who gives her the location of Tyrell's owl. Iris and Vogel furtively obtain unauthorized high-tech weaponry from the LAPD's armory and infiltrate the hideout of the men who possess the owl. After an intense firefight, Iris and Vogel succeed in freeing the valuable fowl. Throughout her mission, however, she's come to distrust Meyer, so she returns to her own apartment with the owl rather than deliver it to LAPD headquarters, hoping to discover exactly for whom this particular predatory bird is so important. As she contemplates her next steps, an unidentified man breaks into her apartment, immobilizes her, and steals the owl.

---

[15] The owl's name is Scrappy. (Yes, really.)

Blade Runner 4: Eye and Talon.

Iris wakes up in the hospital and is confronted by Meyer, who not only informs her that she's been fired but also gives her mysterious GPS coordinates. Despite failing to capture the owl, Iris believes the coordinates may hold the key to determining the owl's current location and who took it from her possession – answers that she feels are important to fulfilling her clouded destiny. Arriving at the coordinates, Iris finds herself amidst the ruins of the Tyrell Corporation headquarters, where Vogel awaits and escorts her to Eldon Tyrell's still-intact, structurally-reinforced private chambers. Oddly, Iris confesses that she knows next to nothing about the infamous Rick Deckard's exploits, Tyrell's murder, or the UN's subsequent destruction of the Tyrell Corporation's headquarters. Surprised at Iris' ignorance, he shows her – using Tyrell's private theater and film projector (!) – Outer Hollywood director Urbenton's latest documentary, *Blade Runner*, which relates Rick Deckard's experiences as a burned-out cop brought back into service to retire four (or is it five?) escaped replicants, complete with CGI "texture-mapping and real-time animated tracking" that make the actors look just like the "real-life" characters.[16]

After viewing the movie, Vogel makes Iris aware that the Nexus-6 replicant Rachael looks exactly like her, and an identity crisis ensues. In one of this novel's several "intercuts," it is revealed to the reader that Vogel works for Urbenton, who has been filming Iris' entire mission/"awakening" (presumably for profit), and that Vogel had gone "off-script" in revealing to Iris her true nature too early. Urbenton's goons then enter the dilapidated ruins to capture Iris and Vogel.

Making their way to the highest point of the collapsed Tyrell Corporation, Iris and Vogel are abducted and taken to a desert compound by someone whom Iris believes is Urbenton. Instead, Iris's abductor/savior is the elderly Carsten, a former Tyrell competitor who went to enormous expense to bring Chew's Los Angeles eye laboratory, piece-by-piece, to his desert stronghold and reconstruct it. In yet another lengthy exposition, Carsten shows Iris a number of Eldon Tyrell replicants in stasis and explains why his group wanted Iris to

---

[16] Jeter seemingly predicted, in 2000, what Ridley Scott accomplished with 2007's *Blade Runner: The Final Cut*, which featured Harrison Ford's son, Ben, assisting Scott in digitally enhancing a scene in which Harrison Ford's mouth movements now match the recorded dialogue, and Johanna Cassidy reprising her role as the replicant Zhora (aka Salome) to replace the face of the obvious stunt double who crashed through plate glass windows during her escape attempt.

recover Tryell's owl. Eldon Tyrell, in an attempt to obtain immortality, had discovered a method by which he could – for safekeeping and future transfer to another Eldon Tyrell replicant – imprint his mental contents onto the owl's brain using each other's eyes as the conduit. ("Windows of the soul" indeed.) Carsten also explains that the UN was behind Roy Batty's infiltration of Tyrell headquarters, and that Batty crushed Tyrell's eyes to stop any further transfer from taking place, unaware that Tryell had, at some point prior to his murder, imprinted his mental contents onto the owl in the event of his premature death.

Carsten then shows Iris a stasis tube containing a Rachael replicant. Using her weapon, which Carsten had given back to her earlier as an act of good faith, Iris shoots and kills the Rachael replicant without a second thought. Immediately thereafter, a firefight ensues in which Meyer enters the freezing laboratory and kills both Carsten and Vogel. Meyer sees the dead Rachael replicant, whom he believes to be Iris, and leaves the desert compound without conducting a further search of the facility.

After Meyer's spinner departs, another spinner arrives and touches down. Exiting the laboratory, Iris spots an owl flying overhead and alighting onto the spinner pilot's arm. The pilot is Rick Deckard, who admits to stealing the owl from Iris' apartment. With him is the young Rachael replicant. Iris asks whether they could take her back to Los Angeles, but Rachael flatly states that they can't possibly "take her back" to a place Iris has never been, implying that the Los Angeles in which she worked as a blade runner is not on Earth, but rather a simulacrum on one of the off-world colonies. Deckard promises to tell the confused Iris everything, and the trio walks back to the spinner.

Finis.

After three novels, Rick Deckard has truly gotten nowhere in life and found only more questions than answers. The replicant Rachael is dead. The Rachael templant, Sarah, is dead. He has Sarah's twin sister Rachael, a second-generation replicant child, whom he has to treat like a daughter, in tow. He's also just picked up a dazed Rachael replicant named Iris (do you get her name now?). And we have absolutely no idea whether the original *Blade Runner* actually took place on Earth, or whether Marty McFly actually saved the day by transporting a copy of *Blade Runner* from the future to 1982 so a Tyrell Corporation could never come into being. If you ask me, Jeter's *Blade Runner* trilogy is pretty darn weird and a boring version of weird at that. If the reader finds my summaries somewhat intriguing or exciting, I'll take that as a compliment.

"More Dick than Dick" is Our Motto

I charged Jeter earlier in this essay with, using Glitz's words, "literary necrophilia." Allow me to delve a little deeper into the reasons behind my indictment by showing how Jeter failed to honor Dick. As Dick related to Paul M. Sammon, author of *Future Noir: The Making of Blade Runner*, "the moral and philosophical ambiguities it [*Sheep*] dealt with are really very profound; *Sheep* stemmed from my basic interest in the problem of differentiating the authentic human being from the reflexive machine, which I call an android. In my mind android is a metaphor for people who are psychologically human but behaving in a nonhuman way." With the Vietnam War's literal and psychological battlefields serving as inspiration, Dick used *Sheep* to explore the danger of humanity turning apathetic if it plunged headlong to the business of cold-blooded death-dealing to eliminate perceived existential threats. In *Sheep* and *Blade Runner*, the existential threats are androids ("andys") or replicants ("skin jobs"), respectively.[17] Could humanity, Dick wonders, become the very apathetic thing it created? Could there ever come a role reversal of sorts in which, biologically speaking, there is very little physical difference while a profound "spiritual" chasm nevertheless exists between the two, with souls eventually emerging in replicants and humanity devolving into something "less human than human"? More to the point, could human blade runners become the very thing they hunted by willfully ignoring the humanity Deckard recognized in a dying Roy Batty?

Like Dick, Scott explored *Sheep*'s core thematic question – *What does it mean to be human?* – but with one significant difference: He dispensed with the psychological vehicles Dick used in *Sheep*, namely conspiracy-fueled paranoia and altered states of consciousness.[18] In *Sheep*, Dick's conspiracy is

---

[17] Sammon, Paul M. *Future Noir: The Making of Blade Runner* (New York: Harper Prism, 1996), p. 16.
[18] Dick used conspiracy-fueled paranoia and altered states of consciousness to propel the story in many of his other works, such as the short stories "The Adjustment Team" (1954; adapted as *The Adjustment Bureau* in 2011), "Minority Report" (1956; adapted to film in 2002), and "We Can Remember It for You Wholesale" (1966; adapted as *Total Recall* in 1990 and 2012), as well as the novel *A Scanner Darkly* (1977; adapted to film in 1996).

relatively simple: Illegally-present androids have established a shadow San Francisco Police Department and fashioned a replicant version of the Civil War-era "Underground Railroad" to protect its own, a concept Jeter runs with very briefly in *The Edge of Human*. The android contingent even goes so far as to employ human bounty hunter Phil Resch (briefly suspected to be a replicant by both he and Deckard) to give the law enforcement counterfeit an air of authenticity.

When Scott dispensed with Dick's atmosphere of paranoia, he changed the *feel* of Dick's original story (I would argue) for the better, for *Sheep*'s conspiracy was nothing more than an obstacle put in the path of Deckard's mission to retire replicants. In contrast, Jeter's sequels put the conspiracy motif front and center. This is not necessarily a good thing. Instead of merely emulating Dick, Jeter puts the conspiracy motif into overdrive, injecting into the *Blade Runner*-verse an *overdose* of paranoia-fueled machinations, altering the reader's mindset to the point that he or she begins to doubt that every character and every locale is not who or what they seem to be. The conspiracies are so intricate – and bordering on the ludicrous – that Jeter ends up sacrificing the action and human drama that Scott employed so well for... talking. A lot of talking.

Jeter's trilogy exhibits a voluminous amount of indulgent exposition, and for good reason: It may have been the only way Jeter could keep track of his own convoluted intrigues. In the end, however, Jeter seemed to succumb to his own impatience and frustration in peering through the web of conspiratorial lies he'd spun, forcing Deckard's various manipulators to unveil each book's primary machination toward the end of each novel in grand Scooby-Doo fashion. These complicated conspiracies are so confusing that Jeter likely couldn't successfully incorporate the required plot threads into the narrative without moving into Tom Clancy-length tomes. Even Iris, Jeter's protagonist in *Eye and Talon*, becomes impatient with her abductor's lengthy monologue while standing, for what seems like several hours, in a laboratory-sized freezer slowly succumbing to hypothermia. In a way, it is a shame Jeter wasn't able to write another *Blade Runner* novel, because *Eye and Talon*'s conspiracy was the least intricate and the most compelling, as if Jeter had learned some, but not all, lessons from his first two installments' poor reception.[19]

---

[19] I must also point out that *Eye and Talon*'s writing style is so different from *The Edge of Human* and *Replicant Night* that I initially wondered if another author had

We Can (Mis)remember It for You Wholesale

Interestingly, the primary source for Jeter's conspiracies lay in his transforming "beloved mistakes,"[20] which resulted from *Blade Runner*'s complex editing process, into intentional plot devices seemingly designed for someone like Jeter to exploit. For example, Jeter's implication that Rick Deckard may be a replicant does not find its origin, as one might suspect, in Deckard's unicorn dream and Gaff's intimation that he knows the contents of Deckard's head by leaving him an origami clue outside Deckard's apartment – a scene Ridley Scott insists is Deckard's *a-ha!* moment. Rather than capitalizing on such low-hanging fruit, Jeter instead chooses a single alternate line of dialogue found only in the theatrical and *Director's Cut* versions of *Blade Runner*. In this particular line, Bryant states that of the six replicants who returned to Earth illegally,[21] only *one* – not two, per the 1982 workprint version and the 2007 *Final Cut* – was killed attempting to infiltrate the Tyrell Corporation, leaving Deckard's job ultimately unfinished. (Deckard's eventual realization in *The Edge of Human* that he possesses poor math skills is quite laughable.) It is as if Jeter lacked respect for the humanness of filmmaking and abused these beloved mistakes like Tyrell abused his niece.

Jeter's second fuel source for the trilogy's overarching conspiracy is, unfortunately, various plot holes that existed in the final version of Fancher and People's screenplay. "How is it," Jeter's characters muse,

> that the weak-chinned Leon Kowalski replicant[22] could sneak a weapon into the ultra-secure Tyrell Corporation headquarters… unless he had help? If Leon were a commonly produced, easily recognizable replicant, why would the LAPD even require Holden to administer the Voigt-Kampff test… unless the LAPD wanted Holden to die? And why would the Tyrell Corporation's sanitation department hire a commonly produced replicant model… unless the conspirators wanted Leon to infiltrate the Tyrell Corporation for the purpose of assassinating Eldon Tyrell?

---

ghost-written it. The presence of Jeter's other literary excesses, however, gave away its true authorship.

[20] A term used by Charles de Lauzirika, restoration producer for Scott's 2007 *Blade Runner: The Final Cut*. This complex editing process resulted in at least eight different versions, five of which found a home in deluxe versions of *The Final Cut*.

[21] This raises the important question of how it is that a replicant's actions can be considered illegal if a replicant has no rights.

[22] Jeter tells us, nearly every time Leon is mentioned, that the replicant is "weak-chinned." Jeter also spares no opportunity to remind the reader that Deckard's hairstyle is "brush-cut." Please, make it stop.

"There must be," various characters claim throughout the Jeter-verse, "a vast UN conspiracy to take over the Earth and the off-world colonies!"

Jeter's over-analysis of Scott's film and overreliance on continuity errors and plot holes to power his books' narratives become a secondary reason, I believe, for the books' poor reception. When one builds a narrative based purely on the shortcomings of *Blade Runner*'s storywriters and film editors, it raises questions about the extent of the author's creative palette. In a twist of irony, Jeter's own *templant* concept, which is completely absent in *Blade Runner*, is called into serious question if identifying replicants – whose physical characteristics are based on known "originals" – is a relatively academic exercise. Why even administer the Voigt-Kampff test when simple facial recognition will do?[23] Whoops.

They're Only "Mostly Dead"

Another significant shortcoming of Jeter's *Blade Runner* sequels is the lack of original characters. Even the trilogy's most interesting character, Iris, turns out to be a Rachael Tyrell replicant. While Jeter's introduction of an original Roy Batty templant (or is he?) in *The Edge of Human* is a somewhat plausible extension of the *Blade Runner* storyline, Jeter unnecessarily resurrects two other characters. The first is J.F. Sebastian. *But,* you ask, *didn't Roy Batty kill Sebastian in* Blade Runner? Yes. Yes, he did. Not only do we witness Deckard use his LAPD-issued Steyr Pflager Katsumata Series-D Blaster[24] to gift Pris with three[25] massive holes in her torso, we also hear Bryant inform Deckard that police discovered Sebastian's body along with Tyrell's in the latter's private bed chamber. By the end of *The Edge of Human*, Jeter's choice to resurrect Sebastian was seemingly nothing more than a plot device for Sarah to blackmail Deckard with the accusation that he carelessly murdered Pris and is a wanted criminal in the eyes of the law.

---

[23] To the lengths Jeter goes to develop his storylines, I am shocked Jeter did not make a conspiracy of Deckard's cheek, which mysteriously appears abraised in pre-Final Cut versions in the scene *prior* to his violent confrontation with Leon, who causes the facial wound.

[24] http://www.imfdb.org/wiki/(Blade_Runner)_-_LAPD_2019_Blaster. Accessed 6 May 2017.

[25] Per the international cut (1982) and Final Cut (2007). Two holes per the U.S. domestic cut (1982) and Director's Cut (1992).

Wait, you demand, *didn't Deckard retire Pris in* Blade Runner*?* Yes. Yes, he did. *And wasn't Pris a replicant?* This is also true... until Jeter causally claimed she wasn't. Not only do I suspect Dick rolled in his grave with this new revelation (Pris was, after all, an android in *Sheep*), I can imagine Ridley Scott returning to Warner Brothers's prop archives, hoping to find Deckard's unfinished bottles of Johnnie Walker and get sloppy drunk. Certainly, Sarah Tyrell's allegation – that Pris was actually a human replicant-wannabe – might sound authoritative given her status as Eldon Tyrell's successor, but I find it impossible to believe. Firstly, given the internal damage Deckard caused Pris, he should not have fallen for Sarah's assertion. Secondly, Pris – replicant or not – would have bled out by the time a revived Sebastian – a genetic designer who would have been able to tell the difference between a "skin job" and a human being[26] – made it back to his apartment to save her. (Even *Sheep*'s Isidore, a "special" not physically or mentally eligible to emigrate from Earth, was able to conclude eventually that a cat he attempted to repair was real.) Throughout both *The Edge of Human* and *Replicant Night*, I had hoped the truth of Pris's replicant nature would have been reaffirmed or, at the very least, Deckard would have dismissed Sarah's claim outright. Alas, I was too generous in my expectations. Not only did Jeter maintain his literary lie throughout his novels, it also resulted in Deckard looking less clever than we know he is.

Absurd Intelligence: The New A.I.

Jeter also seems to appreciate J.F. Sebastian's hobby of designing biomechanical "toys" for companions so much that he once again moves too far beyond the source material – in this case, Scott's *Blade Runner*. In *Blade Runner*, replicants are depicted as extremely high-end, expensive "products," which Scott imbues with more humanity than the humans that created and (ab)use them, a lesson Deckard learns in his paradigm-shifting rooftop encounter with Roy Batty. Sadly, Jeter waters down this motif by introducing an entirely new class of biomechanical A.I. so commonplace that they're available to the masses. In *Replicant Night*, this class of A.I. takes the form of walking and

---

[26] In the *Blade Runner*-verse, Sebastian's ability to revive Pris is absolutely ludicrous, especially considering they are, for the most part, genetically human. However, if Jeter was trying to stay true to *Sheep*, in which androids were more "mechanical" in nature, such ability could be theoretically possible. Of course, since bone marrow analysis was the only sure-fire method to tell the difference in *Sheep* (and Jeter's novels), the Rosens' craftsmanship of androids must have been fine work indeed!

talking clocks and calendars, both of which emote as much as a human butler or replicant slave would, expressing concern for – and fear of – its masters. In *Eye and Talon*, the absurd A.I. is a talking, robotic cat, called – wait for it – a "chat." (Insert eye-roll or groan here.)

Unfortunately, Jeter's sentient timekeepers are, in the context of the story, absurd and annoying, and his imbuing them with human-like personalities ends up cheapening the overarching sociological question Dick and Scott attempt to explore in their respective works. Even viewers of *Blade Runner* are meant to empathize with Sebastian's unique biomechanical creations – bear-faced, button-eyed, Napoleonic Colonel Fuzzy and Pinocchio-nosed, Kaiser Wilhelm-garbed Squeaker Hussar[27] – especially considering their ability to exhibit emotion, such as fear.[28] Admittedly, Jeter's creation of these commercial "devices" has a basis in Sebastian's gene-manipulating hobby, but he turns Sebastian's quirky talent into something any high-tech company could replicate.

It is not just Jeter's talking clocks and calendars that blunt Dick and Scott's concerns about humanity's rapid descent into apathetic inhumanity. It is his equally absurd resurrection of the Roy Batty templant – killed by Holden in *The Edge of Human* – as a sentient, talking briefcase on an alleged mission to recruit Deckard to the rep-symp cause in *Replicant Night*. Unfortunately, the absurdity doesn't end with Briefcase Batty. Jeter dials the level of absurdity to 11 with his second (!) resurrection of J.F. Sebastian, who apparently died "off camera" between *The Edge of Human* and *Replicant Night*. Poor Sebastian now exists as a "dehydrated deity," a packet of sentient, mind-altering drugs capable of not only communicating with its user – in this case, for the purposes of passing along critical information from his rep-symp cohorts to Deckard – but also easily passing the Turing test. (Do not get me started on the metaphysical paradox of Deckard's ability to manifest, while coming out of his drug-induced conversation with Sebastian, a *Salander 3* first-aid kit, physically given to Sebastian by the rep-symps in *The Edge of Human* and later passed on to Deckard... *in his mind!*[29])

---

[27] Colonel Fuzzy and Squeaker Hussar are first named in *The Edge of Human*. While *The Edge of Human* reintroduces these sentient "toys," they do not serve much of a role beyond helping Sebastian scavenge to survive in the ruins of Los Angeles.
[28] At least in Squeaker's case; we cannot read the good colonel's face well.
[29] Yes, *Sheep*'s empathy box can result in psychosomatic injury, but this is not the same as manifesting inanimate objects out of thin air.

"More Movie Than Movie" is Our Motto

If you groaned at Jeter's preposterous idea of Deckard serving as a consultant on a movie about his blade runner career in *Replicant Night*, Vogel showing Iris the movie *Blade Runner* in *Eye and Talon* leaps headlong into face-palm territory. Jeter appears to have been so in love with the idea of transforming our real-life movie-going experience into a simulacrum of the Jeter-verse's film that he nearly breaches the "fourth wall," the literary convention that assumes the existence of an invisible wall between reader/audience and the characters/actors. When Iris responds in the negative to Vogel's question as to whether she had seen the movie, Jeter – with tongue firmly in cheek – has Vogel retort, "You should know about this one. It was a big hit, just about everywhere, got very high ratings. And beyond: it's still got quite a cult following."[30]

Even worse is Vogel's explanation for the movie's realism: "So what you wind up with on the screen is indistinguishable from what you would've gotten if you had been there right on the spot, taping as the actual events were happening. And in some ways... This is *better* than mere reality would have been. Inasmuch as it contains all the information available in reality – faces, the places – but in an enhanced, editable form."[31] Carsten, however, later claims that Vogel was mistaken, that the reason Urbenton's movie is so realistic is that "it was in fact the actual taped record of what happened"! In discussing the scene depicting Roy Batty's murder of Tyrell, Carsten observes, "A very detailed shot, isn't it? ... When the makers of the film edited down the shots from the concealed video cameras, they went for the right close-up, to make sure that we could see exactly what happened. What the Batty replicant did to Tyrell, other than simply kill him. Tell me, what do you see? What *did* happen then? What did the movie show?"[32]

Sadly, it doesn't end there. While Jeter does not have Vogel actually breach the fourth wall, he certainly has him scrabbling to scale it with this revelation: "Oh, this was only the *first* movie... There was actually a sequel, called *The Edge of Human*. That explained a lot more."[33] This degree of authorial self-awareness is not even worthy of a face-palm. It is more worthy of a face-hugger.

---

[30] *Eye and Talon*, p. 123.
[31] *Eye and Talon*, p. 127.
[32] *Eye and Talon*, p. 221.
[33] *Eye and Talon*, p. 129.

Er... Sorry. Right director, wrong movie.³⁴ (Focus, Mike... focus.)

How the Jeter-verse Could Have Been... Modified

Ultimately, Jeter's *Blade Runner* sequels are literary failures. It is not just because they overemphasize exposition to plaster over their flawed conspiratorial foundations (another writer could have condensed the plots of all three novels into one³⁵), but also because they lacked characters with emotional depth and social awareness, as well as the same kind of thrilling action that Scott does so well. In addition to unnecessarily resurrecting *Blade Runner* characters and cheapening his source material's social commentary, Jeter fills out his *dramatis personæ* with one-dimensional characters, such as film director Urbenton, Tyrell acolytes Wycliffe and Zwingli,³⁶ and Iris's owl-knapping companion Vogel. Even Sarah Tyrell's depression is so clichéd that during my first (and unsuccessful) attempt to read *Replicant Night* nearly two decades ago, I found myself unable – until the lead up to *Blade Runner 2049* – to read beyond her overwrought suicidal and sociopathic tendencies.

To write successful literary successors to *Blade Runner*, Jeter should have focused more on Deckard's search for the truth regarding his own identity and explored further the sociopolitical aspects of the rep-symp "replicant rights" movement. While Jeter briefly touched on these themes, they were left untouched in any meaningful way. They were, in a phrase, literary "one-night stands." They didn't even rise to the level of literary "friends with benefits." Either way, Jeter simply did not seem committed to writing about the things that concerned Dick or Scott. Thus, I have to question why the Blade Runner Partnership even allowed these stories to be published in the first place. Was it

---

³⁴ However, Ridley Scott's *Prometheus* sequel, *Alien: Covenant*, comes close to hinting that *Blade Runner* and the *Alien* saga share the same universe.

³⁵ Another common complaint beyond Jeter's wordiness is his constant overuse of personal descriptors. How many times do Eldon Tyrell and his devotees need to be described as owlish? Just about every time the characters are discussed. How many times do we need to be reminded that Iris is wearing a cowboy shirt? Just about every time she's described. Literary Muse, make it stop! It is almost as if Jeter had a word count minimum and consistently repeated characters' descriptions to meet that minimum.

³⁶ Named after 14th-century Roman Catholic dissident John Wycliffe and 16th-century Swiss Reformation leader Ulrich Zwingli, respectively. It is beyond me why Jeter named the Tyrell devotees after, of all things, religious dissidents.

merely Jeter's status as both Dick's friend and colleague and an author in his own right? If so, these are poor reasons indeed.

In the end, what resulted was a trilogy of poorly written *Sheep* sequels dressed up in *Blade Runner* dust jackets. While Jeter attempted as best he could to emulate Dick's penchant for crafting stories featuring conspiracy, paranoia, and illicit drug use, he apparently did so without a true understanding of what made Ridley Scott tick. Although clearly a fan of both Dick's novel and Scott's movie, Jeter was simply not suited to write with *both* in mind.

I do believe, however, that *Eye and Talon* came closest to being a true *Blade Runner* sequel. Its focus on Tyrell's commercial pursuit of "more human than human" as a personal attempt to attain true immortality of the soul was the only aspect of his trilogy that rang true to both Dick's and Scott's visions. Are we, Jeter essentially asks, *gestalt*? Are we more than the sum of our parts? It is unfortunate, however, that it took the majority of Jeter's three novels (his exploration of this theme only comes at *Eye and Talon*'s conclusion) to get somewhat close to *Blade Runner*'s philosophical core.

From *Eye and Talon*'s cliffhanger ending, it is clear Jeter intended to continue the story. However, because of his failure to craft true *Blade Runner* sequels, we will never know what Jeter intended for what must be one of the oddest family units in science-fiction history. Jeter's failures, however, may not be a bad thing. Had his novels been monumental successes, they might very well have served as the basis for new, non-Ridley Scott-produced *Blade Runner* films. This was not too far out of the question, especially considering screenwriter Stuart Hazeldine's aborted attempt in the late 1990s to adapt *The Edge of Human* for the big screen. Perhaps the Blade Runner Partnership, which holds the movie rights, ultimately felt that Jeter's novels failed to ask the right questions or, alternatively, answer the right questions satisfactorily.

Other, more recent attempts by the Blade Runner Partnership to make a cinematic sequel seemed to ignore the Jeter-verse. Nearly a decade after *The Edge of Human*, screenwriters Travis Wright and John Glenn were Batty-ing around[37] *Blade Runner* sequel ideas with Bud Yorkin, ideas that asked questions such as, "What does it mean to be human? That's the central question in life and the paramount question in science fiction. More pointedly: Is or is not Deckard a replicant? What happens to Rachael? What are the off-world colonies like? What happens to replicants once Tyrell is killed by one of his

---

[37] See what I did there?

creations? These are some of the questions we explored with Bud Yorkin for a few years and I believe are a great basis for a story many fans like me are dying to see. Working on them has been a dream."[38] *Wait*, you say, *didn't Jeter touch on these very same questions?* Yes. Yes, he did. Just not very well.

This is Not Called Execution... It's Called Retirement

Now that *Blade Runner 2049* has been released, it is clear that, with the exception of dealing with Rachael's fate, producer Ridley Scott, director Denis Villeneuve, and screenwriters Hampton Fancher and Michael Green chose not to explore in the same fashion many of Wright's and Glenn's questions, which clearly retread Jeter-verse territory. Even *Blade Runner 2049* doesn't establish Deckard's replicant status definitively. However, moving forward, I am interested to see whether future *Blade Runner* movies or spin-off literature will utilize elements of Jeter's novels in much the same way Disney's new *Star Wars* canon exploits material from the massive *Star Wars* Expanded Universe that Disney unceremoniously de-canonized in 2014.[39]

Personally, I'm satisfied that *Blade Runner 2049* has "retired" Jeter's *Blade Runner* trilogy. It is a fitting end to a body of work that not only failed to live up to the spirit of both Dick's and Scott's respective legacies but also failed to release the dove it held in its firm, replicant grip.

---

[38] Sciretta, Peter. "Exclusive: Screenwriter Travis Wright Responds to *Blade Runner 2* Story," Film: Blogging the Real World. http://www.slashfilm.com/exclusive-screenwriter-travis-wright-responds-to-blade-runner-2-story. Accessed 29 Apr 2017.

[39] I am decidedly unhappy about Lucasfilm declaring the Expanded Universe non-canonical. See my essays on *Star Wars: Dark Empire* and *Star Wars* canon in Sequart's *A Galaxy Far, Far Away: Exploring Star Wars Comics* (2016) and *A More Civilized Age: Exploring the Star Wars Expanded Universe* (2017), respectively.

Philip K. Dick on the Screen

by Zaki Hasan

"Pain is temporary, but film is forever."

While the exact source of that phrase has been obscured by the mists of time, it's entirely applicable to the production and aftermath of Ridley Scott's *Blade Runner*. The famously troubled production performed underwhelmingly at the box office during its initial 1982 release, but the ultimate testament to what Scott, writers Hampton Fancher and David Peoples, and star Harrison Ford were able to accomplish with their adaptation of Philip K. Dick's novel *Do Androids Dream of Electric Sheep?* is plain to see in the mammoth mountain of works that have sprung up in its wake.

At least some of the credit for this can go to Scott's conceptualization of future Los Angeles, one that transcended any fantasy cityscape that had been depicted up to that time, and which permanently marked *Blade Runner* as an artifact worth admiration and appreciation for its craft above and beyond its sophisticated narrative. The visual shorthand that Scott established as Deckard goes about investigating the central whodunit was so distinctive that it easily lent itself to imitation and variation.

Indeed, although nearly four decades went by without a true "sequel" to *Blade Runner* emerging (with the ultimate "need" for said sequel still an open question), the project nonetheless proved enormously influential stylistically, tonally, and thematically. Whether 1984's unintentionally hilarious *Runaway*, starring Tom Selleck as a robot chaser in the Rick Deckard vein, Tim Burton's *Batman* in 1989, or Alex Proyas' 1998 *Dark City* taking visual cues from Scott's dystopia, there's been a steady stream of celluloid replicants that have emulated, paid homage to, and otherwise followed in *Blade Runner*'s neo-noir footsteps.

But above and beyond the many stylistic riffs on Scott's film (which followed a very similar pattern of imitation and homage that occurred after his *Alien* in 1979 ignited imaginations by bringing the "Old Dark House" horror movie tropes into the space age), there are also the many, many screen adaptations of Dick's voluminous catalogue that flowed in *Blade Runner*'s wake, none of which would likely have existed were it not for the considerable shadow that it cast in the public psyche.

In a sad irony, the author himself passed away far too young at age 53 (if ever a life burned twice as bright and half as long, this was it), mere months before *Blade Runner*'s theatrical release. He was thus never able to witness the transformative role his original tome would come to play in the annals of cinematic science fiction and the many other projects derived from his work that would follow in its wake.

Now, I grant that the some of these projects were far more successful (creatively and/or commercially) than others, but their sheer ubiquity on the screen for decades now nonetheless speaks to the author's enduring appeal long after his stories first appeared, and nearly 40 years after his passing. They all benefited from his unerring ability to hone in on omnipresent human fears and frailties, all the while incorporating discussions of identity and isolation juxtaposed with dystopian visions of dark tomorrows. The first post-*Blade Runner* Dick adaptation to hit the screens emerged eight years later, with 1990's *Total Recall*.

Based on the Dick short story "We Can Remember It for You Wholesale," *Recall* posits a future world where false memories of experiences are sold like tourism packages. While the rights were scooped up by *Alien* writers Dan O'Bannon and Ronald Shusett before *Blade Runner* was even released, the project spent most of the 1980s kicking around from one studio to another with none quite ready to pull the trigger on the ambitious project (which at one point had David Cronenberg lined up to direct).

Though actors such as Richard Dreyfuss and Patrick Swayze were mooted to star at various points, it wasn't until Arnold Schwarzenegger, then at the absolute peak of his superstar allure, expressed interest in the project that it

The movie poster for *Total Recall* (1990).

quickly came together at (now-defunct) Carolco, with *Soldier of Orange* and *Flesh and Blood* director Paul Verhoeven signed to helm. Verhoeven has a sensibility that's about as distinctly different from Ridley Scott's as possible, but he nonetheless proved the right choice for *Recall* in exactly the same way Scott was for *Blade Runner*.

Upon its summer 1990 release, *Total Recall* received a generally positive reception from critics; it also found the kind of box office success that eluded *Blade Runner*, ending its run with nearly $300 million worldwide against a $60 million budget. In addition to the action and pyrotechnics, it boasted some spectacular and gruesome effects courtesy of Rob Bottin (of John Carpenter's *The Thing*, which opened the exact same day as *Blade Runner*), a terrific, percussive score by the late Jerry Goldsmith, and big Arnold at his most "everyman," as a construction worker-turned-super-spy (or so he thinks).

Upon reflection, and with nearly three decades of remove, a big part of *Total Recall*'s effectiveness stems from one of Schwarzenegger's strongest leading turns, as well as solid supporting performances by Ronny Cox, Michael Ironside, and Sharon Stone (who Verhoeven would turn into a star the following year with *Basic Instinct*). Further, Verhoeven's biting, satirical instinct (so brilliantly expressed in *RoboCop* just a few years prior) was perfectly at home in Dick's futuristic milieu, and broader meditations on the nature of identity and reality itself proved quite the potent mix with contemporary audiences. In fact, in terms of broad-based commercial acceptance, *Total Recall* was arguably the peak for Philip K. Dick adaptations.

Interestingly enough, in a sort of Philip K. Dick feedback loop, a short-lived TV series called *Total Recall 2070* aired for one season on Showtime in 1999, and while it had practically nothing to do with the film whose name it appropriated, it was nonetheless quite obviously (and embarrassingly) indebted to the style and tone of *Blade Runner*. There would also be a far less successful remake of *Total Recall* in 2012 directed by Len Wiseman that managed to lose Verhoeven's aesthetic, Dick's ideas, and any audience interest in one fell swoop.

Nonetheless, *Total Recall*'s rapturous reception in 1990 was just as much a factor as *Blade Runner* (if not even more so, given that it actually turned a hefty profit during its initial run) in the continued presence of Dick's work onscreen for the next several decades. The next such cinematic adaptation arrived in 1995, rooted in the short story "Second Variety," and given the new title *Screamers*. Like *Total Recall*, this one featured a Dan O'Bannon script, and like

Total Recall, it spent several years in development before going into production.

Unlike *Total Recall*, however, *Screamers* came and went without making much of a mark, falling far short of its $20 million budget and getting apathetic notices from contemporaneous critics. Nonetheless, the Christian Duguay-directed film, starring *RoboCop*'s Peter Weller as a hard bitten military man facing off against human-looking murder machines called "Screamers" on an alien planet (that looks a lot like Canada), is a taut, minimalist production whose low budget actually adds to the feeling of isolation and tension that are so central to the piece. For completeness sake, I should mention that *Screamers* also spawned a straight-to-video sequel 14 years later, but honestly, the less said about that one, the better.

2002 would prove especially fruitful when it came to Dick adaptations with two movies hitting theaters within months of each other. Of these, one was remarkably successful, while the other...less so. First came director Gary Fleder's *Impostor*, released in January and based on a 1953 short story. The film stars Gary Sinise as a man who may or may not be who he thinks he is (so, comfortably in Dick's wheelhouse), and while it has an intriguing premise, it feels stretched too thin (understandable, since this is exactly what happened, as it was originally intended as a 40-minute short before its length was extended). *Imposter* cost $40 million to make, and earned only a fraction of that, coming and going from theaters before most audiences even realized it existed. It was an ignominious fate for an intriguing concept that deserved better than what it got. It's worth mentioning that *Impostor* also came to television in a 1962 episode of the British science-fiction anthology *Out of This World*, hosted by Boris Karloff, which gives it the distinction of being the very first Dick adaptation for either big screen or small.

Next came *Minority Report* in summer of 2002, based on the 1956 short story of the same name. In what had by then become a well-worn recurring motif for attempting to make any films from Philip K. Dick stories, this one spent a decade in development before finally going into production. The rights were initially scooped up to serve as the framework upon which to build a *Total Recall* sequel. I guess we should all be grateful that didn't happen.

Minority Report tells of Washington DC's police force in the near future, where crime is prevented before it occurs thanks to the powers of three "precog" mutants who can predict the future. It was one of the author's earlier works, and as such pointed the way towards exactly the kind of narrative

The movie poster for *Minority Report* (2002).

terrain that he'd mine again and again in *Do Androids Dream of Electric Sheep?* and many other works, such as embedded patterns of behavior, systems of control, and what kind of involvement we actually have in the decisions we think we're making.

Given the commercial and storytelling possibilities in that premise, it's not too surprising that the project eventually worked its way out of development hell. What *is* slightly surprising, however, is that the director who helped guide it along was none other than Steven Spielberg. Given Spielberg's specialization in crowd-pleasing, family-friendly opuses (the rousing success of his *E.T.: The Extra-Terrestrial* in 1982 is at least partly to blame for *Blade Runner*'s less-than-stellar box office reception), his decision to film *Minority Report* might have seemed an odd fit.

Nonetheless, teaming with star Tom Cruise as Detective John Anderton, head of Washington DC's "Precrime" unit, Spielberg lent *Minority Report* a visual style that's at least as distinctive as what Ridley Scott was able to do with *Blade Runner*. And while some of the deviations from Dick (via a script by Scott Frank and Jon Cohen) end up lessening some of its overall impact in favor of something a bit more easily digestible by mainstream audiences, it's nonetheless a visual feast, and one that proved exactly as successful as one would expect from a Spielberg-Cruise pairing.[1]

2003 saw another director with a distinct visual style try his hand at the master of psychological science fiction with John Woo's *Paycheck*. Based on a 1953 short story, this one starred Ben Affleck as a "reverse engineer" who guarantees his strict adherence to confidentiality by having his memories erased following the successful completion of his contracts. Also appearing were Uma Thurman as the requisite love interest, and Aaron Eckhardt as the antagonist.

While *Paycheck* is a serviceable enough action entry depending on how charitable one is feeling while watching, it seems to keep the more mind bending aspects of Dick's work (which has an ending that's far grayer than that of the film) at arm's length. It also had the misfortune of arriving just as Affleck had entered the "box office poison" phase of his career (or as I call it "The *Gigli* Effect"), and it died a quick death following its Christmas 2003 release, with neither critics nor audiences warming to its mind game storyline. Its total

---

[1] *Minority Report* also starred Colin Farrell, who'd go on to headline the 2012 *Total Recall* remake, in the Schwarzenegger role.

domestic gross was $53 million, falling short of the $60 million budget, with an international take not much better.

Three years later, Richard Linklater of *Slacker* and *Before Sunrise* fame gave it a go, this time with his quirky and innovative rotoscope animated *A Scanner Darkly*, from the 1977 novel. Featuring an all-star cast including Keanu Reeves, Robert Downey, Jr., Woody Harrelson, and Winona Ryder, *Scanner* is a fascinating examination of the impact of a drug epidemic in a dystopian police state. While it was warmly received by critics, the mind bending animation process may simply have proved a bridge too far from a commercial perspective, and it fell about a million dollars shy of making back its $8 million budget.

Next came *Next*, from the 1954 short "The Golden Man" starring Nicolas Cage. Released in 2007, this one was directed by Lee Tamahori (*Die Another Day*) and co-starred Julianne Moore and Jessica Biel, but its central conceit about a magician with limited precognitive abilities bears only superficial similarities to the source material. And like so many of the adaptations discussed previously in this chapter, the movie largely jettisons the darker, more disturbing aspects of the author's originating work in favor of something a little "safer" and more familiar to audiences, the result being a work without much distinction that failed to measure up to its own pedigree.

In 2011, Ben Affleck's *Good Will Hunting* partner Matt Damon would appear in *The Adjustment Bureau*, writer/director George Nolfi's take on Dick's 1954 short "Adjustment Team." Another of the author's frequent forays into the nature of identity and existence, this one did better than the last few Dick adaptations and actually turned a small profit on its $50 million budget thanks to the box office draw of Damon and a nuanced, twisty script by Nolfi that found the right balance to strike when expanding the original short to feature length.

In what is perhaps an indication of how audience tastes and the cinematic zeitgeist have shifted in the last few years, the most recent Dick adaptations have hit the small screen rather than the silver one, with both appearing in 2015. The less successful of these offerings was Fox TV's *Minority Report*, a sequel that picks up 11 years after the pre-crime division in the Spielberg pic has been dismantled. The main character in the series is Dash (Stark Sands), one of the three freed precogs who now works as a police officer and uses his abilities to help solve crimes.

What was so fresh and unique (and Dick-ian) in both the story and film was drained off for this colorless and bland series that leaned on audience familiarity with the brand name without really doing anything distinctive or noteworthy with it. Premiering in September, ten low-rated episodes quickly came and went, and the *Minority Report* series was gone two months later. In fact, audiences could be forgiven for not realizing the show had even existed at all.[2]

More successful than *Minority Report* on TV, however, is Amazon's *The Man in the High Castle*. Inspired by a 1962 novel positing an alternate history wherein the Allies lost World War II, the project marked Ridley Scott's first return to the Philip K. Dick fold since the original *Blade Runner*, before executive producing *Blade Runner 2049*. Greeted lavishly by critics who appreciate its layered and nuanced take on its subject matter, as well as the breathing room afforded by having a series to play with, *The Man in the High Castle* quickly found a loyal cult audience and was renewed for a second and then a third season of ten episodes each.

Following its *High Castle* success, Amazon also picked up the British co-production *Philip K. Dick's Electric Dreams*, a ten episode anthology series produced by, among others, *Breaking Bad* star Bryan Cranston, and uses its wide canvas to tell stories in the Philip K. Dick vein.

With the continued success of *The Man in the High Castle* and the release of *Blade Runner 2049* greeted with acclaim by critics (if not audiences – yet), it's fair to say that we're not likely to see a slowdown in screen productions drawing inspiration from the work of Philip K. Dick anytime soon. Like replicants, film adaptations are like any other machine: they're either a benefit or a hazard. While Dick's work has been the recipient of adaptations both beneficial and hazardous, the author's demonstrated propensity for creating vivid science-fiction scenarios rooted in all-too-human circles of concern is far too alluring for Hollywood not to continue mining his work for inspiration.

---

[2] I was one of the few people who watched the pilot episode when it premiered, and even I didn't remember the show until I began conducting research for this essay.

Cyberhomages: *Blade Runner*-Inspired Media

by Jean-François Boivin

Although based on Philip K. Dick's book, *Do Androids Dream of Electric Sheep?,* the themes and visuals of Ridley Scott's 1982 movie *Blade Runner* have gone on to inspire many, with some contending that as a futuristic film noir, it propagated the "cyberpunk" sub-genre as a whole. Its popularity also made it part of pop culture, and as such *Blade Runner*, while not as big a franchise as *Star Wars* or *Alien*, occasionally receives some attention in the form of references, homages, or spin-offs in movies, books, comics, and TV shows. This essay will cover some of the major ones.

Alien / Prometheus

Ridley Scott directed *Blade Runner* about three years after his previous masterpiece *Alien*, and while some background elements were re-used from the earlier film (namely, some of the computer screen graphics) and both have android characters in common, there were no overt relations between the two universes. The timelines that later emerged for both series proved interesting, however. For example, in *Blade Runner*'s 2019 setting, the Nexus-6 models we see in the film came into production in 2016. In the *Alien/Prometheus* universe,[1] the Weyland Corp began production on android prototypes in 2025,

---

[1] https://web.archive.org/web/20130210161058/ and https://www.weylandindustries.com/timeline

not far from the time Nexus 8 models were introduced in 2020.[2]

When it came time to produce the sequel to *Alien*, James Cameron and his design team decided to honor both of Scott's earlier science-fiction epics. Cameron's *Aliens* managed to include a reference to *Blade Runner* in the form of, once again, background computer screen elements; this time, a specific name appeared on one of the blink-and-you-miss-it dossiers of the *Nostromo* crew seen on the wall screen behind Ripley as she delivers her report to the board of inquiry early in the film. As the scene opens on a close shot of Parker's file, it shows that the dossiers are incredibly detailed: they include the full names of the characters, their dates of birth, their education and employment periods, and several other dates and details. But for the rest of the scene, viewers can only glimpse out-of-focus or small parts of headshots and files in the background as Ripley walks in front of the wall screen, which left fans curious about that information.

Their curiosity was satisfied with the release of the *Alien Anthology* blu-ray boxed set in 2010.[3] One of the numerous special features on one of the discs is a full view of the character biographies created for the inquiry scene in *Aliens*.[4] It is not confirmed if the character biographies were written by Cameron or by production designer Michael Seymour or any of the design crew, or if they were even approved by Ridley Scott, but they make for a very entertaining read. There are multiple references to *Blade Runner* interspersed within Captain Dallas' file.

According to his in-universe biography, Captain Dallas (full name Arthur Dallas Coblenz) worked for the Tyrell Corporation at age 26[5] as Warrant Officer aboard the transport USCS *Shusett* (named after Ronald Shusett, co-writer of *Alien* with Dan O'Bannon). The rest of his bio and the other crewmembers'

---

[2] http://roadto2049.bladerunnermovie.com/year/2020
[3] "Inquest Dossiers" features under Production menu of the ALIENS section on Disc 6: The Anthology Archives.
[4] Screen captures of which can be found at http://www.platypuscomix.net/hollywood/nostromodossier.html
[5] Dated between 8/1016 [sic] and 1/9/16; the start date is likely a typo, since his employment ended on 9 January of "16" he must have started at least in the previous year. The bios do not reveal which century the information refers to. The year "16" could be 2016, 2116, 2216, etc. The dates don't correspond with the official canon dates established later in which it is now known that *Alien* takes place in 2122 and Dallas' official bio no longer includes Tyrell as one of his past employers.

profiles include a plethora of in-jokes and homages to the original filmmakers and crew of *Alien* in the form of schools and starships named after some of them (as well as starships inspired by the sequel's crew: *Cameron*, *Hurd*, and *Terminator*), but the topical one here is the Tyrell Corporation. The *Alien* universe is a world where major Corporations and Companies are the governing bodies of the galaxy, having created most of the technology and colonized most of the inhabited planets. Although clearly a fun homage to the Tyrell Corporation of *Blade Runner*, it doesn't necessitate that Nexus-6 models or even Dr. Eldon Tyrell exist in that universe, though that's clearly what many fans have inferred.

The connections, however, don't end there. 30 years after *Blade Runner*, Ridley Scott came back to science fiction with his prequel to *Alien*, *Prometheus*. The theater and home video releases enjoyed a wide viral campaign, with a fictitious TED talk from 2023 on YouTube,[6] in-universe websites from Weyland Industries and Project Prometheus, which include a corporate timeline of the company and a space map of the colonized planets, an interactive "Second Screen" smartphone app, a widespread social media presence, and numerous articles in entertainment magazines.

Another expansion of the movie came in the form of special features on the DVD/Blu-ray release. Of interest here is something included in "The Peter Weyland Files." One of Peter Weyland's written logs, dated 2090.01.11, refers to one of his past acquaintances:

> A mentor and long-departed competitor once told me that it was time to put away childish things and abandon my "toys." He encouraged me to come work for him and together we would take over the world and become the new Gods. That's how he ran his corporation, like a God on top of a pyramid overlooking a city of angels. Of course, he chose to replicate the power of creation in an unoriginal way, by simply copying God. And look how that turned out for the poor bastard. Literally blew up in the old man's face. I always suggested he stick with simple robotics instead of those genetic abominations he enslaved and sold off-world, although his idea to implant them with false memories was, well... "amusing," is how I would put it politely.

Once again, we have a reference to Eldon Tyrell and his corporate tower in Los Angeles. Most of the extras and documentaries were produced by Charles de Lauzirika, who also worked on 2010's *Alien Anthology* and 2007's *Blade Runner*

---

[6] https://www.youtube.com/watch?v=dQpGwnN3dfc

Multi-Disc Collector's Edition releases. Managing to bring in a reference to one of his long-time favorite movies, he confessed in an online interview that:

> As a *Blade Runner* fan, and because there's been so much talk before this even occurred with people on the Internet speculating that maybe *Alien* and *Blade Runner* and *Prometheus* could all exist in the same universe, it was just more of a wink at that. Absolutely nothing to be taken seriously. I mean, I sent it to Ridley and he had no comment. [*Laughs*] So, it's just icing on top of icing. It's not the cake. It's a fun, little side thing that's very superficial. And, by the way, it in no way officially establishes that it's *Blade Runner* because, if a lawyer were to comb through that, there's no reference to Tyrell or anything in *Blade Runner*. It's just a very lightly intentioned joke.[7]

Interestingly, however, the timeline seems to jive, since Peter Weyland would have been 29 at the time of Eldon Tyrell's death in 2019.

```
P. WEYLAND/PVM/CXN/LOG-CRG/2090.01.11/TRS-MARS_pkd92

Views: 9
Priority: Low                    Encrypt: High
Links: Weyland RoboDiv, Weyland Archives, W-PR, 9 other private
links

/Dictated but not read/BEGIN

A mentor and long-departed competitor once told me that it was time
to put away childish things and abandon my "toys." He encouraged me
to come work for him and together we would take over the world and
become the new Gods. That's how he ran his corporation, like a God
on top of a pyramid overlooking a city of angels. Of course, he
chose to replicate the power of creation in an unoriginal way, by
simply copying God. And look how that turned out for the poor
bastard. Literally blew up in the old man's face. I always
suggested he stick with simple robotics instead of those genetic
abominations he enslaved and sold off-world, although his idea to
implant them with false memories was, well…"amusing," is how I
would put it politely.

Fortunately, I chose a different trajectory, employing
innovation and ingenuity when launching the Weyland
Robotics Division. Even our earliest synthetics displayed
tremendous intelligence, intuition and compatibility
despite their admittedly unconvincing exterior. But now, several
```

One of Peter Weyland's logs alludes to Eldon Tyrell.

Soldier

This movie was released in 1998 and directed by Paul W.S. Anderson after his previous efforts *Mortal Kombat* and *Event Horizon*, and before his classics

---

[7] http://www.movies.com/movie-news/prometheus-blade-runner-connection/9861

The movie poster for *Soldier* (1998).

Resident Evil and *Alien vs. Predator*. What's relevant here is that the script was written by David Peoples, co-writer of *Blade Runner*. Peoples fully intended it to be set in the same universe as the 1982 movie.[8]

Soldier stars Kurt Russell as Todd 3465, one of the "lucky" few chosen from birth by American Forces to participate in the Adam Project, in which orphans are trained their entire lives to become pure war machines. The prologue shows his progression from infancy in 1996, to his years of classes, boot camp, hand-to-hand combat, until the end of training at the age of 17. After depicting a few of the battles that he fought in, it then jumps to the main story at age 40 in 2036.

The story is simple but enjoyable science-fiction and action fare. While at military H.Q. between wars, Sgt. Todd and his brethren are confronted by a new batch of soldiers who are genetically enhanced, but not combat-experienced, and are set to replace them. After a failed hand-to-hand fight with one of the new soldiers named Caine 607 (Jason Scott Lee), Todd is left for dead and dumped from a ship onto Arcadia 234, a waste disposal planet. It so happens that the planet is also home for a group of families living in a scrap-made village after having crash-landed on the world years before. Todd is taken into a family's home, where he discovers what peace and affection are after having been only drilled for battle his entire life. He becomes infatuated with the wife of the house, and feels a bond with the young son who is mute. One day, the American Forces decide to send the genetically enhanced soldiers to Arcadia to field test them by having them eradicate the unarmed colonists there, and Sgt. Todd is the only one who has the training and knowledge to protect them. The movie ends with lots of action and explosions as Todd fights to protect the ones he's come to know as friends.

The links to *Blade Runner* are difficult to notice. Knowledge of one movie is not required to understand the other. In fact, *Soldier* takes place about 15 years after Deckard's adventure in Los Angeles of 2019, and is set on a different planet. One of the noticeable references to *Blade Runner* relates to Roy Batty's last speech before he died:

> I've seen things you people wouldn't believe. Attack ships on fire off the shoulder of Orion. I watched C-beams glitter in the dark near the Tannhäuser Gate. All those moments will be lost in time, like tears in rain. Time to die.

---

[8] *Cinescape*, Sept-Oct 1998 issue; also see https://www.ranker.com/list/soldier-blade-runner-sequel/john-saavedra

Among the many campaigns that Todd participated in, the shoulder of Orion is listed as one, as is the Battle at Tannhäuser Gate.[9] In fact, Tannhäuser Gate even makes it into dialogue. The woman who nurses Todd after he is found near death mentions the words on his tattoo. Her husband says it was a battle in recent history. In fact, according to the revised 1997 script, the battle took place in 2017, the year after Roy Batty's inception (although most of the dates in the final movie were moved to four years after the dates in the original script).[10]

The second link is found when Todd is banished temporarily from the colony. As he walks through a vast scrapyard, the wreckage of a spinner can be seen. The movie includes other homages to different movies, a few nods to Russell's previous roles, and, interestingly, a couple of Colonial Marine weapons from *Aliens* are listed in part of Todd's combat skills, further strengthening the *Blade Runner/Alien* ties.

Total Recall 2070

Although inspired (and licensed by Universal Pictures) as a spin-off of the 1990 Paul Verhoeven film starring Arnold Schwarzenegger, which itself was loosely based on another Philip K. Dick story,[11] *Total Recall 2070* was more inspired by the Earth-bound, noir environment of *Blade Runner*. Produced by Canadian-American media company Alliance Atlantis Communications Inc., the 22 episodes of the series originally aired on ONTV in Canada and Showtime in the United States during the first half of 1999. It was later syndicated internationally and released on DVD in Canada in 2011.

The Toronto-shot series is described as:

> a sci-fi psychological thriller which centers around police detective David Hume (Michael Easton), and his android partner, Ian Farve (Karl Pruner). Members of the Citizens Protection Bureau (CPB), their investigations will take them from Earth to colonies on Mars. Set in the 2070 global society ravaged by environmental and man-made disasters, this is a world where civil liberties have been exchanged for peace and stability. Six powerful conglomerates known as the Consortium dominate world affairs. The CPB,

---

[9] Tannhäuser and its gate received numerous references in later works of fiction, including an unofficial scenario for *Star Wars: The Roleplaying Game* titled "La Bataille de Tannahäuser" witten by Olivier Némoz and published in the third "Hors-Série" issue of the French RPG magazine *Dragon Radieux* in December 1989.
[10] The revised 1997 draft can be found at http://www.dailyscript.com/scripts/soldier.html
[11] "We Can Remember It for You Wholesale" (1966).

as peacekeepers and defenders of the common citizen, are empowered to thwart corporate espionage and defend innocent parties from the supreme power of the Consortium.[12]

One of the Consortium companies featured on the show is Rekall, a company that created computer technology where people can travel inside virtual reality, and a home version named a Sublimator, where customers can watch recordings of their memories and feel as if they were there. This is pretty much the only link to the movie *Total Recall* (although it could serve as a prequel to the 2084-set movie). Most of the series is set around the CPB station in a multi-layered, heavily-populated, rainy, and polluted city where the agents are sent on various investigations, some of which concern rogue androids. Much like *Blade Runner*, the theme of androids and how they want to become human and how humans react to their existence is very prominent. In fact, the creation of the advanced Alpha android Favre, a flesh and plasma based prototype, is a recurring theme introduced in the pilot episode and is only resolved in the final episode. Detective Hume starts out with a hatred of androids, but the friendship he develops with his new partner, after finding out early on that he is an android, is at the core of the drama on the show.

A forgotten gem of late 1990s television, it is recommended to fans of Philip K. Dick and science-fiction police dramas in general, as it's the closest thing to a *Blade Runner* television series yet, with the CPB agents equaling Blade Runners, and with Beta androids in place of replicants.

Licensed Material

To coincide with the movie's release (during the heavy movie merchandising period of the 1980s), Ballantine/Del Rey re-released Philip K. Dick's novel *Do Androids Dream of Electric Sheep?* as a tie-in using the movie's title and poster on the cover. Marvel Comics put out an adaptation by Archie Goodwin with art by Al Williamson and Carlos Garzon in *Marvel Super Special* #22, followed by a two-issue re-release. Blue Dolphin Enterprises published *The Illustrated Blade Runner*, *Blade Runner Sketchbook*, and *Blade Runner Portfolio*. Also published were the *Blade Runner: A Story of the Future* storybook and the popular collector's item, the *Blade Runner Souvenir Magazine*. The *Illustrated Blade Runner*, *Sketchbook*, and the *Portfolio*, fetch some hefty prices on eBay.

---

[12] From the series' defunct website found at http://web.archive.org/web/20010202212500/http://www.totalrecall2070.com

Other materials include a series of Bantam novels by K.W. Jeter titled *Blade Runner 2: The Edge of Human* (1995), *Blade Runner 3: Replicant Night* (1996) and *Blade Runner 4: Eye and Talon* (2000); Paul M. Sammon's detailed book *Future Noir: The Making of Blade Runner* (1996); Westwood Studios' *Blade Runner: The First Real-Time 3D Adventure* for PC (1997); and BOOM! Studios' 24-issue comic adaptation of *Do Androids Dream of Electric Sheep?* (2009-2011) along with the official prequel series *Dust to Dust* published in 2010 over eight issues.

Now with the sequel *Blade Runner 2049* in wide release, a new generation of filmmakers, writers, and artists may be inspired to include homages in their works.

Here's to the future!

On the Marvel Comic-Book Adaptation of *Blade Runner*

by Julian Darius

In 1977, Marvel Comics launched *Marvel Super Special* (officially titled *Marvel Comics Super Special* for its first four issues). Long before graphic novels became routine, *Marvel Super Special* offered magazine-size graphic novellas, generally containing a 40-ish-page story. The series mostly adapted movies, although early issues featured bands (such as Kiss and the Beatles), and some issues featured other stories, such as Conan tales.

A lot of these forgotten movie adaptations aren't great comic-books, despite some talented creators being involved. There's no doubt opportunism played a part, as movie fans eagerly consumed printed matter related to the films that interested them. At the time, newsstands often featured magazine specials focused on new movies, and the magazine dimensions of *Marvel Super Special* were clearly aimed at this market. Like those magazine specials, most Marvel comic-book adaptations also included text articles about the movie and its production process, with copious photos, at a time when you couldn't Google this stuff. Some of these issues were produced before videotapes became widespread (especially in rural areas). But even *after* you could watch a movie at home, these adaptations came out around the movie's release and were the only way you could relive that experience until the home video release (which took much longer, in those days).

For these largely forgotten adaptations, Marvel seems to have chosen movies that it *thought* would perform well with its readers – primarily science-fiction subjects, although with an almost equal amount of fantasy and a few other genres thrown in. Of course, when adapting a movie in time for its release, it's rarely clear how successful that movie will be, let alone how well it will be remembered. Consequently, the list of movies adapted by *Marvel Super Special* is an odd mixture of movies that went on to be classics, movies that have achieved a kind of cult classic status, and movies that might once have been a big deal but basically disappeared into history.

Of course, hindsight is 20/20. The more successful the movie was, the more one wonders why its studio would stoop to a comic-book adaptation, especially at a time when comic-books weren't exactly mainstream. The less successful the movie was, the more one wonders why Marvel would bother adapting it, or why anyone thought it deserved adaptation.

The studios seemed only too willing to agree to these adaptations, as demonstrated by the sheer variety of material Marvel adapted. One of the title's first adaptations was Steven Spielberg's *Close Encounters of the Third Kind*, adapted in *Marvel Comics Super Special* #3 (1978) by venerated comic-book writer Archie Goodwin and legendary comic-book artists Walt Simonson and Klaus Janson. The musical *Xanadu* got adapted as *Marvel Super Special* #17 (Summer 1980), written by J.M. DeMatteis. James Bond may be the longest-running English-language movie franchise, but he has had only sporadic success in comic-books. Still, Marvel produced an adaptation of *For Your Eyes Only* in Marvel Super Special #19 (1981), written by Larry Hama (of *G.I. Joe* fame) and penciled by Howard Chaykin. Marvel later adapted *Octopussy* in *Marvel Super Special* #26 (1983), written by Steve Moore with art by Paul Neary. The forgotten fantasy movie *Dragonslayer* was adapted in *Marvel Super Special* #20 (1981) by no less than writer Denny O'Neil and artists Marie Severin and John Tartalione. Just a few issues later, the series adapted a fantasy movie that would go on to become a cult classic: *The Dark Crystal*, adapted in *Marvel Super Special* #24 (1982), which included 13 pages of photos and pre-production sketches. While largely forgotten, the movie *Krull* got an adaptation in *Marvel Super Special* #28 (1983). *The Last Starfighter* got adapted in *Marvel Super Special* #31 (1984). *The Adventures of Buckaroo Banzai Across the 8th Dimension!*, which went on to become a cult classic, got an adaptation in *Marvel Super Special* #33 (1984), with Mark Texeira art. The next issue, *Marvel Super Special* #34 (1984), adapted the motion picture *Sheena*, based on the jungle girl character (Sheena, Queen of the Jungle) who had originated in comic-books (not published by Marvel) in the 1930s. The movie bombed and disappeared into obscurity. Marvel also adapted David Lynch's *Dune* in *Marvel Super Special* #36 (1984), written by Ralph Macchio and illustrated by the great Bill Sienkiewicz (who seems like a perfect fit for the stylistic but semi-incomprehensible movie). The adaptation was also serialized as a three-issue mini-series, and it's the only *Dune* comic to date. The cult classic *Labyrinth* got adapted in *Marvel Super Special* #40 (1986), for which John Buscema did breakdowns.

Other choices can seem even stranger. They include the early episodes of *Battlestar Galactica*, which even got reproduced in a tabloid-size edition.[1] *Jaws 2* got an adaptation, as did *Annie* and *The Muppets Take Manhattan*. Disaster movies were popular back then, and *Meteor* got an adaptation (with Frank Miller penciling the cover, no less). Even *Santa Claus: The Movie* got adapted.

Several adaptations had some earlier ties to Marvel Comics. Marvel had long published *Conan* when it adapted the Arnold Schwarzenegger movie *Conan the Barbarian* as *Marvel Super Special* #21 (1982). Marvel went on to adapt the movie's sequel, *Conan the Destroyer*, as *Marvel Super Special* #35 (Dec 1984), illustrated by John Buscema. The movie version of *Red Sonja* got adapted as *Marvel Super Special* #38 (1985).

Marvel didn't have any deeper ties to Indiana Jones when it adapted *Raiders of the Lost Ark* as *Marvel Super Special #18* (1981), written by Walt Simonson, illustrated by John Buscema and Klaus Janson, and featuring a cover by Howard Chaykin. A year or so later, Marvel began the ongoing series *The Further Adventures of Indiana Jones* (#1, Jan 1983, to #34, Mar 1986). While this was running, Marvel adapted *Indiana Jones and the Temple of Doom* as Marvel Super Special #30 (1984), also serialized as a three-issue mini-series.

Marvel also had ties to *2001: A Space Odyssey*, having produced an adaptation and a continuation in the 1970s.[2] After that, Arthur C. Clarke wrote a sequel novel, *2010*, which went on to become a movie. Marvel adapted it as *Marvel Super Special* #37 (1984), written by J.M. DeMatteis, which was also serialized as a two-issue mini-series.

---

[1] As kids, my brother and I got this tabloid edition, and although we'd never seen the show, we adored it – although mostly for its sci-fi content and the comic's size. We bought every tabloid edition we saw, as if on principle.

[2] Covered in my book, *The Strangest Sci-Fi Comic Ever Made: Understanding Jack Kirby's 2001: A Space Odyssey* (Sequart, 2013).

In a more direct Marvel connection, the final issue of *Marvel Super Special* (#41, Nov 1986) adapted *Howard the Duck*, the movie based on the Marvel comic. The adaptation, which was also published as a three-issue mini-series, was written by Danny Fingeroth, with art by Kyle Baker.

Before trade paperbacks were remotely common, Marvel also used *Marvel Super Special* to reprint adaptations it had published elsewhere, using the magazine-size collected editions as a way of appealing to a broader audience who might not purchase comic-books. Thus, issue #15 (Dec 1979) reprinted the first three issues of Marvel's *Star Trek*, which adapted *Star Trek: The Motion Picture*. Marvel's ongoing series *Star Wars* adapted *The Empire Strikes Back* in issues #39-44, and all six issues were also published, all together, in *Marvel Super Special* #16 (Spring 1980), which was sold at some movie theaters like a souvenir book.[3] For *Return of the Jedi*, Marvel published a four-issue adaptation as both a mini-series and as *Marvel Super Special* #27 (1983). Because the magazine-size *Marvel Super Special* wasn't always sold where comic-books were, Marvel routinely serialized later adaptations either as comic-sized one-shots or two-issue mini-series.

Today, comic-book adaptations of movies have fallen out of fashion – even as adaptations of comic-books into TV and movies have never been more popular. If the internet has killed most movie magazines, video-on-demand has made these adaptations into comic-books more of a niche market.

Of course, not all of these adaptations were good, but most were interesting, as even their mistakes often revealed differences between the two media. At the very least, these adaptations are fascinating artifacts from a past era.[4]

It was in this context that Marvel Comics adapted Ridley Scott's 1982 *Blade Runner* as *Marvel Super Special* #22 (Sept 1982). It was written by Archie Goodwin, penciled by Al Williamson and Carlos Garzon, and inked by Williamson, Dan Green, and Ralph Reese, under a cover by Jim Steranko.

---

[3] Thanks to Richard Bensam for this information.

[4] Despite the end of the series, Marvel didn't give up on magazine-sized movie adaptations. Among its more memorable later efforts were magazine-sized adaptations of *RoboCop* (Nov 1987), *RoboCop 2* (Aug 1990, also published as a prestige-format one-shot and a three-issue mini-series... which in turn led into a short-lived ongoing series), and *Darkman* (Sept 1990, also published as a three-issue mini-series).

Today, *Blade Runner* frequently tops the list of finest sci-fi movies ever made. But in 1982, it was just another movie to be adapted alongside *Annie*, *Sheena*, and *Jaws 2*. As an issue of *Marvel Super Special*, it must have seemed like a weak entry compared to *Star Wars*, *Star Trek*, *Indiana Jones*, and *James Bond*. But today, an adaptation of *Blade Runner* can seem almost almost sacrilegious, much in the same way that Marvel's earlier *2001: A Space Odyssey* adaptation can.[5]

The very idea of adapting *Blade Runner* can seem like a difficult proposition since the movie succeeds in large part due to elements that are distinctly cinematic. The movie is known for its slightly slow pace, in which long takes allow the viewer to absorb the cityscape, or the stark and poorly lit interiors, conveying a sense of mood that's often as important as the dialogue. An issue of *Marvel Super Special* didn't have the page count necessary to adapt this kind of mood. It had to focus on plot, not mood-setting visuals.

The movie is also characterized by its dispassionate dialogue and muted performances, which convey a sense that no one's excited to be living in this particular future – except, perhaps, the replicants, who can seem more motivated and "alive" than the humans. Here too, the comic adaptation is at a disadvantage, since its printed dialogue cannot so easily convey tone.

Finally, the movie is also distinguished by its soundtrack, composed by Vangelis. The ambient synthesizer-heavy sounds accent well the movie's stark visuals, conveying a ruminating, even melancholy mood that enhances the visuals. Even the movie's love theme uses a tenor sax that seems to convey an underlying sadness and the distance between the movie's lovers. As a love story, *Blade Runner* feels more like two desperate, sad, and lonely people than an endorphin-spurring jolt of drug-like emotions. The lovers' eyes don't light up, and their smiles at each other are uncertain smirks, emphasizing the tenuousness of their love and their lives. The music seems to capture this same sense of remorse, perhaps suggesting that for these characters no love can be more than this, in this place that has drained life, love, and passion. Like most movie music, the Vangelis soundtrack tells us how to feel. Yet this too is deprived the comic-book adaptation.

---

[5] Of course, it's worth pointing out that *Blade Runner* also got sequel novels (which attempted to be sequels to Dick's original novel and the movie), as well as a 2017 sequel film.

Marvel Super Special #22 (Sept 1982) establishes the story's setting by opening with this splash page.

It's not hard to imagine a comic-book adaptation that addressed these issues. In the 1990s and early 2000s, American comic-books began to embrace a more "decompressed" style of storytelling, with fewer panels per page, as well as fewer captions and word balloons. This might have helped immerse the reader in the movie's world, providing readers with visuals to slowly muse over, much as they might let themselves be absorbed by the movie's music and visuals. Of course, in 1982, this wasn't a realistic option, and the adaptation was limited to 44 pages. But given how the movie has been revised with subsequent releases, it's possible to imagine a revised comic-book adaptation, expanding upon the original art by perhaps doubling its page count and featuring updated, computer coloring, being far more successful.

That's not to say the comic doesn't sometimes take moments to emphasize the look of this future. In fact, it opens with a splash page, prominently featuring the Tyrell Corporation building. The image is lessened by the fact that a thick fog covers its middle ground, preventing a clear shot of the city and making the flying car appear to be drifting in space, rather than grounded in an actual setting. The page is also lessened by its unrealistic colors, typical of comic-books at the time. It seems to reduce *Blade Runner* to the idiom of early-1980s comic-books, rather than being inspired by the material to transcend that idiom.

The image seems to draw a contrast between the Tyrell Corporation's wealth and the poorer areas around it. There's something burning in the distance, suggesting a factory, and the fog recalls industrial pollution. Whereas the Tyrell building and those beyond it are colored orange, the fog-drenched buildings in the foreground are mostly grey and brown, suggesting a grimy setting. The movie isn't without its class tensions, but this establishing shot seems to visually suggest that this is a city of extreme haves and have-nots, a situation more reminiscent of Fritz Lang's classic silent 1927 film *Metropolis* than the dynamics emphasized within Ridley Scott's film.

Later, as the story nears its climax, the adaptation offers a two-page spread, mostly consisting of a single panel depicting the Tyrell Corporation building. The giant screen with a female face on it, an iconic image from the film, is included in this central panel – a fact likely to please fans of the film even today. Yet again, fog is used to avoid depicting a middle ground, and it's not a good sign when a large percentage of a future cityscape is a single, undifferentiated field of color. Here too, the limited colors significantly lower the realism of the artwork and the impression it might make. Nonetheless, the artwork around the fog is good, the detail on the building is remarkable, and the image is good enough to invoke how powerful a comic-book adaptation of *Blade Runner* might be, if it surrendered more fully to the visual potentials of the medium.

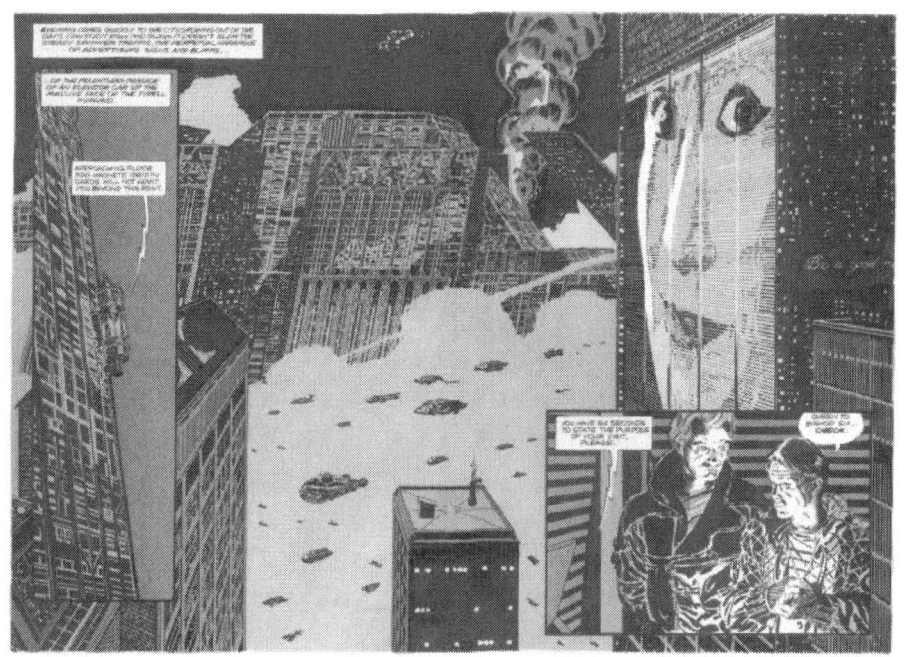

A double-page spread occurs near the climax of the story in *Marvel Super Special* #22 (Sept 1982).

This isn't to say that the art is bad, even if the long list of pencilers and inkers may make us suspicious. Some panels are workmanlike, but others are simply glorious -- even if the colors (by deservedly legendary artist Marie Severin) seem to lessen the overall effect.

One of my favorite sequences in the film is when Deckard administers the Voight-Kampff test to Eldon Tyrell's secretary, Rachael (played by Sean Young). Ostensibly, Tyrell has Deckard test Rachael as a control, but in fact Rachael is one of the new replicant models that Deckard's there to demonstrate the test works on. It takes Deckard far longer than normal, but he's able to ascertain that Rachael is a replicant. Rachael is excused before discussing his finding with Tyrell, but Rachael isn't dumb. She figures out she's a replicant, and this effectively sets the movie's quasi-romantic B-plot into motion. Of course, like all good B-plots, this plot dovetails nicely with the concerns of the more action-based A-plot. In fact, the B-plot is the heart of the film (at least for me).

A beautifully rendered spinner, from *Marvel Super Special* #22 (Sept 1982).

The comic adaptation does a good job here, even if the montage of Deckard testing Rachael feels overly compressed. The page in question begins with an establishing shot of Tyrell's office, illustrated from a distance using a worm's eye view. Besides the extreme camera angle, the panel uses both negative space and reflections brilliantly, and both techniques reinforce the philosophical implications of the scene. Replicants are a distorted reflection of humanity, or vice versa, and the use of flat areas, sometimes without border lines, suggests the austere aesthetic of the movie as well as the emptiness that seems to define this city's inhabitants.

The panel is entirely colored an orange-red, which risks feeling lazy, but this actually works pretty well to accent the wonderful artwork. More "proper" coloring would likely define those areas of negative space too much and would risk distracting from the artwork. As it is, the effect is more like tinting than traditional comic-book coloring, and a strong case could be made that, even were this artwork recolored using present computer coloring techniques, it would benefit from being colored in a single hue (the same orange, or perhaps a blue) ranging only in luminosity. The use of a single color also echoes the darkness of the scene in the movie, suggesting the idea of limited vision in a different way.

One of the movie's most famous sequences is when Deckard guns down a female replicant, who flees in a see-through jacket. As Deckard shoots her, she crashes through a store window in slow motion. The film doesn't hesitate to show her pained face, and her slow-motion death, combined with shattered glass, manages to convey a sense of martyrdom. There's doubtlessly a sexual

Deckard administers the Voight-Kampff test on Rachel, as depicted in *Marvel Super Special* #22 (Sept 1982).

element to the sequence, in which an attractive woman runs in skimpy clothing, and her death suggests the strong connection between eros and thanatos. Yet the death of beautiful women is often used in fiction to represent the death of innocence, or how evil the killer is, or even the unjust, squandering nature of society. These elements are all present in the sequence, which seems surprisingly willing to implicate the movie's main character. After all, she's *fleeing* when she's killed, and she's driven by nothing more than a willingness to live.

The comic adaptation isn't as successful as the movie in depicting this scene. But the comic devotes a full page to the shooting and its aftermath, and it's not afraid to show the female replicant's face as she's shot. The shattering glass doesn't get the space we might wish (much less shard-shaped panels), but it's not cut for space. The shards around her beautiful but dead body still manage to be evocative, and here again the art exploits the reflection motif, as her face is reflected in the shards on the floor. We might wish the sequence were, well, more cinematic, but it's powerful in its own right.

Another of the film's more famous sequences comes at its climax, in which Deckard flees Roy Batty, the lead "villainous" replicant (played by Rutger Hauer). Deckard dangles off a building, but Roy pulls him onto the roof, saving his enemy. Roy then delivers a brief monologue about death, specifically about how his memories will be lost with him. Deckard watches silently as Roy dies – not due to any action on the part of the "hero," but rather due to the artificial time limit placed on replicants' lives. The unorthodox nature of this conclusion pleases on its own terms, but it also works as an expression of how unjust, or at least immune to justice, this world is; there's no sense that the hero triumphs due to his innate cleverness, strength, or worth in any way. If Deckard is even the hero, he "wins" because the villain decides to save him, and the villain would have died at that exact moment anyway.

Precisely why the lead villain chooses to save the lead hero, at the villain's moment of victory, remains debated, but the answer may be a combination of the fact that Deckard's death would bring no added pleasure (the villain has already won, and he's already killed his technological maker) and that Roy wishes to have a witness to his death, so that at least that final memory would be shared and would not die with him.[6]

---

[6] This may well be a part of why we, as humans, don't wish to be alone: we wish to share experiences with others, so that these experiences are not confined to our

The comic-book version of Roy Batty's death uses the literary or printed nature of the medium to good effect. In a film, the viewer can't control the speed at which a story moves, and this can make one feel lost, if one doesn't get a good sense of the landscape in which characters are moving, or precisely where they are in that landscape. This can happen in a comic-book too, but the reader's ability to pause over panels mitigates it, letting one immerse one's self in a landscape until one has a sense of it, or at least as much sense as the panel provides. But it's no surprise that a comic-book would see the drama inherent in a rooftop chase or a character hanging from a building; such melodramatic elements (and the effective ways of visually portraying them) are a staple of comic-book stories, for better or for worse. What's more interesting is that Roy's final monologue, in printed form, arguably brings out its philosophical implications in a way that the movie's dialogue doesn't. The fact that the reader is able to pause, move back, reread, and reconsider aids the sequence, whereas a viewer might have to re-watch the film several times to pick up on the sequence's implications to the same degree.

Other memorable moments from the movie don't work quite as well. Roy gains access to Tyrell's penthouse through the human Sebastian, and the comic-book can't convey the awkward nervousness as Roy and Sebastian wait to see whether their ploy will work. But the comic-book retains the cleverness of having Roy and Sebastian gain access to Tyrell's penthouse through communicating a chess move, which indicates Tyrell's self-indulgent wealth and his detached, cerebral character; chess is more interesting to him than people, again emphasizing how the humans in this world appear to be disconnected and dispassionate, relative to the Replicants, who are arguably more alive. This maneuver used to gain access to Tyrell's penthouse also illustrates how even the greatest security can be penetrated due to human error, a fact now familiar

---

own mortal (and therefore dying) brains, which we interpret as feeling less alone. When my father lost his lifelong friend, what moved my father most was remembering walking with his friend down a street lined on both sides with trees, and how the trees were all shedding their leaves simultaneously. It was a strong memory, and hearing it recounted, I got the sense that my father could still see those leaves, and he could recall how they felt on his body. No one had shared this experience with my father except his friend, and now that this friend was gone, it existed only in my father's brain. Somehow, this was far more touching than the death of a human man who had been deteriorating for some time. His death was no surprise. How much it hurt, knowing this memory was now isolated in a single surviving brain, was a surprise.

to us due to internet and corporate security concerns. And if the comic fails to convey the scene in the elevator very successfully, it excels at depicting Tyrell awakening and going to his chess set. Tyrell's bedroom is lovingly drawn with masterful precision.

Roy Batty kills his maker, as depicted in *Marvel Super Special* #22 (Sept 1982).

Shortly before the climax with Deckard, Roy kills Tyrell. In the movie, this feels (at least to me) impulsive and anti-climactic. That's not necessarily bad, in that Roy's impulsiveness is part of his menace, and it foreshadows his sparing Deckard; he impulsively kills, and he impulsively saves. In the movie, the anti-climactic nature of the scene, in which Roy's squeezing of Tyrell's head feels oddly restrained, may also be read as reflecting how unsatisfying vengeance is for Roy, and perhaps this experience informs his choice to spare Deckard. In the compressed (no pun intended) comic-book, however, the fact that Roy is killing his creator finds emphasis, underlining the mythological truth of the sequence, which evokes how one generation of Greek gods might overthrow the previous one, as well as the psychological truth of the sequence, which recalls how our fathers cast long shadows over our lives until they are literally or symbolically gone. These implications are present in the film, but there's no mistaking the symbolic potency of the murder in the comic-book.

To be sure, the rest of the adaptation is something of a mixed bag, but the more time one spends with it, the more one likes it.

Another advantage of comic-books, relative to cinema, is the presence of page breaks and panel borders. This allows comic-books to control how information is packaged, much in the same way that a paragraph functions in prose. In cinema, footage generally just rolls forward without the same kind of breaks. The captions and dialogue in a panel function with its imagery as a distinct unit, and this encourages the reader to consider it as such, whereas it's easy in film for important moments or lines of dialogue to be lost because the viewer is always paying attention to the next, ongoing sequence. In this way, page or panel borders can act to "bookend" a moment, literally freezing it on the page for consideration.

Thus, when Rachael says that she's not part of Deckard's business (his profession is hunting replicants) but rather *is* his business, the panel includes only this dialogue, combined with Rachael sitting dejectedly. It's a clever line that conveys the depressing consequences of Rachael's realization that she's a replicant, which is, in effect, her reaction to her own objectification. As with the earlier shooting of the female replicant, gender issues mix here with broader, existential ones. In the movie, the same sense is communicated, but is part of a moving tapestry of references, auditory and visual. In the comic-book, it's much easier to turn a bit of that tapestry into what feels like a moment, a unit of its own, surrounded by a nice black box.

While there are several reasons to suspect that a comic-book adaptation of *Blade Runner* might be difficult, *Blade Runner* has one quality that lends itself to adaptation: the movie has Deckard narrating in voiceover – a technique which has since largely fallen out of fashion in cinema. Similarly, captions – especially objective ones – have fallen out of fashion in comic-books. Yet Deckard's voiceover is easily adapted as captions, yielding a comic that can feel literary as a result. Indeed, there are rare moments in the adaptation in which the captions help the comic feel like a comic-book from Europe, where they've remained much more compressed and captions haven't fallen out of favor nearly so much.

Of course, this adaptation preserves a version of the ending narration, which has generally fallen out of favor (I like it, though) in the wake of subsequent revised releases of the film. It does feature Deckard finding the origami unicorn, shortly before the conclusion – although the idea that this proves Deckard to be a replicant remains ambiguous.

It's not hard to imagine that *Blade Runner* could have gotten an ongoing Marvel series, the way another Harrison Ford property – Indiana Jones – did after its own comic-book adaptation (of *Raiders of the Lost Ark*). Marvel also had *Star Wars* at the time, so it could have had three comic-books starring characters played by Harrison Ford! Of course, it might be considered perverse to wish for a 1980s comic-book continuation of *Blade Runner*: the movie is now considered a classic, and there's no doubt that any comic-book continuation would be a bit more pulpy and quite a bit more uneven than purists would wish. Still, an ongoing series, with all the thematic and stylistic incongruities that would have inevitably accompanied it, could have been a most delightful perversion. It could have happened.

Instead, the movie adaptation remains an oddity – a forgotten artifact of the era in which *Blade Runner* was released, when it could be adapted as a comic-book almost as a matter of course. In retrospect, after decades of theorizing and discussions of the movie's depth, *Blade Runner* doesn't feel like a comfortable companion with the Muppets and more obvious franchises like *Star Wars*. But it was another era, when *Blade Runner* wasn't *Blade Runner* yet.

Creating the Graphic Novelization of *Do Androids Dream of Electric Sheep?*

by Bryce Carlson

At age 18, I discovered *Blade Runner* for the first time in a dark classroom. The music and cinematography took deep roots while the story and world became imprinted on my brain. A true film school experience. Since then, I've seen it about a half dozen or so more times. It's a film that was influential and one that I know well, but not half as well as I know the original source material.

I wasn't introduced to Philip K. Dick's *Do Androids Dream of Electric Sheep?* until five years after I had seen *Blade Runner* for the first time. While I had heard of the novel, I had never read it and had little real familiarity with it. That changed dramatically when BOOM! Studios acquired the license to publish *Do Androids Dream of Electric Sheep?* comic books in 2009.

At the time, I was working as the Executive Assistant and part of my five-in-one job was helping the Editorial department with copyediting. They needed all the help they could get so I was tapped to be an extra pair of eyes. That was my initial role on the project.

This comic book series was unique. It wasn't an adaptation because *Blade Runner* was the adaptation and had all the rights that went along with it. And it wasn't an illustrated novel because we didn't have novel publishing rights and it was intended to be much more than a few dozen spot illustrations alongside text. It was something I had never seen before and, to the best of my knowledge, nothing that had ever been done before, at least not on this kind of scale.

It was a "graphic novelization" in the truest sense of the term. It was both full novel and full comic book, coexisting on every page in this experimental, mind-bending way that was strangely and beautifully appropriate for the seminal work of Philip K. Dick.

The parameters of the project were such that we were required to use every word of the novel with the exception of "he said" and "she said," which we could omit when dialogue was being clearly used in word balloons and if there was no additional text attached to it. Otherwise, every single word of that 200+ page novel is in the comic book series.

As you can imagine, it was no easy feat. The first big hurdle was acquiring an editable transcript of the novel. Otherwise, the comic book script would necessitate transcribing the entire novel, which wasn't impossible but would take significant time and create numerous opportunities for error. When taking on a project this ambitious and complex, the last thing you want to do is add anything to the already mountainous pile of odds stacked against you. After all, we were talking about a three-year publishing plan packed with 24 comic-book issues shipping monthly and a six-volume hardcover collection program. Luckily, through exhaustive searching and sheer grit, we were able to obtain an editable transcript that wasn't perfect but infinitely better than retyping an entire novel.

The comic book scripts were generated in-house. It didn't make sense to hire a freelance writer to break down a novel word-for-word and write loose art direction. We didn't need someone to paint a picture – PKD had already done that in spades. So instead, we handled the "scripting" ourselves. BOOM!'s CEO and Founder Ross Richie worked hand-in-hand with Editorial on the scripts and together we put every word of the novel in captions and word balloons alongside loose art descriptions evoked and inspired by the text. Those scripts would serve as blueprints for an artist to work from while having the freedom to improvise as their inspiration from the text saw fit.

We hired Tony Parker as the line artist. Up until that point, he hadn't done much published work in the mainstream comic book industry outside of his work on multiple *Warhammer 40,000* series released by BOOM! He was – and is – talented, reliable, and collaborative. In other words, exactly what you want in any artist if you're an editor, let alone an artist about to tackle an incredibly long and difficult project.

In the same vein, we brought in veteran color artist Blond, who had a strong track record. His style, specifically his use of cooler color palettes, was perfect for a futuristic sci-fi book centered around androids. Since this was a book with mainstream appeal, we thought a more polished and refined approach to the colors would easily greet regular comic book readers while also appealing to non-comic book readers.

To round out the creative, Richard Starkings took on the incredibly arduous task of handling the lettering duties. Not only did he have to letter an entire novel's worth of text, he had to make it fit organically in the artwork. Luckily, he had unique experience as a premier Eisner Award-nominated letterer who had worked on more comic books than I could count and had also served as an editor at Marvel UK, which, if nothing else, meant he understood the audacious insanity we were attempting editorially.

We had comic book luminary Bill Sienkiewicz as the main cover artist accompanied by a suite of diverse talents: Moritat, Scott Keating, Brett Weldele, Dennis Calero, Frazer Irving, and Connor Willumsen. It was a great experiment to do some weirder and more conceptual covers and everyone rose to the challenge, relishing in the opportunity despite one big artistic obstacle…

We were not allowed to do anything that looked like *Blade Runner*.

No actor likenesses. No Syd Mead vehicular or architectural designs. No Japanese influence on the city. Anything that was unique to *Blade Runner* and not in the book was off limits. Anything that crossed the streams had to be redesigned: characters, clothing, weapons, vehicles, everything. It was a challenge because so many of us – myself included – had a strong connection to *Blade Runner* and knew it well. While somewhat daunting at first, this challenge created a distinct set of walls that forced everyone to be even more creative. And dare I say that the restrictions resulted in us making entirely more interesting, important, and lasting art.

The original editor on the project was Ian Brill. He helped put the team together and set the course for the long haul. When this book was being developed and later when it began its run, I was still just the lowly Executive Assistant on the other side of the wall from the Editorial bullpen.

I'll never forget when Ian asked me to proofread that first issue. He handed me a hard copy, full-size proof we had received from our printer and a copy of *Do Androids Dream of Electric Sheep?* I had a decent amount of proofreading experience at that point, but this was an entirely different beast. My assignment was to read the proof of the issue alongside the novel to make sure that every word was there, every word was spelled correctly, and every piece of punctuation was properly represented.[1]

While the task was intimidating, I grabbed my trusty red pen and went to work. Usually when I proofread a single-issue comic book, it would take me maybe 30 minutes. 45 if it was a dense issue or one with numerous errors that required extensive notes.

Do Androids Dream of Electric Sheep? #1 took me two hours to proofread. Maybe more. Probably more. Think about it: I was reading the text twice but in the least efficient way. I couldn't just read through the issue and then read the text in the book. I had to read a sentence here and then read a sentence there. Read a sentence here and then read a sentence there. And through all that, I had to make sure that the words were in the same order, the words in the issue were spelled correctly, and all the punctuation matched up. Not to mention, I still had to do the regular comic book proofreading checks, like making sure that balloons and captions are placed properly, checking that word balloon tails are pointed at the right characters, looking critically at how the information flows from panel to panel throughout the page, checking consistency and continuity in the art – the list goes on.

That first issue alone included over two chapters worth of text. To this day, it is the most intense single-issue comic book I have ever had the privilege of proofreading.

Mind you, at this point in my career, I had no additional copyediting experience outside of the classroom setting and working for my high school newspaper. I just had a natural eye and was filled with the right balance of piss and vinegar.

A month went by and it was time to proofread issue #2. Same thing. Two hours of my workday gone. Maybe more. Probably more. At that point, I knew this was not sustainable. The task of copyediting this book was so monumental it was negatively impacting the core responsibilities of my job.

So I made a decision. I would not proofread *Do Androids Dream of Electric Sheep?* during the workday anymore. Instead, I would tell my boss, who happened to be the CEO, who happened to be working hand in glove with the

---

[1] As a side note, I could have cured the Missing Oxford Comma Epidemic with the amount of commas I caught missing throughout the series.

series scripts, that I was happy to continue copyediting the project but that it would have to be on a freelance work-for-hire basis outside of my standard workday. I would still proofread other projects at the office but this one was a unicorn that needed to run free after hours.

But I never had the conversation. I didn't have to.

Before I could take action to change my work life, work life took action for me. This specific time was when BOOM! was preparing to launch a new line of comic books based on Disney and Pixar properties. We had the license to continue publishing the long-running classic Disney comics like *Walt Disney's Comics & Stories*, *Mickey Mouse*, and *Donald Duck*, and we were the first publisher in any medium to tell brand-new stories with the Pixar properties and characters. It was a massive initiative and one that BOOM! was staffing up for, most notably in the Editorial department.

Matt Gagnon, who was the Managing Editor at the time, came to me one afternoon and asked me if I had any interest in working in Editorial. I told him I was absolutely interested but good luck convincing Ross to let me off his desk. See, Ross and I had a great connection. I was the best assistant he'd ever had – his words – and he saw my potential and had a bigger plan for me that didn't include making a run at Editorial. So that's where I left it with Matt: if he could get it across the plate with the big man, I'd jump into the deep end.

I had underestimated Ross. He taught me a valuable lesson in leadership that day, which was that if you have someone talented in your organization who is an asset with potential and passionate about something, the last thing you should do is be obstructive. People do their best work when they're engaged and excited about what they're working on. I'm a firm believer in that. I mean, I have to be – that's how I got to where I am today.

So, I quickly made the switch to Editorial and had my own slate of books, including *Do Androids Dream of Electric Sheep?* I co-edited issue #3 with Ian Brill, but from there on out, it was all me. I worked on the project for over two years and every single issue shipped on time, for 24 issues. That rarely happens and it almost never happens with a licensed comic book series, especially one that gets printed in Korea on an eight-week print-to-delivery schedule as opposed to a domestic printer's three-week schedule. And that hard work was rewarded with a glowing review from *The Village Voice* and an Eisner Award nomination for "Best New Series." It was an incredible effort and accomplishment by the entire team and I'm grateful to have been a part of it.

Working with the Philip K. Dick Estate came with its own unique set of challenges just like any licensor. Obviously, they were very protective of the material – and rightfully so – which meant the creative team had to find that right balance between personal artistic expression and translating PKD's art from one medium to another. And if that wasn't enough pressure, the main person doing approvals was Isa Dick Hackett, Philip K. Dick's daughter. Imagine the anxiety you already have as an editor and then add the layer of interpreting a deceased great author's work and showing it to that author's daughter. But my anxiety was relieved because the Estate was incredibly helpful and supportive and truly believed in what we were doing.

When it came time to put together the first collected volume, I worked tirelessly with my book designer Erika Terriquez. I remember putting in hours looking at the design of different books and writing a very detailed work order with examples of page layouts that I thought would set this book apart from standard comic book collections and prove appealing to traditional comic book readers as well as casual readers and those who were experiencing the medium for the first time. It came together beautifully, but the hardest part was the copy on the dust jacket. I had to work with Chip Mosher, our Sales and Marketing Director at the time, on the back cover copy because trying to explain exactly what the hell this project was succinctly and eloquently was... an exercise. Turns out that was the easy part. Something much simpler ended up being much more work.

We wanted to put something on the front cover that clearly tied the book to *Blade Runner* without detracting from the main title. We knew telling readers and buyers that this was the book *Blade Runner* was based on would help with sales and garner interest from people who maybe didn't know the film was a loose adaptation. But how were we going to phrase it? It needed to be short and easy to read but it also had to be something the Estate would approve and be happy with. So we bounced a bunch of ideas around and, after a while, we got it: "The Inspiration for *Blade Runner*."

It's amazing how just five words can cause so much pain but also spring a fountain of elation. Now imagine dealing with 60,000+ words of *Do Androids Dream of Electric Sheep?* text.

By the time I finished all 24 single issues and six hardcover collected editions, I had read *Do Androids Dream of Electric Sheep?* cover to cover a total of seven times. Seven times. More times than I had read any other novel. More times than I had seen *Blade Runner*.

I read the novel once at the very beginning just to have a sense of the story – just a free read to get acquainted with the book. I read the novel twice over the course of working on all the scripts, twice more while proofreading all of the pages/lettering of the single issues, and another two times when I copyedited everything again before sending the hardcover collections to press.

Seven times. That's nearly half a million words. And if you count all of the 24 essays we commissioned to run as bonus back matter material in the single issues, I definitely hit that half million-word mark.

So yes, not only did I edit a comic book series that integrated an entire novel's worth of prose, I also edited an entire novel's worth of essay text. Wow! Now that I think back on all this, I have no idea what the hell I was thinking. As I type this, it all sounds quite insane.

It *was* insane. But it was damn fun and rewarding too. Those essays were inspired and revelatory, a glimpse into how this story and Philip K. Dick himself played a role in these remarkable people's lives.

We had a real murderer's row of contributors: well-regarded authors also known in the comic book world in Warren Ellis, Matt Fraction, Ed Brubaker, David Mack, and Chris Roberson; Daryl Gregory, Gregg Rickman, Jack Skillingstead, and Keith R.A. DeCandido, who were authors from the sci-fi world; Tony Parker and Blond who worked first-hand on the art of the complete comic book series; esteemed journalist Graeme McMillan; Philip K. Dick biographer Gabriel McKee; powerhouse author and PKD enthusiast Jonathan Lethem; fan and advocate of the series, BOOM! Studios's former Sales & Marketing Director Chip Mosher; Kalen Egan, my counterpart, liaison, and friend at the Philip K. Dick Estate; television mainstay and creator of *Farscape* Rockne S. O'Bannon; James Blaylock and Tim Powers, Philip K. Dick's sci-fi author contemporaries and close friends; and PKD's daughter, Isa Dick Hackett.

Isa was kind enough to let me interview her for the last essay in the final issue of the *Do Androids Dream of Electric Sheep?* series. It was an incredible moment for me and like everything associated with this project, layered with its own crust of intensity and anxiety. I wasn't a journalist. I wasn't a professional interviewer. I edited comic books. And now I had to discuss a deceased author with his daughter. After I shook my pre-game jitters, it turned into a very pleasant conversation. I learned a lot from it and was happy to provide an outlet for Isa to talk about her father and his work. It was the best way I could imagine ending the long and windy road.

At least, I thought that was the end of the road.

Like every stage of working on this project, there was always something else. This time it came in the form of *Dust to Dust*, the authorized prequel comic book series to *Do Androids Dream of Electric Sheep?*

A limited series that told the story of what the world was like before the events of the novel, it involved not nearly as much reading and copyediting but was still a challenge. After all, we were expanding on a very well-known piece of literature and needed to make sure we weren't taking extreme liberties or negatively impacting the canon source material.

When it comes to well-regarded fiction, especially science fiction, the fan base is incredibly dedicated, which means that they pay attention. To everything. The seemingly smallest inconsistency does not go unseen and there is an enthusiastic crowd of vocal fans that have no problem letting you know when you get something right and when you get something wrong. One thing I really had to keep at the forefront of my mind during this project was that it was imperative that I navigate between curating something for a modern audience that may have found this material through nontraditional means and a core audience that had been living in this world since before I was born. Those kinds of choppy waters can easily push some editors, authors, and publishers to play it safe, which often results in easily forgettable tie-in fiction. But it can also have the reverse effect where you'll see something go completely off the rails and alienate its core base alongside new readers. It's difficult but ultimately rewarding when you can thread that precarious needle.

So it was my job, however subjective it may have been, to look at everything through that lens. I had to trust myself, after being immersed in this world for so long, to be able to look at everything, make a quick judgment as to whether it felt right to the overall universe we were playing in, and ensure that anything that was knowingly out of place had a specific purpose presented clearly to the audience. We could add depth to existing elements but we weren't going to add any backstories or plot points that would change the interpretation of the text in *Do Androids Dream of Electric Sheep?* This was our chance to add a small bit to this incredible world, not change it.

Luckily, I had an incredible team that was right for the job. This time, it was author, comic book scribe, and co-creator of *iZombie*, Chris Roberson. He knew PKD's work well and was an accomplished science-fiction writer in his own right. With Robert Adler on art, Andres Lozano and Javier Suppa doing the color art, and Comicraft's Jimmy Betancourt handling the lettering, we had all the right ingredients packaged in gorgeous covers by Trevor Hairsine, Benjamin

Carré, Scott Keating, and Connor Willumsen. And I had graphic designer Brian Latimer on the book, who used our mutual love of pink and other punchy colors to turn the softcover collections into trippy, psychedelic books worthy of having Philip K. Dick's name on the covers.

We successfully told a new story in the *Do Androids Dream of Electric Sheep?* universe and across eight single issues and two collected paperback editions, we paid our own little tribute to Philip K. Dick. But again, that wasn't the end.

In 2015, I revisited those *years* of my life and teamed up once again with Ian Brill to put together the *Do Androids Dream of Electric Sheep? Omnibus* paperback edition. With over 600 pages, it boasted the entire series, all the covers, and all the essays with a slick new interior book design by Kelsey Dieterich and Scott Newman. It's truly a stunning piece that can also be used as a weapon. But you'd never need to because that cover is the real killer.

The cover to the unabridged *Do Androids Dream of Electric Sheep?* omnibus (front and back).

While putting together the book, we decided we wanted a brand-new cover so I went out to Jay Shaw, a friend and insanely talented artist who also happens to be the Brand Director at Mondo. I wanted him to get inspired and go nuts and what he came back with was this crazy idea to make the book look like a giant computer chip, using intricate line design on top of black. His dream vision was to have all of the line work in foil but he understood that it might be cost prohibitive. I knew we only had one shot at this edition and I knew the foil would make it something really special so I had some conversations, crunched the numbers, and made it happen.

That cover signifies the closing of yet another chapter on this project. Everything about it is new and improved but there is one thing that stayed the same. If you look real close near the title, you can see those five painstakingly crafted words that form that short and deceptively simple phrase that tells a story all to itself.

Earth to Earth: The BOOM! Comics

by Mario Escamilla

Thou Shalt Show Me the Path of Life

In 2008, BOOM! Studios started talks with Electric Shepherd Productions (ESP) to secure the rights to publish *Do Androids Dream of Electric Sheep?*, the 1968 novel by Philip K. Dick, as a monthly series.[1] ESP is the production arm of the Philip K. Dick Estate, managed by his daughters Laura Leslie and Isa Hackett, who have worked alongside several creative teams to provide modern adaptations of their father's work in different media.

The monthly series was an interesting premise, not conceived as an adaptation but rather as a fully illustrated version of the novel, containing the unabridged text with very few edits. The project relies heavily on the letterer, Richard Starkings of Comicraft, to produce a natural flow of the text, inserting the descriptions between the dialogue in the exact order of the novel. All this without making the pages feel cluttered.

Compare the text of the first page of the novel with the first page of the comic (text omissions underlined):

> A merry little surge of electricity piped by automatic alarm from the mood organ beside his bed awakened Rick Deckard. Surprised - it always

---

[1] http://www.newsarama.com/2758-boom-s-ross-richie-on-do-androids-dream-of-electric-sheep.html

> surprised him to find himself wake without prior notice - he rose from the bed, stood up in his multicolored pajamas, and stretched. Now, in her bed, his wife Iran opened her gray, unmerry eyes, blinked, then groaned and shut her eyes again.
>
> "You set your Penfield too weak," <u>he said to her</u>. "I'll reset it and you'll be awake and-"
>
> "Keep your hands off my settings." Her voice held bitter sharpness. "I don't *want* to be awake."
>
> He seated himself beside her, bent over her, and explained softly. "If you set the surge up high enough, you'll be glad you're awake; that's the whole point. At setting *C* it overcomes the threshold barring consciousness, as it does for me." Friendlily, because he felt well-disposed toward the world - *his* setting had been at *D* - he patted her bare, pale shoulder.
>
> "Get your crude cop hands away," <u>Iran said</u>.

Tony Parker (*Mass Effect: Foundation, Elephantmen, Rise of the Planet of the Apes*), a Phoenix illustrator who got his start in the roleplaying game industry, was selected to helm the visual department and does solid, thorough, and above all, beautiful work. The lines are always perfect, whether he's drawing bodies, places, or horizons. The stark, muted clarity of the comic is brought to life by Blond, a talented colorist who infuses the series with palettes appropriate for every scene of the post-apocalyptic world that Philip K. Dick describes.

Harrowing imagery of the San Francisco skyline, the abandoned buildings, the ruined inhabitants, in sum, the decaying Earth, are deliberately reminiscent of the visual style used in *Blade Runner*, to better bridge the two works of art: the novel and the movie, and transform them into a third: the comic.

The aesthetic of the comic is closely reminiscent of the movie, with the city having the same large ad screens, showing the same decay of the buildings, although industrial design and architecture are heavily influenced by the art decó movement, not to mention that the vehicles are flying versions of 1940s car designs with retro-futuristic characteristics.

Retelling the entire novel was no small task, and it required 24 issues published between July 2009 and June 2011. Every issue was accompanied by back matter (bonus material) featuring several notorious writers including Warren Ellis, Matt Fraction, Ed Brubaker, Keith deCandido and even Isa Dick Hackett, who narrate their connections to the author or the novel and the influence the book had on their individual work.

Editors Ian Brill (*Dracula World Order, Zombie Tales*) and Bryce Carlson (*HIT, Wall-E: Out There*) take on the task of dividing the novel into 24 issues, grouping

Do Androids Dream of Electric Sheep? #1 from BOOM!

them into four-issue installments. Their decisions result in the usual comic pacing without regard to the original chapter divisions, sometimes finishing an issue even halfway through a paragraph, but without sacrificing the actual text or flow of the story. For example, issues #1-4 of the comic cover from chapter one of the book up until halfway through chapter seven.

The editors and illustrators worked closely to enhance the novel beyond a mere graphical description. The text provides context in some cases and the art reinforces the comprehension. In other cases, the art provides the context to the prose. A talented group of artists collaborated and shared duties on regular and variant covers, including Bill Sienkiewicz (*New Mutants, Elektra: Assassin*), Moritat (*Elephantmen, Hellblazer: Rebirth*), Scott Keating (*CSI: Secret Identity, Planet of the Apes*), Brett Weldele (*The Surrogates, The Light*), Frazer Irving (*Bedlam, Iron Man: The Inevitable*), Dennis Calero (*Assassins Creed: Templars, X-Factor*), Connor Willumsen (*Wolverine Max*) and Tony Parker.

The comic received an Eisner Award nomination in 2010 for Best New Series,[2] but ultimately lost to Image's *Chew*.[3] Between late 2009 and October 2011, the series was collected in six volumes, each one covering a four-issue installment. Finally, in late 2015, BOOM! published the entire series in an omnibus,[4] a massive 640 page volume that also included all the back matter articles in one section along with a complete cover gallery.

In all, it gives you a completely different experience than simply reading the novel, and will impact your future readings of it. It's hard not to think of the images of the comic the next time you read the novel or watch the movie, thus making this comic series a perfect starting point for those who have watched the *Blade Runner* movie but have yet to delve into Philip K. Dick's written masterpiece. The comic illustrates a path that will not compromise the complexities of the novel in a format that makes it easier to understand and absorb. You could even argue it's easier to stare at Tony Parker's gorgeous art while pondering the heavy questions the novel poses than to take your eyes from the plain text and gaze off into space.

---

[2] http://www.avclub.com/article/eisner-award-nominees-announced-39966
[3] http://www.comic-con.org/awards/eisner-award-recipients-2010-present
[4] http://www.nerdspan.com/booms-do-androids-dream-of-electric-sheep-to-get-omnibus-treatment-this-december/

In Thy Presence is the Fullness of Joy

The critically acclaimed and financially successful BOOM! adaptation prompted the company to negotiate another project with ESP, namely a prequel to *Do Androids Dream of Electric Sheep?* titled *Dust to Dust*. It was proposed by managing editor Matt Gagnon to Chris Roberson,[5] writer of *Cinderella* and *From Fabletown With Love* for Vertigo. The rest of the creative team included artist Robert Adler and Argentinean colorists Andrés Lozano and Javier Suppa, all under the direction of Bryce Carlson.

The 8-issue series starts with Charlie Victor, our main character, reciting the words of the burial rites from the Book of Common Prayer, "ashes to ashes, dust to dust," as if we are witnessing the funeral of Earth. World War Terminus has just ended, the dust has changed the landscape of the planet and few denizens have remained. We are immediately familiarized with recognizable imagery from the *Blade Runner* universe. We see the skyline of San Francisco (where the novel takes place), a flying police car more reminiscent of the *Blade Runner* movie than the retro-futuristic design from the comic adaptation, graffiti related to Mercerism (one of the key concepts from the novel that is missing from the movie), and the decay of animals seen plainly as Charlie encounters a dead owl which lets us know that animals are starting to die in great numbers.

Our next protagonist is a man named Malcolm Reed who has acquired an unusual ability due to the radioactive dust: the ability to receive and experience the emotions of those around him, which not only gives him hallucinations but also brands him a "special," a human being forbidden to emigrate or reproduce, much like J.R. Isidore in the novel. His talent proves useful as he's being recruited to hunt a group of missing androids. If he cannot "sense" a being, then said being must be an android. By that logic, we are privy to the fact that Charlie Victor is a C-V model (hence his name) made by the Grozzi Corporation. His assignment, and the main focus of the comic series, is to capture a number of C-V androids who have become fugitives led by a tyrant named Talus. They're a group of renegade soldiers who fought in World War Terminus plotting to end all organic life on Earth with the intention of having machines inherit the planet. While they're aware that Charlie Victor is a Blade Runner, the term is never used.

---

[5] http://www.newsarama.com/5180-dust-to-dust-what-happened-before-dreams-of-electric-sheep.html

Do Androids Dream of Electric Sheep?- Dust to Dust #1 from BOOM!

Our final main character, Samantha Wu, is a young scientist trying to research a cure for the pervasive dust contamination in order to prevent more animals from dying. Mercerism is highly prevalent in her panels, as evidenced by the graffiti in the subway and her talks with a co-worker who avidly promotes the religion.

Dr. Wu's research is leading nowhere, but she starts suspecting that empathy might be the key to humanity's survival and begins researching Mercerism. Charlie and Malcolm are trying to find the rogue androids by examining the city cameras' facial recognition system which had been disabled by an android posing as a cop.

As Samantha recalls her memories of World War Terminus, we learn that her mother died in 2015, shortly after the end of the war. With a colleague, Dr. Martin Penfield, she intends to investigate how empathy boxes (machines from the novel that control emotions) affect the human brain. This connects to the original novel in that the boxes Deckard and his wife own are Penfield models.

Malcolm and Charlie follow the clues to an abandoned apartment where all kinds of animal carcasses from birds to horses rest, some dead for a while, others recently deceased. Charlie recalls that androids cared little for organics during the war, seeing themselves as superior not only in terms of human frailty, but also in terms of emotion. Malcolm spots an android watching over them and they pursue him to an empty public library. Charlie recounts that androids have the ability to learn from experience, which makes every unit different. His talent is to spot and avoid ambushes, as he is clearly entering a trap inside the library. He dispatches three of the rogues and goes to investigate the workplace of one of them: the Presidio, where Dr. Wu is employed.

Meanwhile, Wu decides to enter the virtual reality world of the empathy box, and meets Wilbur Mercer, the guru of Mercerism, for the first time. Afterward, Dr. Penfield shows her the scans of her brain activity demonstrating that her experience lasted only 30 seconds, but for Samantha it felt like weeks of a transcendental experience. They compare their results to studies which reveal that androids can obtain something similar to feelings when their brains are stimulated with electric charges.

Ecstatic with her experience, Wu goes to find her Mercerist colleague but instead finds Charlie and Malcolm, who tell her there is a mole in the office. Malcolm has a schizoid attack as a result of going too long without his meds that keep him from eternally sensing everyone around him. In the meantime, the rogues and Talus are informed about the failed ambush at the library and the fact that Charlie is at the Presidio. Dr. Wu identifies her own assistant as the android mole, but it's too late, for her assistant has already kidnapped Malcolm at that point.

Halfway through the series, Malcolm Reed has a flashback showing us how he became aware of others' emotions and how the medication he needs not only suppresses his special ability but also his schizophrenic illusions. Then he wakes up among the androids and realizes that he's unable to sense them at all. The group wants to know more about his special abilities, of course. It's then, while he can't sense anything, that he starts to wonder if he might be better off living in a world full of androids.

Charlie Victor, still an android soldier, feels unaccustomed to giving orders to humans, who he considers his masters according to his programming. But he must do so in order to rescue Malcolm and finish his mission. Samantha agrees to help him with his investigation as long as he answers her questions about android psychology.

After checking out her assistant's apartment, the two are attacked once again by the rogue androids. In another flashback, we're shown the process of android creation in the early 21st century, hinting that war was the real motivation that drove the rapid development of the technology, culminating in World War Terminus. Charlie proceeds to neutralize the commandos but is injured.

Malcolm starts to doubt if he will even be rescued and the androids go back and forth between wanting to kill him or wanting to find out how he is able to identify them so easily. In the end, they decide to keep him around for the same purpose he was recruited: to spot other android hunters dispatched to kill them.

Dust to Dust delves into the rationality of emotions – the use of language to define ourselves through our feelings – Samantha Wu decides she doesn't want to be a slave to fear and defeats her last attacker. She heals Charlie Victor with his self-repair kit as they discuss empathy and the human ability to turn it on or off, as well as the concept of androids having feelings.

One thing Talus and Charlie have in common is that they feel emotions are humanity's worst trait. Samantha, who believes otherwise, tries to convince Charlie to experience emotions, but he refuses. Meanwhile, the androids, holed up in the iconic Sentinel Building (occupied by Francis Ford Coppola's American Zoetrope studio since 1972, where we see the name of the Cafe Zoetrope located on the ground floor in the illustration[6]), finally lay out their plan to exterminate all human life in San Francisco. Once that's accomplished, they'll move on to other cities until no humans remain.

Charlie and Samantha arrive and begin their assault while Malcolm remains blissfully calm. Charlie springs the trap by surrendering his weapons, all the while trying to figure out the rogues' plan. Malcolm's Zen-like state is interrupted when Samantha hacks a weapon's power source to produce a surge that forces Talus to experience emotions. Compelled and horrified by these emotions, he agrees to recall the other androids who are busy poisoning the municipal water system. Once they arrive, Charlie Victor reveals that his plan all along was to dispose of them via a bomb located in his torso.

Samantha and Malcolm make a run for it, barely escaping the explosion, which destroys the historical building. They are left to continue their lives as best they can. Samantha turns to Mercerism to cope, demonstrating the rise in popularity of the philosophy/religion that we see at its peak in the novel. Malcolm becomes somewhat of a television junkie, mesmerized by not only the disturbing news, but the many commercial ads that tie in to the novel, like ads for Penfield Mood organs, animal replicas (electric sheep, anyone?), and the premiere of a talk show by none other than Buster Friendly, the tireless host that routinely criticizes Mercer in the novel.

At Thy Right Hand There is Pleasure for Everyone

It is worth mentioning that the covers of the first four issues are reminiscent of the film's aesthetics – not only the main covers by Trevor Hairsine (*Ultimate Six, X-O Manowar*), but more so the variant covers by Benjamin Carré (*Mass Effect: Foundation, Star Wars: Knights of the Old Republic*). Unfortunately, the final four issues were released without variant covers, and Hairsine was only available to work on the fifth issue. Issue six's cover was created by Scott Keating, while Connor Willumsen handled the covers of issues seven and eight, demonstrating a complete departure from the other covers. When published together, the first and second volumes included cover galleries but the second volume came with a bonus sketch gallery.

To me, the ultimate question to ask is whether or not this comic is a fitting prequel to not only the novel, but the entire *Blade Runner* universe. There are

---

[6] Cafe Zoetrope website. Retrieved from
https://www.cafezoetrope.com/introduction

definitely some common themes. There are fugitive androids who try to integrate themselves into human society. There's a hunter who, at a second glance, is more than just a man. There's even the quest to try and extend life. But beside the action and the many cameos, there is little else here that links the series to the bigger picture. If it were not for the mention of things like the Grozzi Corporation, Mercerism, and the string of ads at the very end that include the shout out to Buster Friendly, this could pass as a stand-alone science-fiction comic.

Perhaps the lack of connection was due to the fact that they tried to fit the whole story into eight issues. Some of the more promising threads, such as Dr. Wu's research on empathy and the exploration of supernormal abilities of Malcolm Reed, do not receive any further exploration or closure. One could argue that it was understood that her research could not have been successful because animals are all but extinct by the time the novel takes place. One could also assume that "specials" with enhanced senses may have become extinct since we never see anyone like Malcolm again. These speculative ideas had the potential to fuel the imagination of readers, yet they were cast away.

Stefan Schensag writes in his essay "On Three Comics Adaptations of Philip K. Dick" (featured in *The World According to Philip K. Dick*[7]) that there is an underlying exploration of the definition of reality, demonstrated by things like the Twitter-like part of Samantha (an interesting premise discarded early on the series), and Malcom's inability to trust his senses even when he knows his hallucinations are not really there. Apart from that, there is never an urge to question the philosophical themes Dick is famous for.

In addition, the art is a complete departure from the direction taken by the *Do Androids Dream of Electric Sheep?* adaptation. It's certainly effective in its own way though, with Adler's art taking on a simpler style with many jagged lines and little attention to detail. The use of color is also quite simple, but offering little depth. The color palette is bright and full of stark colors – not very representative of the genesis of a post-apocalyptic, dystopian, and cyberpunk world. But the art pales when contrasted to the previous novel adaptation, further separating the series and hindering its place as an authentic prequel.

Even if the intention of BOOM! Studios was to create an independent project – a companion piece to the *Do Androids Dream of Electric Sheep?*

---

[7] *The World According to Philip K. Dick*, edited by Alexander Dunst and Stefan Schlensag, Palgrave Macmillan UK, 2015.

adaptation – *Dust to Dust* feels like a shallow attempt to interact with and expand the *Blade Runner/Do Androids Dream of Electric Sheep?* mythos. The limited series only has enough space to accommodate a simple detective plot that just happens to have connections to the mythos via flashbacks, and a bit of fan service.

Where the novel adaptation was a true masterpiece, *Dust to Dust* becomes only what BOOM! wanted from it, to be just a "regular comic."[8]

---

[8] http://www.cbr.com/chris-roberson-on-dust-to-dust/

Longevity and Incept Dates: The World-Building of *Blade Runner* Lives on in Multimedia

by R. Lee Brown

It happens every time there's a thunderstorm.

Not big, booming, shake-the-windows thunder, but a distant rumble – the sound of the heavens in discontent. No matter where I am or what I'm doing or who I'm with, the discordant growling of thunder makes me think of *Blade Runner*.

Of course, it's the "Tears in Rain" scene. Tough guy replicant Roy Batty in his last moments decides to spare human Rick Deckard who has been trying to kill him because, in the end, life matters. Everyone's life matters.

It almost makes me cry every time. Not an "Oh no, my sports team lost!" cry or even a "My checking account is empty again!" cry. No, it's a real "Bambi's mom just died and I can't let anyone see a grown man weep" cry. And while the thunder itself is bad enough, if I actually hear Vangelis' heart-touching soundtrack music for that scene, I'm looking for a hanky or a tissue or complaining about how the damn pollen count is making my eyes all puffy again.

It's a true testament to the cinematic world-building of *Blade Runner* that even the sounds of that moment bring everything back. That scene is an amazing culmination of everything that has come before it, of the investment in situations and characters that the film has successfully asked its audience to make. *Blade Runner*'s brilliant direction merges with powerful writing, spot-on acting, creative lighting, exciting sound design, and a spectacular soundtrack to create a "real" science-fiction universe that succeeds in creating its own shorthand, transporting viewers to that dystopian retro world of the future.

It's a world so fully realized, in a way so few movies successfully do, that it actually lives on in the hearts and minds of the movie's fans. It makes us eager to re-experience that world again and again in whatever multimedia forms we can find. Just a few tones of Vangelis' synthesizer or that distant, rumbling thunder and we can hear Roy Batty's quiet, smiling "time to die." Off goes the dove into the heavens.

Where's that hanky again? OK, all good.

It's exactly that kind of ambiance that people embrace; it's what makes a truly great world-building motion picture experience live on well past its incept date.

Despite initial mixed reviews and panicked executives, *Blade Runner* picked up a loyal, thriving audience that has always hungered for more, for a return to the filmic Los Angeles 2019, for the sights and sounds of *Blade Runner* to live on in multimedia over 30 years later.

It took some time for post-release fandom to catch fire, although by 2007 there had been seven versions of the film that had played in different markets. The movie had become a highly popular video rental and was one of the first movies released on DVD. A work print had found a surreptitious release (that won back many disaffected viewers who never enjoyed the extraneous Deckard voiceover attached to the film), a Director's Cut hit theaters, and of course "The Final Cut" version came out in 2007 on just about every video format possible this side of 3D.

Clearly, fans today want to experience more *Blade Runner* so much that studios are willing to invest more big dollars into the franchise, which is an incredible feat when you consider the lukewarm reception the original movie first got in theaters.

There is such devotion to the world created by Ridley Scott, Vangelis, and the incredible sound department of *Blade Runner* that the internet is filled with clips and sound effects intended to replicate the feel of the film. (See what I did there?) Fan Crysknife007 actually posted a 12-hour loop of the ambient sound effects in Rick Deckard's apartment.[1]

Past the initial delight at recognizing the sounds, the various soundtracks and bootlegs quickly become comfortable background noise that you can play while you do other things. After that, all you need is your own Esper Photo Analysis Machine to enhance 224 to 176, enhance and stop. (Don't forget your hard copy.) As a side-note, you'll also find 30 minutes of "ambient sounds of Los Angeles, 2019,"[2] plus 12 more hours of the ambient sounds of the interiors of the Tyrell[3] and Bradbury[4] buildings.

There are even more *Blade Runner* ambient sounds available, but you might be curious about the origins of the clips "McCoy's Bedroom"[5] and "Under the City,"[6] since those locations don't (by my recollection) appear in the film. That's because there was more than one fictional *Blade Runner* hunting replicants in fictional Los Angeles 2019, giving suspects the Voight-Kampff test, enhancing and tracking photos, and wondering about his own human origins.

Surprised? No, you didn't miss a direct-to-video sequel.

In 1997, Westwood Studios let us walk Blade Runner Detective Ray McCoy through the same city, hear the same sights and sounds, and even interact with many of the same characters from the film with the Microsoft Windows release of the *Blade Runner* PC game. (Not to be confused with the 1985 *Blade Runner* game that was based not on the film, but was instead a "video game interpretation of the film score," and featured side scrolling action where your character tries to shoot "replidroids."[7])

Even 15 years after the film's release, fans still loved the movie and its atmosphere so much that computer game producers and publishers staked millions of dollars on a fully-voiced 3D point-and-click adventure game. They

---

[1] https://www.youtube.com/watch?v=O7FhEpif1cA
[2] https://www.youtube.com/watch?v=yrRFx6E9JiQ
[3] https://www.youtube.com/watch?v=2W6tAC8PeCY&list=PL-Qa3JOhMY5eJqVwltfX2KQpLgPJCwzwY
[4] https://www.youtube.com/watch?v=DKHnorlnnqM&list=PLLKrg6lxteen1fcMJ9y-3smq2M-X1yfui&index=5
[5] https://www.youtube.com/watch?v=AyHE5pClfyM&list=PLLKrg6lxteen1fcMJ9y-3smq2M-X1yfui&index=2
[6] https://www.youtube.com/watch?v=CPE14pMGdNg&index=3&list=PLLKrg6lxteen1fcMJ9y-3smq2M-X1yfui
[7] https://en.wikipedia.org/wiki/Blade_Runner_(1985_video_game)

even scored the coup of getting several of the film's actors to voice the in-game version of their characters.

If you didn't get enough of James Hong's eyeball DNA technician Chew being sassy to uninvited guests, you got to revisit his lab and learn more about his devotion to creating eyes (to the exclusion of other distractions.) Imagine playing the object of Chew's impatience:

> **Chew:** What you want? I'm busy. Deliveries to rear.
>
> **McCoy:** LAPD. I've got a couple of questions.
>
> **Chew:** Talk talk. Always talk. You wait. You no take up time. Busy. Busy.

McCoy is much less aggressive with his questioning of Chew than Roy Batty would be later. If you can almost imagine James Hong reading the lines, imagine actually hearing him speaking to *you*.

When Chew is finished giving you his taste of the *Blade Runner* environment, he sends you off to speak with fan favorite J.F. Sebastian ("He do what he always do: nervous system. Very important to Dr. Tyrell.") and you get to spend time in the incredibly atmospheric Bradbury Apartment Building with marching toy soldiers and teddy bears. Sebastian himself is on hand, voiced by film actor William Sanderson.[8] You get the feeling that Pris is already hiding in there, somewhere.

You'll visit many more of the iconic locations from the film, including the golden-hued top floor office of the Tyrell Corporation, recreated from the angles used in the movie. Want to have your own conversation with Rachael about the Tyrell owl? You get your chance, complete with chime-based background music. (Apparently, that owl was pretty important to her; after all, as she says in the game "It's a flawless replica. We used a real one as a model.")

Blade Runner the PC game isn't a prequel or sequel in the strictest sense of the words. The publishers called it a "sidequel." The story takes place *during* the events of *Blade Runner* the film, which is how the character you play gets to meet the likes of Hannibal Chew, Rachael, J.F. Sebastian, Leon Kowalski, and even replicant mastermind Dr. Eldon Tyrell, as he tries to solve mysteries and put together clues. (No appearance by Rick Deckard or Roy Batty, although Deckard's exploits are called out a few times.) What, no Zhora? The game's Blade Runner Ray McCoy spends plenty of time in *other* seedy joints (and his sleuthing takes him by the same shop that identified Zhora's imitation snake scales, so she's lurking around the corner in spirit, if nothing else).

---

[8] https://youtu.be/brGguuW3Cmg?t=1h51m49s

Westwood's *Blade Runner* PC Game.

Blade Runner the PC game was wildly successful: it sold over a million units worldwide, was a critical hit, and was nominated for enough "best game" awards to fill a spinner's trunk... if they, in fact, have trunks. They'd have to, right? The game also won "Computer Adventure Game of the Year," but that wasn't just for its highly repeatable game play (variables changed every time you started a new game, so different characters could either be human or replicant, plus, different game choices allowed for significantly different scenarios and multiple endings). The game was so incredibly popular because *it put the player in the* Blade Runner *world*, recreating the film's atmosphere perfectly, and letting the player interact with just about everything. Every bit of ambience that thrilled fans of the film are in the game.

The game is as authentic aurally as it is visually, and that was no mean feat. The sound effects are spot on; you even get to manipulate photos with the Esper Analysis machine with the telltale "Tick-tick-tick-tick" as the device angles around the images you feed it, with some surprising finds if you point it in the right direction. The *Blade Runner* effects library was available to supply the sounds every fan would expect. But as I pointed out, the music was just as powerful a part of the *Blade Runner* experience as the sound effects and the awe-inspiring visuals. When Westwood went into production on their game, they had to deal with the same frustration that soundtrack aficionados worldwide had been suffering for so many years prior: *the official film score was not available.*

Much can be written about the tangled web of rights surrounding *Blade Runner* (and that's a subject for another article) but even though Westwood was given the license to create the game, use the sounds, and use situations, characters (and actors) from the film, they could not get the rights to access the original Vangelis soundtrack recordings. How was this game going to live up to the name *Blade Runner* without one of the *key elements* that created the atmosphere the player was going to live in?

In the end, not gaining permission to use Vangelis' soundtrack recordings proved to be merely a setback. Westwood *was* given license to use the *music* from the film, just not the *original recordings*. That meant that Westwood composer Frank Klepacki actually had to *recreate* the movie's iconic score by ear – and he did such a superlative job that you'd never have guessed while playing the game. There are several familiar music cues that pop up just when you'd expect them. For example, Detective McCoy takes time out on his balcony for reflection and the same music from Deckard's balcony sojourn swells up in the background. It was immersive.

If you are curious, you can find walkthrough videos of the *Blade Runner* PC game on YouTube and other sites.[9] They'll give you a good idea of how sound, music, and voice brought the streets of *Blade Runner*'s Los Angeles 2019 back to life and let fans finally walk through that world themselves.

Of course, that was in 1997. Back then, we didn't have the luxury of everything we want a click away on the internet. It's no wonder audiences were so eager to pick up adventures that promised a return to the world of *Blade Runner*. There had been two sequel novels by then – *Blade Runner 2: The Edge of Human* (1995) and *Blade Runner 3: Replicant Night* (1996) – and a third would show up a year later. But those required a reader to generate the multimedia "world" of sound and music in their own heads.

Although for all practical purposes, they had been doing that ever since the film came out in 1982. From the beginning, fans had suffered the same multimedia hiccup that Westwood Studios did: *there was no official release of the original soundtrack available to anyone.*

There was a "soundtrack" released; the end credits of *Blade Runner* did promise a soundtrack album from Polydor records and movie scores were extremely popular at the time, riding on the cinematic high delivered by soundtracks from John Williams, Jerry Goldsmith, James Horner, Basil Pouledaris, and other composers who were creating some career-best work.

Because the music was such an integral part of the film, the *Blade Runner* soundtrack was highly anticipated. It was a nearly unprecedented score for an action or science-fiction movie; it wasn't the standard Symphony Orchestra score that had become so prevalent in action and science-fiction movies since *Star Wars*. Vangelis used "spontaneously created," electronic synthesizers to personally create the music for *Blade Runner*, often "on-the-fly" while watching the story from his studio.[10]

From the first booming notes, the score often played at odds with the visuals. While the first images of Los Angeles 2019 were of a hellish cityscape with smokestacks violently spewing flames, the music was grand, almost inspirational, suggesting that there was much more at play than meets the eye. Score-hungry fans flocked to the music store at their nearest local mall to pick

---

[9] https://youtu.be/brGguuW3Cmg?t=1h14m37s
[10] http://www.nemostudios.co.uk/bladerunner/

up the official soundtrack (on cassette tape, LP vinyl, or that newer compact disc fad). They grabbed at the album with the stylized Deckard and Rachael artwork on the front and eagerly took it home for a listen and a trip back to the world they remembered fondly.

It was good, but… something was off. Something wasn't quite right.

And that's because it was *not* the original soundtrack.

It was the official release, all right, but this was not a release of the music created by Vangelis for the film. Instead, it was a release from the California-based New American Orchestra *replaying* the music. It wasn't bad, but it wasn't the original. It was called an "Orchestral Adaptation of Music Composed for The Motion Picture by Vangelis." To make matters worse, there were only eight tracks on the release and two of them were incredibly similar ("End Title" and "End Title Reprise"). Still, there was "Farewell," and the orchestral version of "Tears in Rain." That did the trick. For a while.

Various musical cuts from *Blade Runner* appeared over the next several years, all played by countless orchestral "cover bands" that put together albums based on popular movies. Fans wouldn't actually get the authentic taste of Vangelis from *Blade Runner* for another 12 years – and even then, it wouldn't be a full soundtrack.

The reasons for this staggered release remain somewhat cloudy. The studio clearly wanted to capitalize on the film (which continued to grow more popular and won award after award, including Oscars, Golden Globes, a Hugo, three BAFTAs, Saturn Awards, London and LA Critics Awards, and more). Most other major motion pictures – especially the big science-fiction films – all had official, original soundtracks waiting at the stores. Why not the original Vangelis tracks?

Fans at the time didn't really know what was going on behind the scenes with *Blade Runner*. There was no internet to spill the inside story; it was even before cable's big explosion, before *E! Entertainment Television*, before *Entertainment Tonight* was slinging backstage film news and gossip. Fans had to get their information fix from genre publications like *Starlog* and *Cinefantastique*, and they were printing either studio releases and interviews, or their own wild speculations. The mystery behind the orchestral re-enactment of a few *Blade Runner* tracks versus the actual Vangelis recordings was not a major issue to take up magazine real estate, and definitely not something the studio wanted publicized.

There still hasn't been a definitive statement about the initial soundtrack offering and why the Vangelis tracks were not available. In the years that followed, as more behind the scenes videos were created for subsequent film releases (and as the various parties involved got some emotional distance from the events), it became clear that however much fans loved the film, not everyone involved in the making of the movie was as enthusiastic, and that included various producers who invested money and procured various rights to the film and each of the ingredients that went into it.

It's entirely possible that rights issues tied up the actual Vangelis release tracks. The artist himself says *he* wasn't behind the withholding of the original score. When later speaking of his original 1982 studio recordings in the liner notes of the official full soundtrack release, Vangelis said, "Finding myself unable to release these recordings at the time; it is with great pleasure that I am able to do so now."[11]

Hollywood politics and legalities aside, the scent of atmosphere in the first official soundtrack release wasn't enough to quench fan excitement to revisit the world of *Blade Runner* in all its glory. In hindsight, as we catapulted unknowing toward the Information Age, a release of that actual soundtrack seemed inevitable.

In 1989, audiences got a real taste as Vangelis released his own album *Themes*, which included "Love Theme from Blade Runner," "Memories of Green," and "End Titles." We had heard it before ("Memories of Green" was actually part of the 1980 Vangelis album *See You Later*), but these were the original versions we had been waiting for, so it was a step in the right direction.

Four years later, the floodgates started to open.

A 73-minute bootleg of the authentic *Blade Runner* soundtrack started making the rounds in 1993. It contained 18 tracks in total, and included music from the work print as well as the original version. This was music that would take you back to the movie to experience the atmosphere on your own terms – if you were lucky enough to find a copy, much less even *know* about its release. There was no Google to do an online search 23 years ago to see if someone had uploaded a copy. Still, this was the original music. There was a clear difference from that first album… and this was just the beginning.

Now that the artificial cat was out of the bag, an official release followed soon after. In 1994, Atlantic Records released the first official recording of the original Vangelis score – 12 tracks this time, versus the original eight, resulting in about 25 more minutes of music. "Blush Response" and "Rachael's Theme"

---

[11] https://www.discogs.com/Vangelis-Blade-Runner/release/3198926

made their official debuts, and we finally had the musical version of the powerful opening minutes of the film, including the spinner's descent into police headquarters.

That release also included dialogue snippets from the film. While it was certainly welcome to hear them on initial playback (including the main bits of Batty's "Tears in Rain" speech from the similarly titled track), not all the dialogue was placed in the proper track, which proved disconcerting to purists and distracting to those wanting to experience just the music ambiance. For example, Deckard's ESPER analysis plays over the beginning notes of "Main Titles (From *Blade Runner)*" which in the film itself encompasses the opening title screens and the following introduction to the Los Angeles hellscape.

For those seeking a complete *Blade Runner* experience, the 1993 bootleg version was actually more comprehensive. That remained the case as even more bootleg soundtracks were created and released in the years following. A Romanian version of the 73-minute bootleg from Gongo Music, with a few differences, hit the streets in 1995. There were a few less tracks, but it included "Blimpvert," which any *Blade Runner* fan would recognize instantly, especially if they wanted to travel Off-World.

In 2002, the quintessential bootleg album came out: *Blade Runner: Esper Edition*. Someone, somewhere, got their hands on just about every piece of Vangelis music created for *Blade Runner*. It was two discs, totaling 33 tracks and contained nearly two hours of music, including some very atmospheric background sounds and ambiance. This was a fan's spinner joyride through the world of *Blade Runner*. Want to meditate? Want to turn a ceiling fan on slow rotate? Want a companion piece to the falling rain outside? The *Esper Edition* brought it all home.

There was another shot at an official soundtrack release in 2007 with *Blade Runner Trilogy, 25th Anniversary*. The "trilogy" was actually the addition of a third CD of music – not actually from the film itself, but containing brand new Vangelis tracks "inspired" by the film. A nice addition, even if new music fell outside of the "comprehensive but strictly from the movie" version fans always wanted.

The bootleggers were not to be outdone, however. The *Esper Edition* got its own 2007 upgrade. That version was called the *Retirement Edition* and contained five discs including all of the music missing from the original release, as if the average fan could comprehend that there was even *more* music they hadn't heard yet.

Fans could now hear every note. With the wonder that is the Internet, all these editions have a home online. Most of the official versions are available for purchase on Amazon and other fine music retail websites. As for the bootlegs, they are waiting to amaze and inspire you on streaming sites like YouTube and Spotify. I'll let you find those yourself.

Ridley Scott and the artists involved in creating *Blade Runner* did something that is rarely done successfully in films – they created a fictional universe that lives and breathes and strikes a chord deep within fans in such a way that they want to *revisit* that world over and over.

Few blockbusters have that kind of deep atmospheric resonance and there are fewer directors who can create worlds so fully and skillfully that fans want them to live on. Scott has certainly done it more than a few times; James Cameron (who followed up Scott's *Alien* with one of the best – and few – sequels that matched the original in quality with *Aliens*) has succeeded on that front with both his *Terminator* films and *Avatar*, which, according to Cameron, has four sequels. Certainly, the *Star Wars* films also live on with sequels, prequels, one-offs, books, comic-books, games, and more; everything that capitalizes on successful world-building.

It's no surprise those films have generated so much fan appeal that they are being translated from sight and sound movie experiences to live, *in-person* environments inside theme parks. You can count the number of films that built worlds so successfully that fans would pay to visit them: just look at the current rides at Disney or Universal parks and which new theme park "lands" have just opened and are being built.

Does *Blade Runner* have those kinds of legs? Could there be a *Blade Runner* ride or a cyberpunk theme park area that would extend the brand's longevity even further? Could it drive fans past just wanting sound effects or soundtrack albums to play for their own amusement to go forth, spend more fan dollars, and experience that powerful atmosphere *in person*?

Anything is possible, although the tepid box office reception to *Blade Runner 2049* isn't going to make any theme park investors rush to empty their bank accounts and fast track a "Spinner Ride Through Future Los Angeles" attraction. While *2049* updates the noir feel of the original film, it doesn't bring much extra to the table in terms of memorable, easily-recognizable sounds, music, or visuals... well, perhaps a visual or two come to mind in terms of giant video billboard ads for a sexy Companion A.I., but that wouldn't be the kind of world-building addition you would want exposed to little Johnny Pre-Teen or his Mom – with "expose" being the operative word.

However, if nostalgia and a desire to physically walk through the realized world of a science-fiction classic were to ever win out over return-on-investment, it would likely be the world built from the original 1982 *Blade Runner* and not its 2017 sequel (however damn beautiful it might have looked).

If that ever happens, and the world of *Blade Runner* is finally realized in a theme park, only two things will be certain. One: you'll need to bring an umbrella. Two: if they play "Tears in Rain" over the loudspeakers, someone needs to loan me a handkerchief *fast*.

I Want More Life, Smegger: How *Blade Runner* Influenced *Red Dwarf*'s Revival

by Rich Handley

It's an iconic tale that fans of science-fiction and tech noir know well: Four desperate, disreputable individuals return to Earth from a mining locale in the stars to seek out their bespectacled human creator and ask him to extend their limited lifespan so they can prevent the impending deaths to which they have been fated. The creator cannot grant this wish, however, and the four hapless, helpless travelers are hunted down and killed.

This may sound like a plot summary of Ridley Scott's *Blade Runner* – and, of course, it is – but it's also the premise of *Back to Earth*, a 2009 miniseries, written and directed by Doug Naylor, that served as the ninth season of British science-fiction sitcom *Red Dwarf*. The three-part *Back to Earth* provided a reverent pastiche to *Blade Runner*, while offering a metafictional commentary on Naylor's frustration at *Red Dwarf*'s cancelation and his determination, a decade later, to bring the show back from oblivion. In no small measure, *Blade Runner* helped to shape *Red Dwarf*'s long-awaited return to TV.

U.K. television channel BBC Two aired *Red Dwarf*'s pilot, ironically titled "The End," in 1988. Created by Naylor and Rob Grant, the show was based on five comedic sketches the duo had written four years prior for BBC Radio 4's

Son of Cliché. In those radio sketches, titled "Dave Hollins: Space Cadet," space traveler Hollins (voiced by Nick Wilton) is marooned in distant space seven trillion years in the future, accompanied only by a computer called Hab (Chris Barrie).

Grant and Naylor, after watching Douglas Trumbull's *Silent Running*, a 1972 post-apocalyptic science-fiction film, *Dark Star*, a 1974 sci-fi comedy from John Carpenter and Dan O'Bannon, and *Alien*, also written by O'Bannon and directed by Ridley Scott, were inspired to adapt "Dave Hollins" as a weekly TV series in the tradition of those movies – but with a few alterations. These included adding a few new characters, changing Hollins' surname to Lister, the computer's designation to Holly, and the setting to merely three million years from now. The result, *Red Dwarf*, owed its concept as much to Neil Simon's *The Odd Couple* as it did to these films and *Son of Cliché*.

Dave Lister, an unambitious slob of a soup-dispenser technician (portrayed by Craig Charles of the soap opera *Coronation Street*), now shared a cabin with fellow underachiever Arnold J. Rimmer (*Son of Cliché*'s Barrie). An annoying, self-centered, ineffective, cowardly "smeghead" with delusions of competence and a lust for power, Rimmer had died during an accident aboard the titular mining vessel three million years prior. Though reactivated as a hologram to keep Lister – the vessel's only human occupant, and possibly the sole surviving human in the universe – sane, he thinks only of himself and often complains about the disadvantages of being dead. Like *The Odd Couple*'s Felix Unger and Oscar Madison, Lister and Rimmer are entirely unsuited as roommates and spend much of their time bickering.

Aside from the ship's senile artificial intelligence, Holly (played by Norman Lovett), the two bunkmates' only other companion at the outset is Cat (Danny John-Jules), a single-mindedly vain and superbly stylish individual whose felinoid species had descended from Lister's pregnant pet cat while the technician had spent the millennia in stasis, non-aging and protected from the disaster that had killed Dave's shipmates. Later seasons added two other regulars: Kryten (Robert Llewellyn), a neurotic sanitation robot with a rubbery head shaped, according to Rimmer, like a novelty condom, and Kristine Kochanski (Chloë Annett), an alternate-reality version of Lister's lost love.[1]

---

[1] Hattie Hayridge took over the role of Holly in *Red Dwarf III* after Lovett departed the cast; Llewellyn became a series regular during that same season when the original Kryten, David Ross, declined to reprise his role

Red Dwarf aired eight seasons from 1988 to 1993 and (following a hiatus) 1997 to 1999, before its untimely cancelation after only 52 episodes.[2] UKTV channel Dave revived the series for a ninth season in 2009 as *Back to Earth*, and has since produced three additional seasons,[3] bringing the total episode count so far to 73, with talk of more yet to come. Brilliantly witty and perfectly cast, the show is unusual in that it focuses on a group of dysfunctional protagonists far more likely to display ineptitude, laziness, selfishness, and neurosis than the heroic fearlessness and unwavering morality typical of adventure-based stories.

So where does *Blade Runner* fit into all this? In a commentary track recorded for *Back to Earth*'s DVD release, Doug Naylor claimed that he and Rob Grant were inspired by the film back when they created the show:

> *Blade Runner*... is one of the films which most influenced Rob and I in the early days, when we were trying to create *Red Dwarf*, along with *Dark Star* and *Alien* and *Silent Running*. For the 21st anniversary, it just seemed fitting to revisit some of those areas. There were certainly story parallels with the search for the Creator, and I also thought, 'No one's really done an homage to *Blade Runner* yet,' which is such a wonderfully fabulous film, you know, and greatly, greatly loved. It doesn't ever seem to date, and many *Red Dwarf* fans are also massive *Blade Runner* fans, so I thought that might be a fun thing to do because they would get all the jokes.

To the *Red Dwarf* skeptic, this may seem a bit revisionist, as neither Grant nor Naylor had cited the film as an influence during previous interviews or commentaries, whereas *Dark Star*, *Silent Running*, and *Alien* have all been name-checked. However, Naylor's recollection should not be dismissed simply because the information is new to fans. *Blade Runner* had hit theaters six years prior to *Red Dwarf*'s TV debut, and only two years before *Son of Cliché* first played on the radio, so the movie could very well have been fresh in their minds at the time.

---

following the character's introduction in *Red Dwarf II*; and new-wave recording artist Clare Grogan had guest-starred as Kochanski in earlier seasons before Annett assumed the role in a regular capacity starting in *Red Dwarf VII*.

[2] British television shows, unlike American TV, tend to have much shorter seasons. All seasons of *Red Dwarf* to date have been six episodes in length except for *Red Dwarf VII* and *VIII*, which each span eight episodes, and *Back to Earth*, which contains only three.

[3] *Red Dwarf X, XI, and XII* aired in 2012, 2016 and 2017 respectively. The 13th season, *Red Dwarf XIII*, is slated for release sometime in 2019.

This is especially plausible when one considers the dark, gloomy future that *Red Dwarf* presents, the show's setting aboard a mining vessel, the use in several episodes of such themes as expiry dates and equal rights for synthetic beings, and the fact that *Alien*'s Ridley Scott directed *Blade Runner* as well. Moreover, *Red Dwarf*'s four initial leads could be viewed as analogous to (or even parodies of) *Blade Runner*'s renegade replicants: an arrogant, synthetic leader who laments not being truly alive (Roy Batty, Rimmer), a manual laborer of below-average intelligence (Leon Kowalski, Lister), an attractive person clad in exotic costumes (Zhora, Cat), and a pale individual programmed to serve others' needs (Pris, Kryten[4]).

During the course of its 12 seasons, *Red Dwarf* has featured episodes with a wide range of wacky and often ridiculous (but almost always hilarious) premises, from visiting a universe in which time, actions, and speech all occur backwards to convincing John F. Kennedy to preserve history by assassinating himself from behind a grassy knoll. One of the more unusual and controversial entries is *Back to Earth* – unusual in that it sees the crew discovering that they are merely fictional characters on a soon-to-be canceled television series called *Red Dwarf*, and controversial since the miniseries' unorthodox premise and lack of laugh track did not sit well with some reviewers and fans.[5] Most importantly for the purposes of this discussion, *Back to Earth* provides the show's most significant connections to *Blade Runner*.

Homages to beloved films and novels, both science fiction and otherwise, are common in *Red Dwarf*, as the show has gleefully and unapologetically parodied, satirized, and borrowed elements of *Westworld, 2001: A Space Odyssey, RoboCop, Star Trek: The Next Generation, Citizen Kane, Casablanca, Top Gun, Pride and Prejudice, Rebel Without a Cause, Alien, The Terminator, Easy Rider*, and more. But none have been so deeply referenced as *Blade Runner*, the DNA of which pervades the core concepts of the show's entire ninth season (and, really, the series as a whole). *Back to Earth* mirrors the film's

---

[4] Kryten and Pris, of course, serve extremely different types of needs, since Pris is a pleasure model designed for sexual gratification, whereas Kryten specializes in cleaning toilets. The two *usually* do not overlap – and, in any case, Kryten's "groinal socket," unlike Pris's, is used for vacuuming.

[5] I am not one of them. Even without the laugh track used for most other seasons, I find *Back to Earth* wonderfully funny, especially for its *Blade Runner*-inspired motif and its irreverent willingness to break away from the show's usual mold.

themes, aesthetics, characters, and dialogue so closely that it is, in essence, a metaphorical replicant of Scott's original.

In *Back to Earth*, nine years have passed since the audience last met the not-so-heroic crew, with Lister mourning the loss of Kochanski, whom he believes to have died between seasons (that is later revealed not to be the case). Cat shows up soaked, having been attacked by a sea monster in one of the ship's water tanks. With Rimmer monitoring them from a diving bell, Lister, Cat, and Kryten enter the tank and are besieged by a giant squid, which leaves them covered in purplish ink. Thankfully, they survive (naturally, or else the show would end at that point). Kryten ascertains that the creature can migrate through multiple dimensions, and the squid vanishes in a flash of light.

A holographic woman suddenly appears: Katerina Bartikovsky, the ship's reanimated science officer, who assumes command from Rimmer and announces her plan to use the leviathan's dimension-hopping abilities to help Lister return home. Bartikovsky opens a portal to Earth, but the ship's scanners bizarrely claim that neither they nor their intended destination exist. Instead, the machine sends them to 21st-century London in the nearest viable reality – one in which *Red Dwarf* is a British TV comedy and they are merely dramatis personae on the small screen.

Exiting the portal in a mall department store, the Dwarfers are stunned to find DVDs of televised episodes matching their past adventures. Passersby point and giggle in recognition, and posters hang on the walls bearing their images, along with the name *Red Dwarf*. Not only are they fictional characters, they discover, but the series in which they originated has run its course – the cover text for the DVD of the latest season, *Back to Earth*, notes that they all die at the end. It is here that *Blade Runner*'s influence on the miniseries kicks in.

The quartet learn, from the DVD box's text, that in *Back to Earth*, their characters track down their creators "in best *Blade Runner* tradition" to plead for more life. This amusing breakage of the fourth wall calls to mind *Blazing Saddles*, in which Harvey Korman's Hedley Lamarr learns of his enemies' plans by watching the movie at a theater, as well as *Spaceballs*, in which Rick Moranis's Dark Helmet views a videotape of that film to find out what happens next. In *Back to Earth*, it works just as well as in Mel Brooks' two movies – and with the added *Blade Runner* elements, it becomes something original and new despite also being something the audience has seen before.

The Dwarfers visit a science-fiction collectibles shop full of *Red Dwarf* memorabilia, including Lister's bathtub prop from the show, inside which they find a piece of fake skin from a puppet used in a prior episode to depict a shape-shifting creature that attacked Dave in the form of a giant snake.[6] This, of course, mirrors Rick Deckard's discovery of an artificial snake scale in Leon's bathroom. On the puppet remnant, Kryten discovers the name of a prop maker named Swallow, an allusion to *Blade Runner*'s Hannibal Chew. (Chew and swallow... get it? Naylor's DVD commentary noted that the character's original name was Hachoo, which he admitted he regretted changing.)

Lister notices a *Back to Earth* fan-convention cast photograph, which includes the leads alongside "Swallow" actor Richard Ng. In a sequence that hilariously sends up Deckard's Esper machine scene from *Blade Runner*, Kryten enhances the image repeatedly, with his comrades calling out "frame left," "zoom in," "pull out," "track in," "pan right," "rotate," "flop," and so forth. The funniest moment is at the start of this sequence, when Rimmer instructs Kryten to "un-crop." The mechanoid complies, expanding the image to show details beyond the paper snapshot's edges. This, of course, would be impossible with a printed photograph, but *Red Dwarf* revels in the ridiculous.

The *Red Dwarf* gang visits prop maker Swallow, whose name, look, laboratory, and function pay homage to Hannibal Chew.

After subjecting the image to endless manipulations that include reversing reflections from a doorknob, windows, a water droplet, and even a stylized "H" emblem on Rimmer's forehead, Kryten (who observes, "Uh, sir, wouldn't it have

---

[6] "Polymorph" (*Red Dwarf III*, episode three, airdate: 28 Nov 1989).

been quicker to look him up in the phone book?") uncovers the address of Swallow's prosthetics company, Nose World – named, as *Blade Runner* fans know, after Chew's Eye Works facility. Swallow denies knowing how the crew will die, claiming "I just do noses," referencing Chew's protest, "I only do eyes." Cat realizes the prop maker is wearing his fur coat and makes him remove it (like the replicants disrobe Chew), causing Swallow to shiver in the sub-zero chamber and stammer out Chew's line, "So cold."

The nose designer gives up his boss's address and they follow his directions – which, in a doubly metafictional moment, bring them to the set of soap opera *Coronation Street*. There, the gang come face to face with "Lister" actor Craig Charles, who dismisses them as narcotics-induced flashbacks, a darkly funny in-joke referencing the drug-use issues he'd faced during his younger years.

The Dwarfers finally meet the Creator, who resembles Eldon Tyrell and holds in his hands the lives of his greatest creations.

Eventually, they track down the Creator (as he's called[7]), played brilliantly by Richard O'Callaghan, who closely resembles Joe Turkel's similarly clad and coiffed Eldon Tyrell in *Blade Runner*, including the corporate tycoon's white outfit and memorably large eyeglasses. The creator lives in a lavish residence modeled after Tyrell's pyramidal penthouse, located next to Britain's Houses of Parliament. Towering above the nearby metropolis is an animated billboard

---

[7] In a massively missed opportunity, the Creator is unnamed. This is a shame, as naming him after either of *Red Dwarf*'s parents would have carried the already amusing in-joke even farther.

advertisement of an Asian woman in a *geisha* outfit, one of *Blade Runner*'s most readily recognizable images. Inside his apartment, a pair of diminutive robots bearing Rimmer's face — a clever callback to Bear and Kaiser, the animatronic toys of *Blade Runner*'s genetic designer, J.F. Sebastian (William Sanderson), as well as to a prior *Red Dwarf* episode[8] — serve as his butlers.

The four beg the Creator not to kill them off, and Lister demands, "I want more life, smegger," mirroring Roy Batty's plea, "I want more life, father." He denies the request, however, stating, "A series cancelation sequence can't be revised once it's established" — a clever take on Tyrell's regretful explanation to his "son" that he cannot revise an established coding sequence. The Creator describes his intended death scene for them all,[9] marvelously recreating *Blade Runner*'s iconic sequence in which Deckard shoots Zhora, causing her to crash through several plate-glass windows before falling dead in the snow. He also announces that it's "time to die," referencing a line spoken by both Roy and Leon in the movie, and reveals, "*Blade Runner* is the film which inspired your creation and your death."

If any viewers had somehow failed to recognize what *Back to Earth* was doing, it should have been abundantly clear by this point.

Before the Creator can carry out their cancelations at gunpoint, however, Lister kills the man by gripping his head in the same manner by which Batty kills Tyrell, then uses his typewriter to rewrite the episode's script (à la Tom Mankiewicz's 1991 comedy *Delirious*, starring John Candy) with a happy ending — another possible (though subtle) *Blade Runner* homage, in that the replicants' pasts had been written into their synthetic brains by Tyrell. This culminates in a brilliantly silly series of sight gags in which Dave giddily types out ridiculous scenarios to make fools of his friends.

However, they soon realize none of what they have experienced (not even Bartikovsky) is real, and that they are not fictional TV characters after all — they are trapped inside an illusion created by the squid in the tank, whose ink, secreted as a defense mechanism, caused them to hallucinate their trip to Earth. Cat, Kryten, and Rimmer awaken aboard *Red Dwarf*, but Lister refuses to

---

[8] "Blue" (*Red Dwarf VII*, episode five, airdate: 14 Feb 1997), which features a virtual-reality rollercoaster ride called *The Rimmer Experience*, populated by hordes of singing "Rimmer Munchkins."

[9] The Creator says he has grown wary of them — a possible subtle jab at Rob Grant, who ended his collaboration with Doug Naylor following *Red Dwarf VI*, citing creative differences.

leave after a vision of Kochanski appears. The lovers take a drive in the countryside, mirroring Deckard's escape with Rachael as depicted in *Blade Runner*'s original theatrical cut (though not in subsequent cuts), and Kristine even sports two of Rachael's on-screen hair styles. Lister's desire to stay nearly kills him, but he summons the strength to awaken and life continues aboard the mining ship.

Throughout the illusion, Cat finds himself inexplicably creating origami sculptures of a squid, referencing Edward James Olmos' enigmatic detective character, Gaff. Just as Gaff's origami creations portend the director's-cut revelation that Deckard is a replicant, Cat's paper squids foreshadow the plot twist in the miniseries' final episode that it has all been a dream. The pairing up is one of *Back to Earth*'s smarter homages, as Cat and Gaff (whose sculptures imply that he knows of Deckard's replicant nature and is playing a game of *cat*-and-mouse with his colleague) both wear wildly colorful outfits and tend to walk into and out of scenes quickly, uttering short, memorable lines without being the story's primary focus.

Parallels such as this one lend credence to Doug Naylor's claim that he and Rob Grant had, indeed, partly modeled *Red Dwarf* after *Blade Runner*. Seb Patrick, the writer and editor of reddwarf.co.uk (the official *Red Dwarf* website), in a 2009 posting at *Red Dwarf* fan page Ganymede & Titan, supported this notion:

> I'd argue that since *Blade Runner* was pioneering in showing an onscreen 'future' that wasn't shiny and clean and perfect, but was instead a logical extrapolation of humanity's tendency to keep building on top of things, it was influential on *Dwarf*'s grubby, industrial, sort-of-like-the-present view of the future.[10]

Patrick's stance has merit, for the basic building blocks of *Blade Runner* can be found in *Red Dwarf* right from the start. Lister has robot goldfish in his cabin, alluding to the popularity of electronic pets in *Blade Runner*. A wide range of GELFs (genetically engineered life forms) and simulants (violent androids who hate mankind) roam the stars, mirroring *Blade Runner*'s widespread use of genetic engineering and synthetic laborers, and like the replicants, all live in off-world colonies rather than on Earth. In both series, human cultures of the future are portrayed as hybrid fusions – Eastern and Western in the case of *Blade Runner*, given the large Asian population in 2019 Los Angeles, and British

---

[10] http://www.ganymede.tv/forums/topic/blade-runner-references-pre-back-to-earth/

and American in *Red Dwarf*, as evidenced by the use of currency called the dollarpound. And Rimmer even has an inflatable sex doll named Rachael! The more one examines *Red Dwarf*'s elements, the more one finds *Blade Runner*'s guiding influence.

In an early episode, Kryten discovers that his built-in expiration date has arrived, and that within 24 hours, his shut-down chip will activate, bringing about an abrupt end to his existence.[11] This leads to discussions about the nature of inorganic life; the right of all intelligent beings, even machines, to forge their own destiny; and the electronics version of an afterlife, known as Silicon Heaven. Another tale, which aired a few seasons later,[12] introduces the 3000 Series, a mechanoid model preceding Kryten's line but very realistic-looking, as opposed to Kryten's flat, rubbery cranium. The eerie realism of the 3000s, the episode explains, caused mankind to shun them out of fear that they might successfully impersonate humans. As a result, the entire line was recalled, though several escaped, erasing their own memories and creating new lives un-persecuted by their human masters. *Blade Runner*'s influence on both of these episodes, and on others with similar themes, is unmistakable.

Several episodes during *Red Dwarf*'s earlier seasons utilize the imagery of dreams, illusions, and virtual reality. In two early stories, the crew access the mining vessel's dream recorder, enabling them to capture, playback, and analyze their dreams as they sleep.[13] In another, a computer program called the Armageddon virus causes Kryten to experience bizarre dreams of an Old West town called Existence, in which he, like *Blade Runner*'s Rachael, has manufactured memories.[14] In yet another, the crew become trapped in a hallucinatory film noir-style world, in which they believe they have reached the end of a four-year stint (note the replicants' lifespan) immersed in a virtual-reality game.[15]

The latter example is especially significant, in that *Back to Earth* is a sequel; just as in the miniseries, their dream-like false memories are the result of a

---

[11] "The Last Day" (*Red Dwarf III*, episode six, airdate: 19 Dec 1989)
[12] "Out of Time" (*Red Dwarf VI*, episode six, airdate: 11 Nov 1993)
[13] "Confidence and Paranoia" (*Red Dwarf I*, episode five, airdate: 14 Mar 1988) and "Parallel Universe" (*Red Dwarf II*, episode six, airdate: 11 Oct 1988).
[14] "Gunmen of the Apocalypse" (*Red Dwarf VI*, episode three, airdate: 21 Oct 1993).
[15] "Back to Reality" (*Red Dwarf V*, episode six, airdate: 26 Mar 1992).

squid's illusion-inducing ink. Dream imagery is also an important theme in *Blade Runner*. Not only is the film based on Philip K. Dick's novel *Do Androids Dream of Electric Sheep?*, but in the director's cut, Deckard dreams of a unicorn, implying (in the film's context) that he may well be synthetic himself.

A fifth-season episode even seems to subtly reference Roy Batty's final speech.[16] Here's Roy's dialogue as he awaits his imminent death:

> I've seen things you people wouldn't believe. Attack ships on fire off the shoulder of Orion. I watched C-beams glitter in the dark near the Tannhäuser Gate. All those moments will be lost in time, like tears in rain. Time to die.

Here, by comparison, is Lister's more lighthearted observation:

> I've been to a parallel universe. I've seen time running backwards. I've played pool with planets, and I've given birth to twins, but I never thought, in my entire life, I'd taste an edible Pot Noodle.

Sure, it's not an exact parallel, but it doesn't have to be. What matters is that if, as Naylor maintains, *Blade Runner* did help to shape the direction that *Red Dwarf*'s development took during the show's formative years, then it's likely he and Grant had an ironic eye on Batty's death scene when writing the above gag, given the two speeches' similar phrasings and structures. *Red Dwarf* is often at its best when referencing other franchises, and it's never unintentional.

Other supporting evidence appears in the novel *Red Dwarf: Infinity Welcomes Careful Drivers*, written by Grant and Naylor and published in 1989, when the show was still quite young (its third season aired that same year). A portion of the story takes place on Saturn's terraformed moon of Mimas, the descriptions of which seem lifted straight out of *Blade Runner*. It's easy, when reading such passages, to imagine the grimy colony's locales – for example, the moon's red-light district, Shag Town – taking place within the film's framework. Taxis propelled on mechanical hind legs, known as hoppers, would seem right at home alongside *Blade Runner*'s flying cars, while the movie's animated billboards would not at all be out of place adorning Mimas's streets. Most telling, a brothel on Mimas offers not only human-based android prostitutes to its clientele, but also android sheep!

The novel's sequel, *Better Than Life*, continues the homages by introducing GELF runners, a type of mercenaries who hunt down genetically engineered life forms gone bad, just as Deckard and his fellow blade runners eliminate rogue

---

[16] "Demons and Angels" (*Red Dwarf V*, episode five, airdate: 19 Mar 1992).

replicants. Whether or not the writers had publicly mentioned *Blade Runner* prior to Naylor's commentary for *Back to Earth*, the film's influence is demonstrably present in that miniseries, as it is in prior seasons and even in the Naylor-and-Grant-penned novels.

In the case of *Back to Earth*, it works wonderfully well. DVD Talk's Bill Gibron, in reviewing the miniseries in 2009, praised its parallels to Ridley Scott's film:

> The *Blade Runner* stuff just sings, clearly the work of dedicated fans of the 1982 future shock classic... When we get to the penthouse apartment of The Creator, complete with magic typewriter that can alter the destiny of everyone in the series, we anticipate the creative chaos... and *Back to Earth* delivers.[17]

If there's any drawback to the intricately woven homage-paying in *Back to Earth*, it's this: For someone to truly grasp it requires a working knowledge of both franchises. A *Red Dwarf* fan who has never watched the film could enjoy *Back to Earth*, of course, as could a *Blade Runner* enthusiast unfamiliar with the British TV show. But the miniseries works best when the jokes hit home on both sides of the aisle, enabling a viewer to comprehend and laugh at not only the movie's references, but also the many callbacks to classic *Dwarf* episodes. It's almost guaranteed that someone well-versed only in one or the other would miss some of the punchlines or feel at times confused. In the final chapter of *Back to Earth*, for example, the Creator and crew have the following well-timed exchange:

> **KRYTEN:** Does this mean this is our last episode, sir?
>
> **CREATOR:** The light that burns twice as bright burns half as long.
>
> **LISTER:** Yeah, but... the light that burns *half* as bright burns *four times* as long.
>
> **CREATOR:** But the light that burns *three-quarters* as bright burns *five-eighths* as long as the light that burns a quarter as bright as the light that's gone out.
>
> **RIMMER (aside):** I'd have needed a calculator for that.
>
> **CREATOR:** The point is, gentlemen, you have all burned so very, very brightly and for so very, very long, just like the red dwarf star itself.

This masterfully parallels Tyrell's proud statement to his creation, "The light that burns twice as bright burns half as long, and you have burned so very, very brightly, Roy." But for anyone who has never watched *Blade Runner*, it might seem kind of pointless. The exchange serves a double purpose, as it also offers

---

[17] http://www.dvdtalk.com/reviews/39012/red-dwarf-back-to-earth/

Naylor's reflection (and mirror's the audience's sadness) regarding what was, at the time, simultaneously a celebratory and melancholy moment. The miniseries had ushered in the return of a beloved British sitcom, yet this third episode marked the story's conclusion, and with no new seasons yet announced, *Red Dwarf* fandom – and Naylor himself – had every reason to worry that the series would once again be relegated to its former state of "accelerated decrepitude."

Thankfully, that wasn't the case.

The good news is that *Blade Runner* and *Red Dwarf* are each eminently re-watchable, each a classic in its own right, so for newcomers to either franchise, it would be well worth experiencing both in order to better comprehend and enjoy *Back to Earth*. As an homage to *Blade Runner*, it's spot-on, and as the ninth season of *Red Dwarf*, it does an admirable job of bringing the show back to the airwaves after ten years of cancelation. As a standalone story, however, viewed by someone lacking a strong understanding both of *Red Dwarf*'s prior seasons and of Ridley Scott's film, it could potentially fall flat, and that would be a shame because it is a great achievement.

If you're looking for one hell of a viewing experience, watch *Red Dwarf I* through *VIII*, followed by *Blade Runner*. Then pop in *Back to Earth* so you can fully appreciate what Doug Naylor accomplished with his reverent pastiche to Ridley Scott's timeless classic. Since it's a good bet you will, by that point, be a full-fledged *Red Dwarf* fan, you'll also want to marathon *Red Dwarf X, XI* and *XII*. With *Blade Runner 2049* now available for home-viewing, and with *Red Dwarf XIII* and *XIV* on the horizon, it's not yet time for either franchise to die.[18]

---

[18] Thanks to the late Paul C. Giachetti, my tragically departed best friend and the author of the wonderful two-volume *Total Immersion: The Comprehensive, Unauthorized Red Dwarf Encyclopedia*, for his invaluable assistance. Thanks also to members of the Red Dwarf Posse...!!! Facebook group (www.facebook.com/groups/197048357005295).

Calling Back Cyberpunk

by Lou Tambone

Blade Runner 2049 is an exceptional film, and one that is unique as a sequel in that it can stand on its own, working just as well having not seen the original. Of course, those who *have* seen the original film will benefit greatly from the many obvious callbacks to it. However, there are also subtle references that might slip past the casual viewer. In this essay, I am in no way attempting to create a comprehensive and complete list of such things. I am going to attempt, however, to provide you with a nice variety of such references both outwardly noticeable and somewhat elusive. For example, I'll be excluding things like the appearance of a spinner or neon signs with Asian writing, as they are commonplace in both films and are not necessarily homages or callbacks. So pour yourself a shot of Johnnie Walker, dim the lights, fire up the ESPER, and let's enhance.

Both films begin with a textual preface that sets up the main story, much like the opening crawls of the *Star Wars* films. In *Blade Runner*, it's a little new for us because we've never seen this cyberpunk world before. There's talk of replicants, how they came to be, and how a combat team Off-World was involved in a mutiny and came to Earth, where it's illegal for them to live. We're introduced to the term Blade Runner for the first time as well as the concept of retirement (as opposed to killing). *Blade Runner 2049*'s intro serves a larger purpose since it takes place 30 years after the original. It explains (at a high level) what's happened in all that time and how replicants have evolved under Niander Wallace. So it looks like the template has been somewhat established with the text preface. If there is indeed another film someday, I would be very surprised if it didn't start with some kind of textual introduction.

Speaking of templates, it appears that yet another constant has been established, albeit a much shorter one. *Blade Runner* opens with the now-famous Hades landscape, but within the first few shots, we're shown a large eye in extreme close-up. *Blade Runner 2049*'s very first shot is also the close-up of an eye. In both films, it's never really clear whose eyes these are. I like to think that the first film's eye is Holden's as he's looking out the window of the Tyrell Corporation, watching the world decay before his eyes, but many believe it belongs to Roy Batty. The eye in *Blade Runner 2049* seems to match Officer K's eye, but we don't really know. Oddly enough, in the shots following the open eye, K is shown to be sleeping in his spinner. That disconnect always bothered me a bit.

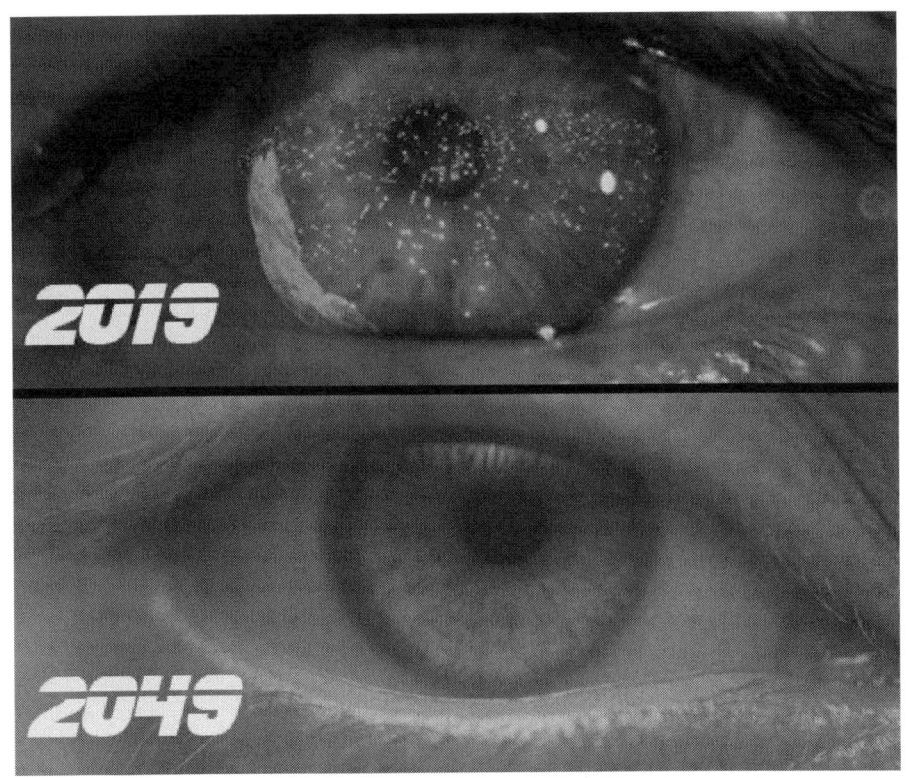

The early shots of eyes in both movies.

Speaking of eyes, any fan will tell you that eyes play an important role in the *Blade Runner* universe. They are the windows to the soul, after all. We've already mentioned the opening shots, but there are many other references to eyes in both films. We'll just touch on a few. The Voight-Kampff test in the original film is not only based on the emotional response of the subject, but on the dilation of the subject's pupil. The eye is studied during the test and always in plain view on a screen.

It's also been noted that many of the eyes in the film (such as Tyrell's owl's) have a whitish reflection in them. This is often referred to as *eyeshine* and is caused by a layer of tissue behind the retina of many vertebrates called the tapetum lucidum, which serves as a retroreflector and contributes to the superior night vision that many nocturnal animals have. As humans don't have a tapetum lucidum, it has been theorized that this is an indication that the character is a replicant or artificial being.[1]

It's a common theory that "reflective" eyes mean the being is a replicant.

When Batty kills Tyrell, he gouges the man's eyes out in a gruesome manner. Hannibal Chew, one of Tyrell's contractors, specializes in making eyes for Tyrell's replicants and owns a shop called Eye Works. While there, Leon plays with the frozen eyes and intimidates Chew with them. Roy playfully holds up fake eyeballs when trying to lighten the mood at Sebastian's apartment. Pris paints a black stripe over her eyes in a fashion similar to that of Native American war paint, knowing a fight is coming. In *Blade Runner 2049*, the way to identify a replicant is via a serial number imprinted on the replicant's eye. This is why K asks Sapper to look up and to the left, something Freysa playfully

---

[1] One of the indications that Deckard might be a replicant is the scene in his apartment with Rachael in which for a brief moment the audience sees the reflective luminous eyeshine effect in his eyes.

mentions later on as well. Freysa herself only has one eye, apparently to evade being identified. Niander Wallace is completely blind, but has little flying devices to help him see when a chip is attached to his neck. It's fun to note that both of the "gods" of the films (Tyrell and Wallace) have vision problems. Perhaps the most interesting eye reference is the one Deckard notices about the newly made Rachael replicant. He's almost taken by her until he notices that her eyes are the wrong color. "Her eyes were green," he tells Wallace. Lastly, when K asks Gaff about why Deckard wasn't "long for this world," Gaff answers, "Something in his eyes." Many took that as further confirmation that Deckard is indeed a replicant.

As mentioned in the prologue, Roy Batty and his team of mutineers were slaves working Off-World when they killed their captors (and who knows who else) and migrated down to Earth. Master memory maker Ana Stelline says replicants lead hard lives, "made to do what we'd rather not." Colonizing new worlds falls under that description. According to *Blade Runner 2049*, Sapper Morton was also Off-World for a time, but as a combat medic and not a slave, though the distinction might be blurred there. He was created for a reason and didn't have much of a choice in the matter. Replicants are no longer illegal, but certain older models, like Sapper (a Nexus 8) need to be retired since they were not programmed to be obedient.

In the original film, Deckard makes use of a machine called the ESPER that gives him the clues needed to find his quarry. The machine takes photos and enhances them for inspection, all the while making clicking sounds and responding to Deckard's voice commands. A similar idea is transferred to *Blade Runner 2049*. First, in the LAPD lab, when Coco the morgue tech is checking out Rachael's bones, the machine he's using makes the same (or very similar) clicking sounds. Later on, when K is using the DeNAbase machine, there are similar noises. K's drone (also known as a pilot fish) responds to voice commands like the ESPER does. In one scene, K directs the drone to fly through the abandoned Las Vegas strip looking for clues or perhaps just scouting ahead for danger.

As regards advertisement and examples of product placement in *Blade Runner 2049*, there's Asian and Russian signage everywhere, neon and otherwise. In *Blade Runner*, there weren't any holograms but plenty of billboard-sized screens, plus the usual sea of neon, including the ubiquitous dragon that was used in many shots. The sequel took advertising a step further adding interactive holograms of all sizes that appear next to you as you walk and even dance in the streets all around you. Many corporate names from the original film show up in Los Angeles including Atari, Pan Am, Sony, and Johnnie Walker brand whiskey. Deckard has plenty of the latter in 2049. There are still loud announcements everywhere you walk (but sadly, no blimp).

A fun parallel worth mentioning is when K is in the bathroom gluing his wound and generally cleaning himself up. Lt. Joshi wasn't going to "pay" for K's medical expenses, stressing the notion that replicants are truly less than human. Perhaps K's salary isn't all that great or he has no medical coverage. Deckard, of course, does something similar in the original film. He chooses not to go to a hospital after retiring Zhora and getting pummeled by Leon, and it may be because he doesn't have medical coverage either.

Sharp-dressed, cane-sporting Gaff makes an appearance in *Blade Runner 2049*. His presence alone is a wonderful callback to the original film in many ways, yet his one scene is short and strange because Edward James Olmos, although incorporating a cityspeak word (*nyugdijas*), doesn't speak with his original accent, which is curious. He sounds tired and old, and perhaps it's because he's in a retirement home or hospital of some kind. The original script describes him wearing a "staff" badge which would explain his all-white outfit, but it's unclear. The best part of Gaff's cameo is that he treats us to one last origami animal, this time a sheep, a likely nod to Philip K. Dick's original novel that started this whole phenomenon. In another interesting Gaff-related moment, his old spinner makes an appearance later in the film at Deckard's place in Las Vegas. When Deckard is trying to make a run for it, he runs to the spinner but it's destroyed before he can get to it. Did Gaff lend it to Deckard? Did he help Deckard at some point?[2]

Outdoor eateries in Los Angeles are still as popular as ever in 2049. K, probably sick of his seedy apartment building where he's taunted as he climbs the steps, grabs a meal in town and thinks about his mission while studying photos from Sapper Morton's home, much like Deckard studied Leon's photos. BiBi's bar is reminiscent of the noodle bar Deckard used to frequent, but on a much larger scale. There are vending machines that span entire walls, advertisements everywhere, and it's conveniently located across the street from a cyber-brothel of sorts just in case one gets the munchies after sowing

---

[2] It's possible that the filmmakers just reproduced the design from old production photos, or that Deckard got his hands on an old model, but in either case, the speculation remains.

some wild oats. Yes, pleasure models (referred to as "Doxies" in the script) are still a thing too.

The classic spinner makes a cameo in *Blade Runner 2049*.

In the original film, Deckard owned a piano decorated with sheet music and numerous photos of vintage quality; an odd contrast in the otherwise futuristic setting. This contrast is carried over into *Blade Runner 2049*, in which Sapper Morton's humble domicile is also furnished with a piano. It seems like an odd choice for a gruff, former combat medic, but perhaps he's an old softie with implanted, latent piano playing ability, much like Rachael. Maybe she even taught him how to play. In any case, hidden inside the piano, K finds a vintage cigarette box with a sock and some old photos inside. Deckard has a piano again in his new home in Las Vegas. In fact, it's the sound of the piano that calls K to the building where Deckard is located.

Much like eyes, animals play an important part in the *Blade Runner* universe, even though real ones are quite rare. In *Blade Runner 2049*, K has a memory of a toy horse implanted in his brain that sets him off on a quest that takes many twists and turns. It's both a macguffin and a red herring at the same time. In the original film (or at least most of the cuts) there are no horses, but there is a unicorn which is of some significance. Deckard dreams of the unicorn (at his piano) and then, at the end of the film, we find that Gaff was at Deckard's apartment and left an origami unicorn there for Deckard to find. This, according to some (such as Ridley Scott), confirms that Deckard is indeed a replicant since Gaff knew of this memory. As we know, Gaff also likes to make origami chickens, and much later, sheep. Zhora owns a snake, Sebastian is seen with rats, and Tyrell owns an owl. Animoid row is a location from the original film where Deckard goes for answers about the scale he finds in Leon's apartment. He mistakenly thinks it's a fish scale, but it's determined to be snake by a vendor. In *Blade Runner 2049*, K and Joi go to see someone called Dr. Badger who has a booth in a place that conjures up aspects of animoid row. Badger makes comments about animals and even offers to get K a "real" horse or a goat. Later in Las Vegas, not only are there living bees (alive due to some kind of science-fiction bee feeding device), but it's learned that Deckard has a dog living with him. We never find out if it's real or artificial. Scattered around Deckard's Vegas apartment are carvings of other animals similar to the horse K finds at the orphanage (where there's also a "horse" ash tray on a desk). There's an elephant, a lion, and a rhino, plus a couple of dogs next to Rachael's photo. It's probably worth mentioning that Ana Stelline is creating a memory involving some kind of beetle-like insect when we first meet her.

Twice in *Blade Runner 2049*, we are taken *directly* back to the original film with actual lines of dialogue. First, Luv takes K to an archive where they listen to audio contained on memory bearings. They hear a fragmented bit of Deckard giving Rachael the Voight-Kampff test. Lines from the original film play out as the replicants listen. Later on, Wallace uses an "audio document" from Deckard and Rachael's first meeting (labeled "Tyrell Archives") in order to manipulate Deckard into helping him. We're taken back even more directly when Wallace ushers out a new Rachael replicant, identical to the old one in almost every way (except for the eye color). Now that's how you do a callback! While we're discussing dialogue, it bears mentioning the replicant Mariette's slightly altered mention of the Tyrell motto, "More Human Than Human," which she changes to "More Human Than Humans." Was this a happy coincidence or did she know the motto?

Over the course of both films, the main characters (in this case, Deckard and K) not only go through a journey of discovery and revelation, but they both get beat up time and time again in a successive series of pummeling right up until the end. Deckard's beatings begin with Zhora, who nearly kills him, Leon, who nearly does the same, Pris, who brutally attacks him, and then Roy Batty, who breaks his fingers (similar to the way Luv crushes Joshi's fingers in what might be another callback) as the two fight their way through rooms and eventually the rainy rooftop where Deckard almost dies yet again. By the end of the film, he's a mess. It's probably good to note that a "final fight" in the rain/water is also mirrored in *Blade Runner 2049*, but we'll get to that soon. K weathers his share of beatings as the film progresses towards the end credits. He, unlike Deckard, doesn't waste any time, though. Sapper Morton throws him through a wall in the film's first few minutes and they violently fight, resulting in a sliced arm, among other injuries. Next, he's shot down and attacked at the junkyard/orphanage site. A quick threesome later and he's off to Vegas where he gets into a knock-down, drag-out fist fight with Deckard, takes a dive over a balcony, and sets off a trip bomb. If that's not enough, Luv and her crew show up and she nearly beats him to death. One round isn't enough with Luv, so he chases her down and they go at it yet again in the water (like Deckard and Batty) in order to save Deckard. This time, she uses her fancy blades on him but he's able to drown her before bringing Deckard to meet his daughter, where K finally succumbs to his wounds and dies. It was a day!

That scene brings us to one of the most obvious, yet also touching callbacks. One of *Blade Runner*'s most famous and talked about scenes is Roy Batty's "tears in rain" monologue on the rooftop. After having saved Deckard's life, the two sit on the roof, clearly exhausted in the nasty rain. Batty knows his time is up and leaves Deckard with some poetic advice of sorts before bowing his head and taking leave for good. The music echoes the sentiment perfectly. Officer KD6-3.7, at the end of *Blade Runner 2049*, also knows his time is up and lies down on the steps outside of Ana Stelline's building. As he does, it's snowing instead of raining, but the imagery is still evocative of the rooftop. The real callback here, however, is the musical cue, which is the same from when Roy died.

I've saved my favorite for last. Did you know that Rachael's birthday is actually in *Blade Runner 2049*? I don't mean her death day of 6/10/21. I'm talking about her incept date, something she specifically asked Deckard for in the original film. When I first saw the sequel, I saw the close-up of Rachael's bones with the serial number and noticed it started with N7, which I took to mean Nexus 7. After a few repeat views at home, I took a closer look and noticed something else. In the original film, when Bryant is showing Deckard information about the replicants he's meant to retire, there's information on them displayed on a monitor. This information includes things like a name, gender, incept date, function, and so forth. However, it also includes a serial number which is in a specific format and can be broken down to reveal information about the replicant without having to look in a database. For example, Roy Batty's serial number in the first film is N6MAA10816. If you look at the rest of the information underneath provided in the scene, you can infer that *N6* means Nexus-6. *M* stands for male. *A* is the physical level, and the second *A* is the mental level. Roy's incept date is 8 January 2016 and that is where the 10816 comes from. When looking at the serial number on Rachael's bones, I noticed that it read N7FAA52318. If we apply the same formula, we can assume that Rachael was a Nexus 7 replicant, female, physically and mentally at level A (smart and strong), and was "born" on 23 May 2018. It's little details like these that make me love the film even more.

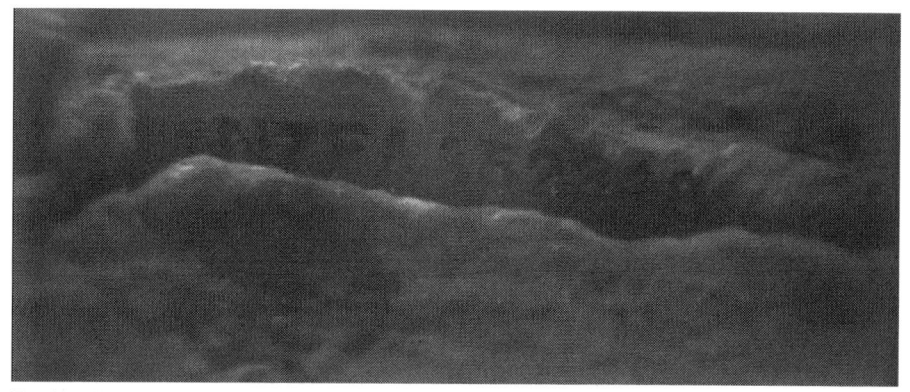

Rachael's serial number gives us clues to her character's makeup.

As I said in the outset, *Blade Runner 2049* works perfectly as a stand-alone film, but it's twice as great when you're able to pick up on all the little bits and pieces that tie into the original. When the sequel was released, one of the many accolades hurled at it was that it evoked the look and feel of the original. In other words, it *felt* like *Blade Runner*. As much as I agree with that to a point, I have to disagree with the overall notion when looking at the entire movie. One of the first things I noticed was that while the scenes in Los Angeles were certainly amazing and gave off the correct cyberpunk vibe, we weren't *in* Los Angeles all that much. I should rephrase that. We weren't *out in the streets* that much. The original film was very self-contained. The sequel moves around a lot and ventures out into places like San Diego and Las Vegas. The opening scenes are at Sapper's farm, outside the city. Then we're in Los Angeles for a while, about 45 minutes or so, but we find ourselves in indoor locations like the LAPD lab, the minimalistic Wallace Corporation, and K's apartment. We don't see too much of the stereotypical cyberpunk neon and so forth. About an hour into the film, we leave the city again. The film even says so with a big glowing sign that reads "Now Leaving Greater Los Angeles." From there, K heads to a waste processing area in the San Diego region which is just a big junkyard, nothing like the original film. Then he's off to Ana Stelline's lab, which the script hints at being located on the outskirts of Los Angeles but looks nothing like the city itself. Inside it's white and sterile. We're only back in the city for another 20 minutes or so before it's off to the yellow-orange tinged Las Vegas, where we spend approximately a good half hour. The rest of the film is spent in various interiors after that, but they're mostly places like Wallace's yellowish rooms, the replicants' hideout, or the sea wall where the big fight happens, before heading back to Ana Stelline's to close out the film.

So while the dark, dreary world of Los Angeles is clearly represented, I don't feel we spent enough time outside to really draw the correct parallels. The spinners and billboards did their jobs effectively but the film is not as cyberpunk as it could have been. After watching the aesthetically similar *Altered Carbon*, it made me wonder if the film should have spent more time out in the streets. Ultimately, it didn't matter because the film works as it is, but it is puzzling to read everyone's comments about how it was *so* much like the first film.

Blade Runner 2049 proves that a sequel doesn't necessarily *need* callbacks to previous installments but they certainly help to fill out some of the blank areas of the canvas, making the overall painting that much more interesting.

"Dreadfully Distinct": The Symbolic Power of K's Baseline in *Blade Runner 2049*

by Kelli Fitzpatrick

Every film sequel faces a similar fascinating paradox: constructively continue the narrative in a manner that is reminiscent enough to appeal to fans of the original, *and* create a story that stands alone as an artistic achievement capable of captivating a new wave of viewers. This is a conundrum faced by nearly all connected movie franchises, including films that arrive hard on the heels of each other (such as installments in the Marvel cinematic universe), but a sequel that releases 35 years after its genre-defining cult classic predecessor will be expected to succeed on an even grander scale. *Blade Runner 2049* does just that. Helmed by award-winning director Denis Villeneuve and acclaimed cinematographer Roger Deakins, *Blade Runner 2049* (hereafter referred to as *BR2049*) pays homage to the most iconic aspects of Ridley Scott's 1982 original *Blade Runner*, but still finds its own identity as a deeply moving new story for a new age. This film is all about being able to tell one thing from another, and the themes of being "interlinked" versus "dreadfully distinct" brought up in Officer K's Baseline tests prefigure the character's major moments of conflict and change in the film. Unlocking the secrets of the Baseline unlocks the very-human heart of *BR2049* and its all-too-timely message about the value of individual action.

The world of *Blade Runner* has always been rooted in literature, and *BR2049* is no exception. Ridley Scott's original film is an adaptation of Philip K. Dick's classic sci-fi novel *Do Androids Dream of Electric Sheep?*, and includes several allusions to other texts, such as nods to Tyrell as a *Frankenstein*-like father of artificial life, and Roy Batty's quoting of William Blake's poetry on rebel angels.[1] Likewise, *BR2049* references several well-known works, including Joi's fixation on the "real boy" theme of *Pinocchio*, Wallace's obsessive Biblical pontificating, and Deckard's quoting of *Treasure Island* (each of which could easily sustain its own full analysis).[2] *BR2049* even references the first film in several ways, including Gaff's reprisal of his role as origami aficionado, as well as Deckard's and K's similar visions — of a unicorn and a horse — which both call into question their nature as a born being or a replicant. But the literary reference that by far defines the film is that of the Baseline and the novel it's lifted from. It's the giant mysterious dead tree that anchors the entire story.

Fans of *Blade Runner* may recognize the Baseline test as similar in some ways to the older Voight-Kampff test that Deckard used to identify replicants, but this new test is significantly different in its purpose and tone. The Voight-Kampff test seen in the original film is a series of hypothetical scenarios used to distinguish replicants from humans. When Deckard questions Rachel to determine if she's a replicant, he assumes a methodical, almost conversational tone, even encouraging her to "relax" while she casually smokes a cigarette. Conversely, the Post-Trauma Baseline Test in *BR2049* is utilized by the LAPD as a regular controlling check on their Blade Runners' psyches, to ensure the replicant agents do not become emotionally affected by their work (and therefore volatile and dangerous). Administered to Blade Runners immediately following retirement missions, the Baseline test involves a series of rapid-fire questions delivered from an unseen interviewer and is meant to "wrong-foot" its subject in a "hellishly aggressive" verbal assault, as film editor Joe Walker states, in order to root out any forbidden emotional entanglement.[3] Do the job,

---

[1] Worra, Bryan Thao. "William Blake, Orc and Blade Runner." On the Other Side of the Eye, 24 Nov. 2009. Accessed 24 Feb. 2018.
[2] Wenzel, John. "Review: 'Blade Runner 2049' is a force of nature, constructed to precision." The Know, 4 Oct 2017. Accessed 28 Jan 2018.
[3] Lapointe, Tanya. *The Art and Soul of Blade Runner 2049*. Los Angeles, Alcon Entertainment, 2017. p. 114.

but don't break, and don't, under any circumstances, feel — this is the inescapable charge of a Blade Runner in the year 2049.

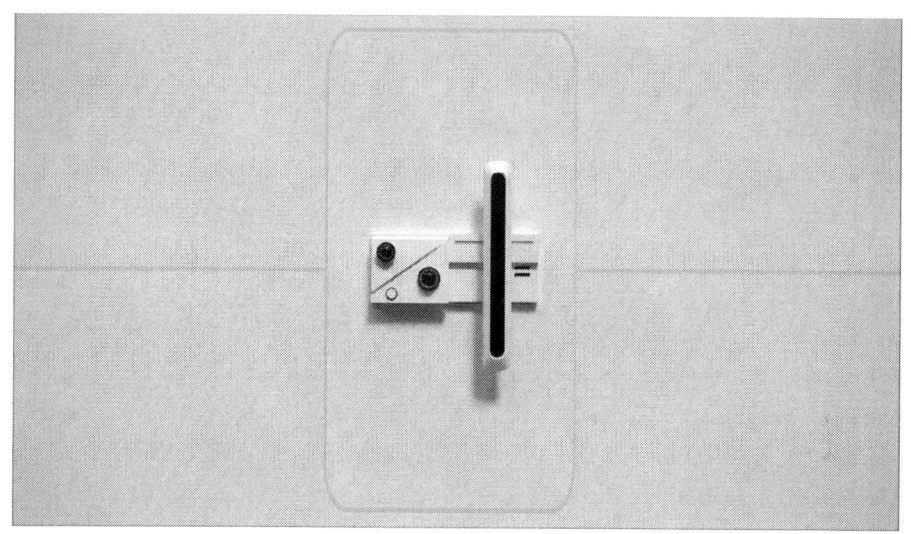

The Baseline Test Machine used to interview K at LAPD Headquarters.

This Baseline process, introduced less than 15 minutes into the film, is quickly characterized as cryptic and cruel and serves to establish Officer KD6-3.7's primary desire — to be interlinked with other people in meaningful relationships, something the system seems determined to deny him. It's never explicitly stated whether there is one single Baseline text used in the testing of all Blade Runners, or if each individual is assigned their own unique passage. Since the Interviewer says "Recite *your* Baseline" instead of "Recite *the* Baseline," I'm inclined to think it's uniquely assigned like their serial number names. Given the general lack of liberties in K's life, it is highly unlikely he was allowed to *choose* the text himself, though that raises the question of who did? Lieutenant Joshi? Niander Wallace? Ana Stelline? In any case, upon his return to the station after killing Sapper Morton, we hear K recite his Baseline text (the first of two such tests depicted in the film), and though it is short in length, it is dense in poetic imagery:

> *And blood-black nothingness began to spin,*
> *A system of cells interlinked within cells interlinked within cells*
> *interlinked within one stem.*
> *And dreadfully distinct against the dark,*
> *a tall white fountain played.*

No indication is given in this scene as to the author or source of these lines, but we don't have much time to contemplate that, as we are instantly dragged into a cyclone of harsh interrogation. In a voice callous and curt, the Interviewer on the other side of the wall asks things mostly related to isolation and emptiness, like "Do you long for having your heart interlinked?" and "Do you feel that there's a part of you that's missing?" The question "When you're not performing your duties, do they keep you in a little box?" mirrors the claustrophobic nature of the test room: a tiny white cell, with a bug-eyed monitoring apparatus mounted to the wall. K is not allowed to *respond* to the questions in a human manner. Instead he must repeat back certain words and phrases so the crucible-like chamber can get a read on his vital signs and brain waves.

K passes his first Baseline test with no issues, but the scene serves as a gateway into the tortured world of replicant servitude and the ways they are kept "dreadfully distinct" from humanity. He arrives at the LAPD station streaked in blood and visibly exhausted, but must go directly to the test room. That might be rational if the point of the test was to diagnose injuries and help him heal. However, this "post-trauma" check has nothing to do with treating the very real physical and psychological trauma that arises from this kind of work; it's a dehumanizing maintenance inspection that is utterly unconcerned with the welfare of the *person*. K's arm is cut fairly deep from the fight, and his seemingly joking quip to Lieutenant Joshi of "I'll glue it" turns macabre when we watch him do just that in his bathroom mirror because his boss won't pay for medical care. Whatever salary the LAPD does give him allows him to rent a cubicle-sized spartan apartment in a crowded converted office building,[4] which is admittedly more than many people in this world can afford, but it's still a dismal existence of two-second showers and rehydrated worm protein. He catches sleep in his spinner on the way to jobs and may only own one good shirt, since Joi, his AI romantic partner, offers to fix it when it gets ruined. While Joi does bring some actual joy to K's life, it is a life that is routine yet far from comfortable.

But replicants are not engineered to live fulfilling lives, they are engineered to be obedient tools of imperialism, and the Baseline test is an essential mechanism in that system. Niander Wallace, the father of the modern replicant lines, is an unabashed colonialist. "I have taken us to nine new worlds," Wallace boasts. That is not enough to satisfy his ambition, though, as he feels humanity

---

[4] Lapointe, Tanya. *The Art and Soul of* Blade Runner 2049. Los Angeles, Alcon Entertainment, 2017. p. 80.

"should own the stars" and admits he's willing to get there on "the back of a disposable workforce." To keep his replicant workforce in line, Blade Runners are created. To keep the Blade Runners in line, the Baseline test is created. It's a vicious cycle of manipulation, benefitting only those humans at the very top. It's unsurprising, then, that the Baseline process would qualify as torture under the United Nations definition, since it intentionally inflicts "suffering, whether physical or mental" on a person to obtain information.[5] The Baseline test purposely puts Blade Runners in acute psychological distress — over, and over, and over — and somehow the justice system has sold this to the population as normal and necessary.

It isn't just Wallace or Joshi who are to blame, though; most of the world of *BR2049* has internalized this societal segregation, which becomes evident in the ways others interact with K. Ridley Scott calls it "a condition of apartheid" in which the replicants are "a new race of people who should be accepted, should be equal" but clearly are not.[6] K's colleagues harass him harshly; he has to sidestep an aggressive snarl of "Fuck off, skin job" from one of his fellow LAPD officers, and even unassuming lab technician Coco makes multiple prejudicial insults. His neighbors are no better. K is heckled as a "tin-plate soldier," "prick," and "bastard" on the long climb up to his apartment, and finally arrives home to find "Fuck Off Skinner" scrawled across his door. He is also hated by his kind. Mariette's pleasure model companion calls him a "fucking Blade Runner" upon recognizing him and saunters away in disgust. K is clearly used to such reactions to his nature, as he is shocked that Mariette keeps talking to him, saying, "Don't you know what I am?" *He* may not know what he is for the first half of the film, but he knows *exactly* how society views him — as an outcast, an untouchable island — and it shows in his facial expressions. In the special feature "Designing the World of *Blade Runner 2049*," Ryan Gosling (who plays K) comments that Roger Deakins' cinematography is so effective that one can watch the film on mute because the shots tell the story. I would argue Gosling's nuanced depiction of K's reactions contribute just as much. Watching his face while Joshi tells him he doesn't need a soul, or when the orphanage warden calls him less than a man, there is no question: K keenly feels every spurn and slur hurled his

---

[5] "Convention against Torture and Other Cruel, Inhuman or Degrading Treatment or Punishment." *United Nations Human Rights Office of the High Commissioner*, OHCHR.org. Accessed 28 Jan. 2018.

[6] Lapointe, Tanya. *The Art and Soul of Blade Runner 2049*. Los Angeles, Alcon Entertainment, 2017. p. 24.

way. In letting that hurt flicker silently on the surface of his performance, Gosling skillfully advances the franchise's assertion that replicants are indeed "more human than human."

K's humanity is perhaps most evident in how he chooses to use his bonus pay, which hints at the selflessness that will be critical in his character's later moments of growth. At the conclusion of the first Baseline test, he is told he can "pick up [his] bonus." It's unclear whether the reward is for retiring Sapper Morton or acing the Baseline, though probably the former, as successful tests seem to be a non-negotiable expectation. Either way, Officer K spends the extra money on an Emanator for Joi, allowing the hologram some coveted freedom from her ceiling-mounted projector. He needs a new shirt and a trip to a surgeon, but he opts to buy something for her instead. It's a touching gesture of empathy, a tiny spark of compassion in a bleak world ravaged by utilitarianism and capitalistic greed. K cannot free himself from the LAPD, but he finds meaning in doing for others what they cannot do for themselves. There's no question that K is "interlinked" with Joi, at least to some degree, in an entirely non-human but tender relationship of mutual care.

While the Baseline source text is not explicitly identified in-film, it does make a cameo in a moment when K and Joi are together, and its plot bears uncanny resemblance to K's journey. Right before Joi is given the gift of mobility (where her first experience is — what else? — rain on a rooftop), she picks up a book, one of K's few possessions, and asks him to read to her in an effort to cheer him up. The book is none other than Vladimir Nabokov's 1962 novel *Pale Fire*, the source of K's Baseline text. The story of *Pale Fire* focuses on the autobiographical tale of fictional author John Shade, a man with a "spirit stripped and utterly alone"[7] who writes mostly of dealing with the loss of his daughter, as well as a mystical vision that he becomes determined to interpret. Writer Andrew Dyce characterizes *Pale Fire* as a novel that plays with "the idea of what is real, what is not, and who gets to decide."[8] There are many parallels to *BR2049*, from a "ghostly tree" where the "phantom of [Shade's] little daughter" lingers, to a "blood-orange sun," to a reference to being "artistically caged."[9] The chunk of text that forms K's Baseline appears at a point in the

---

[7] Nabokov, Vladimir. *Pale Fire*. New York, Alfred A. Knopf, 1962. p. 42.
[8] Dyce, Andrew. "*Blade Runner 2049*: Every Easter Egg & Clue." Screen Rant, 8 Oct 2017. Accessed 30 Jan 2018.
[9] Nabokov, Vladimir. *Pale Fire*. New York, Alfred A. Knopf, 1962. p. 38, 26, 28.

story when Shade has a heart attack and collapses; the Baseline describes the vision (of a system of interlinked cells and a white fountain) that Shade sees in those moments of unconsciousness. In general, Shade is a man who is trying to find meaning in a life he doesn't understand, and seeks answers anywhere he can find them.

K's copy of Vladimir Nabokov's 1962 novel *Pale Fire*, the origin of the lines of poetry he recites in his Baseline.

Pale Fire lends thematic backdrop for the film not only in the content of the lines used, but also in the structure of the source text as metafiction,[10] which mirrors K's existential quest to understand his purpose and place in the world. Nabokov's novel defies genre; it is not really a novel at all in the traditional sense, as it breaks all rules and expectations of novel plot and form. It is a text inside of a text: a long poem written by the fictional character John Shade, that is framed by an even longer set of annotations by another fictional character, editor Charles Kinbote. Together, the two narratives overlap and intertwine, sometimes quite confusingly, to weave the complex story of these two men's lives and relationship. The metafiction moment in *BR2049* comes when Joi suggests K read to her from *Pale Fire,* and K says "You hate that book," implying he *doesn't* hate it, and reads it often enough for her to be tired of it. He is referencing part of his own story. K is subjected to Baseline tests on a regular basis (perhaps even daily, if his standard missions mirror the Sapper Morton case), and one can only imagine how deeply these lines of poetry are ingrained into him, how sick he must be of reciting them. Yet he chooses to spend *more*

---

[10] A type of postmodern storytelling that is aware of its own creation, where the text literally references itself in some way, asserting that fiction is sometimes more real than reality. Cambridge Dictionary. 2018. Accessed 23 Feb 2018.

time analyzing them off the clock, searching for "why poetry is meaningful to us," as Shade writes.[11] K owns little, but he owns this book. It matters to him, because he wants to better understand his existence and the power structure he is (an unwilling) part of. His process of trying to understand himself through the lens of this text sets up the identity quest he follows for most of the film.

The might of that power structure comes crashing back to the scene during K's second Baseline, when we learn a failed test earns a Blade Runner an execution. When Officer K gets confirmation from Ana that his memory is "real" in that it was indeed lived by someone, he assumes that means he is the child he was sent to hunt down and destroy, and therefore must try to make sense of the fact that his entire existence has been a lie, and that the two most powerful organizations in L.A. want him either dead or dissected. He reacts as any person would in such a scenario — emotionally, with the only uncontrolled outburst we see from him the entire film. Of course, it is in that moment he is picked up by police and brought back to base to be interrogated. No longer a jaded pawn, K is a walking repository of everything the system forbids replicants to be, but he *can't hide it*, and the system immediately flags the aberration to Joshi, who watches in horror as her model officer swallows anxiously and stumbles through questions. The scans of his brain on her computer show his synapses firing like manic sparklers. None of this is shocking to viewers who just witnessed K walk up to a furnace that wasn't supposed to exist and pull out a piece of a hallucination. Any sane individual would be shaken by that, let alone the implications it has on his identity. Nonetheless, the test is tense and terrifying to both K and to us because of what's at stake — his life. "What's it like to be filled with dread?" the Interviewer asks in a ruthless tone. At this point in the movie, we don't have to guess.

Realizing the gravity of the situation, K cleverly bends the truth to Joshi after the test, implying that he succeeded in retiring the child, which buys him some leeway with her. "I can get you out of the station alive," she tells him, "but you have 48 hours to get back on track. Surrender your gun and badge, and your next Baseline test is out of my hands." The Interviewer calls him "Constant K" earlier in the story, meaning this is the *first* time he's ever been "miles off [his] Baseline," and after a mission in which he was ordered to murder an innocent child at that. Despite his exceptional record, despite the disturbing nature of his orders, the system allows for zero compassion, and K is

---

[11] Nabokov, Vladimir. *Pale Fire*. New York, Alfred A. Knopf, 1962. p. 46.

automatically condemned, requiring Joshi to bend her own rules to keep him alive. This is not just prejudice, it is abject authoritarian subjugation: replicant lives are regulated, devalued, and deemed disposable by those in power. This injustice of a "near-fascistic system," as *The New Yorker's* Anthony Lane calls it,[12] is the "dark" against which K must distinguish himself by the end of the film.

This harrowing process of carving an identity from a backdrop of brutality is amplified by the striking visual contrast leveraged in the film's cinematography, especially in the use of lighting and the frequent onscreen juxtaposition of life with non-life. The light in the film is classic noir: stark, moody, and enigmatic. As reviewer John Wenzel writes, "Cinematographer Roger Deakins' use of lighting — whether in sharp, parallel bars, undulating pools or saturated waves — is as brilliantly considered as any film of the high-def, digital age."[13] These lighting choices perfectly compliment the emotional thrust of each scene, from the cool ambiance of Ana Stelline's lab as she creates, to the thick shadow that K sinks into as he realizes he's just another unremarkable slave. Added onto superb lighting is the thematic contrast achieved by repeatedly depicting symbols of life alongside symbols of death, such as the Nematode grubs that squirm next to K's gun in Sapper's kitchen, the animated nail designs that dance on Luv's fingertips while her drone missiles obliterate the landfill dwellers, and the glitching holographic Elvis that croons while Deckard tries to kill K. Each of these pairings highlight the paradoxical nature of what it really means to be "alive." There is one juxtaposition that emphasizes connection: the precipitation that falls on the hands of Joi, K, and Ana at different points, indicating in all instances a moment of heightened appreciation for the simplest pleasures that make us human. Despite K wanting more than anything to be interlinked to others to a greater degree, especially through a family and real heritage, the majority of the artistic visual composition of the film effectively reinforces the fact that he is and will remain "dreadfully distinct," though perhaps not as we might first assume.

One of the most unforgettable elements of visual contrast in the film is the use of color, particularly yellow. Each of the two *Blade Runner* films uses a very

---

[12] Lane, Anthony. "'Blade Runner 2049': The Mysteries Deepen." *The New Yorker*, 16 Oct 2017. Accessed 28 Jan 2018.

[13] Wenzel, John. "Review: 'Blade Runner 2049' is a force of nature, constructed to precision." The Know, 4 Oct 2017. Accessed 28 Jan 2018.

different overall color palette with which to tell its story. This is not hard to pick up on just by watching the films, but I found more definitive evidence of the difference by comparing the color spectrum posters for the two films created by Charlie Clark of The Colors of Motion website.[14] He uses software algorithms to extract the average color of frames in a film, which then print into a series of thin bars showing the progression of color through the movie. The palette of the *Blade Runner* poster is overwhelmingly blue-toned, its color continuum full of lines of teal and hazy azure, with a few stripes of warm brown for the scenes in Deckard's apartment. The *BR2049* poster, on the other hand, which I commissioned, is a study in contrast: mostly stripes of drab green-grey cut through by several bright gold bands representing the shots of the data archives, Wallace's offices, and of course, the iconic Vegas environment. There are even some bars of "blood black nothingness" (mostly corresponding to the dark depths of the orphanage). The two posters, while both beautiful, look extremely different from each other, with the original a relatively homogenous set of tones, and its sequel a fiery spectacle of contrast. This use of sudden yellow serves a purpose that supports the theme of becoming "dreadfully distinct against the dark." Yellow stands out against the greyness of the brutal, urban-industrial environment in Los Angeles; indeed, one of the most unforgettable shots in the film is when we cut from the cold silver light of Joshi's office (where Joshi lies dead) to the radioactive orange haze of Las Vegas (where K searches for life). Director Denis Villeneuve stated in an interview that he intentionally used the color yellow symbolically throughout the film to represent a connection to "creation and childhood and mad desires" that starts with Sapper Morton's farm and flower, and which "K [then] follows all the way through until the very end."[15] Without this expert application of hues, the film would lose some of its symbolic power that is so carefully crafted around the Baseline allusion.

For K, the "dreadful" part of the Baseline prophecy comes in the form of the subverted myth of the Chosen One on which he stakes so much of his hope. The idea of being "distinct" is set up initially in the film as the traditional path of the Hero's Journey, the classic structure of Western storytelling defined by

---

[14] Clark, Charlie. "Blade Runner." *The Colors of Motion*, thecolorsofmotion.com. Accessed 6 Feb. 2018.
[15] Desowitz, Bill. "'Blade Runner 2049': The Most Difficult Craft Challenges for Director Denis Villeneuve." IndieWire, Penske Business Media LLP, 24 Nov 2017. Accessed 23 Feb 2018.

Joseph Campbell in which a seemingly common person answers a call to greatness and discovers their grandiose destiny. Author Aliette de Bodard explains that by the rules of this narrative, "you have to be special to matter,"[16] and we are led to believe, as K is, that he *is* special, the replicant child who is "born, not made," as Joi says. And then, a solid two hours into the film, that myth is unexpectedly shattered when K learns the special child is female, and deduces it is Ana Stelline, the memory-maker whose own memories were implanted in him. That truth is devastating to him (he collapses upon hearing it), and disorienting to the viewing audience (who are set up to ask, what now? How can this possibly end in a satisfying way?) For *BR2049* to "[blow] the Chosen One narrative wide open,"[17] as author Tod VanDerWherff puts it, is a bold move from a screenwriting perspective, but it's one that pays off, because it allows the film to make an important point: being special is not required to make a difference.

K's difference takes shape at the climax of *BR2049*, where he faces off against Wallace's agent to rescue Deckard, and where the meaning of the "white fountain" from his Baseline is made manifest. This scene directly maps onto the context of the white fountain in *Pale Fire*. After Shade has the vision of the fountain, he goes on a quest to determine its meaning, seeking out other people who have had similar experiences. He tracks down a woman who reportedly also had a vision of a fountain, and excitedly hopes that his mystery might be solved, only to discover in his investigation that it was a misprint — she saw a *mountain,* not a *fountain.*[18] Shade's quest for understanding yields false results, just as K's does. However, in the wake of his disappointment and the resultant existential crisis, Shade decides that "it sufficed that I in life could find [...] some kind of correlated pattern in the game." He realizes there is no destiny, no certain purpose for his life, but it doesn't matter because he sees meaning around him and has the ability to exact change as he chooses, no different than the powerful beings who are "playing a game of worlds." By the fight scene with Luv, K knows there is nothing special about his nature, but he now knows the game that the LAPD, Wallace, Freysa, and even Deckard are playing, and decides to *act anyway,* and not in accordance with the desires of

---

[16] de Bodard, Aliette. "Chosen Ones, Specialness, and the Narrative of the One." *Aliette de Bodard – Fantasy and Science Fiction*, 2015. Accessed 24 Feb. 2018.

[17] VanDerWerff, Tod. "The best thing about *Blade Runner 2049* is what it isn't." Vox, Vox Media Inc, 9 Oct. 2017. Accessed 21 Feb 2018.

[18] Nabokov, Vladimir. *Pale Fire*. New York, Alfred A. Knopf, 1962. p. 50.

any of these people, but on his own. He chooses his own path, one that is unique, *distinct,* and extremely difficult. He succeeds, but in true noir form, it's not a clean victory. As Tod VanDerWerff of *Vox* points out, "K, who began the movie killing his own kind at the behest of the human power structure, ends it killing his own kind so that others of his kind might live."[19] There's a heavy cost to squaring with reality, but for K, it is worth it.

Some critics argue that the toy horse is K's metaphorical fountain,[20] and it could certainly be read that way as it does prove to be a misleading object. But in a film that clearly takes its symbolism seriously, I maintain it's no coincidence that K first flies past the flowing Sepulveda Seawall when he thinks he is the child, and later returns to that very spot right after learning the truth. The Baseline text reads *"and dreadfully distinct against the dark, a tall white fountain played,"* and this scene of the film brings these lines to life. K and Luv duel at night (*against the dark*), silhouetted by the yellow taillights of the Wallace limousine (*dreadfully distinct*), at the foot of the immensely high Sepulveda Seawall that has white water cascading over the top (*a tall white fountain*). It doesn't get any more literal than that.

It may seem excessive to dig so deep into the meaning behind a few lines of the film, but research into the circumstances of the Baseline scenes' filming prove otherwise. Admittedly, the literary connections and symbolism unearthed in this analysis of K's Baseline are in no way necessary to understand the plot of the movie, or to be moved by it. The filmmakers likely had no expectation that audiences would have read Nabokov's esoteric and highly academic novel, or that those who had read it would draw connections between the lives of Shade and K. However, the people involved in producing the film *did* delve into their own deep analysis of the Baseline scenes in ways that reinforce the idea that this film is interlinked with its heritage, and yet distinct. The most notable example is the fact that Ryan Gosling revised the original Baseline text he was given to read, lengthening the dialogue exchange considerably with much deeper questions. To do this, he utilized a technique from voice coach Natsuko Ohama called "dropping in," in which an actor explores the meaning of their lines by exhausting every possible interpretation

---

[19] VanDerWerff, Tod. "The best thing about *Blade Runner 2049* is what it isn't." Vox, Vox Media Inc, 9 Oct. 2017. Accessed 21 Feb 2018.
[20] Bustillos, Maria. "*Blade Runner 2049* is revealed through the novel *Pale Fire*." Medium, 17 Oct 2017. Accessed 28 Jan 2018.

of the words.[21] Much of that exploration made it into the final cut of the film, when Villeneuve decided to give Gosling's version a try. It was reportedly a long, grueling scene to shoot, but both actor and director told interviewers that the filming of the Baseline scenes served as a thematic touchstone for the rest of production. Gosling said it "unlocked [his] understanding of K, but also provided insight into the state of mind of those who would force this burden upon him." Likewise, Villeneuve said, "There's always a scene that makes you feel you've made contact with the soul of the story. This was it, and it became our own Baseline for the rest of principal photography."[22] The Baseline text was clearly a nexus of meaning for the creation of *BR2049*, both for the storyline and the production process.

The use of this alternate dialogue in these scenes becomes even more significant when considering that Gosling is not the first actor playing a replicant to re-write his own lines. In the early morning hours before the shooting of the iconic climax scene in the original *Blade Runner,* Rutger Hauer, the actor who played Roy Batty, shortened his rooftop monologue and added the now-infamous "tears in rain" line, with the blessing of Ridley Scott.[23] Two different films, two different actors, two very different scenes, interlinked by a willingness to "play" outside the rules. One actor found enhanced meaning by condensing the script, the other by expanding it; in both cases, the deviation proved memorable and moving.

While I have heretofore been mostly focusing on interpreting the *words* of the Baseline, the strongest symbolic connection to *Pale Fire* occurs at the end of the film in a moment ironically *absent* of words. K successfully frees Deckard from Luv's custody but is mortally wounded in the process, and as the two men stand outside Ana's center, Deckard recognizes the selflessness his fellow Blade Runner has exhibited in saving him. "Why? What am I to you?" Deckard asks. K does not respond, yet the answer is obvious: Deckard is not a father, not a comrade, not even a hero. To K, Deckard is simply a person (replicant or no) with relationships that matter and deserve to be protected. We don't need to hear K's answer to understand his intent; unspoken, it's just as powerful.

---

[21] Lapointe, Tanya. *The Art and Soul of* Blade Runner 2049. Los Angeles, Alcon Entertainment, 2017. p. 117.

[22] Lapointe, Tanya. *The Art and Soul of* Blade Runner 2049. Los Angeles, Alcon Entertainment, 2017. p. 114.

[23] *On the Edge of Blade Runner*, directed by Andrew Abbott, Channel 4 Television Corporation, 15 July 2000. Accessed 1 Feb 2018.

Likewise, the last line of the *Pale Fire* poem is left unwritten by its author, but the rhyme scheme implies the final line is meant to be an echo of the first: "I am the shadow of the waxwing slain." K could very much be read as an analog for the waxwing, a bird that dies by colliding with "the false azure in the windowpane," the reflection of a sky that wasn't really there. In his life, K chases after a dream (of having been born, of being special) and is let down by reality, and appropriately, no dove rises at his death, as it does with Roy Batty. Author Maria Bustillos suggests that while K bleeds out, he is dwelling on these very lines of the poem,[24] on the utter uncertainty of life, but I contend his last thoughts are likely something much more hopeful. As he leans back and watches "each drifting flake shapeless and slow,"[25] as Shade writes, K is undoubtedly aware of the coveted "azure" of connectedness that he will now never reach, *but he knows someone else will* thanks to his actions. Deckard and his daughter will be reunited. Freysa's replicant rebellion will not be betrayed to Wallace, and will still have a chance to end the oppression of his people. In a clever callback to the original film, we are reminded, poignantly, of Roy Batty's quiet rooftop expiration, but the two scenes are very opposite in tone: from tears in rain to blood in snow. From an empty, pointless loss to a sacrifice, a gift, a *choice*. As the distinctly unspecial hero of *BR2049* breathes his last, he isn't pondering his own death; he's seeing a miracle, as Sapper Morton foretold — a miracle that only he could have wrought.

Through its intensely smart anchoring of the story around a passage of literature rich in imagery and symbolism, *Blade Runner 2049* effectively tells a tale both personal and universal. The Baseline tests, though brief in screen time, are absolutely integral to the film's message, and I would argue no other passage could replace Nabokov's text and retain the unique symbolic power it provides. Those few lines of poetry that are repeated, recited, *exhausted* over the course of the story provide necessary semantic grounding for nearly every other visual and narrative element of the film, from the high-contrast noir lighting to the protagonist-sidelining plot twist. But most importantly, the Baseline text serves as a persistent symbol of K's quest to determine what it means to have a soul, what it feels like to "have [his] heart interlinked," and what it costs to become "dreadfully distinct" from a corrupt, unjust system. The

---

[24] Bustillos, Maria. "*Blade Runner 2049* is revealed through the novel *Pale Fire*." Medium, 17 Oct 2017. Accessed 28 Jan 2018.

[25] Nabokov, Vladimir. *Pale Fire*. New York, Alfred A. Knopf, 1962. p. 25.

Baseline test is brutal and unforgiving, as is his character arc — he dies alone on cold cement steps. And yet, in sacrificing his life to save Deckard's, he heals a separation 30 years in the making. In stepping outside of the system, K defies the Baseline mockery, knocking a crack into the "wall that separates kind" that has kept replicants beating themselves to death against it for decades.

As Freysa tells K, "dying for the right cause is the most human thing we can do," and in K's case, it's an act that very well might break the world for the better.

Building the World of *Blade Runner* without Breaking It: Why Unasked Questions are Answered but Our Most Enduring Question is Not

by Nathan P. Butler

Modern movie audiences have it easy. No, really, we do. More often than not, a movie that manages to achieve financial or pop cultural success is virtually guaranteed a sequel within a few years. Why would a studio place bets on new intellectual property when an existing franchise could be farmed for more profit with a ready-made audience? A modern audience rarely finds themselves having to wait a single decade, let alone three and a half, for a sequel in hopes of getting answers to questions left dangling in a groundbreaking film of its time.

Such was the case for *Blade Runner* fans, who waited (and debated) for 35 years to discover whether Rick Deckard, the film's namesake Blade Runner, was as human as he first seemed or a replicant as later hinted. Fandom investigation into this seminal question in science fiction was complicated repeatedly by alternate versions of the film, most notably the 1992 *Director's Cut* and 2007's *Final Cut* (which made the jump to 4K Ultra HD Blu-ray in 2017 for the film's 35th anniversary). Thankfully, the very same mentality that makes modern sequels for recent films such an obvious choice for studios has also led to a resurgence of long-dormant properties, as the urge to profit from nostalgia seems to be creating an entertainment market in which "everything old is new again." For *Blade Runner* fans, this renaissance of franchises from the 1980s and 1990s meant finally seeing a sequel, *Blade Runner 2049*, and at long last the chance of getting an answer to their most pressing question: Is Deckard a replicant?

To borrow a turn of phrase from Lt. Joshi, though, ongoing interest in a film is often built on a wall that separates the questions that *are* answered and those that are not. Answer the wrong question (or the right question in the wrong way), and you've bought an online flame war among fans, or a loss of the very ambiguity that has helped your film remain a subject of discussion for decades.

That is where *Blade Runner 2049* and the short films that form a bridge between it and the original *Blade Runner* have succeeded marvelously.

They have given us answers to questions few of us ever asked, while entirely denying us the answer we have sought since 1982.

Wiping the Slate Clean: Answers from 2022

By 2017 (or at least *our* 2017, rather than the dystopian 2017 we would expect when looking back from *Blade Runner*'s 2019), the internet had become a prime location for releasing free content as a means of promoting upcoming films, but few have done so as elaborately as the lead-up to the October 2017 theatrical premiere of *Blade Runner 2049*. In August and September, three short films were released, detailing the world of Ridley Scott's (and now Denis Villeneuve's) gritty future. The short films were created by artists whose talents *Blade Runner 2049* director Villeneuve had long respected, and each expanded the universe of the franchise to answer questions raised by the second movie, yet which were not crucial to understanding the film itself.

The first of the short films chronologically (but the last released) was the animated *Black Out 2022*, directed by Shinichirō Watanabe. (Yes, the title made *Black Out* two words, rather than the grammatically correct one found in its final text.) Set just three years after Deckard's fateful clash with Nexus-6 replicant Roy Batty and escape from Los Angeles with Rachael (the saga's only Nexus-7 model replicant, as far as we know), *Black Out* seeks to explain its namesake power outage that led to the loss of electronically stored data in the gap between the two theatrical films.

The young replicant Trixie in *Blackout 2022*.

The story focuses on a pair of Nexus-8 replicants with open-ended lifespans. *Black Out* confirms they were created almost immediately after the 2019 death of Eldon Tyrell. Edward James Olmos' Gaff makes a reappearance (with Olmos reprising the role to provide his voice, just as he reprised the role for *2049*), while Sapper Morton gets a brief name-check amongst the replicants appearing in computer records. We also indirectly learn a bit more about Sapper's own backstory by way of replicant rebel Iggy Cygnus being one of only five known surviving veterans of the same military campaign on Calantha. While we do not know whether Iggy and Sapper were on the same side in the conflict, we learn that it was a battle fought on both sides by replicants as disposable combatants, raising ethical questions about the use of troops who are "nothing more than toy soldiers in a sandbox."

If the Calanthan campaign provides a macro-scale doorway into exploration of the line between replicants being human or subhuman, it is the peril faced by "young" (by design?) replicant Trixie that provides a micro-level version of the same when a group of human thugs attempt to sexually assault her, claiming that "this is what you're made for." (If true, this would make her a "Doxie" replicant like Mariette in *2049*.) Iggy brutally puts a stop to the rapists' assault (and lives, for that matter), then recruits Trixie to join him in the attack that will become the basis for the loss of data described by the Wallace Corporation file clerk to K in *2049*.

A viewer who skips the short films would perhaps be forgiven for criticizing the idea that a simple blackout could cause massive data loss. Fortunately for *Blade Runner* continuity, we learn in *Black Out 2022* that it was not a typical power outage. It was accomplished through the detonation of a nuclear missile (ironically manufactured by Tyrell Corporation) high over Los Angeles, which caused an electromagnetic pulse (EMP) that resulted in widespread data loss. Moreover, magnetic backups of records relating to Tyrell Corporation's replicants, particularly to the Nexus-8 line, were simultaneously destroyed by Iggy, who detonated a fuel truck to devastate the building housing Tyrell's servers. Other cells also carried out strikes at similar data centers. This explains how "every machine stopped cold" and "when the lights came back" after "ten days of darkness," as the file clerk describes, "we were wiped clean. Photos, files, every bit of data… gone. Bank records too." The data loss was apparently profound, as society "had everything on drives. Everything, everything, everything."[1]

Interestingly, the final narration of the 2022 tale states that it was in the aftermath of the blackout (and the attack that caused it) that replicant production was prohibited and the Tyrell Corporation subsequently went bankrupt. This appears to limit the "series of violent rebellions" mentioned in the opening text of *Blade Runner 2049*, as well as the rise of "human supremacy movements" described in the short's own opening to only about three years of such activity after the acts perpetrated by Roy Batty, Pris Stratton, and Leon Kowalski in the original film. This also suggests that the data Niander Wallace acquires through purchasing the Tyrell Corporation must have been backed up *somewhere* for him to have access to it, while also providing a motivation for the mogul to become a "data hoarder," as Luv describes him.

We are also treated to an unusual pairing of human views on replicants in *Black Out*. We learn that the human supremacy movements that began between 2019 and 2022 "used the replicant registration database to identify and kill replicants" (as seen with cries of "They're not human! They're replicant!"), but we also see a diametrically opposite view in the form of Ren. This young man, drawn into a love for Trixie that was likely just manipulation to

---

[1] That apparently included irreplaceable, adorable baby pictures of the file clerk himself that his mother still cries over.

convince him to take control of the nuclear missile for the strike, refers to humans as "selfish, stupid liars," while seeing replicants as "pure" and "perfect," even going so far as to reverently echo the Tyrell slogan, "more human than human."

Were these answers that viewers really needed to understand the new movie? Not particularly. The short film was inspired by a small segment of dialogue and suggested events within the theatrical sequel, then built its own narrative to provide backstory that solidified the movie's foundations while not being truly essential. It is a story that is nice to have, yet whose impact is handled well enough in a smattering of film dialogue that it need not have existed in the first place. It is a piece of sci-fi dessert or a pre-meal snack, not the meal itself.

Steve Jobs with a Dash of Josef Mengele: Answers from 2036

The first short film to launch online, *Nexus Dawn*, takes place in 2036, making it the second chronological bridge between theatrical releases. Luke Scott's first live action short brings fans the story of how Jared Leto's Niander Wallace (*Blade Runner 2049*'s visionary businessman with a morally questionable god complex) managed to convince the lawmakers of 2036 to overturn the ban on replicant production that has stood for over a decade so that he can produce his new line of Nexus-9 models.

Niander Wallace goes to extreme measures in *Nexus Dawn 2036*.

In *2049*, we only learn that Wallace was responsible for the technologies that saved humankind from famine in a period of ecological collapse that began in the mid-2020s (which suggests ecological disaster piling on top of the chaos already unleashed by the technological disaster of the aforementioned blackout and resultant data loss). This made Wallace wealthy in the extreme, and he was able to purchase the remains of Tyrell Corporation, using its facilities and intellectual property to develop a new line of (supposedly) fully-obedient replicants.

In *Nexus Dawn*, we finally see that this was not simply a matter of lawmakers forgetting the past and dooming society to repeat its mistakes. The officials remain fully aware of the reasons behind the ban on replicants and in fact inform Wallace that "the prohibition of replicant technology is not subject to debate, nor is its repeal" and that they have only granted Wallace a hearing "in deference to [his]... essential contributions." The lead lawmaker even reminds Wallace that he is breaking the law by having one of his new, illegally-developed Nexus-9 models at his side for the hearing. It is Wallace's actions in the meeting, both in terms of simple intimidation and a rather gruesome proof of concept in the form of ordering his own replicant to choose between harming its master or killing itself, that manages to swing the lawmakers toward abolition of the replicant ban. His position is further bolstered by the argument that such slave labor could help expand human colonization of other planets, something we learn is indeed true when in *2049* he notes how his creation of the new breed of replicants was "how I took us to nine new worlds." His arguments and brutal demonstration are apparently successful, as production of replicants begins under the Wallace Corporation.

Moreover, we get another example here of Niander Wallace as a man who relishes playing God, seeing himself as a creator of life (what Luv calls "a gift... from Mr. Wallace to the world"), yet one who perceives little to no value in the life he creates beyond the financial benefit of a sale or the "free" labor replicants can provide in building and expanding civilization for their human "betters." He sees their creation as "breeding," a term usually used for animals rather than sapient beings. Of course, those in political power are shown here in a similar light, if not as starkly so, given that their concerns remain on matters relating primarily to obedience, rather than to any of the broader moral questions that arise in creating "artificial" humans. (They do, at least, repeatedly state that "This is wrong" when faced with Wallace's demonstration of replicant loyalty, albeit without any real effect on the outcome of the hearing.)

Wallace, meanwhile, views replicants as products for sale and tools for human expansion, valuable in terms of whatever use their owners might choose for them. As he puts it, "Every leap of civilization was built off the back of a disposable workforce," which must be his replicant "angels" since humankind has "lost our stomach for slaves, unless engineered." In Sapper's words, natural humans have replicants "scraping the shit."

Again, is this an encounter we needed to see in order to understand the change in policy toward replicants or Wallace's version of a god complex? Not particularly, given that we learn about the change in policy in the opening text of *Blade Runner 2049* and simply take it for granted from then onward, and Wallace provides plenty of evidence of his mindset within the film itself, even going so far as to kill a newborn, sterile replicant (described as "barren pasture, empty and salted") to illustrate a point to Luv. More specifically, Wallace's own words in the same scene confirm his self-perception, as he refers to his creations as "good angels" existing "in service of civilization" and his office (or presence) as the "kingdom of Heaven," wishing Luv to proclaim (in full Messianic fashion) "a child is born" upon the presentation of a new replicant model. Once more, we have learned more about the universe by receiving answers to the kinds of questions fans weren't really asking, but the universe is at least a little richer for it.

Setting the Stage: Answers from 2048

Luke Scott's second *Blade Runner* outing, *Nowhere to Run* (AKA *No Escape* in China and *Nowhere to Escape* in Taiwan), is another live action short, set in the year 2048, about a year before the beginning of *Blade Runner 2049*.

As the second theatrical tale opens, Blade Runner K has discovered the location of Sapper Morton, a Nexus-8 replicant and veteran of Calantha (like Iggy Cygnus). The film provides no information as to how Sapper was found, only his reason for being hunted, which is as simple as existing at all, since any living Nexus-8 is to be "retired" (Blade Runner speak for "killed"). Over the course of the film, we learn a bit more about Sapper through implication, since we know that he was a combat medic and apparently tried to save the life of Rachael during childbirth. He seems somewhat gentle and reverent toward the "miracle" he witnessed (i.e. replicant procreation, what Niander Wallace calls Tyrell's "final trick"), and his lifestyle as a simple nematode farmer (since 2020) would seem to suggest that he is not currently a threat to anyone, yet is still targeted primarily because of what he is, rather than who he has chosen to be.

Nowhere to Run serves to both reinforce the positive nature of this post-Calantha Sapper and to provide a somewhat tragic rationale for how he was put on K's radar after about 30 years in hiding. We learn that he is what he claims, a simple farmer. Moreover, he is at a disadvantage, given that he must accept lower prices than others in his field or risk a confrontation with buyers like Sultan that could blow his cover. We find that his willingness to put himself on the line for the sake of a child is not limited to the "miracle" child of Rachael and Deckard but also to a young girl named Ella, when she and her mother are accosted by thugs intending to rape them.[2]

It is, in fact, this act of heroism that brings to light Sapper's true nature and leads to a witness informing the Los Angeles Police Department (for whom K works) that he has discovered a wanted "skin job." In essence, it is an act of protection that starts the domino effect that will come close to "breaking the world."

Sapper Morton shares some light reading with a friend in *Nowhere to Run 2048*.

Did we need to know how K learned about Sapper, other than his name being on a list of replicants to be retired? No. Did we need further evidence that

---

[2] Rape appears to be an ongoing theme in the franchise, owing perhaps to the nature of dominance, devaluation of the individual, and victimization inherent in both sexual assault and the very nature of a Replicant's existence.

Sapper seemed to be a good "man" prior to being placed in a situation of desperate self-preservation by K? Not really, but seeing Sapper acting in defense of Ella makes his fate the next year all the more distressing as the audience for *Blade Runner 2049* is introduced to K as the saga's new "hero," then almost immediately witnesses him kill the short film's own protagonist.

When One Step Forward Means Two Steps Back: The Lack of an Answer in 2049

All of this brings us back around to the year 2049 and the true sequel to the original *Blade Runner*. Most of the audiences who have seen *Blade Runner 2049* will never see the short films that bridge the theatrical tales, nor will they truly need the answers to unasked questions presented therein. However, anyone who has seen *Blade Runner* in the decades since its theatrical run, especially those who saw the later Director's Cut or Final Cut on home video, is likely to still have a single burning question in relation to the film: Is Deckard a replicant or not?

This was a mystery that became the focus of discussion about the film even more with the advent of internet fandom and Ridley Scott's attempts to bring the publicly-available movie in line with his original vision. In 1982, viewers of both the U.S. and international theatrical releases were "treated" (though I'd argue "rankly abused," as Hamlet would say) to a version of the film that included explanatory, detective noir-style narration by Deckard, along with a final scene that explained a sort of "happy ending" in which Deckard and Rachael drove off (north, we assume) and it's implied that they lived long, happy lives together, thanks to her lack of a termination date. In this cut, the hints that Deckard might be a replicant are there but subtle, and the inclusion of the driving scene after he and Rachael leave his apartment draws attention away from that question by the time credits roll.

The 1992 Director's Cut (which Ridley Scott had limited control over) ditched the narration for a more subtle and deliberate form of storytelling that required the viewer to think a bit more in order to follow the film's progression. It also dumped the theatrical cut's studio-imposed final scene, instead ending the film immediately after Deckard discovers the origami unicorn left by Gaff. This is an important moment, as the Director's Cut also restored (at least partially) the sequence in which Deckard dreams of a unicorn. Debate was sparked immediately as to whether there was a connection between the dream and Gaff's origami unicorn, including the notion that Gaff may very well have known of Deckard's dream because it was a programmed experience implanted into replicants.

Ridley Scott was finally able to have full restorative control for 2007's Final Cut. This edit, which remains the current canonical version of the original film, provided a full version of the unicorn dream sequence, retained the origami endpoint, and lacked the narration of the original cut. This home video release and its subsequent reissue on 4K Ultra HD Blu-ray to roughly coincide with the theatrical launch of *Blade Runner 2049* in theaters has added further kindling to keep the fires of debate raging over Deckard's status.

Surely, fans believed, the presence of Harrison Ford's Deckard alongside Ryan Gosling's Officer K in the new film would require the filmmakers to finally provide a definitive answer on Deckard's status. Was he human or replicant, and would whatever answer provided by Denis Villeneuve's film (via a script by Michael Green and Hampton Fancher) be in line with the intentions of original film director Ridley Scott (and original screenwriters David Peoples and, again, Hampton Fancher)?

Fans waited with baited breath for 6 October 2017, and disappeared into darkened cinemas to finally get a definitive answer to the Deckard mystery after over a third of a century!

They received no such thing.

Blade Runner 2049 provided no clear answer as to Rick Deckard's true nature. If anything, the film went out of its way to avoid answering the question. Instead, it tantalizingly seemed to provide an answer when Wallace tells Deckard, "You are a wonder to me," and asks the former Blade Runner, "Did it never occur to you that's why you were summoned [to meet with Eldon Tyrell in 2019] in the first place? Designed to do nothing short of fall for [Rachael] right then and there? All to make that single, perfect specimen." Mere seconds later, though, this potential revelation is called into question once again, when Wallace continues, "That is, if you were designed. Love or mathematical precision?" As far as the new movie was concerned, Deckard was simply Deckard, and his actions both during and after the original film were what mattered, not whether he was born or manufactured. Deckard simply answers Wallace with, "I know what's real."

Some fans were aghast. Others were ambivalent. Others, like me, saw this as precisely the right call. For these fans, the issue of whether we should have been given a concrete answer came down to two fundamental questions: would it have added to the story, and would it have served the franchise well?

I would argue that the answer to both is no.

Deckard's Nature in Relation to *Blade Runner 2049*

At its core, *Blade Runner 2049* is a film that considers the nature of what makes someone (or something) "alive." What defines a living thing or gives that life value in both individual and societal terms?

For the humans of the film, most notably Lt. Joshi and Niander Wallace, lives of value are human lives. Joshi sees K as a favorite servant (whom she can "sometimes forget" is a replicant) and speaks down to him in much the same way that a slave owner might talk down to a slave, while seemingly agreeing with K's assertion that artificial humans lack a fundamental aspect of humanity: a soul.[3] However, Joshi doesn't let K's lack of a soul stop her from wondering aloud what might happen if she finishes a bottle of alcohol, suggesting that she would welcome a sexual encounter with K. To her credit, voicing the notion as a vague question instead of a command provides K with a choice in the matter, and he immediately voices his need to return to work. Given the prevalence of rape in *Blade Runner*'s dehumanization of replicants, this perhaps makes Joshi a "good" slave master, if such a thing is not unshakably oxymoronic.

Among the human characters, Dr. Ana Stelline could potentially provide another avenue for exploring the nature of "life," given that we initially understand her to be a human with a compromised immune system living her life in a "bubble" to protect her from potentially deadly pathogens. Even before learning that she is actually the replicant (or half-replicant, depending on Deckard's nature) child of Rachael and Deckard, she presents the unique case of a supposed human confined to a "cage" since age eight by her own body, limiting her freedom and raising questions as to whether one could live a fulfilled life under such circumstances. Her true nature does nothing to deter these lines of inquiry, it just alters the parameters of her physiology. Ana also provides a bit of a blind spot for Wallace, as we realize that the megalomaniac had the key to procreation that he was seeking right under his nose as a subcontractor for years and never even knew it, putting the lie to any omniscience inherent in his god complex.

For K and the other replicants in the film, the answer is not as simple as their natural-born human "superiors" would claim. While subjecting himself to

---

[3] This Replicant self-perception is echoed by Iggy in *Black Out* when he tells Trixie that there is "no heaven or hell for us. This world is all we've got."

the authority of Joshi and other humans (with a Nexus-9's supposed inability to disobey) and claiming that replicants lack souls, K nevertheless makes individualistic choices once confronted by the possibility of Rachael's miracle replicant child and the brief belief that he himself could be that first-born child of his kind. Over time, he ceases to obey expectations and finds means by which to skirt authority through the letter, if not the spirit, of the rules, and through lies of both omission and commission. When asked about the circumstances that bring K to Wallace Corporation to access Rachael's records, he only tells the suspicious Luv that "Everyone just sleeps better when they know where [replicants] got to." After reporting on the investigation to Joshi, he neglects to tell her the connection between the date from the tree and that on the wooden toy in the story he shared with her. Joi describes this as K not "liking [Joshi] enough to tell her the truth," a lie of omission. He further perpetuates this willingness to lie through a lie of commission with his intent to inform the authorities that Deckard has died in the spinner crash, thereby allowing him the freedom to meet his daughter. Whether or not that actually happened remains unknown.

Luv also stretches the bounds of her obedience as Wallace's "best angel." When speaking to a client about the purchase of new replicants, she advises, "I wouldn't waste your money on intelligence, attachment, or appeal unless you'd like to add some pleasure models to your order," which viewers hear as a statement of devaluation of replicant life, yet Luv seems also to see little value in some (most?) humans. When confronting Joshi, she refers to the human as a "tiny thing," while considering a procreating replicant or her child to be "the fabulous new." Unlike K, who begins if not content then at least accepting of the status quo, Luv foresees revolution. She refers to the potential for "great change" while noting that "you can't hold back the tide with a broom." But is it a change to benefit replicants that she seeks or simply the future for self-replicating replicants that Wallace envisions as a means of increasing the slave population? One has to wonder, given that she (even more overtly than K) is willing to lie, informing Joshi that she will tell Wallace that Joshi tried to shoot her before killing her outright. One could argue, though, that it is a lie in service to obeying the wishes of her master (and creator). Perhaps all of the film's characters should take Deckard's advice: "Don't lie. It's rude." (Among manufactured beings that have trouble avoiding telling lies, Pinocchio appears to be in good, albeit dystopian, company.)

The rebel replicants, as one would expect, take a more clear-cut view of the humanity and value of their kind. Rebel leader Freysa (the other of the three identified Calanthan campaign veterans of the five noted in *Black Out*) argues that the child of Deckard and Rachael means that replicants "are more than just slaves," for "if a baby can come from one of us, we are our own masters." Procreation, in her eyes, is not just a means of perpetuating a species but also an active ability to control one's own destiny and a proof of replicants' humanity. As a modern abolitionist, Fresya taps into our collective history of struggles against slavery and oppression by openly advocating for revolution and seeking to recruit K. As she tells him, "A revolution is coming, and we're building an army. I want to free our people. If you want to be free, join us." Still, as much as audiences can agree with her goals, there linger hints of potential danger. Mariette, who has introduced K to Freysa's rebel cell, hears Freysa's description of what the baby means for replicants and seems to suggest a thread of replicant supremacy in her use of the Tyrell company line, "more human than humans." Are all of the replicant rebels seeking equality, or is the society of *Blade Runner* facing a potential reversal of fortune in which the oppressed become the oppressors? We are left to wonder.

K further provides us with a glimpse into another test case for a debate on what constitutes "life" (particularly artificially-created life) through his interactions with Joi, a "very realistic" artificial intelligence consumer product sold by the Wallace Corporation. (Luv unintentionally emphasizes her nature as a mere program when she first asks K if he is "satisfied with our product," which she would also use as a verbal blade later.) Joi seems to be K's only "friend" and the closest thing to a romantic interest in his life. Always acting in ways that serve K, yet doing so in a fashion more akin to a lover seeking to please than a servant required to obey, Joi gives K comfort and companionship. This relationship acquires more freedom of movement through K's purchase of an *emanator* (a sort of remote holographic projector and memory device) for Joi, while further bringing physical contact into play through the use of a surrogate body ("Doxie" replicant Mariette) to house Joi's A.I. "essence" during a sexual encounter. For her part, Mariette draws a distinction between replicants and Joi when, upon hearing the Wallace Corporation notification music from Joi's emanator, she declares that K doesn't like "real girls." Despite not being "real" in Mariette's or even her own eyes (as evidenced by her desire "to be real for him," suggesting that she is not), Joi is the one who initiates that encounter, apparently hiring Mariette without K's knowledge (whether part of Mariette's broader rebel goals or not). It is an act that is unquestionably K physically having sex with someone who is not Joi, yet the fact that it would've been defined by all involved as an intimate encounter between K and Joi herself is also without question.[4]

One could argue over whether physical intimacy that requires one's "partner" to have sex with another person, even if as a shell for one's self, could be seen as an act of sacrifice, giving up physical fidelity to act upon emotional fidelity. Joi's choices after that encounter, however, more clearly put his needs and safety above her own, "sacrificing" for love. Whereas she could easily have either remained in K's apartment computer or even paired her essence with the emanator with the apartment computer as a backup, it is Joi herself who suggests to K that he download her into the emanator and delete her program from the apartment, putting herself at risk of "death" if the emanator is damaged, destroyed, or even simply has its memory erased. This potential sacrifice becomes all too real when Luv's team assaults Deckard's hideout. With K momentarily incapacitated by Luv and Deckard unconscious and unable to help, Joi does the only thing she can: she speaks up and implores Luv to stop harming him. It does indeed distract Luv from possibly delivering a killing blow to K, only for her to deliver a "death" blow to the emanator, causing K's Joi to vanish from existence with a final declaration of love. Her sacrifice provides one of the film's most overt examples of humanizing the Joi A.I., as Freysa describes "dying for the right cause" as "the most human thing [one] can do," a sentiment which K (and the viewer) applies to Joi's final act.

Joi's individuality and apparent "emotions" toward K come into question late in the film as K, battered and having lost the emanator (and thus Joi's program), encounters a giant holographic advertisement for the Joi product line. The advertisement interacts with K as a potential customer, making comments (including calling him "a good Joe," the very name "his" Joi had chosen to call him upon insisting that a "real boy" would have a "real name") that bring into question whether anything Joi ever said or did was anything other than programmed responses meant to convince an arguably gullible customer that they were somehow real or unique. Even their act of quasi-physical intimacy is called into question, as the consummation of their

---

[4] K, for what it's worth, does not seem to need this form of consummation. When Joi briefly justifies the encounter by telling him, "I want to be real for you," he replies in no uncertain terms, "You *are* real for me."

relationship is juxtaposed by a cut to a similar (or the same) holographic advertisement for the Joi product line that proudly proclaims that "Joi is anything you want her to be. Joi goes anywhere you want her to go." Presumably, that includes becoming a sexual partner going where, if you'll pardon the phrase, no personal A.I. has gone before (at least for K, that is).

For her part, Joi does get her own moment of apparent introspection on the nature of life. As K searches the *DeNAbase* for records of supposedly human children born on 10 June 2021, she notes that "Mere data makes the man," describing how DNA (represented by the initials of its four nucleobases: A, C, T, and G) are "the alphabet of you," creating both humans and replicants "all from four symbols," whereas she, as a program, has only two base symbols: 1 and 0.[5] Despite being an A.I., even Joi recognizes the significance of replicant procreation, employing phrases like "a child of woman born, pushed into the world, wanted, loved," "born, not made," and a "real boy," when considering the notion of whether K, who she "always knew" was special might be that child. Her love and concern for him is even apparent when the emanator begins to glitch after K crashes their spinner and she attempts to rouse him back to consciousness, only to find herself unable to be heard or physically touch his door. Her distress is on full display in her expression, even as her hologram glitches. More than any other character in the film, Joi challenges the viewers' perceptions of what it means to be an individual and the very definitions we hold for "life."

Of course, the broader plot of the film is driven primarily by the revelation that Rachael, last seen by audiences leaving Deckard's apartment with him in 2019, has had a child with Deckard. Rachael's death in childbirth and Deckard's disappearance lead K on a search for the child and answers about it (including whether the child is K himself). K may be driven to a degree by personal motives, but his quest has broader implications. As Joshi puts it, "The world is built on a wall [that] separates kind" (i.e. humans and replicants). To tell either side that such a wall no longer exists (i.e. that replicants can breed like humans and thus have children who are not manufactured and are therefore, arguably, "real" humans) would kick off a war between humans and replicants or a

---

[5] K continues his apparent belief in her "life" by complimenting her in response that she may be "half as much" in terms of symbols, but she is "twice as elegant." It is also one of the few responses in which he refers to her by a term of endearment, in this case "sweetheart."

slaughter of one side by the other. (Joshi defines the act of hunting down and killing the child as euphemistic "erasure," and part of her duty to "keep order.") The truth would, in essence, be a similar revelation to those who have historically undermined the foundations of every form of slavery that has ever existed: the understanding that the slaves are no less human than the slave masters.

It is a film fraught with avenues for discussion, debate, and introspection about the nature and value of life, presented within a deliberately-paced piece of science fiction. With this in mind, we have to ask whether knowing if Deckard was human or replicant would have mattered in the least to *Blade Runner 2049* or the intriguing questions it raises? Deckard's actions are dictated by his desire to protect the daughter he barely knew, who is eventually revealed to be Dr. Ana Stelline, whose creation of artificial memories for replicants appears to have provided an opportunity to implant memories in K (and possibly other replicants) that would help eventually reunite her with her father. Would Deckard have acted differently toward his child, based on what type of being he was? Would his love for Rachael (or his daughter, for that matter) have been fundamentally different if he were a replicant overcoming his programming instead of a human overcoming his prejudices against replicants? Would it have somehow changed the path K had to take in order to find him after years in hiding? Would it have made Deckard's peril when captured by Wallace's sinister assistant Luv or nearly drowning while shackled inside her spinner any less real, any less a life or death situation? In other words, would Deckard's motives and actions be any more or less human if he were manufactured rather than born?

For fans invested in these characters and who enjoy the thoughtful ride of both the original film and its sequel, I would argue that the truth is that in the grand scheme of things, no, it would not have mattered. If anything, the possibility that Deckard could be either human or replicant might cause the audience to look at any given moment in either film with an eye toward how he displays his humanity, regardless of whether he is a natural-born human. He proves himself a man and a father, without us needing to know whether he is truly a "man" at all in the eyes of the society churning along around him.

Perhaps Deckard says it best when K inquires as to whether Deckard's dog is real: "I don't know. Ask him." Maybe what matters is self-perception, rather than what others, whether fictional or real world viewers, believe a character to be.

In any event, Deckard's nature is not even remotely at the core of the film's examination of the nature and value of life. There are a plethora of characters already inhabiting that space in *2049*'s narrative.

Deckard's Nature in Relation to the *Blade Runner* Franchise

Of course, Deckard might also ask, as he does to K, "Why are you making it complicated?" Frankly, fans raise questions about Deckard's nature because it intrigues them, but if revelations about Deckard's nature were not necessary in relation to *Blade Runner 2049*, then what about in relation to the franchise as a whole? After all, the question remained unanswered for 35 years and will now continue to lack any kind of definitive answer for the foreseeable future. Surely, after so long, one of the most hotly-debated, lingering questions of science-fiction film *needs* an answer.

That would certainly be true to form for most franchises. After all, the hallmark of a money-making sequel tends to be to give the audience what it wants. Well, unless the franchise is *Star Wars*, in which case an abundance of fan service, or none at all, seems to be met with equally vigorous outrage. *Blade Runner*, though, has always stood out as the "thinking fan's science fiction." It did not serve up answers on a silver platter or spoon feed us information until plot points were obvious and overdone. Instead, it took us on a slow-burn ride through a dystopian society that caused us to consider the very nature of humanity. It was less "pop" and more "pulp." It could defy conventions by refusing to provide the one answer nearly everyone expected.

And that is precisely what it did, to the benefit of the franchise as a whole.

A large part of what has kept *Blade Runner* fandom alive and engaged, especially online, has been the ongoing, never-ending, mind-bending, and sometimes mind-numbing debate over the nuances of scenes, the multiple hints (both purposeful and entirely unintentional), and how they impact our perceptions and conclusions about Deckard's nature. That essential question has provided fuel for the fires of *Blade Runner* fandom, while other contemporary films have faded into memory. Most films invite nostalgia, while *Blade Runner* also inspires *discussion*.

To have provided a definitive answer as to whether Deckard is a replicant might have been a step forward in terms of clarification, but it would also have been a significant blow to the very debate that has kept the franchise alive for decades. When a particular conclusion is already determined, all debate becomes merely academic and far less engaging. ("I'm right because the filmmakers say so" is a bit of a discussion nuke that is both technically correct and the antithesis of a debatable point.) To borrow a turn of phrase again, what would it profit a franchise to provide fans with answers yet lose its longevity? To have definitively proclaimed Deckard a human or replicant, regardless of the answer, would have been taking a single step forward while taking two steps back, to the overall detriment of the *Blade Runner* franchise as a whole.

Skin Jobs and Snow Jobs: *Blade Runner 2049* as Cli-Fi Noir and Race Erasure

by Leah D. Schade

What I first noticed about *Blade Runner 2049* is that it *feels* like the original *Blade Runner*. Denis Villenueve's cinematic masterpiece of "future noir" layers superb visual effects upon an absorbing storyline peopled with fascinating characters who wrestle with poignant religious and philosophical themes.[1] Visual and aural "quotes" from the original 1982 *Blade Runner* film are embedded into stunning, high-concept scenes to create grim, poetic beauty worthy of Ridley Scott's original dystopian vision. Flying cars swoop across vast desiccated landscapes. Glowing umbrellas and oversized neon ads illuminate garish urban cityscapes. The churning, vibrating soundtrack by Benjamin Wallfisch and Hans Zimmer pays homage to Vangelis' masterpiece (complete with a key musical cameo from the original soundtrack) while adding its own mystique with soaring strata of synth-sound. The film even furthers the climate and environmental storyline presciently rendered in the 1982 film, thus securing both films' place in the emerging subgenre of *climate fiction* (or cli-fi,

---

[1] See: Sammon, Paul M. *The Future Noir: The Making of Blade Runner* (Revised and Updated). Dey Street Books, 2017.

for short), which is literature and art that addresses or is informed by climate change. With its brooding, pessimistic interplay of light and shadow against the backdrop of extreme climate breakdown, I suggest that *Blade Runner 2049* (hereafter, *BR2049*) is part of a new genre-fusion we might call "cli-fi noir."

But *BR2049* also continues a failing of its predecessor – the erasure of race, even as it appropriates the black experience of slavery, oppression, and the struggle for personhood and freedom. As I watched both films from the perspective of the Black Lives Matter movement,[2] I realized that the *feeling* I savored from both movies was largely premised on the reality of my occupying a racial, socio-economic position as a middle-class Caucasian who benefits from the privilege of my white race. Because, as writer Nicholas Podany points out, neither film requires white people "to leave their comfort zones of white fragility to enjoy a compelling story about bigotry and persecution."[3] In other words, while each film can be viewed as a metaphor for racial oppression, they give barely a nod to the reality of racism itself, because despite a few token characters of color, the main roles in both movies are filled by white actors.

Whitewashing in science fiction is, of course, nothing new.[4] But *BR2049* had an opportunity to engage the reality of racism in a much more honest and straightforward way than its predecessor. The fact that that opportunity was squandered is more than just a disappointment. It actually reinforces a narrative and underlying artistic structure of white privilege precisely at a moment in our history when such narratives need to be interrogated, deconstructed, and placed within a larger context of eco-racism and the climate crisis that is having enormous impacts on communities of color. This essay will critically explore *BR2049* through the intersections of race, technology, climate

---

[2] https://en.wikipedia.org/wiki/Black_Lives_Matter
[3] Podany, Nicholas. "*Blade Runner 2049*: White Appropriation of Black Oppression." *Medium*, 19 Oct 2017, medium.com/@nicholaspodany/blade-runner-2049-white-appropriation-of-black-oppression-76a5e20ca324. Accessed 6 Feb 2018.
[4] See: Rieder, John. *Colonialism and the Emergence of Science Fiction*. Middletown, Connecticut: Wesleyan University Press. 2008. See also: Berlatsky, Noah. "Why Sci-Fi Keeps Imagining the Subjugation of White People." *The Atlantic*, Atlantic Media Company, 25 Apr. 2014, www.theatlantic.com/entertainment/archive/2014/04/why-sci-fi-keeps-imagining-the-enslavement-of-white-people/361173/. And: Berlatsky, Noah. "Star Wars and the 4 Ways Science Fiction Handles Race." *The Atlantic*, Atlantic Media Company, 25 Mar. 2014, www.theatlantic.com/entertainment/archive/2014/03/-em-star-wars-em-and-the-4-ways-science-fiction-handles-race/359507/.

change, and economic exploitation. I will make the case that if "cli-fi noir" is, indeed, to become a new subgenre, then directors, producers, and actors must forthrightly address the reality of raced bodies if there is to be any integrity to their art.

Blade Runner as Early Cli-Fi

Cli-fi is a subgenre of fiction in which the emerging realities of climate change are brought to life in present-day settings or imagined in a future world.[5] It appears that the term was first coined by author and freelance news reporter Dan Bloom in 2007.[6] As early as 2005, however, Robert Macfarlane called for artists to provide a "creative response" to the impending, yet slow-moving catastrophe of global warming:

> Where is the literature of climate change?... Where are the novels, the plays, the poems, the songs, the libretti, of this massive contemporary anxiety?... The question is pressing. For an imaginative repertoire is urgently needed by which the causes and consequences of climate change can be debated, sensed, and communicated.[7]

Since that time, authors such as Margaret Atwood, Barbara Kingsolver, Ian McEwan, and Jeannette Winterson have incorporated the theme of climate change into their works. According to American studies researchers Susanne Leikam and Julia Leyda, "Over the last two decades, the global landscape of cultural production has been teeming with a cornucopia of fictional texts, in print, in live performance, and on the screen, engaging with the local and global impact of advanced human-induced climate change. In academia as well as in popular culture, this rapidly growing body of texts is now commonly referred to by the catchy linguistic portmanteau 'cli-fi.'"[8]

---

[5] Tuhus-Dubrow, Rebecca. "Cli-Fi: Birth of a Genre." *Dissent Magazine*, Summer 2013. www.dissentmagazine.org/article/cli-fi-birth-of-a-genre. Accessed 9 Feb 2018.
[6] Glass, Rodge. "Global warning: the rise of 'cli-Fi.'" *The Guardian*, Guardian News and Media, 31 May 2013, www.theguardian.com/books/2013/may/31/global-warning-rise-cli-fi. Accessed 9 Feb 2018.
[7] Macfarlane, Robert. "The burning question." *The Guardian*, Guardian News and Media, 23 Sept 2005, www.theguardian.com/books/2005/sep/24/featuresreviews.guardianreview29. Accessed 9 Feb 2018.
[8] "Cli-Fi in American Studies: A Research Bibliography." *American Studies Journal*, 9 July 2017, www.asjournal.org/62-2017/cli-fi-american-studies-research-

Released in 1982, the original *Blade Runner* was ahead of its time as a prototype of cli-fi. Set in 2019 Los Angeles, director Ridley Scott's dreary, polluted film-scape was eerily prophetic of the consequences of the actual climate and environmental crisis already underway in real-time. In the movie, loosely based on Philip K. Dick's novel, *Do Androids Dream of Electric Sheep?*, the city was enshrouded by smog-stained clouds that muddied the sun and dumped perpetual rain on the detritus of humanity left behind on a dying planet. As the rains fell, towers of flaming gas erupted into the sky, pumping even more heat-trapping gasses into the atmosphere.

"Fiery the angels fell. Deep thunder rolled around their shores, burning with the fires of Orc," intoned Roy Batty, a genetically engineered humanoid known as a replicant, in one scene of the film. He was slightly misquoting a line from William Blake's 1793 mythological narrative poem, "America a Prophecy." The epic poem, originally meant to describe the rebellion of the American Colonies against England, contains chilling imagery that is eerily vatic of our present age of fiery fossil fuels and tumultuous climate change. Science-fiction critic Bryan Thao Worra describes the mythological figure of Orc in Blake's narrative, relating it to the replicants in *Blade Runner*:

> Orc's activities are driven by emotion, and gradually degenerate into unpredictable chaos, terrorizing those around him. So, too, the degeneration of the replicants even as they seek vindication or redemption for their excesses. It's a matter of some interest to consider what it means for the angels to fall, according to Roy Batty. With whom, then, does he feel the replicants should identify, even as they're shackled with such limited time remaining to them?[9]

We might ask the same question of ourselves as the clock is ticking on the time remaining for humanity to curb its fossil-fuel excesses and transition to a saner, cleaner, more just economy.[10] As catastrophic weather events, ocean acidification, glacial melting, droughts, and rising sea levels increase due to a

---

bibliography/. Accessed 9 Feb 2018. See also Dan Bloom's *The Cli-Fi Report*, www.cli-fi.net/.

[9] Thao Worra, Bryan. "William Blake, Orc and Blade Runner." *On The Other Side of The Eye*. 24 Nov. 2009. thaoworra.blogspot.com/2009/11/nam-william-blake-orc-and-blade-runner.html. Accessed 27 July 2017.

[10] Wallace-Wells, David. "When Will the Planet Be Too Hot for Humans? Much, Much Sooner Than You Imagine." *Daily Intelligencer*, 9 July 2017, nymag.com/daily/intelligencer/2017/07/climate-change-earth-too-hot-for-humans.html. Accessed 27 July 2017.

changing climate, *Blade Runner* warns us of a world perhaps best described in another passage from Blake's poem:

> I see thee in thick clouds and darkness on America's shore. Writhing in pangs of abhorred birth; red flames the crest rebellious And eyes of death...

Do You Like Our Owl?: *Blade Runner*, Climate Change, and the Commodification of Life

In classic film noir style, the shadowy, dripping atmosphere of the 1982 movie reflected the sense of alienation and world-weary demeanor of the anti-hero, Rick Deckard. Played by Harrison Ford, the grizzled Blade Runner police detective was on a mission to "retire" (kill) rogue replicants. That sense of alienation was as much environmental as it was anthropic. The skies, lands, and seas became so toxic, and humanity had wiped out so many species, Earth was rendered uninhabitable for any creatures save for humans, rats, and bugs.[11]

When Deckard pays a visit to the Tyrell Corporation to test one of the replicants created by the company, he has an exchange with a woman named Rachael (who later becomes his paramour) which reveals even more bleak details about this futuristic world. Standing in the great hall of Eldon Tyrell, the company's founder and genius neuroscientist, Deckard watches an owl take flight across the room.

> "Do you like our owl?" asks Rachael as she enters the room.
> "It's artificial?" Deckard asks.
> "Of course it is."
> "Must be expensive."
> "Very."

When considering the "sixth great extinction" currently underway in our own world, the future animal-less world of *Blade Runner* seems tragically possible.[12] It is a planet devoid of anything but manufactured life, leaving the world with nothing but "Memories of Green," as Vangelis titled one of the bittersweet songs from his soundtrack. Genetic engineering has rendered life a commodity to be bought and sold to the highest bidder – including human life engineered for hard labor in the "Off-World" colonies.

---

[11] Recall one scene with rats scrounging for food on J.F. Sebastian's table, and Deckard in another scene pulling a bug out of his mouth from his drink at the bar.
[12] See: Kolbert, Elizabeth. *The Sixth Extinction: An Unnatural History*. New York, New York: Henry Holt and Co., 2014.

Blade Runner 2049 continues the saga of Earth in ecological ruin. The film takes us into a world where the only real tree that exists is dead, kept upright through stakes and ropes.

Blade Runner 2049 continues the saga of Earth in ecological ruin. The film takes us into a world where the only real tree that exists is dead, kept upright through stakes and ropes, Las Vegas is a red-tinted ghost town recovering from toxic levels of radiation, and San Diego is nothing more than a massive dumping ground for metallic refuse. Set 30 years after Deckard and Rachael escaped from Los Angeles, the planet is affected by dramatic shifts in weather and climate. Gargantuan sea walls have been constructed between L.A. and the

Pacific Ocean to protect the city from rising sea levels. The desertification of Las Vegas is stark and total (at least at first glance). The only greenery is seen in the holographic bubble of a scientist who designs replicant memories. But, oddly, snow squalls swirl unexpectedly in L.A. How can this be?

BR2049 is premised on an environmental twist. According to the movie's timeline, a nuclear detonation explodes in 2022 over the West Coast which obliterates electronic data and shuts down cities for weeks. Data and financial records are lost, and communications are severed, leading to chaos and mass hunger. Presumably, this also leads to a kind of nuclear winter and ensuing sub-arctic blasts that periodically turn L.A.'s rain into snow.

There is debate about whether the science behind such a scenario is possible or even plausible. Bloom asks, "Was this movie about global warming or global cooling? Is this 'The Day After Tomorrow' all over again? Great movie, bad science?"[13] While these are interesting questions, the truth is that scientists are unclear as to the how effects of human-induced climate change are going to unfold. The more important question concerns how communities will be affected, and in what ways those in poverty – particularly communities of color – will suffer. Both the original *Blade Runner* and *BR2049* – like all good cli-fi – show us what it might look like to find our humanity amidst a dire environmental scenario. But one aspect of humanity is conspicuously missing from both films that leaves a gaping lacuna – the reality of racialized bodies.

Blade Runner So White?

Both *Blade Runner* movies have been recognized as modern iterations of the classic film noir genre for their visual and thematic hallmarks that align with the noir style.[14] Philosopher and film critic Mark T. Conard identifies the classic noir period as falling between 1941 and 1958, and describes the typical setting of a noir film: "The claustrophobic settings are awash in deep shadows, the streets are rain swept, it always seems to be night, and the atmosphere is

---

[13] Bloom, Daniel. "*Blade Runner 2049* is about global warming or global cooling? Great cli-Fi movie, but bad science? Critics are having a field day!," 6 Oct 2016. http://thefutureofreading101.blogspot.com/2017/10/blade-runner-2049-is-about-global_6.html. Accessed 8 Feb 2018.

[14] See: Narcisse, Evan. "Like the Original, *Blade Runner 2049* is Scifi Film Noir at Its Finest." io9, 23 Nov 2017, io9.gizmodo.com/like-the-original-blade-runner-2049-is-scifi-film-noir-1820549771. Accessed 10 Feb 2018. See also: Pugh, Garreth. "*Blade Runner* as Film Noir / Neo-Noir." *ScreenSense*, 3 Mar 2010, screensense.wordpress.com/blade-runner/genre/genre/. Accessed 11 Feb 2018.

charged and angst ridden. We know the stories; we love the noir style, at once romantic and pessimistic; we sympathize, maybe even identify, with the doomed antihero; the anxiety and sense of alienation are uncomfortably familiar."[15] *Blade Runner* and *Blade Runner 2049* certainly contain these settings in which first Deckard and then Officer K embark on their tortured detective work in dark, rain-swept cities. Conard denotes the characteristics of the film noir style as marked by:

> the constant opposition of light and shadow, its oblique camera angles, and its disruptive compositional balance of frames and scenes, the way characters are placed in awkward and unconventional positions within a particular shot, for example. But, besides these technical cinematic characteristics, there are a number of themes that characterize film noir, such as the inversion of traditional values and the corresponding moral ambivalence (e.g., the protagonist of the story, who traditionally is the good guy, in noir films often makes very questionable moral decisions); the feeling of alienation, paranoia, and cynicism; the presence of crime and violence; and the disorientation of the viewer, which is in large part accomplished by the filming techniques mentioned above.[16]

From the perspective of critical race theory, however, the fact is that while white audiences thrill to film noir style, they are often oblivious to the underlying "racialized structuring of the noir idea."[17] Michael Boyce Gillespie interrogates the subgenre of film noir through the lens of racial theory and notes that:

> A common feature of classical film noir is its consistency as a racialized mode of white masculinities in crisis. Often this normative focus on whiteness, masculinity, and racial privilege codes difference as aberrant, a potential threat, or a mark of hierarchal contrast. This measure of difference as deviation from and threat to the standard manifests in figures such as the strong-willed woman, the homosexual, the Hispanic, the Greek, the Italian, and the African American.[18]

Or, in the case of *Blade Runner* – the replicant, which, as we will learn, symbolizes the black experience while obscuring racism by coming at it from a racially oblique angle. As Gillespie explains, "Issues of narrative authority,

---

[15] Conard, Mark T. *The Philosophy of Film Noir*. Lexington, Kentucky: University of Kentucky Press, 2007. 1. See also: Conard, Mark T. *The Philosophy of Neo-Noir*. Lexington, Kentucky: University of Kentucky Press, 2007.
[16] Ibid, 1-2.
[17] Gillespie, Michael Boyce. *Film Blackness: American Cinema and the Idea of Black Film*. Duke University Press, 2016. 84.
[18] Ibid.

racialization, and power deeply inform noir beyond its aesthetic profile as a high-contrast play of light and shadow."[19] The result is that the "black" energy of noir films is morally ambiguous because of its associations with race: "'Film noir is in this sense a sort of whiteface dream-work of social anxieties with explicitly racial sources, condensed on film into the criminal undertakings of abjected whites.'"[20] Thus while noir depends on racial difference as "an exercise in 'white pathology' it renders black bodies as socially invisible."[21]

The problem with both *Blade Runner* movies is that while each film is an extended allegory for real-life racism and oppression, the fact that there are so few people of color in the films themselves effects an erasure of non-white people. Film critic Zeba Blay notes the ways in which science-fiction and fantasy movies "play on the black experience while erasing black people."[22] In her critique of the movie *Fantastic Beasts and Where to Find Them*, part of the *Harry Potter* series, she writes, "So often these films create very little room for the presence of black people and other people of color. The irony of this (and what makes it so incredibly frustrating) is that these narratives mirror the real-life oppression of marginalized groups." Yet, while "real-life oppression is metaphorized in stories of dystopian worlds... race almost never comes into the equation." This is precisely the case with both *Blade Runner* and *Blade Runner 2049*.

"Skin-jobs" – White Replicants as "Niggers"?

Atlantic writer Noah Berlatsky suggests that there are four ways science fiction handles race.[23] One is through *extended metaphor* in which characters, plots, and symbols suggest or represent the analogy of racial oppression (such as *District 9*'s extended allegory on apartheid). Another is through *tokenism*, where a few actors of color are sprinkled into the cast (think Lando Calrissian of *Star Wars*). A third approach is *diversity*, using a cast that intentionally decenters whites and includes actors of many races. An example is *Star Wars:*

---

[19] Ibid.
[20] Gillespie, 87. Quoting Lott, Eric. "The Whiteness of Film Noir." *American Literary History* 9.3 (1997). 551.
[21] Ibid, 87-88.
[22] Blay, Zeba. "How Fantasy Film Plays On The Black Experience While Erasing Black People." The Huffington Post, 2 Dec 2016, www.huffingtonpost.com/entry/how-fantasy-film-plays-on-the-black-experience-while-erasing-black-people_us_583f36e6e4b09e21702c5de2. Accessed 4 Feb 2018.
[23] Berlatsky, Noah. "Star Wars and the 4 Ways Science Fiction Handles Race."

Rogue One, which featured cast members of various ethnicities. Such an approach, however, can still enable a disingenuous attitude toward race if it assumes the myth of "color-blindness" which ignores the realities of racism. The fourth and ideal way for science fiction to deal with race is the *direct* approach. This is seen in movies such as *The Hunger Games* and *The Dawn* which deal forthrightly with prejudice, segregation, inequities based on racialization, and racial profiling and brutality by police.

Blade Runner utilizes the *extended metaphor* approach for dealing with racism. In the original theatrical release of the film, Deckard's overdubbed narration provides a bit of insight into the way in which humans regard replicants: "Skin jobs, that's what Bryant called replicants. In history books he is the kind of cop used to call black men niggers." This is the one reference to race in the film. Replicants are the "niggers" of the *Blade Runner* world. They are engineered to *look* like humans, but without the essential human quality of feelings and emotions. Their labor enables humans to relocate to the Off-World colonies. They were created to serve, doing the dirty and dangerous work. The women are "pleasure models" intended to provide sexual gratification. And both the male and female replicants are designed to be violent killing machines for "death-squads" when necessary. The allusion to African slaves is intentional. People of African descent were – and often still are – regarded as servile, subhuman, devoid of emotions, dangerous, and no better than animals.

The philosophical conundrum of both movies is that replicants do, in fact, develop feelings, and thus self-awareness.[24] When they come to realize they are nothing more than slaves, they naturally rebel against their state of servitude. They turn on their owners and do everything they can to escape and secure their freedom (including killing humans if necessary). Thus, they are deemed too dangerous for Earth itself.

Similarly, when people of color "get out of hand" by being too emotional (especially displaying the emotion of anger) or demanding their freedom and equal rights, police and military forces are sent out to use any means necessary

---

[24] Judith Barad points out that more than mere emotion – which all human experiences from birth – the Nexus-6 models are unable to develop emotional *maturity* due to their four-year life span. The inability to respond with empathy to another's distress is why the Voigt-Kampff test is effective in determining whether a being is replicant or human. (Barad, Judith. "*Blade Runner* and Satre: The Boundaries of Humanity." In: Conard, Mark T. *The Philosophy of Neo-Noir*. Lexington, Kentucky: University of Kentucky Press, 2007. 21-34.)

to maintain "law and order" – including the use of deadly force. "You not come here! Illegal!" cries the ocular genetic designer Chew in the 1982 film when two replicants enter his workshop. Replicants on Earth are "illegal," and cops in the Blade Runner unit, reminiscent of Immigration and Customs Enforcement (ICE) officers pursuing "illegal aliens" today, are sent to kill any that dare invade the space of the truly human.

Ironically, while the movie intends to invoke the experience of dehumanization and oppression experienced by people of color, *Blade Runner* has only white actors in the main roles. With the exception of Edward James Olmos (who plays Gaff, a fellow detective in the Blade Runner unit), and James Hong (playing Chew, the eye-designer), any ethnic characters occupy minor roles in the film. Notably, the Nexus-6 replicants are all white. Blay's question is pertinent here: "Genre films are all about shifting perspective and pushing the limits of our imagination... So, why is it so hard to believe in a future... that includes people of color?"[25]

It also raises questions specific to the story line and the film itself. Did the Tyrell Corporation (or the film's creators) deem it unsavory to create black replicants? Would dark-skinned replicants be too uncomfortable a reminder of the slave history of this country? Are replicants of the caucasian flavor somehow more palatable? Or, as a mixed-race friend of mine suggested, perhaps the replicants were white because, in the hopes and dreams of the American psyche, people of color will have been eliminated in the future.

Obviously, these are not questions the film addresses. And maybe it's understandable that such issues were not on the minds of the director and producers, given that the Black Lives Matter movement was still 20 years in the future. Also, the hashtag #OscarSoWhite, used to protest the underrepresentation of people of color in the annual Academy Award nominations, only came into use during the 2015 award cycle. But *Blade Runner 2049* was released in 2017, in the midst of these movements, so the stakes for this film are much higher when it comes to handling racial realities.

---

[25] Blay, Zeba. "How Fantasy Film Plays On The Black Experience While Erasing Black People."

Tokenism and Extended Metaphor: Two Approaches to Race in *Blade Runner 2049*

BR2049 combines two of Berlatsky's categories in the ways it deals with race: extended metaphor and tokenism. Tokenism is the more patronizing approach, because filmmakers can point to the casting of a few actors of color and believe they have paid the diversity fee. In Villeneuve's film, there are admittedly a wide range of secondary characters played by actors of color (including Wood Harris, Lennie James, Ana de Armas, Barkhad Abdi, Hiam Abbass, and Dave Bautista). The problem, however, is that the primary characters around which the plot of the film revolves are played by white actors (Ryan Gosling, Harrison Ford, Jared Leto, Robin Wright, Sylvia Hoeks, MacKenzie Davis, and Carla Juri).

Why is this a problem? Podany describes the results of such "diversity tokenism":

> White audiences watching a white character being subjugated to sci-fi racism can invest safely. We're obviously now in the land of make believe if anyone is randomly pulling over Ryan [Gosling]. Moviegoers can pick and choose what parts of the African-American experience they want. They cheer the underdog, they hiss at the police force, but once the movie's over, they will go home, and post #blacklivesmatter from a distance. If you want the movie to truly be about Replicants vs. Humans representing a futuristic Cowboys vs. Indians, put actors of color on both sides to represent what 2049 will look like. If the filmmakers believe that 2049 Los Angeles will be somehow practically ethnically cleansed, that's another movie. As the film stands now, it succeeds at targeting a white audience who can comfortably dip their toe in what it feels like to be systematically persecuted.[26]

Podany's critique leads us to consider the movie's other way of dealing with racism, that of using extended metaphor. Like its predecessor, this approach appears to be borne of positive intentions but has unintended consequences. As Berlatsky explains: "[M]etaphor may be used to try to understand or condemn racism," but it often makes the misstep of "borrow[ing] for white protagonists the experiences of the marginalized."[27] In other words, the movie uses analogy "to express virulent racism without having to own it."[28] For the

---

[26] Podany, Nicholas. "*Blade Runner 2049*: White Appropriation of Black Oppression."
[27] Ibid.
[28] Berlatsky, Noah. "Star Wars and the 4 Ways Science Fiction Handles Race."

white viewer, such a movie creates a certain kind of experience, as Podany describes:

> It's guilt free, heart-racing, artistic... it even occasionally makes you feel gleefully socially conscious when you notice parallels of modern day racism in the movie. But that glee is a very safe pat on the back. The Replicants are literally called slaves... it's not very hard to miss. We should instead pay attention to how the story is being told and by whom it's being told.[29]

In the movie, Officer K is derisively called a "skin job" and "skinner." Wallace's description of his project to engineer replicants capable of sexual reproduction is meant to recall the white slave-owners of early America: "Every leap of civilization was built off the back of a disposable work force. We lost our stomach for slaves unless engineered." He goes on to say, "We need more replicants than can ever be assembled. Millions, so we can be trillions more."

But how can we take seriously a film that implicitly raises the specter of African slavery of the past, while the replicants are being portrayed by a mostly white cast? How can the film talk about the Off-World colonies without acknowledging the actual history of colonization, the Middle Passage, the slave ships, and the auction blocks? The result of addressing the theme of racial oppression through a white-washed extended metaphor is a movie that teeters on the fence of a post-colonial narrative that could fall one of two ways, depending on one's interpretation.

On the one hand, we sympathize with replicants who, like colonized and brutalized African slaves, revolt against their human masters. Such a metaphoric device utilizes what Berlatsky calls a "colonial inversion." In this case, "the reverse colonial stories in sci-fi can be used as a way to sympathize with those who suffer under colonialism."[30]

But such an approach can just as easily justify an imperialist stance. "[R]everse colonial stories can erase those who are at the business end of imperial terror, positing white European colonizers as the threatened victims in a genocidal race war, thereby justifying any excess of violence."[31] For example, one might imagine a white supremacist watching *Blade Runner 2049* and assenting whole-heartedly to Wallace's repugnant logic. In light of white supremacist apologists such as Richard B. Spencer and Milo Yiannopoulos, Wallace's hubristic reasoning seems a natural extension of white-identity

---

[29] Podany.
[30] Berlatsky, Noah. "Why Sci-Fi Keeps Imagining the Subjugation of White People."
[31] Ibid.

ideology. Wallace is obsessed with creating replicants that can reproduce on their own, in order to implement his masterplan to create an army of enslaved replicants who will enable him to "storm Eden and retake her." When his experiments fail, he kills his creations without mercy. Certainly, the intent of this storyline is to create fear and loathing of such sadistic supremacy and create sympathy for the oppressed replicants. But by sparing the viewer the discomfort of seeing this plot play out without actors of color, the film is disingenuous and inadvertently reinforces the vision of white supremacists for a future scrubbed clean of inferior races.

Why does it matter that the film shows a world where the main actors are white? Bertlasky explains: "Sci-fi is at least in part a dream of a different world and a different future. When that future unthinkingly reproduces current inequities, it seems like both a missed opportunity and a failure of imagination."[32] Blay concurs: "Genre cinema is about escape, so some might argue that acknowledging and exploring race in less oblique, metaphorical ways isn't necessary. But genre cinema is also about imagining new worlds in order to make sense of our real world. If we can imagine lightning speed space-travel and monstrous dragons, why can't we imagine scenarios that don't erase or decontextualize race in hypothetical futures and make-believe pasts?"[33]

Deconstructing the Wall that Separates Kind

It's not entirely accurate to say that the movie has no value as an extended metaphor for exploring race and oppression. For example, a major theme in both *Blade Runner* and *Blade Runner 2049* is the way in which humans engineer and construct their conceptualizations of themselves and each other. This has parallels in the study of race theory. The idea that one human being can own another is a notion that has itself been engineered – constructed – in human consciousness since the beginning of civilization. Replicants, like people of color in American history, are the forced labor that enables humanity to survive and the wealthy class to thrive. The fact that they are genetically engineered to be obedient servants – and that their copyright is owned by a corporation – is simply the end result of race construction taken to its science-fiction extreme.

On top of that, the concept of a "black" person is also a construct. In Africa, the natives did not think of themselves as "black" until white Europeans

---

[32] Berlatsky, Noah. "Star Wars and the 4 Ways Science Fiction Handles Race."
[33] Blay, Zeba.

invaded their continent and enslaved their people. Only then did the category of *black* come into being. Eventually blackness became a cipher for all the negative qualities of humanity – aggressiveness, wildness, hyper-sexuality, superhuman physical abilities, and ferocious anger. These are exactly the qualities that humans in the *Blade Runner* world fear from replicants.

Further, we could say that those constructed as "black" humans have historically functioned as replicant-type automatons. They were expected to perform their duties of hard labor, domestic chores, and sexual servitude without question, without feelings, and with total obedience. But of course, they *are* human. And they know in every cell of their bodies that their inhumane treatment is intolerable. Even after the Emancipation Proclamation of 1863, and the Civil Rights Movement a century later, people of color continue to find themselves regarded as "less human than human" (to recalibrate the motto of the Tyrell Corporation) by their white counterparts.

BR2049 invites us to make that association and consider those historical realities. But what if the director and producers had decided to take a more direct approach to racism in the film? What if, for example, Villeneuve had imagined a scene between Officer K and Mr. Cotton, the black orphanage manager, in which the two had an exchange that noted the irony of a black man enslaving white children, even while Officer K was himself a slave? Or what if the actress playing Luv had been brown-skinned? What layer of complexity and intersectionality would that have afforded as she watched Wallace ruthlessly slit the empty womb of a naked newborn replicant woman, or if the newborn replicant had been black? Consider how much nuance and texture could have been layered onto Lt. Joshi, Officer K's overseer, if she had been a woman of color instead of white? This is not a question of calling for "diversity" for diversity's sake. This is about missed opportunities.

"Painful to Live in Fear, isn't It? Nothing is Worse than Having an Itch You Can Never Scratch."

At a diversity and inclusion training seminar I once attended, one of the participants, a black man, shared how it felt for him to be treated as "less than" because of his race. "I have felt inhuman," he admitted. "I feel that I'm regarded as disposable, replaceable, that my existence doesn't really matter. I know that when I go certain places and encounter certain people, I'm perceived as a threat, even though I intend no harm."

As a white person, this was necessary for me to hear. Because for hundreds of years, society has conditioned both whites and people of color to think of blacks as dangerous, even murderous. Our interactions have been "colored" by mistrust, fear, and overreactions to perceived threats. This has become blatantly obvious in the stunning number of murders of blacks by police officers over the years, especially high-profile cases where unarmed blacks are shot without provocation.

There is a particular scene in *Blade Runner* which portrays this kind of police brutality. Deckard discovers one of the replicants named Zhora working as an exotic dancer in a bar. Zhora makes a run for it, trying to lose Deckard in the crowded city streets, but he catches up with her and aims his gun right at her back. He fires, and she falls through breaking plate glass, fake snow swirling around her bloodied body. When I recently watched this scene, I could not help but recall the 2015 video of Walter Scott, an unarmed black man, being shot in the back eight times by Officer Michael Slager in Charleston, North Carolina.[34] Slager pled guilty to violating Scott's civil rights – a rarity in law enforcement where only 35% of cases of fatal on-duty shootings end up in convictions.[35] In most cases, the scene is similar to the one in the movie where Deckard simply shows his badge to the other officer and walks away. Meanwhile, a recorded voice from the police cruiser drones repeatedly: "Move on. Move on. Move on." There are no consequences for Deckard shooting an unarmed woman in the back.

Similarly, Officer K in *BR2049* is sent to find rogue replicant Sapper Morton with the intent of either arresting him for disassembly, or "retiring" him on the spot – which is the outcome of their encounter. In any case, it was never a question of whether Morton or Zhora would be afforded due process of law.[36]

---

[34] Blinder, Alan. "Michael Slager, Officer in Walter Scott Shooting, Gets 20-Year Sentence." *The New York Times*, 7 Dec. 2017, www.nytimes.com/2017/12/07/us/michael-slager-sentence-walter-scott.html. Accessed 8 Feb. 2018.

[35] Park, Madison. "Police shootings: Trials, convictions are rare for officers." CNN, 24 June 2017, www.cnn.com/2017/05/18/us/police-involved-shooting-cases/index.html. Accessed 8 Feb. 2018.

[36] It could be argued that since both Zhora and Morton initiated violence against the Blade Runners, they deserved to be killed. However, this raises the question of what recourse they had given their plight. As it was, they had little choice but to use aggression to stop the men who represent the implacable will of the state and an existential threat to their very being.

Their killings are not considered murder in the eyes of the law, because, ultimately, neither Zhora nor Morton were considered to be human. Thus, they did not enjoy the rights afforded the truly human. Like people of color in the off-screen world, their lives did not matter.

But of course, both Morton and Zhora *were* persons. British philosopher Mary Midgley identified three defining qualities of personhood: 1) the ability to suffer, 2) the capacity for emotional fellowship, and 3) that they "mind what happens to them – that they are highly sensitive social beings."[37] In the *Blade Runner* franchise, all replicants meet these qualifications. They experience emotions, have friends with whom they share mutual care, experience suffering, and desire nothing more than to live their lives free of captivity and without fear. So it is with every person of color, every undocumented resident, every refugee, every person "othered" by the white hegemonic system that undergirds all aspects of culture, economy, and social structures.

Why, then, is there a problem with the movie's handling of race through the metaphor of replicants? Shouldn't we applaud a movie that gives viewers an opportunity to explore the complexities of racism and oppression in a way that gives creative expression and space in which to contemplate these realities? Blay explains the troubling nature of this approach: "There's a kind of danger in using racial oppression as a model, because it is, by its very nature, *not* universal."[38] As with the *X-Men* franchise, the replicants in *Blade Runner 2049* are hunted down and exterminated for their superhuman abilities. But just as with *X-Men*, the movie continues the practice of "borrowing the social and political discrimination of people of color as fodder" for its mostly white replicants.[39] Such a practice not only continues the normalization of white colonization and appropriation of black experience, it unnecessarily insults and alienates people of color who might otherwise appreciate the film. Blay explains:

> Fantasy and sci-fi films that exclude or glaze over race even as they tell stories of fighting against oppression do an extreme disservice to the people of color who are just as eager for the latest blockbuster as anybody else. There is no point, no value in asking us to empathize with

---

[37] Midgley, Mary. "Is a Dolphin a Person?" *The Essential Mary Midgley*. New York: Routledge. 141.
[38] Blay, Zeba.
[39] Ibid.

hypothetically oppressed people if people who are actually oppressed in real life are excluded from the narrative.[40]

No More Snow Jobs

In the final scene of *Blade Runner 2049,* Officer K escorts Deckard to meet the child for whom he sacrificed everything to save and keep hidden. As Roy Batty did in the previous film, yet another replicant has given Deckard what he was not able to obtain on his own – life, hope, and meaning. As "Tears in Rain" plays plaintively while K lays down on snowy steps to die, we recall Roy's final words and might imagine them transposed: "All these moments will be lost in time, like footsteps in snow." The pathos evoked in this scene is at once filled with grace, but also irony. Snow lightly covers all in a blanket of white, just as the film obscures the footsteps of actual oppressed people in a coating of whiteness. It is beautiful, but chilling.

In *Blade Runner 2049*'s final scene, Officer K lays down on snowy steps to die. We recall Roy Batty's final words and imagine them transposed: "All these moments will be lost in time, like footsteps in snow."

I make the case that including narratives of brown and black-skinned bodies must be a moral imperative for the future of cli-fi because the fact is that for people of color, an environmental dystopia is not just a ghost of future

---

[40] Ibid.

imaginings, but an all-too-present reality. Consider, for example, the movie's orphanage scene with rows and rows of sick white children disassembling electronic equipment. The scene is meant to disturb us. But most of us are ignorant of the fact that our own electronics are picked apart by non-white children in other countries, particularly the Global South.[41] Their tiny fingers are put to work "recycling" our discarded cell phones and computers, and in the process, they are exposed to lethal metals and toxins that wreak havoc on their young bodies. Like the machines they pry open with their delicate hands, the children are disposable. We are horrified by this in the movie, but when it comes to children of color off-screen, most of us will conveniently ignore or forget this reality. Like footsteps in snow, they are erased from our consciousness both by the movie and by globalized structures of racist inequality.

The same is true when it comes to toxic dumping grounds, industrial wastelands, superfund sites, and areas affected by the realities of climate change – all of which are depicted in the extreme in *BR2049*. Disproportionately, communities of color suffer the most from the effects of cancer-causing pollution, fine particulates that trigger asthma and lung disease by virtue of the fact that they are deliberately targeted as ideal locations for polluting industries.[42] Similarly, suffering from extreme weather events, floods, agricultural blights, and droughts due to climate disruption is unevenly distributed to countries and communities of black and brown-skinned people.[43] But this reality is not even alluded to in *BR2049* or most cli-fi for that matter. As

---

[41] For more on "trans-boundary dumping" of electronic waste, see: Moe-Lobeda, Cynthia. *Resisting Structural Evil: Love as Ecological-Economic Vocation*. Minneapolis: Fortress Press, 2013. 27-30. Referencing: Pellow, David Naguib. *Resisting Global Toxins: Transnational Movements for Environmental Justice*. Cambridge: MIT Press, 2007. 186.

[42] Bullard, Robert D. "Race, class, and the politics of place." *Dumping in Dixie: Race, Class and Environmental Quality*. Boulder, CO: Westview Press, 1990. http://www.ciesin.columbia.edu/docs/010-278/010-278chpt2.html#fn27. Accessed 12 Feb 2018.

[43] See: Kelbert, Alexandra Wanjiku. "Climate change is a racist crisis: that's why Black Lives Matter closed an airport." *The Guardian*, 6 Sept 2016. www.theguardian.com/commentisfree/2016/sep/06/climate-change-racist-crisis-london-city-airport-black-lives-matter. Accessed 12 Feb 2018. See also: Schade, Leah D. "Let's Make Earth Day about the Earth Martyrs." *The Christian Century*. 18 Apr 2017. https://www.christiancentury.org/blog-post/lets-make-earth-day-about-earth-martyrs. Accessed 12 Feb 2018.

it stands, what whites fear as they gape at a screen depicting an apocalyptic future eco-cide is already being experienced where non-white bodies systematically undergo eco-racism. Whites feel dread for their own future while ignoring the reality already experienced by people of color. Thus Lt. Joshi's wall metaphor for the division between replicants and humans is actually the movie's own – it builds a wall to separate viewers from the stark realities of actual racism and oppression.

But as with every slave saga, from the Bible's Hebrews to America's slaves, the truth eventually reveals itself to us. No matter how strong, how high, or how wide we try to build our walls to keep out the "undesirables," we discover that we have actually been imprisoning ourselves. The ones we fear turn out to have eyes looking back at us from the mirror.

Conclusion

Is there hope? A single bee answers that question. As we watch bee colonies collapsing today – canaries in our climate-crisis coal mine – I couldn't help but note the ironic juxtaposition of seeing a bee on Officer K's hand as he walked through the Las Vegas desert. He then discovers an entire thriving apiary there among the dunes. How is this possible? Bees need flowers. They need pollen, sunlight, and greenery. Their presence must mean that somehow, somewhere, in this apparently god-forsaken world there is a resurgence of organic life and hope.

Villeneuve explains that the bees derive their sustenance from bee-feeding machines designed by Deckard – indicating that there is hope for both manufactured and organic life to co-exist and flourish.[44] The bee colony can be seen as a metaphor for the replicants who have escaped their human captors to

---

[44] "If you look closely, there's like a bee-feeder science fiction gadget there that we see. The bees are going out of their hives, and they are feeding on a machine that I designed with [production designer] Dennis Gassner, which is like a bee-feeder. It is a machine designed to feed the bees, so the bees can produce honey and feed Deckard. I love the idea that Deckard is a beekeeper – but you cannot raise bees in the desert. The bees were not in the screenplay to be honest, it's an idea we were storyboarding, and I said 'yeah, but how do bees live in the desert,' and then I came up with the idea for the bee-feeders and Dennis Gassner designed those machines. For me, that's beautiful science-fiction, I must say that I love it – it's not about weapons, it's about a new way of farming." Skrebels, Joe, quoting Denis Villeneuve, "*Blade Runner 2049* Director Answers 9 WTF Questions." IGN, 26 Jan 2018, www.ign.com/articles/2018/01/26/blade-runner-2049-director-answers-9-wtf-questions. Accessed 12 Mar 2018.

form a community of resistance, rising to claim their humanity, their love, and their freedom. In *Blade Runner 2049*, as in the original *Blade Runner*, the ones who show the most humanity, are, ironically, those whose origins are manufactured. As Mariette proclaims to Officer K, replicants are "more human than humans." From this we can draw an important insight. When it comes to living with ethical integrity in this fraught time of racial injustice and eco-cidal collapse, it matters less where and what you come from, than who you are intending to be.

Looking for Love in Cyberpunk Places: Examining Love in *Blade Runner 2049*

by Lou Tambone

    Love is not a tangible thing. It's a feeling. It's something inside of us. It's not always romantic. It's more than that. It comes in many forms. We use words to describe it like fondness, tenderness, intimacy, devotion, adoration, empathy, passion, desire, lust, infatuation, and so many others. Because it's a feeling, we might hypothesize that it's based on stimuli. We may love our children, but when we are at work or away from them, we go on with our lives. When we see them again, we are filled with emotion that sometimes manifests itself physically via hugs and kisses. That warmth, the contact between two beings, regardless of relationship, is where love lives. It's a beautifully understood feeling that we often tend to overcomplicate when layered on top of things like relationships, marriages, and especially sex. Love dominates us as human beings. This is why it's usually the focal point of much of the entertainment we see and hear. It's something we can all relate to. The *Blade Runner* universe is no exception.

    You might think of *Blade Runner* as simple science fiction, but love is there, lurking under the hood, in many facets. I believe the underlying and elusive love themes are the most interesting aspects of the films. Most of the characters and story threads are intertwined with themes of love. The genius of *Blade Runner 2049* (and science fiction in general) is that you don't always notice it. There are layers of subtext and social commentary that sometimes make the love hard to find. As my co-editor Joe Bongiorno is fond of saying, real science fiction is the exploration of *ideas* and *Blade Runner 2049* is chock full of them.

With that in mind, if we remove love as the driver of all the various aspects of the film, we're left with nothing but some lovely visuals.

Deckard and Rachael

"Sometimes to love someone, you gotta be a stranger."

Replicants have come a long way since the original *Blade Runner*. According to official *Blade Runner* lore,[1] in 2028, Niander Wallace acquired what was left of the Tyrell Corporation and made swift advancements in genetic engineering, resulting in more obedient Nexus 9 replicants that do not lie, run, or disobey. Can they love, though?

It appears that love transcends all kinds of beings, even those created in a facility. In the case of Deckard and Rachael, things are a still bit hazy since the question of Deckard's existence has yet to be definitively answered. We're not really sure if it was love or programming in his part, but in the end, does it matter? Love is still love, and perhaps that's something Tyrell didn't think about in his machinations. One thing we know did come out of Tyrell's work is replicant procreation. While it's of course possible to procreate without love involved, Deckard and Rachael were clearly in love by the end of the original film, awkward as it was. Much like Wallace's right hand, Luv, Rachael was emotionally inexperienced. Kissing and sex were foreign to her. One might assume she had never done these things before. It made for an intense encounter in Deckard's apartment, which many viewed as a rape scene, but I felt Deckard was teaching her how to be physically involved with a person. His approach was certainly suspect and she did seem fearful, but not of Deckard forcing himself on her, but of confusion and panic in not knowing how to react in that situation.

It raises the question of whether or not Deckard manipulated her or took advantage of her state in order to have her to himself and then run away with her. I think that's going a little too far, though. It's clear that they both needed to run and he was saving her just as much as he was saving himself. Their love

---

[1] http://roadto2049.bladerunnermovie.com/

might have started out rocky, but in the end it was true and deep love, something many humans long for yet never achieve.

So Deckard and Rachael represent true, deep, romantic love. However, in *Blade Runner 2049*, we learn a lot more about what Deckard's been up to for the last 30 years; more importantly, the first few years after he departed Los Angeles with Rachael. It's unclear if the two had any idea they could conceive a child, but I like to think that it was a surprise to all parties involved.

Deckard's fatherly love is also very evident in the film. Anyone who has a child knows what it's like to be without them. I can't imagine never even meeting a child I had a hand in making. The love between parent and child is a strong one. The great thing about K's conversation with Deckard (after their fistfight, of course) is that K believes he's interviewing his own father. He's under the impression that he's the first child born of a replicant. He's special. The question here is whether or not he feels some kind of love for Deckard, or if he's just looking for a definitive answer to the question of his origin. We don't really know.

Rachel reborn.

As for Deckard, when the miracle child was born, everyone knew it was important. Rachael was dead, and Sapper would take care of hiding the body. Freysa would take care of hiding the child. Deckard had to take care of hiding himself. K seems surprised when Deckard reveals he never met his own kid, but Deckard explains the dire situation: "Because that was the plan. I showed them how to scramble the records; cover their tracks. Everyone had a part. Mine was to leave. Then the Blackout came, paved over everything. Couldn't have found the child if I tried." He goes on to explain that he didn't want the child found and dissected.

He only wanted what any loving parent wants, for their child to be safe. His love for the child cannot be doubted. For him to have torn himself away from his child had to have been difficult, even if he left before the baby was born. It's hard to distinguish how long Deckard was around as the events unfolded. He explains that he was "long gone" by the time the baby was in the orphanage, but did he see the birth? Did he see Rachael die? I don't believe he saw either event. What's most likely is that Deckard and Rachael had some sort of goodbye resulting in his ending up in Vegas and her living on the run, probably with Freysa and Sapper, until she died. It's a sad story but one rooted in love. All that happened did so out of love and protection of the child.

Then there's the dog. Deckard, despite his gruffness, is a loving guy, it seems. His love for Rachael ran deep and his love for his child was so profound that he went into hiding to allow her a chance to survive. In the midst of all this, he came across a dog and adopted it. You could say it was out of loneliness if you like, but he treats the dog with respect and love, like a good guardian should. This type of love and respect for life is compassionate love. It makes us respect Deckard as a character who, although he's been through some hard times, still knows how to be compassionate and loving to living creatures, be they real or not. It's a quality he seems to have unknowingly passed down to his daughter.

Compassion, paternal love, romantic love: they're all embedded into the character of Rick Deckard.

K and Joi (and Mariette, Oh My!)

"I want to be real for you."

I found the love story of K and Joi to be fascinating for one major reason: the two *least* human characters in the film are the two most interested in having a human, loving relationship. The real humans in the film are the coldest beings we encounter.[2] They seem like the machines. The replicants come off as emotional and true. They want what all humans want — basic rights and

---

[2] Robin Wright's Lieutenant Joshi or Lennie James' Mister Cotton are two good examples.

equality. They don't want to be slaves. Perhaps they really are "more human than humans" as Mariette says, slightly altering a line from the original film.[3]

K may be considered an artificial person without a soul, but when you get down to it, Joi is even less. She's basically an app, or a product as Luv states various times in the film. She isn't even physically *there*. K goes through a journey of transformation in the film, but I believe that his journey started long before then. At some point, K decided he wanted to be more like a human being. Perhaps this was triggered by his peers, or maybe his shame at being shunned for what he is – the lowest of the low in the replicant food chain, since he kills his own kind. That raises the question of whether or not he can even feel shame, but we won't focus on that. He seems to handle being bullied or teased, both at work and in his apartment complex, quite well. Maybe he just wants to feel like a human with a soul who is capable of love. So he creates the perfect companion in his version of Joi.

Joi and K share a loving moment.

The two characters act like a happy couple interacting the way any human couple would. They talk about how their day went. She tells him to "go scrub" when he gets home and asks about his "meeting." She even offers to repair his clothing. She gives him the impression she's been hard at work all day trying a new recipe that she hopes he likes, even after he tells her not to fuss. As music plays in the apartment, she offers data on the song, including its release year and record label. She lights his cigarette and they talk to each other using pet

---

[3] "More human than human" is the Tyrell Corporation's motto in the original film.

names like Baby Sweet and Honey. She breezes through her virtual outfits, perhaps trying them out to gauge his reaction, making notes for future reference. She wants to read (not really, but she offers, even though she hates the book) or dance, whatever it takes to make him happy.

Two people in love should try to make each other happy, of course. It should be reciprocal, and K knows this. He buys her a gift, pretending it's their anniversary. "Is it?" she asks? "No," he replies. "But let's just say that it is, okay?" The gift is an emanator, which allows Joi to be free of the ceiling contraption that keeps her symbolically locked in a cage. Wherever K goes with the emanator, she can follow along, just like the ads for the Joi product announce throughout the film: "Joi goes anywhere you want her to go."

The first place they go is to the roof where Joi experiences rain for the first time. Normally she can only see it from behind glass. As she twirls with wonder at her new discovery, K actually smiles, something we don't seem him do very often.[4] He's happy that he's made her happy. However, the important part of this scene is that it sets up something later on. On the roof, they try to touch and kiss in a physical way which is very limited, like trying to hold onto a cloud of smoke. We can only assume they've done this before and they've both accepted this is the only way they can show true love for each other.

The moment is ruined by Joshi, unfortunately, in a 2049 version of a voicemail. Joi is frozen in place, bringing back the harsh reality that she's just a construct, a customized application. In any case, he goes back to work, but so does Joi. She has a plan. The abilities of her new emanator allow her to listen in on K's conversations. This comes in handy in her never-ending quest to make K happy. Free of her puppet strings, she can now monitor K's conversations out in the world in order to further a plan she's concocted to "be real" for him. It will bring their love to the next level.

Enter Mariette. A "doxie" or "pleasure model," she's a replicant who strikes up a conversation with K in BiBi's Bar. This is no chance conversation, of course. She's sent by Freysa to try and glean information. She makes no headway and leaves, but soon has a stroke of luck when Joi hires her come to the apartment to allow herself to be synced for sex, thus creating a real, physical, love experience with K. It's something she could not offer before. The love that K

---

[4] Even Mariette notices this, saying, "You don't even smile," when she meets K for the first time.

and Joi share via Mariette is only briefly physical, but most certainly romantic, empathetic, and compassionate.

Joi syncs with Mariette (seen here) to please K.

Although Joi's love evolves as the film goes on, you have to wonder if she's just telling him what he wants to hear because she's made to, instead of being truly supportive. It's Joi who pushes the suggestion that K might be more than who he is, based on his memory of the wooden horse. When they're in DeNAbase together, Joi (after mildly suggesting that Joshi might make a good sex-surrogate) starts putting the pieces together in his mind. In a way, she's passively to blame for him pursuing the mystery of his origin. Every time he seems content to go on with his work, she pops up and starts talking about his memory of the horse. "I always knew you were special. Maybe this is how. A child. Of woman born. Pushed into the world. Wanted. Loved." Again, the theme of love comes into play, this time coming from a potentially unseen parent he never knew. Joi almost dares him to take the search for his origin further. Is it because she's evolving beyond her programming or simply following it?

When it's clear that K has to leave in order to avoid being hunted (and to find answers to the questions he has), Joi offers to come with him, putting her entire existence at great peril. She knows that everything about her is housed in the main console in the apartment. She tells K to put her inside the emanator so that no one can access her should they check the console. It's the 2049 version of deleting one's browser history. This, of course, has disastrous results later on when Luv comes across the emanator on the ground after abducting Deckard. Joi appears as Luv looks like she's about to kill K and tries to save him by yelling, "Stop!" Luv seems amused and before she stomps the emanator into oblivion, Joi is barely able to blurt out her last words to K, "I love y—," her love for him demonstrated in the ultimate sacrifice.

Not long after, K is back in L.A. thinking about his next move, a risky venture, given that just about everyone is after him. He's tasked with killing Deckard in order to save the replicant uprising. This is so K doesn't inadvertently lead Wallace to Freysa and the rebellion. It's why Sapper Morton allowed himself to be retired. "Dying for the right cause," as Freysa says.

While walking and thinking, K comes across one of the larger-than-life sized interactive (and naked) Joi advertisements. She tries to sell her product to him, as she would any other person walking by. I often wonder what's going through his mind at that moment. I like to think it's one of two things.

Firstly, he could be saying to himself, "What a waste of time all that was." His attempts at creating love, or a loving relationship, were really just automation and advanced machine learning. She was customized to be what he wanted and needed. He's probably looking up at that Joi hologram regretting all the time he spent customizing her. Today, if we get a new phone or device, we go to great lengths to customize it to the point that if we replace it, we want those same exact settings transferred over. Why go through all that again? All of his Joi settings are gone, along with all her memories and their entire history. She's lost forever, at least in the previous form. A Joi with default settings would be a lot of work.

Secondly, he could be thinking that it might be worth it to start over with a new Joi, if he ever got out of his current predicament. She's the future of gadget-lust. The emanator proved that K was trying to customize her even further, whether it was for his own selfish reasons or because he simply wanted her to be happy, insisting in his mind that she was "real for him." Without Joi, he has no one. He'll be alone again. It might be okay for a while, but he'll eventually need something to contrast the dreary life he leads, mocked by his fellow officers, teased by tenants as he climbs the steps to his apartment, hated by other replicants who see him as the ugly face at the bottom of the totem pole. Either way, he's focused on the love he's lost, artificial or otherwise.

K's love of his work might be worth discussing. To me, it was debatable if he really loved his work at all. What was there to love? Being spat upon by other police officers? Called a skin-job on a daily basis? When he tried to take Sapper

Morton in, he showed no emotion at all and even seemed a little regretful at having to be there. "I'm sorry it had to be me," he says. He even goes so far as to make a class division between the replicant models saying that he doesn't retire his own kind because they don't run. When Luv asks him if he enjoys his work, he deflects the question and leaves. Maybe he didn't love the job at all, but it was the job he was made to do. He had to be a good boy and obey his programming. So maybe this love is forced, if it's love at all. Maybe that feeling of being trapped in a job he's not fond of (something many people can relate to) is what led to his pursuing the Joi product in the first place.

The book *Pale Fire* by Nabokov plays a dual role in the film. It's there in K's apartment in the guise of light reading. However, lines from the book are also part of K's baseline test, to gauge his emotional stability. This is interesting because the book contains within it a certain element of duality. It's presented as a long poem by poet John Shade, but it also contains a foreword and some commentary written by someone named Charles Kinbote. Perhaps the book was given to K so he could learn to recite his baseline, or perhaps K found out what the lines were from and tracked down the book out of curiosity.

In any case, I appreciate the contrast between the unseen baseline test administrator and the lines of the test. We never see the test administrator, only the gadget on the wall. For all we know, he could be off-world somewhere, working remotely. He could also be artificial, just a ghost in the machine. His voice provides the wonderful contrast I'm speaking of. He comes off as cold, mean, even incendiary. It's like he's daring K to fail the test, but the lines he reads are often times about love. He asks questions like:

> What's it like to hold the hand of someone you love?
> Did they teach you how to feel finger to finger?
> Do you long for having your heart interlinked?
> Do you dream about being interlinked?
> What's it like to hold your child in your arms?
> Do you feel like there's a part of you that's missing?

Again, we see love takes center stage. The first time K's asked these things is after his confrontation with Sapper. "Constant K" recites his answers flawlessly. He's under no more emotional duress than after any other mission, we assume. Morton was just another job, but it was the beginning of something else that had yet to blossom. The second time we see him take the test, the administrator is still aggressive (though he speaks slower for some reason) but K's answers are more delayed. Something is off after his visit with Ana Stelline. It's no surprise since he just found out that the memory of the horse is a real memory. He wrongly assumes it's his, but it shakes him to his artificial core. It's the one time in the film we see him lose control, even if it's just for a hot minute. Emotionally rattled, he fails his baseline, which sends him down a new path of discovery, but marks him as a target at the same time.

As you can see, there's a lot of love in K, but it's mostly out of reach. It's about longing, wanting, wishing, and yes, emulating.

Niander Wallace

"You think I have nothing to offer but pain? Only, I know... you love pain. Pain reminds you the joy you felt was real. More joy, then!"

Niander Wallace is an intriguing character. He's the blind, eccentric, and very rich innovator with a God complex, even more so than Tyrell, and that's saying a lot. He comes across as meek, even humble sometimes, walking around in a robe and sandals, quoting pertinent Bible verses. Yet, sometimes his dark side takes over and he starts to display megalomaniacal tendencies, wanting to own the stars and such. It's hard to imagine someone like that displaying love, but we must remember that love takes many forms and has many uses.

Wallace *uses* love as a weapon. More specifically, he uses both love the emotion and Luv his replicant assistant as weapons. You have to applaud the filmmakers for creating such a delicious parallel.

Luv is Wallace's *physical* weapon. She's loyal and ready, beautiful and deadly; all by design. Wallace keeps her in line with subtle manipulation, feeding her young ego by telling her she's the best "angel" of all, yet another example of Wallace's God complex. He's so powerful, he makes angels! She's the one who will get her hands dirty for Wallace.

In using the *emotion* of love as a weapon or tool, Wallace tries to manipulate Deckard into helping him during one of the most haunting scenes in the film, alluding to the fact that Deckard might be a replicant right before tempting him with a newly created, ersatz Rachael:

> Is it the same, now as then? The moment you met her.
> All these years you looked back on that day, drunk on the memory of its perfection.
> How shiny her lips. How instant your connection.
> Did it never occur to you that's why you were summoned in the first place? Designed to do nothing short of fall for her right then and there.
> All to make that single, perfect specimen.

That is if you were designed.
Love or mathematical precision.
Yes.
No.

If Deckard was summoned to the Tyrell Corporation as opposed to having been sent there on assignment, then this suggests a larger plan at work, hatched by Tyrell who, as we now know, unlocked the secret to replicant procreation. Although it's not spelled out in the film, it's implied that Rachel was a Nexus 7 prototype, and the only one capable of procreation.[5] The secret died with Tyrell, and subsequently his company. We can assume any private information related to the procreation of replicants was lost somewhere along the line, perhaps in the blackout of 2022.[6] That means, in order to speed up his research,[7] Wallace needs to find Rachael (and her child, after he learns that there is one) to try and reverse-engineer the process.

These moments in the film feature the evil genius of Wallace. He doesn't get loud or threatening. He knows what emotional buttons to push in order to get the right reactions and achieve the desired result. He pushes a series of small buttons first, playing audio from Deckard and Rachael's first meeting, bringing out Rachael's actual skull (while once again quoting Bible passages), and offering Deckard great rewards in exchange for his help. Then he hits the big, shiny, red button and out walks the remade Rachael.

Of course, her dialogue is all about love. "Did you miss me?" she asks a bewildered Deckard. "Don't you love me?" Deckard is nearly drowned in his own emotions, a symphony playing on his heartstrings, until he sees her eyes are the wrong color. The eyes, the windows to the soul, are symbolic in the *Blade Runner* universe, of course. The wrong eyes give Deckard a flaw to focus on, taking him out of the moment. I like to think it's his love for the child he never knew that keeps Deckard strong here. The eyes were just an excuse; a back door. Wallace, clearly disappointed, uses Luv as his weapon once again and destroys Rachael since she can be of no more use.

Wallace's true love is a love of power and excess. As with many people in a seat of power, even something like love can become corrupt and decayed, called upon when needed to be a means to an end, nothing more.

---

[5] The serial number on her bones begins with N7.
[6] https://www.youtube.com/watch?v=rrZk9sSgRyQ
[7] In the film, Wallace mentions that he has so far been unable to successfully breed replicants.

One of my favorite lines from Wallace is his reply to Deckard when he asks, "You don't have children, do you?" It's Deckard's one attempt at taking Wallace down a notch, insinuating that Wallace is devoid of love since he doesn't know what it's like to have children. Wallace is having none of it, though, and retorts quickly with, "Oh I have millions." Unfortunately, we all know that *fathering* a child and *being a father* to a child are two completely separate things.

Lieutenant Joshi

"Are you telling me no?"

As with Wallace, it's hard to imagine Joshi being a loving person, but we don't really know her well enough to make that assumption. She's this film's Captain Bryant, who was Deckard's boss in the original. He was a hardened, crass, demanding, manipulating jerk of a man. We don't know if he was married but if he was, I could easily imagine him going home, getting drunk, and beating her on a routine basis. He's not what you'd call a sympathetic character. Zero love there.

The thing I love about Joshi is that she takes all those police captain stereotypes and turns them on their heels. Usually the big cop boss is an overweight man, angry at the world. Now, Joshi isn't a ray of sunshine, but that's part of the magic. When we see her, we expect a compassionate, easy-going, person because that's what we're used to seeing in Hollywood. The woman isn't in a position of power and usually needs rescuing. Not here. She's no nonsense from the get-go. It's her job to keep order. She's rarely seen without a drink in her hand. She wears no make-up (that I can tell). It's all turning the tables and role reversal, and it works well without hitting you over the head.

Joshi is K's boss and she knows that K is designed to obey without question. When she shows up at his apartment to inform him that Rachael's bones were stolen and Coco is dead, she ends up having an extended visit. A few drinks later, a tipsy Joshi makes a pass at K. It may seem out of place at first, but it's not so out of the question if you swap her gender. A man, someone like Bryant, for instance, wouldn't hesitate to make a pass at a female subordinate. In fact, events like that are all too commonplace and not limited to the confines of someone's apartment.

K is designed to be obedient. Joshi knows this. Just moments before, she "ordered" him to share one of his memories with her, which he reluctantly did. She admits, in a passive way, that she finds him attractive by saying, "I've known a lot of your kind. All useful, but with you, I sometimes forget." It's subtle, but it's there. She could easily forget that he's a replicant. He must seem more "human" to her than the others she encounters in her daily routines. She moves from subtle to forward quickly, though. "What happens if I finish that?" she asks, nodding to the bottle she's been slowly emptying. K politely rejects her, saying he should be getting back to work.

The big thing to note here is that Joshi makes her pass, is rejected, and then moves on. She reads his reaction, knows what it means, and leaves. Perhaps she realized what she was doing and stopped herself from making a potential mistake.

Joshi, it appears, is longing for love. Maybe it's just physical. It would certainly fit her character. She doesn't seem to be someone who has time for a partner. She's married to her work, trying to keep the world from breaking. Maybe she saw a fleeting chance to experience some kind of love, even if it was in the form of sex. She could, for a short time, be close to someone. She could pretend to be in love, much like K and Joi.

She could technically order K to have sex with her and he would have to submit, as per his programming, but she does not do this. I think someone like Bryant wouldn't think twice about manipulating a replicant female into doing his bidding. In fact, he'd probably make a habit of it.

The lesson here is that while she may be in a stereotypical man's shoes as far as her role in the film goes, she's better than that kind of man. She rises above and takes the high road.

Freysa/Sapper Morton

"We all wish it was us. That's why we believe."

Sapper Morton is one of the first characters we meet in the film. He doesn't have a lot of screen time, but his role in the story cannot be understated. We also know that he is a compassionate, loving replicant. In the short film, *2048: Nowhere to Run*[8], we learn a little more about Sapper's backstory and the events that result in him ending up on the police's radar. In short, he risks being discovered as a rogue Nexus-8 in order to save a girl and her mother from being assaulted. He kills some thugs, drops his ID papers, and a witness calls the police with Sapper's address, which we assume is how K knows where to go at the beginning of *2049*.

---

[8] https://www.youtube.com/watch?v=aZ9Os8cP_gg

Sapper's love is borne out of protection, much like Deckard's paternal love for his child. Sapper was affected deeply when Rachael had her child, it seems. He refers to the baby as a "miracle." This miracle of the child, who would grow up to be Ana Stelline, becomes a legendary story, much like a fairy tale. It's the only fairy tale the replicants have, actually. It belongs to them and them alone. Freysa and Sapper, we assume, have passed it down like an old folk tale, most likely by word of mouth for their own protection, and perhaps as a recruitment tool. This is probably why the only known photo of the child was hidden in an old cigarette tin inside a piano, along with a small sock. These items are important to Sapper. All other knowledge of this miracle lives in his head.

Photos are a common thread in the *Blade Runner* films, it seems, though not all replicants value them. In the original film, Leon even goes so far as to return to his hotel to retrieve his "precious photos" because they're all he has. K's drone takes photos for him. Deckard examines Leon's photos in his Esper machine to help him with his case. Deckard has photos all over his piano and apartment. Rachael tries to prove her humanity to Deckard by showing him a photo of her as a child. Photos are like evidence, but they have sentimental value as well. They bring back feelings of love and warmth.

Sapper's love for Rachael was reverent. She was the mother of the miracle and therefore a type of replicant deity in a way. Sapper helped deliver the child with his medical training and tried to save Rachael, but he couldn't. He meticulously laid her to rest in one of his own foot-lockers. One can only imagine the bittersweet grief and guilt Sapper felt afterward. He was able to save the miracle child but not her mother, someone we assume he knew for some time. He carried that guilt with him for years. In the end, he allowed himself to be destroyed in order to keep the secret safe. In doing this, he most likely feels a sense of redemption, however brief. He died for the right cause, as Freysa says later on.

Speaking of Freysa, her displays of love also appear to be few and far between, but if you look closely, you'll see that, while harder than Sapper, she can also be a loving person. She has taken on the role of leader in her group of replicant rebels. It's somewhat of a maternal role, when you think about it. It's most likely the role Rachael would have played, had she lived. Rachael's death resulted in her receiving a martyr-like status. She surely would have been worshipped as a goddess-like being had she survived.

Rachael's position at the top was filled by Freysa, who saw the child born and did the legwork necessary to keep her hidden, going as far as to gender-swap her and scramble all the records, as per Deckard's instructions. From there, it was just a waiting game, but someone had to rally an army while Sapper lived an honest and inconspicuous farmer's life. Freysa's love is both maternal, toward her replicants and the young baby Ana, and protective, as with Sapper.

"Dying for the right cause is the most human thing we can do," she tells K while trying to recruit him as one of her soldiers. Her love for Ana and the rebellion runs so deep, she'd not only die for it, but kill for it. She orders K to find and kill Deckard, lest he lead Wallace to her. Her love is also expressed in hope for the freedom of her replicant race. She explains that if a baby came from a replicant, it meant they were more than slaves. They were their own masters.

It's unclear if Freysa knows what happened to Ana after she was given away. One hypothesis is that Freysa kept track of the child all this time and was just waiting for the right time to approach her with the news of who she was. She speaks to K about showing her to the world when the time is right. However, another hypothesis is that no one knows where the child is. Not Wallace, Freysa, K, Deckard: no one. In an alleged version of the script with some alternate dialogue, Freysa's relevant (and altered) line is, "I wish I could find her... I show her unto the world. And she lead an army!"[9]

So in the end, yes, Freysa loved the child, but she also loves her people and the idea of their freedom. When Ana finds out that everyone's looking for her, she's sure going to feel special.

Ana Stelline

"Someone lived this, yes."

To me, Dr. Ana Stelline represents the purest love in the film, innocent and compassionate. She has a love for all life regardless of its origins. She's a kindly, soft-spoken, empathetic business person, trapped in a life of freedom behind glass. We feel even more sympathetic toward her when we learn she was locked in a sterile chamber at eight years old because of her compromised immune system. Despite all this, she's made a successful life for herself creating the memories that live inside the heads of replicants.

---

[9] https://scriptslug.com/assets/uploads/scripts/blade-runner-2049.pdf – Freysa speaks in very broken English in this version of the script.

Dr. Ana Stelline.

She's the best at what she does because she cares. She's not just doing her job, as she explains to K:

> Wallace needs my talent to maintain a stable product. I think it's only kind. Replicants live such hard lives, made to do what we'd rather not. I can't help your future, but I can give you good memories to look back on and smile.

She feels genuine empathy toward replicants. For such a long time they were looked down upon mainly as slaves. Many still look down on them, even the new models, in the shadow of the repealed replicant prohibition which followed the blackout. Ana doesn't really concern herself with all that. If something is alive, she shows it respect and love. If she can make a hard life a little easier by making the memories enjoyable, she's more than happy to do so.

She even goes so far as to illegally use her own memories as the basis for implants, which gives them a greater level of authenticity. "If you have authentic memories you have real human responses," she says. We find that out soon enough when K has a "real human response" to Ana telling him that the memory in his head is a real one.

Ana's presence in the film at times leaves us with more questions than answers. Did her parents move off-world without her? How did she survive the orphanage, and how old was she when she lived there if she was locked in a sterile chamber at eight? Are parts of her backstory fabricated? It doesn't matter, really. What matters is that she's a special person, not only because she's the first replicant birthed, but because she's the film's embodiment of pure love, born not made, special in every way. She's a love MacGuffin.

Luv

"I'm the best one."

Wallace's best angel of all, Luv, maintains a flat composure throughout much of the film. She's like K in that aspect, however she does tend to get riled up much easier when Wallace isn't around. It makes you think about the ways love is represented through her. Being a replicant, you might think it difficult for her to love, but think about Deckard and Rachael. Think about Roy Batty and Pris. Love finds a way, yet there's something off about Luv, isn't there?

Luv gives the impression of being a teenager trapped in an adult's body. I don't believe her emotional palette is fully formed and that manifests itself in various ways. At one point, she tells K, "It is invigorating being asked personal questions. Makes one feel… desired." She states this as if she doesn't really talk to many people outside of clients. The next thing she does is ask K a personal question. "Do you enjoy your work, officer?" she asks. At first, I thought that perhaps she was being flippant, asking if he likes killing replicants, her being one. Sapper asked him the same thing. After a few viewings, however, I started to wonder if she was just testing her hypothesis that being asked personal questions makes one feel desired. Perhaps in an odd way she was making a pass at him, as if saying, "Look, I'm asking *you* a personal question!" Like Joshi, maybe she saw a fleeting chance at a quick display of love and went for it. Maybe under all that sternness, Luv longs for love too.

Luv usually sheds a tear when death looms, whether by her own hand or not. We see it happen when Wallace kills his new replicant model with a scalpel. We see it again before she kills Joshi. Some might think it's empathy in the first example, but the second example negates that for me. She has no empathy toward Joshi, whose dead body she slams on the desk after using it for facial recognition. There was always tension between the two. So why the tears?

I'm of the opinion that replicants evolve, but differently than humans. Their evolution is more akin to machine learning, yet underneath it all there are these emotions that crop up, maybe even at the wrong times. I like to think that even she doesn't know why these tears suddenly well up in her. She's confused and doesn't know what's happening. It's as if Wallace put seeds of humanity inside her, and once in a while, they bloom, but does she learn from them? I think we're seeing a work in progress with Luv. Professionally, she's up to snuff, but emotionally she has a lot to learn.

Tyrell, it seemed, was always playing with his creations. He created testing scenarios to see what happened. Rachael wasn't told what she was. He needed to see his experiment play out in the real world. Who knows what other "experiments" he had in progress? Wallace, it seems, was a big fan of Tyrell so it makes sense that his methods mimic that of the bespectacled recluse. He's given Luv the ability to feel emotion and though she might not know it, she's feeling love or empathy or sadness at any given time. How will she evolve as a result? That's what he wants to see. If he's not happy, he can always destroy her and start over.

Luv is most definitely a right hand to Wallace, but is there more to her than we see in the film? She clearly worships him. "What a gift, don't you think, from Mr. Wallace to the world?" she tells K. "The outer colonies would never have flourished had he not bought Tyrell. Revivified the technology." She's in awe of him. You might say she loves him, but in what way?

By definition, Wallace is her father. Surely, she loves him in that respect. He's also her master and employer. She's obedient without question, but is there something more? She's strikingly beautiful. Wallace could have made her look any way at all. It raises the question of whether or not she's also his lover. Does she love him as both a father figure and a lover? Replicants have no frame of reference for family life unless implanted in memories. Does she even have memories? It's unclear. She's all business. According to Denis Villeneuve, "She has a massive Oedipus complex with Wallace, she wants to be loved by him, she wants to please him, and she's very crystallized - in that she didn't evolve at all, so she's confused."[10]

---

[10] http://www.ign.com/articles/2018/01/26/blade-runner-2049-director-answers-9-wtf-questions

I wonder if replicants can evolve past certain elements of their programming. Is it a customizable thing? The ability to fall in love and express love in different ways must be something learned, you would think, but what about something like lying? There are at least two occasions in the film where it appears that an otherwise obedient replicant appears to be lying.

First, K cleverly skirts the issue of his assignment to eliminate "all trace" of the replicant child. "I found the kid. He was set up like a standard replicant, put on a service job. Even he didn't know who he was," he tells Joshi. From a certain point of view, this is true. K, at the time, believes that he is the child in question. When Joshi inquires further, he simply tells her that it's done. "What you asked. It's done," he clarifies. He's clever, that K.

Later, Luv confronts Joshi when her search for K hits a dead end. Joshi is flippant, and Luv starts to come undone. Her love for Wallace will not let her fail because she's the best angel of all. Before she kills Joshi, she says, "You're so sure. Because he told you. Because we never lie. I'm going to tell Mr. Wallace that you tried to shoot me first. So I had to kill you." She says "we never lie" but then immediately does just that. If you take her at her word, it means she's admitting to a future lie. Maybe her intent is to never follow through with the lie, but wouldn't that in itself be a lie? She's either lying about lying, or will lie later on to Wallace, who I'm thinking wouldn't care either way. It's all a little confusing, really, but then again, love and loyalty can be quite confusing, especially to someone who hasn't had a lifetime to develop and fine tune such things.

When K first meets Luv, he remarks that she must be special since Wallace actually gave her a name. That's true, but her name is also symbolic, as is Joi's. Love is something K longs for desperately, in both its emotional and physical form, simultaneously. What he has, however, is joy (Joi), which you could argue is closer to a form of general happiness, but does he know the difference? Is there a difference? Is love greater than joy? When Luv calls K a "bad dog" before she beats the holy hell out of him and destroys Joi, it suggests that this is indeed the case.

Later on, when K is drowning Luv, her words come back to bite her as she disturbingly growls like a dog under the water. It reminded me of Pris' death in the original film when she goes into violent spasms after being shot, screaming like a banshee, trying to hold onto life because she just isn't done with it yet. In the end, K is forced to kill love (Luv) in order to survive and save Deckard. K could buy as much joy (Joi) as he wanted, but love, in both its emotional and physical form, would remain an unattainable goal.

Conclusion

In many ways, *Blade Runner 2049* is a very brutal film. It begins with a fight that takes two replicants through a wall. The violence is realistic and isn't only limited to physical abuse. However, it's love that makes *Blade Runner 2049* work. When you really look at these first two films, stripping away the layers of cyberpunk and violence, you find that the entire thing is, in essence, a love story.

Love is present in almost every scene if you look hard enough. It might be a casual mention, or it might be symbolic. Love is the bright yellow flower that Sapper leaves by the tree, clearly visible in an otherwise gray environment. Love is the baby's sock he kept in the piano with the photo. Love is the lock of hair he kept in the makeshift ossuary. Love is in Joi's voice, telling K he's special. Love is in K's eyes as he watches Joi experience rain for the first time on the roof. Love's there in the picture of Rachael in Deckard's home. There's love in Ana's tears as she sees her memory play out via K's implant. There's love in Mariette as she looks at the little wooden horse on K's night stand. There's love in Deckard's hand as it touches the glass that separates him from his daughter.

Love is what set the plot in motion back in 2019. Had Deckard and Rachael not fallen in love (whether by design or simple fate) and created that perfect specimen of a child, there would be no story to support the events of 2049, and all we'd be left with would be some lovely, but empty visuals.

Beyond 2049: An Afterword

by Lou Tambone

From the moment we pitched this book to the moment of its release, much has happened. *Blade Runner 2049* was released to critical acclaim, although, like its predecessor, it did not perform well at the box office (not managing to crack the $100mil US domestic market). Three online short films were released to prime audiences for the new theatrical film. Both theatrical films were released for home viewing, looking better than ever (*2049* containing the short films as bonus features). After all this, the future of the *Blade Runner* universe sits at a crossroads.

The underwhelming box office take will surely hamper the efforts of the parties involved, or at least cause them to rethink how they go about making another film. There have been no literary tie-ins or online shorts since the release of *2049*. In fact, there's been little to no buzz at all about anything *Blade Runner* except the standard marketing for the home releases, and that soon died out as well. Even the fact that the film won two well-deserved Oscars for Visual Effects and Cinematography in early 2018 resulted in a few headlines (mostly about Roger Deakens) that came and went.

Denis Villeneuve almost immediately turned his attention to adapting *Dune* for the screen once more. Ridley Scott became busy with other films and seems more concerned with keeping the *Alien* franchise alive than anything else. So where does the *Blade Runner* universe go from here?

When *2049* was released, people involved with the project seemed hopeful and were even entertaining the idea of more films. In a Metro article by Gregory Wakeman, Villeneuve said, "Of course if the movie is well received, then I would easily bet that they would do another one. For this time it is a one off movie." Co-screenwriter Hampton Fancher added, "I had an old idea that I liked, and I might play with that and see what everybody thinks. It would involve Deckard in another world, culturally so to speak, other than the USA. It would take him to another country." Even Harrison Ford seemed willing, saying, "if they came up with something equally as good as this I would be involved."[1]

The original film, though not initially greeted with open arms, found a second "cult" life after a number of years, most noticeably after its first release on DVD. *2049* may be subject to the same treatment as the years go by, but by then it may be too late. Will we have to wait another 30 years until someone decides it's time for another entry? At the risk of sounding morbid, by that time most of the principal cast and crew could be gone. Ridley Scott has surpassed 80. Harrison Ford is over 75. Denis would be around Ridley's age at that time. The chances of seeing Ford reprise his role as Deckard grow increasing slim as each day passes.

The filmmakers seemed prepared for failure (of the film and the franchise), making *2049* into a mostly stand-alone feature while simultaneously setting up new possibilities among its many twists and turns. The film left the door wide open for a replicant rebellion on the horizon. That, coupled with the notion that replicants can reproduce is fertile ground for visionaries to formulate a satisfying storyline. That could include what Deckard and his daughter, Dr. Ana Stelline, do after the film concludes. Where do they go? Do they lead a replicant rebellion along with Freysa?

In a December 2017 ScreenDaily.com article, Villeneuve was asked if he'd return to the *Blade Runner* universe again. His reply was coy: "The door is not closed. I know, to my great admiration and excitement, that for [Production Company] Alcon the journey goes on. They're proud of the movie and they're not closing the door."[2]

---

[1] https://www.metro.us/entertainment/movies/will-there-be-a-blade-runner-sequel

[2] https://www.screendaily.com/features/denis-villeneuve-looks-back-at-blade-runner-2049-talks-sequels-dune-and-bond/5125161.article

In January 2018, Ridley Scott told DigitalSpy.com, "I think there is another story. I've got another one ready to evolve and be developed, so there is certainly one to be done for sure."[3]

In a February 2018 *Variety* article, Alcon Entertainment's Co-CEOs Broderick Johnson and Andrew Kosove, addressing the company's 2018 job cuts, said, "We fully expect our company to thrive with our upcoming IP, including the expansion of the *Blade Runner* universe."[4]

It definitely feels like there are many more stories to be told as long as there are writers and filmmakers willing to tell them. The Los Angeles in *Blade Runner*'s future is a neon cyberpunk minefield just waiting to be quarried. Will anyone bring out their picks and shovels? Only time will tell.

Until then, we now have more than we had previously, and this author is extremely grateful for that. If the story ends there, so be it, but (strange as it sounds) I look forward to a dystopian future where many more installments of the *Blade Runner* universe exist.

Acknowledgements

Joe Bongiorno: Special Thanks to my buddy Lou Tambone for introducing me to a wider world than I knew existed... and setting me loose in it!

Lou Tambone: I would like to thank the following people involved in bringing this book to life. Julian Darius and Mike Phillips at Sequart who greenlighted the project before I could even think twice. My co-editor Joe Bongiorno for all his hard work and friendship. Rich Handley for referring Joe Bongiorno. The contributors who really rose to the occasion and delivered top-notch essays. Extra special thanks to Matt Busch for painting such an extraordinary cover that immediately blew everyone away. Extra, extra special thanks to respected *Blade Runner* "historian" Paul M. Sammon for a wonderfully poetic foreword.

And of course, my wife Louisa and my kids Zack and Isabella, who inspire me in ways they don't even know.

---

[3] http://www.digitalspy.com/movies/blade-runner/news/a846834/ridley-scott-has-plans-another-blade-runner-sequel/
[4] http://variety.com/2018/film/news/alcon-entertainment-job-cuts-operations-1202694160/

About the Contributors

Mike Beidler is a retired U.S. Navy commander whose combination of military aviation experience and *Star Wars* fandom pedigree launched him, beginning in the mid-1990s, into a decades-long relationship with numerous *Star Wars* authors. His direct contributions to the *Star Wars* universe include work on Tom Veitch's *Dark Empire* saga, A. C. Crispin's *Han Solo Trilogy*, and John Whitman's *Galaxy of Fear* series. These days, he lives in the Washington D.C. Metro Area with his wife and three children and serves as the Navy's Deputy Director for International Affairs. In addition to creating the *Star Wars Literature Compendium*, the earliest (1995) and—at one time—most comprehensive literature timelines on the Internet, he is considered the father of *Star Wars* chronologies and the inspiration for more recent and comprehensive timelines. He contributed essays to two Sequart *Star Wars* anthologies: *A Galaxy Far, Far Away: Exploring Star Wars Comics* (2015) and *A More Civilized Age: Exploring the Star Wars Expanded Universe* (2017). Mike once had a face-to-face conversation with Harrison Ford during which Ford claimed Deckard was, in fact, [redacted by the Wallace Corporation]. It doesn't get any more authoritative than that, folks!

Jean-François Boivin is a life-long collector of all things *Star Wars*, Cthulhu Mythos, *Aliens*, *Predator*, *RoboCop* and *Godzilla*, as well as a horror movie aficionado. He is a part-time writer, and has assisted other authors with research for their works. His first short story, "Calamité," was published in the small-press 1991 French Canadian anthology *H-3027 Rouge*. He also co-wrote (with Abel G. Peña) "Echoes of the Jedi", the fourth adventure of the *Star Wars:*

Dawn of Defiance RPG campaign for Wizards of the Coast in 2008, and he was a contributor to Sequart's *A Galaxy Far, Far Away: Exploring Star Wars Comics* and *A Long Time Ago: Exploring the Star Wars Cinematic Universe*.

Joe Bongiorno is a Long Island native and the creator of The Royal Publisher of Oz (www.theroyalpublisherofoz.com), which publishes new books in the universe started by L. Frank Baum. He is author of the eight volume series *Black Sabbath: The Illustrated Lyrics*, creator of the Star Wars Expanded Universe Timeline (www.starwarstimeline.net), the Royal Timeline of Oz (www.oztimeline.net), and the X-Files Chronology (www.xfilestimeline.net). Joe has written short stories and essays for *Oziana* magazine, *Star Wars Gamer* magazine, and several Sequart anthologies.

R. Lee Brown has spent nearly half a century crafting effective, engaging stories for clients, corporations, and characters, from original tales in comic, novel, or screenplay form to advertising and marketing via print, video, or website. He's run the gamut from a career as corporate Director of Marketing to producer of award-winning commercials to creator of acclaimed genre websites to helping others realize their creative impulse as a professional ghostwriter and script doctor. But, mostly, R. Lee Brown is a storyteller.

Robert Meyer Burnett has worked professionally in Hollywood since 1989, where he received his first screen credit as the Production Assistant on *Leatherface: The Texas Chainsaw Massacre III*. Known primarily as the writer-director of the cult film *Free Enterprise*, starring Emmy Winners Eric McCormack, and William Shatner, he's also been a producer on the *Agent Cody Banks* films for MGM and developed and produced *The Hills Run Red* for Warner Premiere and Joel Silver's Dark Castle Entertainment. He's recently edited the feature films *Paradox*, *My Eleventh* and the upcoming *Tango Shalom*. As a special features producer, he's created documentary materials for the Home Video releases of such films as *Snow White*, *Fantasia*, *The Lord of the Rings*, *The Usual Suspects*, *X-Men*, *X2*, and *Star Trek: The Next Generation*. Since 2015, he's appeared weekly on Collider's YouTube series *Heroes*.

Nathan P. Butler is the author of *A Saga on Home Video: A Fan's Guide to U.S. Star Wars Home Video Releases*. He has contributed to the *Star Wars Legends* continuity, publications like Sequart's *Star Wars* essay anthologies, and the *WARS: The Battle of Phobos* novella series. He is an avid YouTube video producer and has been a podcaster since before "podcasting" had a name. By day, he is a professional educator with his county's innovative virtual learning program. He resides with his wife and pets in the Atlanta area, where the traffic makes a futuristic dystopia look tame.

Bryce Carlson is the author of the multiple Harvey Award-nominated crime noir comic book series, *Hit*, and the Managing Editor at BOOM! Studios, where he has spent a decade editing an array of critically acclaimed titles such as the Eisner Award-nominated official graphic novelization of Philip K. Dick's seminal work, *Do Androids Dream of Electric Sheep?* His other comic book works include Cartoon Network's *Adventure Time* and Disney-Pixar's *WALL-E*. He lives in Los Angeles with his wife and son.

Julian Darius founded what would become Sequart Organization in 1996, while still an undergraduate, to promote comics and popular culture as legitimate forms of art. With dozens of books and seven documentary films to date, Sequart played an important part in the acceptance of comic books as literature. After graduating *magna cum laude* from Lawrence University (Appleton, Wisconsin), Darius obtained his M.A. in English, authoring a thesis on John Milton and utopianism. In 2002, he moved to Waikiki, teaching college while obtaining an M.A. in French (high honors) and a Ph.D. in English. In 2005, Darius published the first scholarly book on Christopher Nolan's Batman films. He has also published books on (among other subjects) *Batman: the Killing Joke* (which elaborated a theory on the book's plot that was praised by Kevin Smith); Jack Kirby's comic-book continuation of *2001: A Space Odyssey*; and *Mai, the Psychic Girl*. He also co-authored, with Kevin Thurman, a book on Warren Ellis. In 2015, he released *Classics on Infinite Earths*, a massive study of the Justice League and DC's shared universe. In 2011, Darius founded Martian Lit, which publishes creative work, including his acclaimed indy sci-fi comic *Martian Comics*. He currently lives in Illinois.

Ian Dawe was initially educated in the sciences (Molecular Biology and Biochemistry), but soon came to his senses (well, after ten years of teaching College genetics) and finished his MA in Film at the University of Exeter with a dissertation on the work of Terry Gilliam. His work has subsequently been published in books about James Bond, *Breaking Bad*, *Star Wars*, *Star Trek,* and Alan Moore. He has served for two years as the webmaster and Supervising Editor of Sequart.com and has written over 400 articles for the site. He lives in Vancouver, BC.

Joseph Dilworth Jr. is the co-host of *The Flickcast* podcast (theflickcast.com), a contributor to several pop culture books published by the Sequart Organization, and a regular writer for *Long Island Pulse* magazine . He has an unhealthy obsession with obscure 1970s and 1980s television. Joe resides in the Pacific Northwest where he spends time with his family, brews beer, writes, reads, and expresses his opinion to whomever will listen. Just be warned: never, ever feed him after midnight.

Mario Escamilla is a computer systems engineer who has loved science fiction ever since picking up his first book, a Jules Verne classic. Since then, he has devoured sci-fi and fantasy in every possible media: comics, novels, movies, TV shows, and more. During the constant search for just a bit more *Star Wars* he stumbled upon a Harrison Ford feature, *Blade Runner*, and was awestruck. Collecting most home media versions of the movie, from VHS and Laserdisc to DVD and Blu-ray, he continued to search for more of the story in the novel, comic adaptations, and other media. He currently lives in sunny Veracruz, Mexico, with his wife, Gaby, and their daughter, Montse.

Kelli Fitzpatrick is a science-fiction author and English educator with an obsessive love of libraries and outer space. Her *Star Trek* story "The Sunwalkers" is published in *Strange New Worlds 2016* from Simon and Schuster, and her essay analyzing an episode of *Star Trek: The Next Generation* appears in *Outside In Makes It So* from ATB Publishing. She runs a creative writing group for teens, serves on multiple community nonprofit boards, and is a passionate supporter of the arts in all their forms. She can be found at kellifitzpatrick.com and @KelliFitzWrites.

Sabrina Fried has been a contributor to the many worlds of fandom for over 20 years as a writer, editor, blogger and all-around creative person. Her latest publication is a contribution to *A More Civilized Age: Exploring the Star Wars Expanded Universe* from Sequart. She currently lives in British Columbia, Canada.

Rich Handley is the editor of Hasslein Books (www.hassleinbooks.com) and the author or co-author of *Timeline of the Planet of the Apes*, *From Aldo to Zira: Lexicon of the Planet of the Apes*, *Back in Time: The Back to the Future Chronology*, *A Matter of Time: The Back to the Future Lexicon*, and *Watching Time: The Watchmen Chronology*. Rich co-edited and contributed to *Planet of the Apes: Tales from the Forbidden Zone*, a short fiction anthology published by Titan Books, as well as five Sequart essay anthologies to date about the *Planet of the Apes* and *Star Wars* franchises. He has contributed to IDWs five *Star Trek* comic-strip reprint hardcover books; Sequart's *New Life and New Civilizations: Exploring Star Trek Comics*; and ATB Publishing's *Star Trek* anthology *Outside In Boldly Goes*. In addition, Rich has contributed to numerous magazines and websites, including StarTrek.com, StarWars.com, *Star Trek Magazine, Cinefantastique, Movie Magic, Sci-Fi Invasion, Cinescape, Dungeon/Polyhedron,* and various Lucasfilm *Star Wars* licensees. By day, he is the managing editor of *RFID Journal* and *IOT Journal* magazines. If only you could see what he has seen with your eyes.

Zaki Hasan was born and raised in Chicago (with a decade-long detour in Saudi Arabia) before settling in the San Francisco Bay Area. Zaki Hasan is a professor of communication and media studies, and the co-founder of Mr. Boy Productions, a Los Angeles-based independent film and video company. A lifelong pop culture buff, Zaki has been a media scholar and critic for more than 15 years. His film reviews and analyses have appeared at The Huffington Post, Philadelphia Weekly, Fandor, and Sequart, and he is a member of the San Francisco Film Critics Circle. He is co-host of the *MovieFilm Podcast, Nostalgia Theater,* and *Diffused Congruence: The American Muslim Experience*. He is also co-author of *Quirk Books' Geek Wisdom: The Sacred Teachings of Nerd Culture*, and has appeared as a panelist on Al Jazeera America's *The Stream* and *HuffPost Live*. Since 2004, the Zaki's Corner website has been his one-stop forum for musings on news, media, politics, and pop culture. He was included in 2010's Top 35 Political Blogs by BestBloggers.org, and has been nominated for "Best Blog" and "Best Writer" in 2010, 2011, and 2012 by the Brass Crescent Awards, receiving an Honorable Mention for "Best Blog" in 2011.

Steven Slaughter Head's middle name is really Slaughter; it's not a joke. He co-created the much-loved movie news website IGN FilmForce (now IGN Movies), was a writer and content producer for IGN Entertainment, America Online, Netscape, and Propeller.com. From 2011-2018 he hosted the *Diabolique* magazine Podcast. He earned a B.A. in History from Providence College. He also helped make movies, including *Little Monsters* and *Teenage Mutant Ninja Turtles II: The Secret of the Ooze*, most of which are listed on his IMDb page. You can find Steve online at instagram.com/cinemanitrate.

Tom Lennon is a UK-based freelance writer and humorist with a lifelong weakness for the geekier end of the pop culture spectrum. His work can be found at www.tomlennon.com.

Bentley Ousley is an award-winning composer, film maker, producer, and musician and is considered the go-to source for minutia regarding the *Blade Runner* soundtrack. As a composer, Ousley created the score for the immersive film *Once and Future Cities: A Fractal Journey* and Warner Brothers Pictures awarded his composition "Deckard's World" Grand Prize in their "Inspiring the

Future" competition. *Once and Future Cities* is slated to be re-released as a virtual reality experience with the score for the film to be released as a stand-alone musical work under the title *Once and Future Cites: Under the Influence of Blade Runner*. You can find him at bentleyousley.com.

Nelson W. Pyles is novelist living in Pittsburgh, PA. His latest novel is Spiders in the Daffodils. His fiction has appeared alongside Neil Gaiman, Harlan Ellison, F. Paul Wilson, and many others. You can find his short stories in the collection *Everything Here is a Nightmare*. He is also the creator of the popular podcast The Wicked Library (where he is also the voice of The Librarian). You can find him online at nelsonwpyles.com, on Twitter @nelsonwpyles, and on Facebook at www.facebook.com/nelson.pyles. His first novel *Demons, Dolls and Milkshakes* will be re-released late 2018, and the sequel is due in 2019.

Brian Robinson has been a film tutor for five years, and a screenwriter/filmmaker for far longer than he cares to remember. A science-fiction and fantasy nut since before he could read, his was a childhood spent with "The Doctor", various Kaiju, and normally "in a galaxy far, far away" before becoming involved in splatter films as a teen. His teaching work currently focuses on Expressionist and Noir film techniques while his writing and filmmaking revolve around dark comedy, science fiction and horror. He currently lives and works near Edinburgh, Scotland with a plethora of animals and a very patient wife.

Paul J. Salamoff has been working for over 25 years in film, television, video games, and commercials as a writer, producer, director, executive, comic creator, and make-up FX artist. His film & TV writing credits include *The Dead Hate The Living*, *The St. Francisville Experiment*, and *Alien Siege*. He also wrote and directed the sci-fi/drama *Encounter*. He was recently named one of The Tracking Board's Top 100 up & coming screenwriters and has developed projects with Warner Bros., Mosaic Media Group, Hollywood Gang, Silver Pictures, Valhalla Motion Pictures, Vertigo, Unstoppable Entertainment (UK) and Eclectic Pictures. Salamoff is the author of *On the Set: The Hidden Rules of Movie Making Etiquette*, *The Complete DVD Book* and the graphic novels *Discord*, *Tales of Discord*, *Logan's Run: Last Day*, *Logan's Run: Aftermath*, *Logan's Run: Rebirth* and issues of *Vincent Price Presents*. His short stories have been included in acclaimed anthologies including *Midian Unmade: Tales From Clive Barker's Nightbreed* and he is a two-time Bram Stoker Award Nominee.

Paul M. Sammon is an author, filmmaker, Hollywood insider and one of the most respected and knowledgeable writers on film working today. He has published numerous articles, short stories and books. His many film journalism pieces have seen print in *The Los Angeles Times*, *Empire* magazine, *The American Cinematographer*, *Cahiers du Cinema* and *Cinefex*. Sammon is also the author of the books *The Making of Starship Troopers* (1997), *Ridley Scott: Close-Up (1999)*, *Alien: The Illustrated Screenplay (2000)*, *Aliens: The illustrated Screenplay (2001)*, and *Conan the Phenomenon (2007)*. But Sammon does not only write about films, he works in them as well. He first entered the industry as a publicist in the 1970s, before becoming a producer, director, special effects coordinator, computer graphics supervisor, second unit director, still photographer, electronic press kit producer, and Vice President of Marketing: Special Promotions for a major studio. Some of the scores of films on which he worked include *Robocop, Platoon, Blue Velvet, Conan the Barbarian, Dune, Return of the Living Dead, The Silence of the Lambs, and Starship Troopers*. He was likewise among the first "genre marketers" to present studio film promotions at the San Diego Comic-Con international, and Sammon also co-wrote (in Moscow, 1988) *Stereotypes*, the first animated coproduction between Russia and the United States. In addition, for four years, Sammon was the American co-producer of a number of Japanese television shows, including the long running entertainment program *Hello! Movies* (1988-1993). Sammon was closely involved with the 2007/25th anniversary rerelease of Ridley Scott's *Blade Runner* on DVD and the Internet. Among his other contributions, he was extensively interviewed on camera for *Dangerous Days*, the definitive 3 ½ hour *Blade Runner* documentary. Paul M. Sammon still writes today, still loves movies, and travels the world giving public appearances to talk about films, pop-culture and books. He also remains fascinated by *Blade Runner* and is honored to have written *Future Noir: The Making of Blade Runner*, which many have called the "*Blade Runner* Bible" as well as the definitive book on this film. *Future Noir* (in continuous print since its initial publication in 1996) was updated and revised for a brand-new third edition, published by HarperCollins in 2017.

Rev. Dr. Leah D. Schade is the Assistant Professor of Preaching and Worship at Lexington Theological Seminary in Kentucky. She earned both her MDiv and PhD degrees from the Lutheran Theological Seminary at Philadelphia (now United Lutheran Seminary), and completed her dissertation focusing on homiletics (preaching) and ecological theology. Leah is the author of *Creation-Crisis Preaching: Ecology, Theology, and the Pulpit* (Chalice Press, 2015). Her "EcoPreacher" blog for Patheos explores environmental issues, politics, religion, race, gender and women's issues, and popular culture: www.patheos.com/blogs/ecopreacher.

Timothy Shanahan is Professor of Philosophy at Loyola Marymount University, Los Angeles, CA, USA. He is the author of *Reason and Insight: Western and Eastern Perspectives on the Pursuit of Moral Wisdom* (Belmont, CA: Wadsworth, 2003), *The Evolution of Darwinism* (Cambridge: Cambridge University Press, 2004), *Philosophy 9/11: Thinking about the War on Terrorism* (Chicago: Open Court, 2005), *The Provisional Irish Republican Army and the Morality of Terrorism* (Edinburgh: Edinburgh University Press, 2009), *Philosophy and Blade Runner* (Houndmills: Palgrave Macmillan Publishers, 2014), and over two dozen scholarly papers.

Lou Tambone is an independent musician, freelance writer, and UI/UX designer from New Jersey. A lifelong fan of pop culture, he was an early HTML adopter, creating and maintaining some of the first *Star Wars* fan sites under the Starwarz.com banner. As well as the occasional magazine and web piece, he's been published in anthologies from Sequart on the *Planet of the Apes, Battlestar Galactica,* and *Star Wars* franchises. His editing credits include *The Cyberpunk Nexus: Exploring the Blade Runner Universe* and *Somewhere Beyond the Heavens: Exploring Battlestar Galactica*. When he's not reading or writing, he's usually making music or rehearsing with one of his many bands. During his "spare time," he tries to remember to eat and breathe.

ALSO FROM SEQUART

A LONG TIME AGO: EXPLORING THE STAR WARS CINEMATIC UNIVERSE
A GALAXY FAR, FAR AWAY: EXPLORING STAR WARS COMICS
A MORE CIVILIZED AGE: EXPLORING THE STAR WARS EXPANDED UNIVERSE

NEW LIFE AND NEW CIVILIZATIONS: EXPLORING STAR TREK COMICS
THE SACRED SCROLLS: COMICS ON THE PLANET OF THE APES
BRIGHT LIGHTS, APE CITY: EXAMINING THE PLANET OF THE APES MYTHOS

BOOKS ON GRANT MORRISON:

GRANT MORRISON: THE EARLY YEARS
OUR SENTENCE IS UP: SEEING GRANT MORRISON'S *THE INVISIBLES*
CURING THE POSTMODERN BLUES: READING GRANT MORRISON AND CHRIS WESTON'S *THE FILTH* IN THE 21ST CENTURY
THE ANATOMY OF ZUR-EN-ARRH: UNDERSTANDING GRANT MORRISON'S BATMAN

BOOKS ON WARREN ELLIS:

SHOT IN THE FACE: A SAVAGE JOURNEY TO THE HEART OF *TRANSMETROPOLITAN*
KEEPING THE WORLD STRANGE: A *PLANETARY* GUIDE
VOYAGE IN NOISE: WARREN ELLIS AND THE DEMISE OF WESTERN CIVILIZATION
WARREN ELLIS: THE CAPTURED GHOSTS INTERVIEWS

OTHER BOOKS:

THE BRITISH INVASION: ALAN MOORE, NEIL GAIMAN, GRANT MORRISON, AND THE INVENTION OF THE MODERN COMIC BOOK WRITER
HUMANS AND PARAGONS: ESSAYS ON SUPER-HERO JUSTICE
CLASSICS ON INFINITE EARTHS: THE JUSTICE LEAGUE AND DC CROSSOVER CANON
MOVING TARGET: THE HISTORY AND EVOLUTION OF GREEN ARROW
THE DEVIL IS IN THE DETAILS: EXAMINING MATT MURDOCK AND DAREDEVIL
TEENAGERS FROM THE FUTURE: ESSAYS ON THE LEGION OF SUPER-HEROES
THE BEST THERE IS AT WHAT HE DOES: EXAMINING CHRIS CLAREMONT'S X-MEN
AND THE UNIVERSE SO BIG: UNDERSTANDING *BATMAN: THE KILLING JOKE*
MINUTES TO MIDNIGHT: TWELVE ESSAYS ON *WATCHMEN*
THE WEIRDEST SCI-FI COMIC EVER MADE: UNDERSTANDING JACK KIRBY'S *2001: A SPACE ODYSSEY*
WHEN MANGA CAME TO AMERICA: SUPER-HERO REVISIONISM IN *MAI, THE PSYCHIC GIRL*
THE FUTURE OF COMICS, THE FUTURE OF MEN: MATT FRACTION'S *CASANOVA*
MOVING PANELS: TRANSLATING COMICS TO FILM
MUTANT CINEMA: THE X-MEN TRILOGY FROM COMICS TO SCREEN
GOTHAM CITY 14 MILES: 14 ESSAYS ON WHY THE 1960S BATMAN TV SERIES MATTERS
IMPROVING THE FOUNDATIONS: *BATMAN BEGINS* FROM COMICS TO SCREEN

DOCUMENTARY FILMS:

DIAGRAM FOR DELINQUENTS
SHE MAKES COMICS
THE IMAGE REVOLUTION
NEIL GAIMAN: DREAM DANGEROUSLY
GRANT MORRISON: TALKING WITH GODS
WARREN ELLIS: CAPTURED GHOSTS
COMICS IN FOCUS: CHRIS CLAREMONT'S X-MEN

For more information and for exclusive content, visit Sequart.org.

Printed in Great Britain
by Amazon